She stood in the midd[...]
black men held her arm[...]

This wasn't happening. This wasn't happening. She shook her head, hard. Held her breath. Sometimes either of those was enough to take her out of a nightmare. This was a dream. In fact, she remembered that she had had this dream before. The worst part was that she already knew how it ended.

A man stood in front of her, a tall, ruddy man with flaming red hair. His breath stank of whiskey. His eyes were fever bright.

She felt her mouth open, and heard herself speak, not knowing where the words came from. The voice wasn't hers. It was a woman's voice, and she was shocked to hear that it sounded like her own mother's.

"Please," her mouth said. "Please don't kill my babies."

The man reached out and slapped her. Hard. And said, in the angriest voice she had ever heard, "Did you think you could get away from me, *bitch?*"

TOR Books by Steven Barnes

Achilles' Choice (with Larry Niven)
Beowulf's Children (with Larry Niven and Jerry Pournelle)
The Descent of Anansi (with Larry Niven)
Firedance
Gorgon Child
The Kundalini Equation
Streetlethal

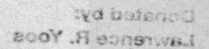

BLOOD BROTHERS

Steven Barnes

TOR®

A TOM DOHERTY ASSOCIATES BOOK
NEW YORK

NOTE: If you purchased this book without a cover you should be aware that this book is stolen property. It was reported as "unsold and destroyed" to the publisher, and neither the author nor the publisher has received any payment for this "stripped book."

This is a work of fiction. All the characters and events portrayed in this book are either products of the author's imagination or are used fictitiously.

BLOOD BROTHERS

Cover art by Waldo Tejada and Shelley Eshkar

A Tor Book
Published by Tom Doherty Associates, Inc.
175 Fifth Avenue
New York, NY 10010

Tor Books on the World Wide Web:
http://www.tor.com

Tor® is a registered trademark of Tom Doherty Associates, Inc.

ISBN: 0-812-54807-8
Library of Congress Card Catalog Number: 96-20706

First edition: November 1996
First mass market edition: October 1997

Printed in the United States of America

0 9 8 7 6 5 4 3 2 1

*To Sonia Barnes, who cared for my father
in his darkest hours, and never faltered*

Acknowledgments

This book is for:

The Kirleys: JoAnn, Michael, and Janette, who were family to me when I needed it most.

The Saturday morning Silat crowd—wild people all, but most especially to Steven Plinck and his wife, Kim, for sharing their home, their hearts and their considerable skills.

Brenda and David Cooper, with hopes that life will bring them all of the wonder and beauty they deserve—I love you both, and always will. *Vaya con Dios.*

My incredible wife, Toni, who had the sense to dare me to move to Washington, and my daughter Nicki, who daily continues with the arduous task of teaching me to be a proper daddy.

My uncle Carver, and cousin Ike, who both helped. And always, for my wonderful sister, Joyce, and her family— Stevie, Shar, and Mitz.

My editor, Beth Meacham, who has always understood. Harley Reagan, Dianne Nightbird, Jamie Charles, Jan Holmes, Pippin Sardo, Richard Dobson, Jeff Learned, Robert Sheckley, Larry Niven, Ray Bradbury, Harlan Ellison, Clive Barker, Jerry Pournelle, and John Truby. Sue and Jeff Stone, the Wizards Tai Chi group—especially Meg and Shannon. Cat Pryde, for a tour of Chicago's underside.

And to all of the shoulders I've leaned on and ears I've bent concerning this project for the last three years—thanks for being there.

And to my readers: comments, questions or requests in the form of e-mail will reach me at LIFEWRITE@AOL.COM. or DJURU@TELEPORT.COM

Soul and skin are linked: Soul can lead skin. Skin can call soul. Both soul and skin can be stolen or torn apart. Shun the man who would tear skin—for he is evil. But fear the man who steals the soul, for that man can steal stars from the sky.

—Congolese saying

Lancaster, California
Thursday, November 27, 1980

The high desert's cool evening breezes lied—they promised peace, not violent death for a woman and two small children. The air was crisp and chill, circling an eye of calm seventy miles north of a swirling urban chaos called Los Angeles. It was an evening for gentle fires, for the slow, warm digestion of turkey, dressing, cranberry sauce and homemade biscuits. And beyond that sweet satiation, for contemplation of a greater holiday soon to come.

Distantly, cars rumbled on Highway 14, heading south to Canyon Country or north to Tehachapi. Somewhere up in the foothills, a coyote yipped for its mate, and a chorus of German shepherds and retrievers answered.

Vista del Mar was a middle-class neighborhood. Its neat rows of prefab Cal-Mex ranch-style houses resembled egg cartons stapled together for a grade school Cinco de Mayo celebration. Every thirty feet, the shadows along the avenue were broken by sodium-arc streetlamps. Yellow-white pools of light washed together in overlapping tides.

Vista del Mar terminated in a palm-tree-shadowed cul-de-sac. Bicycles splayed carelessly across manicured lawns. Plastic guns and dolls lay in untidy heaps on porches. The local children knew each other, and each other's toys, well enough to discourage petty theft.

A stretch of brownish grass and bushes separated one house from the others. Its walls were faux adobe, its roof low and tiled with overlapping clay ringlets. The porch light was dimmed, but the living room lights blazed brightly.

Three human shapes emerged from the shadowed bushes. Male shapes. They slid through the night, ghosted across the lawn. Approached the house closely enough to hear the television playing inside.

The men paused, communicating only with brief, fluttery

hand gestures. They moved stealthily, paused, listened, scurried closer, slipped back into shadows.

One paused at a side window. He raised a small tinted mirror at the end of a telescoping wand, and squinted at the reflected image. The bedroom was a typical little girl's, crowded with bunk beds, clothes chests, and posters for Barbie's latest adventures. Toys and dolls and crumpled dresses littered the floor.

A girl with pale red hair slept in a canopied bed. Her name was Dahlia Tucker, "Dolly" to her family. Her skin was as fine as porcelain. Tears shimmered jewel-like, at the tips of her long, thin lashes. One thumb was thrust deeply into her rose petal mouth.

Her perfect face clinched in a frown, as if gripped by a nightmare. Her eyelids fluttered without opening, and two whispered words fell from her lips like stones: *"They're coming."*

Major Austin Tucker drained his bottle of Anchor porter and glanced toward the kitchen. Just visible was the yellow plastic trash can. Within it, six dead soldiers already lay at rest. He pitched the bottle over his shoulder. He didn't need to watch, he instinctively knew the precise trajectory it would travel. Tucker closed his eyes and visualized its lazy spin, heard it crash-tinkle home. "Two points," he said, engulfed by a warm and rosy glow of satisfaction.

Austin Tucker was an enormous man. Wiry, sporting a heavy red beard worthy of a Viking, he stood over six foot three, and possessed the shoulders and arms of a professional athlete. His face was lean and leathery, and sometimes gave the impression that his skull was too big for his skin. When in peak condition, his facial skin stretched tight. In the wrong light or mood his high forehead and jutting cheekbones suggesting the way he might look a month after his own death.

His chest was thick, his gut corded with muscle despite a love of fermented beverages. Some people collected stamps, some collected rocks. He collected memories of Tuborg Gold and Henry Weinhardts. Lately, he had become enamored of a delectable liquid bread called Anchor porter. He managed to squash about half of a cheerfully beery belch.

His massive right arm nestled around the slender shoulders of his wife, Crystal. She sighed in resignation, and brushed a strand of light red hair from her eyes. "I guess it doesn't get much better than this, hmmm?"

He felt good. Perhaps a quarter of a truly enormous turkey was presently basting in his beer-diluted digestive juices. His son, Billy, had trounced him in a game of chess and was presently absorbed in a television show of some kind, something with gunshots and car chases. Eight-year-old daughter Dolly had wobbled off to bed early, propelled by the soporific effect of turkey, Neapolitan ice cream, and having Daddy back in the house after six months of legal separation.

Preoccupied children times holiday spirit times a thoroughly relaxed Mrs. Tucker was the secret formula to a jolly, early Christmas.

Ho ho ho.

"It could get a *lot* better than this," he said, and whispered a suggestion in Crystal's ear. She turned in his arms, and looked up at him, green eyes narrowed. She was a hundred and thirty pounds of strawberry blond fire. Although five pounds above her high school best, her cheerleader's skirt and blouse still fit perfectly—it took *muscle* to retain the firmness of youth, and muscle added weight.

"You think you can handle me, buster boy?"

There was a spark of challenge in her voice, in the cant of her head, in the gleam of those green eyes.

And he wasn't fool enough to mistake her meaning.

You're getting a chance here, she was saying. *Your son wants you here. God knows Dolly wants you here. But convince me. Show me that I should still want you here. Make me want you.*

It'll take everything you've got, but I'm worth it, buster boy.

And she was, too. He wasn't drunk enough to forget the good times. No man could be drunk enough to forget Crystal in her cheerleader skirt. In her prom dress. In the white chiffon ruffles of her wedding gown. In her silk negligee on their honeymoon night, in San Francisco. In his arms in their suite at the Hyatt, with the Golden Gate Bridge sparkling in a bank of silvered fog just beyond their balcony.

He had been the problem. He and the army, and his mistress, that damned beret. Something inside him felt as though he had to earn its emerald blessing—and the respect of his men. And if that meant drinking more than they could drink, brawling harder than they could brawl, partying louder than they could party, well, then, that was what he had to do.

Duty was a jealous bitch.

The home he and Crystal built together eventually became Crystal's fortress, with Austin Tucker perennially on the wrong side of the drawbridge. Every disappointment anchored another bar into place, every canceled vacation added another twist of barbed wire. Although neither had intended to build a keep so cold, both had labored mightily in its construction. Brick by daily brick, one broken promise at a time, the walls grew so strong that neither could climb over, tunnel under, or find any door at all. That was the way love died. One brick at a time.

The living room mantle was heavy with his medals and commendations. An oak showcase in the hall between kitchen and bedrooms held trophies: Light-Heavyweight Interservice Boxing Championship, Heavyweight Karate Championship. Small arms competition, "Top Gun" Award at the GunSight Shooting Academy. And on. And on, testifying to his coordination, endurance, and aggression.

At that moment, he would have traded all of them just to know what Crystal would say to him in the morning.

This will either be the best Thanksgiving we've ever had, she'd said to him. *Or our last. No more games, Tucker. I'm too old for games.*

Can you handle me, buster boy?

"Give me the chance," he whispered, surprised by the husk in his voice, certain that there would be some guile, some lust, some manipulation there. Hearing nothing but a prayer that it still wasn't too late.

Her face, only inches away from his, softened, and he leaned forward to kiss her. Felt her lips warm, soften and part beneath his, and he fell into her, into her willingness to believe in him one more . . . one *last* time.

From the corner of his slitted eye, he saw twelve-year-old Billy at the kitchen table, working very hard to ignore them.

Billy leaned forward, elbows on the speckled blue Formica breakfast table, studying a *Man from U.N.C.L.E.* rerun. His unblinking intensity suggested that Napoleon Solo might possess the secret of eternal life. Or if not that, perhaps something even more immediately important to his redheaded, densely freckled existence: the secret words that induce girls to open their mouths when they kiss. Billy pressed his hands tightly over his ears, and concentrated on the screen.

Crystal's eyes opened, and for a moment he wondered what she was thinking. Maybe saying an early good night to Billy?

No. She was looking behind him, and he followed her gaze. Dolly stood in the hallway leading back to the bedrooms. Her little hands were clenched into fists. Her face was flushed and red. She gulped for air. A feather of alarm reached through the booze and tickled the base of Tucker's spine.

When she finally spoke, her voice was strained, and ragged, and *aged*—insanely, the voice of an older woman. There was something else about it as well, something that he couldn't put his finger on. Something disturbing as hell.

"Danger," Dolly said. *"Get out. They're coming."*

Her mother walked over to her slowly, somewhat stiffly. "What's the matter, baby girl?"

The word "danger" wrenched Tucker alert faster than ten cups of espresso. "Who's coming?"

Once again, Dolly answered in that odd, altered voice. It reminded him of someone. Who? His mother? His sister? Just a little bit. *"They're coming for Billy,"* she said.

That caught Billy's attention, tearing him away from the sight of Ilya Kuriakin orbiting a pair of uneven parallel bars. The Russian-born U.N.C.L.E. agent dismounted, bowling over a clutch of T.H.R.U.S.H. hoodlums in the process. "Who?" Billy asked. "Who's coming for me?"

Crystal pressed the back of her hand flat against her daughter's forehead. "She's warm."

Tucker's first thought was that they should bundle Dolly back to bed. Then the first tendrils of smoke wafted from her hair.

At first, he assumed it was a trick of the light, or the mild hallucinogenic effect of seven beers. For the rest of his life, Tucker would ask himself what might have happened had he perceived the truth five seconds sooner.

Dolly stiffened. Her rosebud mouth twisted with sudden pain. *"Dangerrrrr!!!"* She prolonged the single word exquisitely, almost ecstatically.

Tucker scooped Dolly up. She was fever hot. Too hot, so hot it felt like brushing his arm against a stove. Her eyes rolled up under the lids, exposing the sclera. Her teeth clattered. Dolly opened her mouth impossibly wide and shrieked. She howled and wailed until the entire world seemed ready to explode.

"Dad?" Billy quavered. "What should I do?"

Crystal broke free of her momentary paralysis. "Billy—help me with the bathtub." She didn't wait for him, but ran down the hall and dove left. An instant later came the sound of water rushing against porcelain.

Tucker pressed Dolly tightly against his chest. Waves of heat seared him, flowed from her like air shimmering above a Mojave highway. He staggered toward the bathroom. No more than fifteen or twenty seconds elapsed, but Tucker felt as if the entire world drifted in syrupy slow motion.

Tucker took two halting steps toward the bathroom, and then made a mistake:

He looked down, into Dolly's open, screaming mouth— *"Daddy, helllllp. It hurrrrrts."*—and watched as a tiny blue flame flickered to life at the back of her throat.

At that moment, all rational thought ceased. He gawked, although his skin seared as if he held an electric skillet. Although her nightclothes were untouched, her pale skin fried, darkened, shriveled. He felt nothing, experienced nothing but pain and terror. He staggered onward.

Somewhere up ahead of him, water sounds beckoned.

Only an inch of water stood in the tub. Crystal tore Dolly from his hands, and thrust her beneath the water. Steam boiled away from her skin. He ignored the searing pain in his arms and rolled her in the water, the words *Dolly-DollyDollyDolly* repeating over and over again in his mind. All of the rest of the world collapsed like a dead star.

A world of steam and dwindling screams, then—

Dolly arched up, arms shooting straight out of the mist and the churning murky water. She grasped at her mother once, then fell away, leaving a long, charcoaled smear along her dress. Her eyes crumbled to nothing, her face collapsed to ash, leaving a core of glowing coal in the wet nightclothes. Her remains crumbled through his hands back into the water.

Within Tucker's mind, a chasm yawned. Madness coiled and hissed in that dark and abscessed place. Two emotions exploded within him, shrieking like twin express trains:

Rage. And grief.

Behind him Billy screamed, then made a *"Hhhhh—"* sound, and fell silent.

Tucker grabbed Crystal's shoulders, and pulled her away from the tub. She ripped at him like a scratching, screaming wildcat, struggling to reach the blackened, sodden knot of ash in the tub.

Suddenly, something in Tucker's overloaded brain, some atavistic trip wire clicked. All fear, doubt, confusion and grief vanished.

Something in the house had changed. Billy had stopped screaming in the doorway. Tucker ran back through a multitrack recording in his head, and replayed the despairing aspirate *"Hhhhh—"*

Strange how clear that memory. Even, perhaps especially, in the midst of chaos a part of Tucker remained utterly professional, waited patiently for anything at all within rational experience. And once that single thing was found, Major Austin Tucker became terribly calm.

Crystal screamed. Tucker pivoted in time to see Billy complete his slump to the ground. A tiny red dart protruded from the right side of his neck. In the same moment, the first of two men turned the corner.

Snapshot appreciation: Two men. Negro. Muscular. One built like a linebacker, rifle held high. The other stiletto thin. Rifle low. Fit. Camos and night-vision gear. Laser-sighted Remington .38 dart rifles. Stepping well, very professional. He automatically labeled them Lowball and Highball, for the rifle positions. Lowball already had Crystal in his sights.

Phut-Phut.

She stiffened as the dart slammed into her breastbone. She pawed weakly at its plastic fletching—

Tucker was already in the hall, moving toward Highball. Crystal partially blocked the line of fire. In the narrow hallway there was little room to maneuver. He swung her to the side, slammed his shoulder into the oak trophy case and knocked it into the thin man. Tucker vaulted it, stepped on the middle of the thin man's back and was on Highball a moment later. The big man tried to swing his rifle around, but Tucker pinned his hand in a crushing grip, pivoted and spun in a hip throw. The back of Highball's head crunched into the wall, crushing lath and plaster. Instead of releasing the big man's arm, Tucker twisted. He smashed the flat edge of his right hand into the elbow joint, snapping it like a bread stick.

Highball's arms were tangled around the rifle, and it would have taken a vital moment to extract the weapon. Tucker had a better choice: a knife swung in the invader's belt sheath.

No conscious decision had been made, but Tucker snapped off the safety strap, and slid out the knife as if his fingers were magnetized. He spun it in his grip, and caught Lowball as he came up with the second rifle.

With a single liquid slice, Lowball's arm opened from elbow to wrist. Blood squirted everywhere. Tucker grabbed with his left, stabbed with his right, taking Lowball in the armpit, puncturing the lung. He jammed it to the hilt and left it there, grabbing the rifle. He spun—

Just in time to take a dart in the neck from a third black man, just now entering the hall.

Tucker jerked back, hurt, but his adrenaline was high enough to resist the toxin. He tried to tug the rifle up, but Lowball was still holding on to it. Even dying, the bastard held on. Tucker heaved at it, ripping it away from the weakening fingers—

Phut-Phut. Two more darts in chest and neck. Tucker staggered back, gave up the fight for the rifle, and ripped the bloody knife out of Lowball's armpit, threw it underhand in a flickering throw, burying it in the third man's throat.

The full load of three anaesthetic darts hit Tucker like an avalanche, and his world slid sideways. He crashed back into the wall, pawing at the darts in his chest. All of the strength in his calves and thighs evaporated, and he slid down. The floor struck him hard enough to make him bite his thickened, furry tongue. He felt as if he were floating in ice water.

A few feet away, Crystal lay slumped and motionless. Billy stretched out on the floor like a broken doll.

The night seemed absurdly peaceful. He heard a groan. Highball. He hoped the big bastard was dying. Tucker felt as if he were a balloon, floating up and up and away from himself.

He thought of Dolly. Wanted to cry. Wanted to kill. Wanted to die.

Just before darkness claimed him, a fourth man stepped through the door. Black, like the others. He held some kind of fancy video rig on his shoulder. The fourth man panned the camera back and forth, surveying the damage. An odd symbol was graven on the camera's side, something that looked like a genie in a bottle, next to the words "Advanced Graphics."

The man grinned at Tucker as the camcorder whirred.

The man's lips moved, but Tucker's ears registered nothing. Above himself, outside himself, Tucker wondered at the words. And wondered what death would be like.

In his last moment of consciousness, he understood what the man was saying.

The man said, "Watch the birdie."

Los Angeles, California
Tuesday, April 28, 1992

1

Shadowless, two amazons fled silently across a torchlit corridor. Before they reached the ironclad door at its end, the portal slammed open. They shrank back, cursing.

From behind the door shambled six and one half feet of leering mutant anthropoid. Thick, yellow foam oozed from the corner of its mouth. It waved a whirring chain saw overhead, chortling with unholy glee. The gargoyle laughed as the amazons spun and ran back the way they had come—

To find their path blocked by thirty feet of emerald dragon. Its body coiled and rippled like a sack filled with snakes. Crimson flame shot from saucerlike nostrils.

The taller of the two women reached to a scabbard at her side, drawing three feet of glowing silver sword. She held it high. It shimmered, power boiling forth until the very air about it seethed in a whirl of sparks. She struck at the dragon—

And the blade slid harmlessly *through* it.

"Damn!" Derek Waites said emphatically. He pushed his chair back from the computer terminal, and thumped the screen with a dark forefinger, disgusted.

Derek downed a warm, syrupy sip of Jolt cola. He repressed the urge to regurgitate the mouthful at the screen, or into the computer circuitry itself. In spite of his best efforts, the damned monsters were winning again. That wasn't the way the world was supposed to work. It was especially embarrassing when something like this happened at his daughter's seventh birthday party. Not a pleasant image to remember: a room filled with seven- to nine-year-olds, all eager to challenge the newest leg of Dungeon Quest.

Dee's bright little eyes widening: "Daddy *wrote* this part!" she said gleefully.

Eager laughter. And then the friends begin to play. Everything fine. Isn't it fun? A dozen kids wearing goggles and VR gloves, all hooked into a central desktop machine, which is in turn hooked to a central machine in Malibu Canyon. Each kid sees a representation of himself, or herself. They choose names: Conan, Wonder Woman, Sir Mix-a-Lot, Eddie Murphy (the kid wouldn't be persuaded otherwise).

They settle down to some serious play. They enter the computer-animated world of Dungeon Quest, the most realistic arcade adventures money can't buy, a secret world of monsters and wizards and magic, scheduled for its premiere in summer of '93. . . .

The kids are thrilled. Awed. Even their parents are impressed, and this is especially wonderful because most of them made the southeast trek from Beverly Hills under protest. They consider his mother's house—his new residence—located five miles south of Hollywood and La Brea, an area he often referred to as NorthWestSouthCentral Los Angeles, to be Hell's Penumbra.

The kids giggle and play eagerly. There is only one problem: their weapons don't work. Oh, they wave their arms and mutter spells, but the monsters just walk through the fireballs. Virtual swords slash bugbear butt, but the Uglies merely grin and eat the guests. Conan the Barbarian flexes his video muscles and attacks a puny-looking Ork. The Ork proceeds to perform virtual judo on the hapless Cimmerian. Poor old Bob Howard would toss his cookies.

It was ghastly. In five minutes, the living room went from a dozen cheering kids to a wasteland of sniveling, crying, moaning little casualties. Their parents made swift, lame excuses and performed a magic act of their own. Abracadabra. Why, where *did* the guests go? Door slams. End of party.

Derek sighed.

He was a thin man, about five foot ten, with horn-rim glasses and a distracted air that led seven out of ten complete strangers to guess that he made his living programming computers. At thirty-three, he retained the resemblance to Johnny Mathis that had won him a mild but steady popularity in high school.

Derek tilted his glasses to get a slightly better view. From his wallet, he extracted a sliver of silvered plastic the approximate size and shape of a Visa card. On it the words "Dungeon Quest Commander's Key" were embossed in large, raised letters. Below a half-inch magnetic strip appeared the words "Advanced Graphics, Ltd."

He inserted the key into a slot at the side of the computer case and waited. The computer wasn't a model available from any store or mail-order catalog. It was a custom job, with a central processor faster than anything available for under a quarter million dollars. The entire system was completed by a gigabyte Winchester cartridge system, and a Kodak color laser printer. The setup was a loan from Advanced Graphics Corporation, the machine was reserved for those lucky few engaged in the creation of Dungeon Quest.

It was actually too powerful for the old wiring in his mother's house: he couldn't run the computer, the printer, the Winchester drive and his ceiling lights at the same time.

The words "Debugging Mode" flashed onscreen. Dragon and amazons froze. Their flesh melted away, becoming skeletal lines, mere framework images. Derek extracted a laser pen from a cluster of tubes in his pocket, licked reflexively at the tip and directed its hair-thin ruby laser beam at the screen. Screen sensors registered the light as he drew here and there with the sensitive hand of a master craftsman. He traced along the edge of the dragon, at the place where the sword sliced through it. As he did, a column of alphanumerics scrolled along the left vertical edge of the screen.

Derek pared and drew, each stroke registering in the hard disk. When the sequence was perfected, it would be uploaded via modem to the central system in Malibu, and integrated into the main game.

He loved this. It was as real as anything else in his world, and more real than most.

His daughter Dee stumbled up against him, rubbing sleep from her eyes. She watched him for a while, leaning her head against the wall, not speaking.

She was dark as a Hershey's bar. Her heart-shaped face would be breathtakingly lovely one day. Her nose seemed too small until you looked again and realized that it only appeared so because her eyes were huge.

Dark brown ringlets of hair hung down on her forehead. At the moment, confetti and bits of glitter were sprinkled among the strands. She watched her father work with wide, worshipful eyes. He laughed to himself while he worked. Derek was completely absorbed, as if machine and man fed off each other, each becoming more alive through the interaction.

He hit another combination of keys, his fingers blurring. The message "Game Mode" flashed on-screen. The bare skeletal lines of women and dragon and ogre grew flesh again. Animated flesh, but flesh nonetheless. The taller woman slashed her sword again, and this time the dragon roared in pain and reared back. Cartoon claws pawed the air in animated agony.

Her father thrust a fist into the air and yelled, "Captain Africa strikes!" Dee leaned against him adoringly. Light from the twenty-inch monitor bathed his face in a coruscating rainbow. She gazed up at him and hugged his arm. "Daddy?" she said softly.

He spun. "Dee?" His thin face split in a huge smile. "Did you see that?! I got it working!"

Dee nodded happily, sleepily. Behind him on the screen, the chain saw-wielding monster took center stage again.

"Daddy," Dee said. "I think you've got a problem."

"Nuts!" He turned back to the screen in time to watch the shorter woman whirl a bola in a propeller motion overhead, and then release it at the monster. "What are you talking—?"

The woman released the bola. At the end of their leather thongs, the triple balls whipped through the air. And right through the monster, without disturbing a single square inch of fur.

Waites sagged in frustration. Dee sleepily laid her head on his arm. It took him a few moments to recognize the weight, and for its significance to pierce his veil of concentration.

She tugged at his arm, gaining his attention and distracting him from thoughts of cathode mayhem. She yawned. He glanced at his watch. Almost two in the morning. He sighed. "Why aren't you asleep, honey?"

"Bad dream," she said quietly.

He lifted her onto his lap. She was a warm, soft weight against his chest. His lips brushed her forehead. "Do you remember anything about it?"

She shook her head no, then stopped. "It was a woman," she said. "She was screaming. There was blood." She squeezed her eyes tight. "That was when I woke up."

Derek cursed himself silently. He should have heard her tossing out in the living room, been more aware. But it was just so damned easy to disappear into his work.

As his fingers rubbed her shoulders, he realized that she wasn't wearing her usual nightgown, the one with Fat Albert and the Cosby Kids spiraling around a field of blue flannel in an endless soapbox derby. Tonight she wore something special, a slip woven of cotton and some darker, finer fiber, something old and passed down his wife's side of the family for generations. A present from Grandmama Lula, now gone for three years.

The nightgown had appeared at Christmas three years ago, with instructions for his wife to give it to Dee on her eighth birthday.

He rubbed the cloth between his fingers. It was rougher than her usual nightgown. Maybe a bit scratchy? "Are you sure you want to wear this?"

She nodded drowsily. "Can I sleep with you?" she murmured. All children know that daddies are a sovereign remedy for nightmares.

On screen, the chain-saw monster walked right through a hail of bolas thrown by the shorter woman. He raised his whirling weapon on high.

Derek winced as the saw came down. Flesh parted. Fluorescent arterial blood gushed.

"Daddy," Dee murmured, "you're *sick.*" She giggled with sleepy delight, and her head melted into him again. A contented smile curled her lips. She had come between Daddy and his work, and that was enough for her.

It shouldn't have been. There shouldn't ever be a question in her mind as to the relative importance of children and computers. But there *was* a rivalry, and he was the one who had let it creep into his family.

And eventually, let it destroy his marriage.

"No more. Not ever again," he whispered.

"Oh, I like it when you're sick," she said.

"Not that," he said. He held her tightly and heaved himself to a standing position. "Something else."

"Can I sleep with you?" she asked again.

Derek Waites rubbed at his eyes. Now that he considered it, an eight-hundred-pound fatigue gorilla was banging against the wall of his concentration. One part of him wanted to make it an all-nighter, to work and work until the job was done. . . .

But there was a small, living miracle in his arms, a warm and loving someone who needed him, and needed him now.

And the hell of it was that he even had to reason it out like that.

Damn.

"Sorry, ladies." He pressed the mouse button, drew down a menu from the top of the screen and selected "Quit."

The computer produced a card cautioning him to check his LAN and modem connections upon resumption of activities, and blinked off.

"Whee!" She giggled. Dee smiled dreamily as Waites carried her out into his modest living room.

The lampposts beyond his front window cast pools of pale light out onto West View Street. He had grown up here. Over the years, both he and the street had changed. Yellow light glowed behind the curtains of the house across the street. That would be Mr. Rossini, who seemed to have lost the knack for sleep since Mrs. Rossini's death, a decade earlier. Strange, that. The Rossinis were estranged at the time, kids grown, nothing in common but the roof above their separate bedrooms. Still, her death forced Mr. Rossini to turn some cold and lonely corner of his life. Perhaps he, too, had nightmares. Perhaps he, too, was afraid of the dark.

Confetti littered the entire living room, remnants of the afternoon's birthday party. He remembered the faces of the parents as they brought their children up to the door. West View Street was a long way from Doheny Drive, the site of last year's party.

But that was before the divorce. Before a lot of things. Right now, Derek Waites was glad his mother had left him this house. He wondered what might have happened to him if she hadn't, and didn't like the answer.

An avocado green L-shaped couch snuggled into one corner of the room. Rafts of makeshift bedding stretched across it in happy disarray. Dee's side, with the Mr. Elephant blankets and the Lego-block pillow covers, was empty. On the other side of the L slept a boy. He was twelve, almost thirteen—in less than two weeks he would celebrate his own birthday, and all of the fuss and muss would be repeated. Fuss and muss that Derek awaited as a drowning man craved his next breath of air.

The boy's hair was cut very short, with a razored arrow drawn almost to the scalp. He was small for his age, but wiry and awesomely quick on the basketball court. There was an innocence that seemed almost out of place in this age of playground crack dealers and pederastic TV evangelists. His

name was Troy, and in some small way, he and Dee were
Derek's bridges to another, better life.

He bent, kissed the boy gently, just below the brow line,
tasting moisture and a thin salty film of sweat. Troy's open
lips emitted a steady purring sound. With one hand, Derek
tucked the sheet up around Troy's neck, and murmured,
"Sleep well, sweetheart."

Derek carried Dee back through the house, through the
hallway he had walked so many times as a boy. All of those
years he thought he had left behind him. Years of climbing
up and out, years of college, and then owning his own company, Prometheus Engineering, Ltd. Years of marriage and
happiness, and some fine homes and a fine family.

And then . . .

Shit. He didn't want to think about it.

They entered his bedroom, the same bedroom he had
grown up in. Some of the same books crowded the shelves.
Tom Swift and His Atomic Jetmarine by Victor Appleton
II. *Conan the Usurper* by Robert E. Howard. *Tunnel to the
Stars*—

He had to giggle a little when he saw the Heinlein title. It
had been ghost-checked out of the school library in third
grade. One of these days he was going to walk back to Alta
Loma, and see if Mrs. Stewart, the librarian, was still there.
He wanted to see the expression on her face when he brought
Tunnel back and presented his head for a pat. See? I'm not
bad. I brought it back. . . .

The bedside clock read 2:05. A more serious and insistent
yawn racked his body. He laid Dee carefully on the bed, and
stood back up, straightening his spine, listening to it crackle.
Snap, crackle, pop. Jesus. His back never used to do that.
Maybe he needed to get more exercise. A feverish meta-
bolism kept him thin as a rail, but it was a kind of *soft* thin.
His body had always been utterly competent at its most important job, namely, carting his brain and penis from one
adventure to the next. Derek was beginning to suspect that
God had erred on the basic locomotive design. Dammit, *he*
could design a better body than this one, so why couldn't
the Almighty?

Oh, well. His body needed sleep, and food, and Jolt cola

(Nectar of the Nerds), and occasional sex. Aside from that it gave him very little trouble, so he supposed he should feel grateful.

He stopped himself. That was the compulsive programmer in him talking, the part that had almost destroyed his life. He had to stop that, to fight against it, or he would lose his family.

And he would rather die than do that.

He laid Dee softly on the bed. Almost instantly, she opened her eyes and rolled off.

Scammed again.

"Hey! Where are you going now?"

"Brush my teeth," she said. "Got to brush my teeth."

He nodded. He sat on the edge of the bed, another, darker, wave of fatigue gnawing at him. Equations and flow lines coiled in his thoughts like snakes in a swamp. He desperately ached to get back into his office, but he dared not give in to it. If he hadn't the strength to do it for his own beaten body, then for Dee: if he wasn't in bed when she got back, she would just come looking for him.

Derek felt the gears of his mind engage, grinding against each other as they clawed their way to a decision. Thank God, the parental part of his superego could still keep his ego under control. That was Freud's gig, wasn't it? And what part of a programmer was the id? Christ, he was tired. He lay back against his pillow and closed his eyes for an instant.

Water bubbled distantly in the bathroom, and the sound of small, delicate scrubbings. *Up and down, up and down, side side side side side.*

Dee was very conscientious. He lay back on the bed, and closed his eyes. Just for a moment. The bed felt so comfortable, and the pillows so soft. And it felt good beneath his sore back. Very good. It felt as though the bed were dissolving under him, and he was falling into a deep, deep hole. . . .

Dee spat very politely, completing her dental ablutions. She had to stand on tiptoe to hit the drain precisely. She liked to hit it as precisely as possible, because she really didn't much like the way it looked when a mouthful of peppermint foam splashed against the side. Yuck. When she straightened, she saw the small color print stuck into the corner of the mirror. It was a little bent at the corner, and had been taped back into place. It was a picture of her, and Troy, and Dad, and Mom. Maybe two years old, an image of the house in Hollywood. That was before the trouble. It was easy to look at Mommy, so pretty and smiling, but something in her eyes said that she wasn't as completely happy as a mommy should be.

She was happier now. Uncle Medford wasn't Daddy, but he made Mommy happy, and that earned points. Sometimes this was confusing, but Dee was learning to live with it.

Daddy hurt almost all the time, but kept trying to act happy. Daddies were ridiculous like that. He wasn't fooling anyone. He didn't fool her. Dee knew what Daddy needed, which was to forget everything and play more. That was what the whole world needed. Sometimes daddies just needed someone to remind them of the important things in life.

She looked at herself in the mirror. She liked the new nightgown, but she couldn't tell her daddy the real reason why. Somehow, it just felt *right*. Daddy would think she was crazy if she said it, but the nightgown seemed to *tingle* a little bit, especially the dark threads running through the white. Grandmama Lulu said that it belonged to Great-great-grandmama Dahlia, Dee's namesake. It smelled old and felt old, and after tonight, Dee would put it back in its cedar chest and maybe just take it out now and then, and then maybe give it to her own daughter someday. . . .

But tonight it felt good.

Really good. It actually *tingled*, but she wouldn't tell Daddy about that. Maybe it would keep the nightmares away.

Dee turned off the bathroom light, and went back to bed. Even before she entered the room, the harsh burr of Daddy's snore made her flinch. Daddy lay on his back, mouth open, eyes closed, sawing logs.

She pulled the cover over him, and crawled in next to him, fitting to him like a baby spoon to a daddy spoon. Her tiny arms went around him, reveling in the warmth, safety and comfort of her father.

She felt all tingly, and was sure that there wouldn't be any more nightmares tonight. She hardly *ever* had them.

Dee's eyes fluttered closed. Not all the way closed. The lower arc of her pupil was still visible beneath the lash. It vibrated back and forth, back and forth violently within a minute or so after sleep overcame her. Her tiny body spasmed, and she moaned softly.

A thin sheen of perspiration beaded her cheeks.

She spoke without waking, and her voice was no longer a child's voice. It was older by years, perhaps decades. A mature woman's voice. An old woman's voice.

"Please don't kill my babies!" Her voice was filled with a terror somehow made more horrible by the tender age of its source.

"I couldn't let you murder the babies. . . ." Her face grew slack. Her head jerked to the side, as if slapped. *"No . . ."*

And then she screamed, *"Don't kill my babies—"*

Tehachapi State Prison,
Tehachapi, California

2

"Don't kill my babies! Don't kill—" Austin Tucker awoke on his bunk, screaming. His recent dreams sloughed away like hot, sticky sand. He struggled to orient himself. *Where? . . .*

Who? . . .

The dream. That damned dream again. A dream of killing some black woman. Strange, though—he was watching himself do it, almost like a spectator.

Sounds around him, outside of him. Echoes along the shadowy cell block. The other inmates hooting at . . . something. At him.

The yells shivered into echoes, reinforcing each other, swelling into a cacophony shrill enough to awaken the entire prison. Cries filled with anger and ridicule, mocking his fear.

Austin Tucker was forty-five years old. His blazing red hair, still thick, receded from his forehead and temples a bit.

Although his chest was still a barrel, his belly hung heavy now, something he had never thought would happen. There were a lot of things he'd never thought would happen. But they had, hadn't they?

"Shut the fuck up, *killer!*" someone yelled from down the block. The word "killer" echoed mockingly.

Tucker inhaled hard and held it. He exhaled, struggling to orient himself in his cell. It was six by ten, standard size in the Tehachapi max block. For the past six years, it had been his home. A calendar was tacked to one wall, the dates pale rectangles beneath a garish nude blonde. He wasn't certain why he kept it there. Maybe to remind him that time actually did pass. Sometimes it felt as though it never would. Nights felt like months. Days like weeks. Hell would be a relief, after a life like this. The calendar page read "April 1992." He felt as if it were a century too slow.

Or too fast. God, the nightmare was so real—and he was the star of the show. Only a little younger, and without the beard, or the scars he had won in Southeast Asia. Weirder still, he almost seemed to be watching the nightmare, experiencing it from the position of the black woman. What kind of Freudian bullshit was this?

" 'Sa matter, tough guy? Bad dreams?"

He finally managed to make out one of the voices. Then another, and another.

"Screaming like your fuckin' wife screamed, baby killer?"

His palms blazed. He felt them shake. All he wanted was peace. All he wanted was peace. All he wanted was—

"All right. Quiet. Shut up, everybody. Back to sleep. Show's over, show's over." Parker's voice, one of the three guards who worked the block. Parker looked like a shaved rottweiler, but was a decent guy.

Parker stopped at the cell door. His flashlight shone like a glittering metal eye. Tucker reflexively sucked his gut in a little. God, he felt old and tired and sick. Why couldn't he just get numb like so many of the other cons? *Because they don't serve Percodan in hell,* he tells himself.

He looked down at himself as the flashlight played over him. His hands, clutching at his knees, were great calloused, knobby things. His arms and legs were corded with muscle. Once his entire body had been like that. That had been a long time ago. Another life. There was almost nothing left of the man he used to be.

God. Let me die.

"Tucker. *Tucker!*" Parker yelled.

Tucker shielded his eyes with one flat, hard, callused hand. "Dream," he muttered. "Another . . . bad dream."

Parker nodded. "Keep it down," he said sympathetically, but not taking any shit, either. That was Parker. "Get some sleep."

Tucker climbed heavily back into his bunk, and curled onto his side. He stared into the darkness, trying to find . . . something.

"Don't kill my babies!" Someone in the block above him laughed. "What a pussy!"

"Maybe it's your *kids,* Tucker. That how you earned that beret, killing kids?"

Parker slammed his heavy flashlight into the wall next to Tucker's cell, and yelled, "I said, shut the fuck up!"

The laughter continued to echo up and down the block, ceasing to be words, or even identifiable human sounds. Became fragments of his own nightmare, all of the light and sensation squeezed out of them, a solid wall of pitiless sound.

The max block cafeteria of Tehachapi State Prison can seat four hundred and fifty prisoners at a time. The entire room is painted an institutional, sickly green. Guards pace a catwalk ringing the walls. From this high vantage point they watch the convicts with care, directing the floor guards into trouble spots with swift efficiency. By common agreement, the room is generally divided along racial and cultural lines. The two largest slices of the room's pie go to the white and the black inmates, a smaller but still substantial section to the Latinos. The Asians have barely a table to themselves.

Tucker carried his tray into the food line, deaf to the laughs and whispers around him. He pushed his tray at the man behind the counter, and received a pile of steaming glop for his efforts. It could have been hash, or oatmeal, or horse puke. He barely cared. Reflexively, he put a carton of milk on his tray, considered and then replaced it. He waited for the crowd to thin, and picked his way to a half-empty table. Even as sparsely occupied as it was, the others scooted down to make additional room for him.

Tucker was by far the largest man at the table, a shambling bear of a human being. He hunched over his food and ate one slow spoonful at a time, weighing each carefully.

Two men made their way through the room over to him. They didn't carry trays. Tucker figured they had already finished eating. By mess hall rules, they should have filed out into the yard as soon as they were finished, along a sickly green corridor and past the metal detectors that prevent uncreative inmates from smuggling spoons.

The men were a Mutt and Jeff pair, bearded types reminiscent of extras in a Corman biker flick, palookas who might have given Jack Nicholson or Peter Fonda problems on the *Easy Rider* highway.

The bigger one's beer belly made Tucker feel downright petite. His name was Trench. The lean weasel of a man was named Murray.

Trench sidled up to him, whispering in low, confident tones. "It's going down, Tucker."

Murray bobbed his head up and down, up and down, so excited Tucker thought he might pee his pants.

Tucker ate, saying nothing.

Murray's tight little eyes sparkled. "They found someone to go against you. Some kick-boxing pimp who came in last month." He paused, as if building up dramatic effect. "Have you ever heard of Ahmed?"

Tucker looked out across the room, his eyes drawn as if by magnets to the largest, loudest table in the room. Black men crowded the table. They laughed raucously. Most of their attention was focused on one enormous man. He was dark-skinned, huge, almost as big as Tucker. From across the room, Tucker could tell that the man was harder than he, leaner. Corded with bouncy muscle.

Ahmed.

Almost as if Ahmed sensed Tucker's sudden interest, he turned and grinned, lifting his milk carton in ironic salute.

Ahmed was sugar-pimp handsome, his body so brutally

hard he might have controlled a bevy of hookers single-handedly. Pleasure and pain in one gaudy package.

Tucker returned to his food.

Trench slammed his palm on the table, almost feverish with hatred. "Are you gonna do it?" He dropped his voice a bit. "You gonna use that vibrating palm thing? *Zing?* Stop his fucking nigger pump?"

Tucker felt as if the words were flying over him, away from him, far away. Floating overhead. He could have glanced up and plucked them out of the ether if he cared to, but he didn't.

Didn't need to. He was more interested in another mouthful of food.

He could taste the way it broke down in his mouth, taste every little lump and flake, right down to the fiber. It was awful. It was fascinating. Down and down and down. When the liquid light pumped in his mind, it seemed he could break down the complex proteins into their most basic amino acids, and the carbohydrates into their individual chains long and short, the fats into individual globules and from there right down to the molecular level . . .

Distractedly, he realized that they were waiting for an answer. He didn't have one for them. Murray slapped him on the back.

"Hell, boy," he said, all chums now. "Any way you want it. You saved Krause, the main man! That's good enough for the Brotherhood."

Krause was the leader of Lightning Dawn, the largest and craziest right-wing militia in California. Convicted on charges of conspiracy to murder Senator Dwight Nelson. He had been right at home with the Aryan Brotherhood, the neo-Nazi power controlling the California penal system. The Aryan Brotherhood hated Senator Nelson as a Commisymp race-mixing nigger faggot. Far more liberal than the AB, Lightning Dawn simply hated Nelson because of his gun control stance.

But the AB had only *talked* about killing Nelson. Krause had blown up the senator's beachside love nest. The senator had required stitches, burn treatments, and the best divorce lawyer in Century City. The senator's nineteen-year-old lover had sold his story to the *Tattler* for six figures.

Krause had gone to jail, becoming an instant hero to the AB. It was a marriage made in hell.

And Tucker had saved Krause. If he had it to do over again . . .

The two men laughed, making light of the discomfort they felt around the huge man, telling themselves that they'd gotten the responses they wanted from him. They slapped his back, and left the table.

Tucker continued to shovel the tasteless food into his mouth, continuing to feel the textures right down to an impossibly fine level. He wondered if he were the only one in the world who tasted food, who felt time, who sensed life in this bizarre manner. Certainly, he was tired of asking others if they shared this or that perception. He had wearied of the odd expressions, the polite laughs. Those responses had dogged him since the moment, coinciding with (and, he suspected, resultant of) puberty, when he woke up watching odd lights coursing behind his eyes, and realized there was something special about him. Something that made him better at football. At unarmed combat.

And at the deadlier games played by the Special Forces units. He was tired of trying to explain what was different about him, especially since even the best and the brightest seemed blind to his world. Scum like Murray and Trench weren't even worth trying to educate.

Tucker caught a flash of glittering metal. He didn't even have to tell his body what to do. In a single seamless motion, he pivoted up from the table. His right hand swept around, blocking, grabbing the wrist, still wheeling, throwing the man to the table. Smooth as snatching a roller-skater off a greased rink.

He whipped the man around, and brought his own elbow to within an inch of the attacker's Adam's apple, within a tick, a breath, a heartbeat of just allowing his weight to fall forward to crush the vulnerable trachea.

A voice within him said, *Why not? How many more life sentences can they give you?*

But the feverishly terrified kid beneath him was just that. A kid. And the "weapon" was a spoon. Blunt. Harmless.

The kid had simply tripped, slipped, fallen against Tucker fast enough to trigger his freak reflexes, response patterns that should have been dead and gone, long ago.

They weren't so damned fast that night you were drunk, were they? They weren't so fast the one time you really needed them, were they, killer?

The kid was so terrified that he could do nothing but rattle away in machine-gun Spanish. Tucker recognized enough of it to know that the kid was begging for his life. Swearing that he hadn't meant anything. It was a mistake. Please, please don't kill him. . . .

Tucker looked up. The entire room was silent. The men at the table around him had stopped eating, staring with fear and astonishment.

They had probably blinked and missed the action. Or worse: hadn't blinked, and *still* missed it.

The kid was thin, terrified, maybe eighteen years old. Maybe. A guard hurried toward them. Two guards. Three.

Tucker stood, and released the boy.

His hands felt hot. He remembered the dream.

Something was happening to him. Something was coming. He didn't know what, or when.

He knew only that it had something to do with death.

And a black woman who seemed oddly, impossibly familiar.

Wednesday, April 29

3

The sweet aroma of espresso wafted through Derek's sleep, lifting him up to consciousness, out of a dream that had begun in darkness but through some odd alchemy become lighter and brighter as it rolled on.

Derek woke up smiling, stretching. He stretched out his arm, checking on Dee without turning his head to look at her.

He yawned hard, feeling as if his blood had congealed in his veins overnight. Derek rolled out of bed, only then really looking down at Dee. She was still asleep, curled into a ball like a little kitten, and he simply couldn't bring himself to wake her up.

He splashed water on his face, examined himself in the mirror and performed the daily job of adjusting the muscle tensions until his mirror image looked like someone he'd want to know. Then, armed with the knowledge that he had taken the first huge strides toward wakefulness, he went out to face the coffee.

Troy was puttering around the kitchen, absurdly small in one of Derek's T-shirts, trying to organize the components of breakfast.

He greeted his father with a huge grin. " 'Morning." Derek sniffed at the espresso machine (a DeLonghi Caffè Pronto, sixty bucks if it was a penny, and last Christmas's present from Dee and Troy), which had just ceased its happy gurgling.

A cup of hot milk sat next to it, lightly steam-frothed. Derek started to extract the little glass pot to draw off its dark nectar, but Troy waved him away. The boy was good at this: he sniffed at the steam, waved it under his nose, and gave an okay sign.

"The coffee is exceptional this morning," he said in a splendidly faux British accent. He poured the dark fluid into the steamed milk, sprinkled a little cinnamon on top, and handed it to his father. Derek tasted, and purred in satisfaction. Life was good.

He let Troy push him down into a chair. "Let me. I never get to do this for you anymore."

"You're going to make someone a wonderful wife—"

Troy balled up his little fist, and screwed his face up tightly. "Sit down, shut up, or I *punch!*" The Asian accent wasn't bad at all. Two whole months of Hapkido. Bruce Lee lives.

Pop-Tarts levitated in the toaster, and Troy scooped them onto a napkin and brought them to his father. "Another minute for the eggs." Troy sat down and stared into his father's eyes. The boy looked so earnest.

Both Dee and Troy looked like little Derek clones. On more than one occasion Rachel had sworn that they weren't hers, had probably budded off Derek's rump. They were no spawn of *hers*.

"What we've got to do," Troy said, "is get you and Mom back together."

"Troy—"

"Nope. I think this whole thing with Medford is just a bluff." He narrowed his thirteen-year-old eyes. "It's time to move in for the kill."

"Is that what the breakfast and the espresso is all about? I've told you before—I don't really have a say in it. Really."

Troy cocked his head. "I've got a plan."

"What plan?" Derek asked, exasperated.

"You'll see," Troy said. He got up hurriedly. "I've got to take a shower."

"What plan?"

"Oops! Gonna be late!" And he was gone before Derek could haul him back. He sighed, and took a bite of the eggs. Damn, they were good.

He eased into a luxurious breakfast, listening to Troy's toneless singing as the shower water began to run.

Well, whatever Troy had up his sleeve, it was bound to be entertaining.

Derek dropped off Dee first. She attended St. Helen's, a fairly pricey school just north of Santa Monica. Its gates and white towers seemed ostentatious for an elementary school, but he felt a pang of pride when she scampered off toward the front door. She paused on the steps, and turned, as if knowing that he would be there to watch.

She blew him a kiss, and then waved at Troy, and pirouetted, her red-and-black skirt twirling in the sun.

"Dad?" Troy said in the seat beside him. Derek didn't really hear his son. Damn, but that little girl was pretty. "Dad? It's time to go."

Derek nodded, and pulled his Toyota Tercel back out into traffic.

He piloted his car on automatic, taking it through a swarm of BMWs and Lexuses. He kept remembering the way Dee looked, only pulled from his reverie by the sound of Troy clucking in the seat next to him.

"You know, I think you love my sister more than you love me."

"She's just prettier."

"Yeah, but I'm more mannish. Check out my mustache."

"That's dirt."

"Well, yeah, but under the dirt, there's hair."

Troy's school was only five minutes farther, Fairfax High School. A public school, it still had the best electronics program in the state, and a computer lab endowed by an alumnus who had gone on to eight seasons as TV's toughest private eye. Someone Derek had a very special reason to dislike.

Oh, well . . .

Derek pulled up in the line of parents waiting for their opportunity to drop their kids off. A tall, thin man strolled by, ducked his head to look in the window. Derek recognized him instantly. That was Mr. Fiscus, Troy's science teacher. He grinned and ran with surprising, storklike grace around to the other side of the car.

"Mr. Waites!" He said, and pumped Derek's hand. "So glad we'll have you for Career Day. Hello, Troy."

"Hi, Mr. Fiscus."

"Career Day?" Derek asked blankly.

"Why, yes—we've already heard back from your wife. Next Wednesday. You're going to talk about setting up your engineering firm."

He looked over at Troy, who smiled innocently. "Well . . . sure," he said. "If she's willing to be there. Absolutely. I'm not much of a public speaker, though."

"I'm sure you'll be fine." Fiscus's Adam's apple performed an exercise in linear equilibrium, and he smiled with genuine warmth, waving his hand as he jogged back toward the school.

"Career Day?" Derek asked quietly, when Fiscus was out of earshot.

"Yep."

"Me and your mom? Talking about the good old days, eh?"

Troy had a fascinating resemblance to a Siamese cat.

Derek shook his head. "You have *got* to stop this."

"Any day now," Troy said, and hopped out of the car. He leaned his head in, and spoke in a pretty damned fair imitation of Fiscus's voice. "I'm sure you'll be fine," he said, and scampered off.

Derek pulled out into traffic, shaking his head.

Career Day.

Not bad, kid.

Derek drove down Sunset to La Brea Avenue and turned right. He had driven this path so many times that it felt completely automatic. The number of times he and Rachel had stopped at Pink's hot dog stand and savored their chili, the number of times they had counted the hookers trolling Melrose, or taken a side trip at three o'clock in the morning to window shop . . .

That was early in their marriage, the really good times, when he and Rachel shared dreams, peered in the crystal ball they were casting together. They spoke of their glorious future. Those were the times they would talk about at Career Day.

Afterward, they would go to lunch, laughing and talking. And her eyes, those unforgettable brown eyes, would sparkle and be so full of life. And she would laugh. And at some point, because she was happy, and remembering the good times between them, her hand would steal across the table . . .

A chill actually ran up his spine.

Damn you, Troy. You're *good.*

The farther south he went, the tackier La Brea became. South of Wilshire Boulevard car washes and doughnut stands proliferated. The pastry stands had once been Winchell's franchises, but now sold mystery muffins of unknown pedigree. There was a Taco Bell which had once been a part of the now defunct Pup 'n Taco chain (hot dogs and tacos fifteen cents, chili or kraut five cents extra). He still remembered when Taco Bell had also charged fifteen cents for a crisp corn shell and a generous dollop of greasy meat. Now, after massive publicity that attempted to position Taco Bell as one of the big three quick-nosh dealers, prices had skyrocketed to fifty-nine cents for a taco. Four hundred percent inflation. Economics are most concrete when they affect your appetite.

On his car radio, the announcer was saying something about the Rodney King beating case. So a bunch of cops had beaten the hell out of some poor drunk. Nothing new there. Big difference this time—they'd gotten caught on video. *Watch the birdie*. They'd fry. The verdict was due later today, and Derek was already bored with the whole thing.

By the time he reached Pico, the neighborhood had begun to look positively sleazy.

Derek turned left off La Brea, onto Washington Boulevard, to West View Street, and turned right, past the liquor store. Once, this had been a nice corner. A little shopping center: laundromat, liquor store, paint store. The paint store was filled with the sharp smells of turpentine and water-based paint and wallpaper and paste, staffed by nice brown-skinned women who operated the jiggling machines, mixing perfect colors for his mother. Nice parking lot, where he and his friends had skateboarded for hours on end, losing themselves in friendly challenges and scraped knees and elbows and general summer-day delirium.

Derek had never had the nerve to take his skateboard down the hill cresting West View Street. Never gone faster and faster, out of control, swooping down toward Twenty-first Street. He was always too afraid of losing control, and spinning out into traffic.

He paused at Twenty-first Street to let a green Datsun putt past, and drove on down. Three houses from the end of the block, he pulled into the driveway of a white house with a blue-green arched roof. A white wrought-iron fence embraced the yard. Once, the yard had been neat and green. Now it was matted and brown.

The neighborhood was pretty quiet. As he lifted a single bag of groceries from the car he heard music from a television a few doors down. A dog barking. Traffic rumbled along the Santa Monica Freeway, only a block farther south.

He balanced the groceries on his hip as he opened the front door. The streamers and party decorations were still everywhere, still reminded him of the previous day's truncated celebrations. He sighed. He put the groceries away, pulled a

Jolt from its plastic holder, popped the tab and sipped deeply. It tasted better than the promise of heaven.

The living room was small. A green couch divided it from the dining room. A piano sat against the wall, unused except when Dee tinkled its keys. A long time ago he had taken lessons. Long neglected. Forgotten.

His mother's bedroom was his office now. It seemed sacrilegious to make her bedroom his own. After inheriting the house, he had imagined bringing women home and making love to them on his mother's bed. The notion was nauseating. He had thrown the mattress away, and purchased a water bed.

It still didn't make any difference. After his divorce from Rachel, the legal problems, and the two years away from his family, he'd never brought a woman home anyway. Something had just gone out of him, and he didn't know where to find it. He hadn't had sex in over a year. He didn't miss it.

Yeah, sure.

He walked into the office, and turned the computer on.

The prototype's special screen allowed direct laser-pen input to the graphics programs. The Advanced Graphics logo on the side of the machine looked like an abstracted, ugly genie in a bottle. He didn't know who did their artwork, but he figured they ought to be stabbed with paint brushes until they looked like a revisionist St. Sebastian.

While the computer booted up, he leaned back in his chair, staring at the certificates on the wall. There were thirteen parchments, etched with curlicues and stamped with gold seals. There were also clippings and magazine cuttings.

"National Merit Scholar," one of them said. Another read, "Most Innovative Software Design." Another, and in some ways the one he was most proud of, perhaps more proud of than anything else he had ever done in his entire life, was the one that read "Cal Tech Valedictorian, Class of '81."

There was a picture below that one, of a young man in a blue robe, with a tasseled cap, the tassel already switched from the left to the right side. He stared into the face in the picture. Just a boy, really. So young. So damnably young and confident.

And optimistic.

There were other awards and certificates, including his business license for Prometheus Engineering, Ltd., and a framed photostat of a two-hundred-dollar check. First profits of the company. He remembered that. Too damned well.

And finally, as if to remind himself of something he was afraid of forgetting, there was a picture torn out of another magazine. It was in a plastic protector sheet, and it depicted him in handcuffs, hustled out of the Santa Monica house. The caption read, "Captain Africa Strikes—Out." The type was gaudy, as if there were a special pleasure in announcing the arrest.

And perhaps there was. A few of his covert actions had caught the media's fancy: arranging to have David Duke send e-mail to the entire membership of Compuserve's gay interracial dating service had a certain newsworthy panache.

"Notorious computer hacker Derek Waites, known as Captain Africa, was convicted today on charges of grand larceny and . . ."

He wrenched his mind away. Enough of that crap: he had work to do.

For hours he worked, his single telephone line hooked into the main system in Malibu.

He lost track of time, of tension, of everything except the work. This was the easy part. What was hard, had always been hard, was people stuff. Machines were easy. There was a mathematical sanity about a machine. You hit a 3, the screen said 3. If it didn't, there was something wrong.

With people, you punch in a key, and you get a string of random symbols. There was no way to open them up and see what was wrong. In fact, there wasn't really anything wrong. That was just the way people were, and he had to get used to that idea.

The amazons were battling with an on-screen dragon, this time with considerably greater success. With each sword stroke, the dragon roared in pain. Derek clicked a button, and the three-dimensional images became skeletal lines. He traced the dragon's outline with the bright, hair-thin beam of his laser pen. He rotated the model, examining it from all angles.

Everything looked good. "Captain Africa strikes!" he yelled, and wearily thrust his fist into the air.

He speed-dialed Rachel's work number at CBC and was faintly surprised to get a busy signal. Strange—he rarely got that irritating beep this time of night. It was almost nine, and while Rachel was usually supervising taping until ten or so, he would have expected to get her beeper, and then, finally and somewhat irritably, Rachel herself. Somewhere in the back of his mind it registered that sirens were blaring. Hmm.

Maybe a fire or something.

He tried the number again, and this time rang through. "Extension four-four-two, please," he said when the operator answered.

He dredged the name of the night operator out of his memory. "Ina?" he asked. "This is Mr. Waites. Is Rachel still there?"

"Mr. Waites?" she asked. She sounded breathless.

There was something in her voice that chilled him. "Yes?"

"Ms. Childe left a message for you." Pause. "Two of them. She went to pick up the children. And the children are safe. She couldn't reach you on the phone. . . ."

The sound of sirens was oppressive now, something akin to the sensation of an express train bearing down. "Is there something wrong?"

He was already walking to the window. So many sirens. To the north, something glowed in the night sky. His skin crawled. Something was terribly, terribly wrong, and somehow he had missed it entirely.

Rachel's secretary was still saying something when he hung up the phone.

Derek turned on his radio, and stood staring out at the street, listening to the news commentator as he did.

"And what began as an isolated disturbance at Normandie and Seventy-seventh Street has swelled to include other sections of the city, as reactions to the verdict—"

The verdict? What?

He twirled the dial.

"And in the wake of a not-guilty verdict in the Rodney King beating trial—"

Derek felt numb. What? Not . . . guilty?

Distantly, he heard sirens. Screams. But more than anything, he felt the cold hand of fear at his throat.

Not . . . guilty . . . ?

"This isn't happening," he whispered.

4

It took him another hour to raise Rachel on the phone. By the time he did, his blood pressure felt as if it were under boil, and the sound of police sirens had grown to an almost omnipresent, shrill whine, weaving in and out of the background noise, worming their way into his consciousness at the oddest and least appropriate times.

But he kept calling, kept dialing, hoping that one of the calls would get through. When it finally did, he was taken by surprise.

Until then, all of the lines had been busy. And busy. And as the disturbance that began in South Central L.A. spiraled further and further out of control, Derek felt increasingly weak and nauseated.

He wasn't the only one. On every channel, news commentators black, white and Asian expressed two common attitudes: shock at the not-guilty verdict, and absolute horror at the violence breaking out across Los Angeles.

He could understand that. This wasn't even a racial issue. It was something older, and uglier. It was *Shall we have law?*

The question is, what happens when a large section of the population feels that there is no justice?

Anarchy.

Derek was almost paralyzed, and while he fought with that awful sensation, Los Angeles blazed. Derek was hypnotized by real-time television images: not six blocks away, a liquor store was being smashed and looted. He felt as if his hands were melting into the arms of his chair.

"Hello?" Rachel said.

"Hi," he replied weakly. "Rachel?"

He heard her exhalation. It was easy to imagine her exquisite body slumping in relief. "Thank God," she said. "I'd been trying your line for hours."

A long pause. Sirens blared.

"Are the kids all right? Are you—?"

"All fine. Derek—stay home. It's bad out there. It's worse than we're saying on the news."

"What do you mean??"

"I've heard things," she said. "Through some of the news contacts at CBC. It's weird. But just . . . be careful."

He thought for a moment, and then said, "Put Dee on the phone, would you?"

"Sure." She paused, and then said awkwardly, "I guess this kind of screws up dinner tomorrow, huh? Do you want to come over here?"

"Ah . . . is Medford still in Cannes?"

"No, he got back in last night."

Derek resisted the impulse to grind his teeth. Enamel was so fragile. "Perfect timing."

"Let's push it back a couple of days, all right?"

He could hear the smile in her voice.

"I love you," he said carefully.

"Thank you," she said.

There were a couple of clicking sounds, and then Dee was on the line. "Daddy?"

"Sweetheart? You're safe now, you know. Are you scared?"

"Troy said that the martians are coming."

"I think the technical term for that is a lie."

"I know. Check mark for Troy."

"Yeah. Major league check mark. Listen. I want you to just relax and play, and let all this pass, all right?"

"Okay. Daddy? Love 'oo."

"Love 'oo, too," he said.

And he hung up.

Feeling sick at heart, Derek started his Toyota and backed out of the driveway. The news asked those without urgent business to remain in their homes, but morbid curiosity was a persistent itch. He just couldn't help himself.

Smoke muddied the sky above the entire L.A. basin. Fire sirens blared from all directions. There was little vehicular traffic, but people were running, some of them carrying boxes or armloads of groceries. Windows were broken, doors torn down and hauled into the street. It looked as if the city had been hit by a blitz.

A new sound, this one in the car. "Ohmigod. Ohmigod. Ohmi—'' He finally recognized the rattling litany as his own voice. "Ohmigod. Ohmigod. Oh, my . . .'' It took a violent mental effort to tear himself out of that pattern.

The radio whispered to him. He turned it up.

The announcer spoke briskly. "In the wake of the Rodney King beating verdict, violence has broken out in several sections of Los Angeles, beginning with a riot at the corner of Vernon and Vermont. Mayor Bradley is expected to announce a state of emergency. At least seven major fires have been reported, and four dead . . .''

Derek felt clubbed, brain-dead. The entire city, the place that he loved, had dissolved into nightmare. He drove with no conscious thought of where he was heading, drawn by the sound of sirens, the smell of smoke, the expressions of fear.

His eyes seemed to record individual images as concrete things, without relating them to anything else in his mind or experience, as if they were strips of film lying side by side:

Waves of angry brown- and black-skinned people smashing windows.

A man—perhaps white, perhaps Asian, beaten to his knees.

A minimall near Western and Beverly, where frightened shopkeepers guarded their stores with shotguns.

The police. He saw them to the sides, their patrol cars pulled to the curb. Their radios buzzed with calls and reports. The men and women of the LAPD were omnipresent, but oddly withdrawn. Derek recognized the strained, carefully neutral expressions. The restlessly shifting eyes. The hands caressing the butts of their revolvers as they watched the violence and rage without acting.

Fear. They were police, but they were also human, and they were afraid.

He had never had more empathy with police officers in his entire life.

In the next block, the police were acting: four looters knelt on the sidewalk, fingers interlaced behind their head.

That might have been comforting, except that everywhere, everywhere, buildings burned. The smoke of their destruction drifted across the streets in acrid curtains.

The flames reflected on his windshield. He saw rioters attacking the firemen who struggled to quell the blazes. Derek felt the kind of deep, quiet despair that makes one feel nothing at all, a kind of despair he had hoped never to feel again.

Everywhere, everywhere around him, violence seethed.

A small pale child sat on skinned knees, crying in the street and nearly trampled by the people running around her. Men rushed past her, carrying loot, television sets, armloads of clothes, as if participating in some kind of end-of-the-world fire sale, as if someone had jabbed an electrode into the acquisition lobe of their brains and superstimulated them. As if just the mere response, the *reflex* to possess and possess and possess was stronger than the hardwired urge to protect the young and helpless.

The hunger, and raw desperation, fear and self-loathing on their faces was almost unendurable.

But in a few faces, there was something like a sense of complete and total betrayal, as if they had entered into a world not of their understanding. As if there were no response to the engulfing insanity except to join it.

Tears streaked the little girl's face. A man carrying a television set stumbled blindly toward her. Without thought, Derek set his emergency brake and leaped from the car. He was buffeted by the crowd, but ignored the screams and ugly words. Five steps later she was burying her face in his chest. Her breath was hot and frightened, as Dee's would have been.

Tears drooled out of the huge blue eyes. Derek wanted to say something comforting, but his mind was somewhere beyond words.

A plump blond woman ran up, staring at the child in his arms. Derek held the girl out to her. The woman didn't know what to say or do. She looked like a big pale balloon, swollen with fear and anger and discontent—but mostly fear. She snatched her daughter from Derek's hands, and half turned. Then their eyes met again. Her mouth worked, as if trying to force out words, but ultimately, words failed her.

The girl stared at him over her mother's shoulder. She raised one small pink hand, waving good-bye before she was completely swallowed by the crowd.

He felt sick.

Derek flinched as a storefront window behind him shattered into slivers. The crackle of crushed glass filled the air. In the display sat a row of television sets, all tuned to the same news channel. As the rioters surged in to steal them, the images winked out.

Derek watched, until every television set was gone. Looters, black, white and brown buffeted him on all sides as they descended on the department store.

Shaken, he returned to his car. He made a U-turn in the middle of the street, heading south once again.

A looter ran in front of his car, lugging an armload of furs. Derek slammed on the brakes. The man yelled something unintelligible, laughed, and ran on.

Derek stared at him. He had seen that face before. Years before. Often, it had worn a football helmet. That face belonged to Raymond Cross, fullback for the L.A. High School Romans. Derek had cheered as Cross dashed across the goal line. He had shaken his head in admiration as Cross won a girl Derek lusted after. What was her name? He couldn't remember. Could only remember her smile, and the Certs-sweet breath as she kissed him. Then she was with Ray Cross, and he hadn't even been pissed. It was just natural. Guys like Ray Cross got everything.

And there was Ray Cross, with an armload of furs. And that wasn't natural at all.

The Tercel stalled. He started it again, and drove on through the middle of the riot-torn street.

Afraid.

This was not his world. This was not any world he had ever known.

This was madness.

Raymond Cross ran across in front of the nigger in the Tercel, carrying an armload of top-flight furs boosted out of a fancy-assed clothing store on Beverly. The four-eyed asshole in the Toyota slammed his brakes hard. Far from grateful, Cross yelled, "Muthafucka! Lucky I don't bust a cap in your ass," and kept going.

This whole riot thing was a piece of luck. Hell, there hadn't been a lot of luck in Ray Cross's life. First there was the busted leg that screwed up his tryouts for the Miami Dolphins (everybody said he would have made it) and then Georgia Washington got pregnant. That wouldn't have been an enormous problem except that Georgia's father was a cop.

When nineteen-year-old Ray expressed a lack of enthusiasm about the joys and duties of impending fatherhood, the elder Washington had taken the hulking fullback into the backyard and administered an exquisite ass whipping, notable for its efficiency, intensity and complete absence of tissue damage. No marks remained behind, anywhere except in Ray Cross's heart.

So Ray Cross's world suddenly telescoped: one minute he was future NFL MVP, and the next, the assistant manager of a dry cleaner at the corner of Olympic and Crenshaw. From the young stallion whose sexual conquests were limited only by his body's capacity for hydraulic recuperation, he became a plough horse, returning every night to a woman he didn't love and a family he didn't want. It wasn't fair, it just *wasn't*.

And soon after Officer Washington caught a disabling bullet in the line of duty, Ray Cross ditched Georgia and Ray Junior, and began a series of misadventures that brought him to the inevitable attention of both the local criminal element and Officer Washington's compatriots. Time at various local and state-level facilities followed. His lack of good judgment now a matter of official note and public record, Ray Cross found it increasingly difficult to find honest work the few occasions he searched for it.

The last few years, he had lived on food stamps and two skinny crackhead skeezers he ran at the Sundowner Motel. It was enough. When the Rodney King thing happened, he was outraged. A black man just didn't have a chance, but this time, the motherfuckers were caught on video. Ray was sure he'd run into one of those cop bastards in lockup one day, and was going to stick a blade up his ass so far the punk could pick his teeth with it.

But then the fucking verdict, and he had shaken his head. No justice in the world. Ray Cross watched on TV as a bunch of righteously pissed-off brothers pulled a white man named Denny out of his truck down at Normandie and beat the shit out of him. Hell, the newscasters were all fucked up about that, but Denny was lucky they didn't bust a cap in his ass.

When the rioting spread north, Ray realized that the initial shock and outrage triggered an orgy of freelance capitalism. Cross declared it his civic duty to protest the unjust legal system by grabbing an armload of furs from a store around the corner from his apartment. Hell, maybe he could dress up those skeezers he was running, attract a better clientele. Couple more good breaks, he'd be printing that *crazy* paper.

So after a decade of strict neutrality, Ray Cross made a political statement with a brick. Smash and run. He had places to go, people to see, furs to fence, bitches to pimp.

Ray Cross had almost made it to his car when he felt something strike him in the back. At first he thought he had been shot, and the icy sensation sweeping through his body did nothing to disabuse him of the notion. But as he turned, another smashing blow took him in the chest. He looked down, and saw the dart. He saw the street beyond the alley, filled with running men, and he saw the police van parked just beyond the turn of the alley. He saw the two big cops coming toward him. One kind of fat. The other one thin, and tall. Very wiry. Hawk face.

Like an Indian.

The world spun. Ray Cross was outraged. *Since when do cops use stun darts? What is this shit?*

And then there was only darkness.

Thursday, April 30

Thursday, it was impossible for Derek to do much more than watch television. He could see the smoke from his front porch. Sections of Wilshire Boulevard's Miracle Mile were burning. Much of the downtown area was sealed off, closed down. Los Angeles was aflame, and shock settled over him in a numbing shroud.

The images were hypnotic. The schools were shut down, and Rachel was home with the kids. At her security condo, they were safe as houses—he didn't need to worry about that, but something about what was happening just drained all of the strength out of him.

He should have stayed at his desk—there was money due him. All he had to do was finish the project, but the fire, and the news reports, and the endless speculations and comparisons with the '65 riots just drained his strength and will.

So instead of working, he walked the neighborhood, listening to the sirens, smelling the smoke. Peering into broken windows.

Something inside him had been certain, *certain* that this kind of self-destructive energy no longer plagued his community. But a nightmare of broken glass, and blackened walls told him that the rot was deeper than he had ever dreamed.

It had only required one grotesque miscarriage of justice to squeeze the pus to the surface.

He sat across the street from Vendome Liquor. Derek had bought comic books there as a kid. Read the latest adventures of Spiderman and Daredevil and Batman. An old Jewish couple owned Vendome first, and then a black family who ultimately bought a dry cleaners on Wilshire, selling out to a Korean family. He had stopped in a couple of times. The cola was too warm, but they were nice, hard-working people.

Vendome was rubble now. Windows shattered, steel security grille twisted out of true. Raped and empty.

It felt as though someone had ripped out a piece of his

childhood, and squeezed it dead. He kicked at a fragment of brick, pushed it with his toe. He picked it up. His hand shook. A fragment of something bright blue and red was stuck to the underside of the brick. Derek peeled it away: a comic book. It was a picture, a fragment of a cape. He couldn't figure out which hero it belonged to. And he wanted to. He really wanted to know.

There were too few heroes left.

Derek walked home, alone.

Saturday, May 2

5

The offices of Advanced Graphics were seven steel-and-glass structures built into the Malibu hillside, about two miles north of where Sunset Boulevard met the Pacific Coast Highway.

Derek pulled off the Pacific Coast Highway about two miles north of where it crossed Sunset Boulevard, at the outskirts of Malibu. A sign to the right indicated a narrow gravel road and a street number. Just up the road was a stone tablet reading "Advanced Graphics." Beneath the words was the AG corporate logo, a symbol that reminded him of a genie in a bottle, abstracted almost beyond recognition. Something about this always made him feel a bit uncomfortable, but he managed to get over it by the time he cashed his check.

Advanced Graphics was one of the mystery success stories of the computer industry. Apparently spun off from one of the Wang think tanks, they had obtained funding from sources rumored to be anything from Arab oil money to Japanese kieretsu cash, American technology being developed and surreptitiously shipped overseas.

The foreign story had proven untrue when Advanced Graphics snagged a small defense contract providing virtual reality gear for jet fighter simulations. At that point the funding became known to the government. Neither he nor anyone else outside a very tight loop knew exactly where it originated, but it wasn't from overseas—at least the DoD was satisfied of that.

They may have still had defense contracts. God knew their security was good. A few months before, large rectángles of sod had been cut out of the lawn and stacked like tiles. He managed to peer in the holes, and glimpsed a wire mesh pressure plate system beneath.

In the backseat of his Tercel, Troy and Dee were playing one of their one-upmanship games. Troy, by dint of superior years, could win on almost anything that required knowledge. Dee could usually win out on silliness. Therefore, any game that the two played more than once had to award points for both qualities.

Derek turned into the parking lot, parked next to a green Karman Ghia and set the hand brake. A vast expanse of green lawn stretched out ahead of them, manicured, set with picnic benches and a jogging path. Advanced Graphics was said to be the best work environment south of Microsoft.

"This'll just take a minute." The kids were too absorbed in a hand-held video game to pay any attention. They were playing an odd variant—how low a score can you get, without actually getting killed out of the game. It was silly and smart enough for both of them.

Troy suddenly glanced up, immediately sensing the possibilities of an empty lawn. "Wow." His mouth remained in O position for an extended moment. *"This'll* work."

He reached up under the seat and pulled out a folding Nerf Frisbee. It popped into saucer shape although Derek thought that it made a rather limp disk. Troy was something of a miracle worker in managing to get as much range from it as he did. "Go long, Dee!" He called, and she squealingly obliged.

"You guys stay out of trouble," Waites said, watching Dee dash off.

"Trouble is my middle name," Troy said, in a bad Sean Connery. Maybe an imitation of Rich Little doing Connery. Or Rich Little doing Little Richard doing Connery.

Troy threw the Frisbee before Dee managed to fall off the edge of the world.

It wobbled through the air with an endearingly offbeat

approach to aerodynamic stability. The disk swooped low to the ground, then back up again. Dee dove for it, missed, and hit the ground rolling like a little rubber ball. She giggled.

God, he loved them. He hurried through the front door of the main building.

The main lobby was a meld of earth tones and stainless steel, somehow both primitive and briskly modern, a combination that Derek found uncommonly alive and dynamic. The employees always seemed to be moving at a pace motivated by some galloping internal engine, as if working in such a wonderful place were, by itself, sufficient reward.

The receptionist's desk was a half acre of blinding white faux marble. It felt like stone to the touch, but had to be some kind of composition material. It grew right out of the wall without a seam, and he couldn't even imagine what something like that would have cost, had it been genuine.

The receptionist herself was hardly less spectacular, a blonde who seemed to have been cast in one piece with her desk. He had never seen her stand, so he had no idea about her legs. But the upper half of her body was so utterly flawless that he didn't really want to see her stand, almost dreaded the idea of seeing her come to her feet, and being disappointed by her legs, or hips.

Her badge said Carol. "Can I help you?" she asked.

"I'd like to see Mrs. Prentice," he said nervously. He resisted the urge to peek over the edge of the desk.

Carol smiled. "Well, you're lucky to catch her on a Saturday, aren't you? Do you—?"

"I have an appointment," he said.

She nodded, as if that explained everything. "Fine. Would you take a seat?"

Carol didn't use the intercom, instead she rose from her desk, walked to the center of three doors set into the wall behind her, and knocked. Derek had plenty of time to look at the legs, and wasn't the slightest bit disappointed. He sighed. Sometimes, Nature knew what she was doing. Even if the design for backs *was* completely tacky.

He looked out through the side window, and could see the kids. They couldn't see him, not from this angle. It gave him a somewhat delicious sense of mystery to be able to watch them. Dee tossed the Frisbee to Troy. It bounced off the ground at a crazy angle, and hit Troy squarely in the groin.

Troy grabbed himself, hit the ground, rolled, and ran after Dee, who fled laughing with mock fright, squealing. Happy.

God, he missed them both so much. He just had to get his act together. True, the last few days had thrown him off a bit—but they had thrown all Los Angeles for a loop—

There was a commotion behind him, and he turned to see a cluster of men walking through the lobby. The largest of them, the man in the center, was also by far the darkest. Almost blue-black. Derek couldn't make out many of his features. The man wore sunglasses and a fedora, and a deer-skin vest with a collar high enough to hide most of his features. And he walked swiftly, speaking in a bass rumble that seemed to reverberate through the floor.

Derek couldn't hear the conversation, but fervently wished he could. The five or six shorter men were hanging on the big man's every word, completely absorbed.

Derek hadn't realized it, but the secretary had returned now. She stared after the men, and one of the other secretaries sidled up and whispered, "Isn't that Mr. Niles?"

Carol shrugged. "I think so. I've never actually met him. But I think so. Who else would have Jacoby and Erhardt so stirred up?"

There was something in their voices that Derek coveted. Some interest in the power, in the force of the mysterious Mr. Niles that he wished he could hear in someone's voice when they talked about him. Just once. Just one time.

"Isn't that Mr. Waites?"

"Mr. Waites?" The voice came from behind him, and he jumped to his feet, pivoting. Mrs. Prentice stood there, a middle-aged woman with the beginning of gray hair fringing a tightly controlled face. She was about five four, as rounded and solid as a potato, and was the one constant he had dealt with since first coming to Advanced Graphics.

"Glad to see you again," he said, extending his hand.

She took it and pumped it dryly, twice. Not enough to imply warmth, not little enough to be rude. As precisely measured as her smile.

"Umm-humm," she said. "This way, please."

He glanced over his shoulder one more time as the elevator doors closed, sealing the mysterious Mr. Niles away from view.

She led him through that center door and along a familiar corridor to her office, a room that would have seemed spacious but for a full-sized Dungeon Quest arcade prototype in one corner. It looked a little like a chrome gazebo, a platform with room enough for four adults, with video masks for five. It wouldn't accept coins, it performed its miracles at the urging of magnetic dollars, credits encoded on key-card tape strips. The financial information was encoded along with all of the other statistics that made the game unique: hours played, number of kills, characters in play, powers, abilities and experiences of each character . . .

And also, importantly, the ages and clearance levels of the players as well. There were secret rooms that you simply couldn't access until you earned your way up to a silver key. Gore effects that you couldn't enjoy until you were over eighteen. Seraglios that could only be accessed by those over twenty-one. Oh, Advanced Graphics knew *exactly* what they were doing. They had a money machine here that would buy Porsches for the next decade, and leave Nintendo slicing sashimi in the rain. No one understood American vices and weaknesses like other Americans.

Wall posters sang the glories of Advanced Graphics's forthcoming video projects. Some featured animals, some aliens, some fantasy creatures that had never walked, or swum, or crawled. All were designed to make Advanced Graphics the most powerful game company in the world. And he was a part of it.

Mrs. Prentice's voice jarred him from his reverie. "Frankly, Mr. Waites," she said, "I was surprised by your request. Your contract was explicit. It stated a specific schedule of payments in exchange for specific Dungeon Quest modules completed. As we are both aware, you missed your last deadline." She paused, and it was a deadly pause indeed. She showed him her teeth. They weren't filed. He hoped that was a good sign. "I hope that you have something to show me."

He shriveled under that gaze, then managed to straighten up. "Mrs. Prentice, I should have had the work to you yesterday. I . . . I've been paralyzed. I'm not going to lie to you about it."

The corner of her mouth twitched down, then up.

He plunged ahead. Hesitation could be fatal. "I'll have everything debugged and on-line by Tuesday." He watched the fractional inclination of her head which might, just *might* mean that she believed him. "You'll love it, I promise. It's wicked. It's just that . . ."

He was running out of steam. He needed her to say something here. To interject a word, to provide a more definite sign that she was in some kind of harmony with him. Not a big sign, just anything. A polite cough. A smile. Scratching at her mustache. Anything.

"Yes?" she inquired politely.

It would have to do.

"I'm out of money. I know that it isn't your problem, but if you could just see your way to another advance—"

God, he hated the whine that was creeping into his voice. This shouldn't be happening, he shouldn't be pleading for money at this stage in his life. It was degrading and humiliating. It was also reality.

God, it was hot in here.

The clock mounted on her desk was digital, but he would have sworn that he could hear it tick. Mrs. Prentice watched him, as if wondering if he might cough up a frog. She sighed. "Mr. Waites. You came with very high recommendations." Pause. "When you perform, you are very good indeed. If I were to consider the present situation to be part of the overall pattern, it would be the third time you have failed to make a deadline. However, this is a very special circumstance."

She was trying to smile. "Has it been bad? Down where you live?"

"Everything's gone to hell." The words tasted like rusty iron.

There was a long pause, as if Mrs. Prentice were trying to decide what to say. "Well," she continued, "Tuesday is another day. Today is the second of May—you need a new key card, don't you?" She smiled, and he was amazed to see that the smile was genuine. He had been excoriating himself, and she was assuming he was like other human beings. He made mistakes. What a concept.

It still hurt. He was so weary of having *potential*.

Mrs. Prentice reached into her desk drawer, and pulled out a silver plastic card. She hesitated, then smiled and extracted two bronze cards as well, each on necklace chains.

She handed all three to him.

"I don't understand," he said, mystified.

"For your children," she said. "For . . . ah, Dahlia and Troy, is it?"

He nodded. He hoped that she had scanned his file recently. The thought of that much RNA in one brain was a little scary. He might start to like her entirely too much.

"The cashier's office will have . . . say two hundred dollars? For you?"

"That would be wonderful." He tried to think of something else to say, but there really wasn't anything. He rose to go.

Mrs. Prentice's quiet smile stopped him. "Mr. Waites?" she said.

"Yes?"

"Wish your daughter a happy birthday from Advanced Graphics. Take her someplace nice."

He nodded dumbly, and backed toward the door, afraid that he was going to babble again if he wasn't very, very careful.

He exited the building just in time to see Troy make an incredible catch, one of those hummingbird-reflex efforts that amazed Derek. It seemed that Troy had gotten faster just recently. A *lot* faster. Those reflexes certainly hadn't come from *his* side of the family.

Dee ran to him. "Daddy!" she yelled happily. "How did you do?"

"They love me," he said. He wagged the envelope mockingly at Troy. "Two hundred dollars, cash money."

He slipped a twenty out of the envelope, and held it just above Troy's head. Troy reached for it, and Derek pulled it up just a little, making Troy jump higher, an old game. Troy squinted at him, and popped up like a flea on a griddle, snatching the bill from the air so fast it nearly seemed to vanish. Derek had to whistle. With reflexes like that, he could hardly wait for Troy to get the rest of his height. The kid was going to be *murder* on the basketball court.

6

The cellular phone in Rachel Childe's silver Jag beeped plaintively, deep-sixing her good mood. She was thirty-four, with lush hair, dark olive skin and faintly Latin features. Her body was as lean and tight as that of a talented semipro bodybuilder. She seemed completely unaware that her beauty captured the attention of men and women alike. Rachel's was the kind of slow-ripening sensuality that might not peak for another twenty years.

She was also the youngest vice president at CBC. The sky was the limit, and she had contempt for glass ceilings. This morning she had sneaked a new Henson animated series away from ABC, and negotiated an extension on the Schwarzenegger option. No one knew quite how Arnold might muscle up a Saturday-morning cartoon lineup, but the first executive to figure it out had her bonus in the bag.

She pushed the blinking button. "Hello, Derek. I know, I'm running late."

It sounded as if he were calling from a telephone booth. She heard laughter and car sounds behind him. The zoo.

"It's only your daughter's birthday, for Christ's sake." He sounded exasperated, but not angry. That was good. This wasn't going to be an easy birthday, no matter what. "It's Saturday, for Christ's sake. Who works on Saturday?"

"People who have careers instead of jobs," she said calmly. "I said I'll be there, and I'll be there."

He sighed. "All right. We're going to go ahead and eat. Are you sure you can spare the time?"

No, I can't.

"Of course," she said. "I'll be there. Besides," she added. "We need to talk."

Something in her voice must have caught him off guard, because suddenly he was no longer attacking. "Sure, Rache," he said warily. Almost subdued. "I love you."

"I'll see you," she said, and depressed the receiver as softly as she could.

Rachel pulled into the parking lot, cruising for a place to park. Out of the corner of her eye she noticed a police car cruising past in the next aisle. For just an instant she noticed the driver speaking into a microphone. She couldn't see much of his face, except that his eyes were intense, his nose hawklike. She wasn't completely certain why she noticed the black and white at all. Something had brought it to her attention, and there it remained.

Odd.

She spotted a parking space ahead of her in the twenty-acre lot, but a little VW squeaked in ahead of her Jag.

She was feeling the first warning signs of irritation when she heard a familiar sound, the *Dum-dum DUM DUM dum-dum DUM DUM* of the *Mission: Impossible* theme. Well. Only one maniac in Los Angeles had *that* tune wired into his car horn. She followed the sound as it swelled and then repeated, and emerged in a picnic area.

She spotted Derek's little red Tercel quickly, and found a space four cars farther down. She parked, locked up, hurried over. Troy and Dee were feasting on pizza and Coke while Derek stood against the fender. He leaned on the car horn, triggering his favorite music one more time.

Dee crammed the last scrap of pepperoni into her mouth, and ran to her Mother.

"Mommy! Mommy!" she yelled as if they had been separated for years instead of hours.

Rachel gave her an enormous kiss. "Sweetheart. Have you had a good birthday?"

"The best." She looked up hopefully. "Are we going to the zoo now?"

Troy had joined them. He smiled, but was entirely too cool

to give his mom a hug. "Nope, we're here because we like the smell of elephant shit."

Dee was incensed. "Ooh! Troy said a bad word! Troy gets a check mark, doesn't he, Mom? Doesn't he?"

Rachel considered. Dispersal of check marks was serious business indeed. " 'No cursing' is technically a house rule. Since we aren't in the house, we can't technically give him a check mark. However—" She cautioned, flicking the tip of Troy's nose with her finger. "We will make an attempt to watch our language, Troy. Elephant *poop,* if you don't mind."

"Not a bit," he said in his finest pseudo-English accent.

Rachel gave Derek a polished cheek to kiss. He smelled like English Leather Lime, and popcorn salt.

She took Dee's hand, and the four of them marched off into the zoo, playing family.

7

One of the first exhibits was the meerkat area. Meerkats were little furry beasts about the size of prairie dogs, with similar habits and habitats. You could watch the exhibit for an hour and not catch sight of even one of the little monsters. Dee leaned against the low rail, peering at the sculpted terrain where, no doubt, an entire colony of the fiends was hiding maliciously, having heard that the Waites children had chosen this day for their zoo outing.

Dee's lower lip pooched plaintively. "Why do they call them meerkats?" she asked no one in particular.

Troy was quick to answer. "It should say 'nearcats,' actually, because they're almost cats, you see?"

She turned and searched his face, not certain if he was teasing.

His expression was very sincere.

"What?" she said blankly.

"Raoul is a mere cat, like, he's only a cat, you know? Like you're a mere child."

This time she caught the sarcastic inflection, and immediately stiffened. "Well," she said, "you're a mere toad."

"You're a mere brat."

"Mere nerd."

"Mere *snot.*"

"Daddy!" Dee shrieked. "Troy gets a check mark!"

Rachel and Derek ignored them. Troy pinched Dee's bottom and ran off chortling, his little sister in hot pursuit.

Rachel laughed quietly. "Have you gotten much work done, the last few days?"

"Vast amounts. A tribute to your husband's rare organizational skills."

"Ex-husband," she reminded him, not unpleasantly.

"Oh, come on. We can still work things out." He looked exasperated, gave her one of those oh-why-can't-you-see-reality expressions that drove her to distraction. "Things are great now. Really! Everything is changing for me. I'm getting my old chops back. After the Dungeon Quest contract, I'll be set. Rache, we can get back together, you can stop using your maiden name—"

Her look froze him in midsentence.

"I *like* my maiden name," she said flatly, then changed the subject. "Does Advanced Graphics know that you're Superhacker? You remember: 'Captain Africa strikes'?"

He chuckled ruefully. "Black Avenger of Cyberspace?" He waved his hands in dismissal. "That's ancient history, Rache. I want to talk about now. About us."

Very gently, she laid her hand on his arm. "I need the papers signed, Derek. Medford and I are getting married."

That stopped him short. The air around him congealed, grew too thick to breathe. How had everything so good gotten so damned bad? He needed time, or he might blurt out the first thing that came to mind.

Behind him, Troy was talking to another kid. The other kid was blond, a couple of inches taller, wearing purple Reeboks and a T-shirt that said "He Who Dies with the Most Toys Is Fucking *Dead.*" He examined the plastic key card chained around Troy's neck, his naked envy undisguised. "I saw a picture of that in *Gaming Times*—it isn't supposed to be on-line till the end of the year!"

"Well," Troy admitted, "I'm play testing. My dad works for Advanced Graphics. I beta test a lot of their stuff."

"You're kidding!" The blond kid groaned, so jealous he could barely stand it. "Wizard Lair? Just came out."

"Got it last October."

"Jesus. Vampire Maze?"

"Last June."

"Arrgh!" He tore at his hair. "Is Dungeon Quest really rad?"

Troy looked at him, and assumed his very sweetest expression. "It's your worst nightmare."

"Arrgh!!! Come on. Let me come over. I wanna—"

The kid's mother was watching from nearby. A short woman with dark roots and support stockings, she had grown steadily more concerned as her son became more involved in the conversation. She watched Troy and his parents nervously, and approached, her polite smile frosted on her face.

"Mom! He's got Dungeon Quest!"

"I'm sure that's very nice, dear."

"Listen. I wanna go over and play with it. Would you take me over?"

His mother's face was a warring mask of emotion. "I'm not sure we want to go down there yet, Mitchie. Maybe when things settle down a bit."

"Aw, Mom." But she coaxed Mitchie firmly away. Before Mitchie and Derek could exchange phone numbers, Derek noted.

Derek watched Troy's relaxed, calm reaction proudly. The kid had social skills, resources that Derek wished desperately to possess at this moment.

Rachel still watched him, her brown eyes soft, compassionate. There was nothing in those eyes that wanted to hurt him. Dammit, it would have been easier if there were. All that mattered was he still loved her, still remembered everything about them together, even loved the away she looked and smelled first thing in the morning. Still ached with the memory of holding her. And if that was obvious, if he felt that with every fiber of his being, it was just as obvious that love him though she might, Rachel was no longer *in* love with him. And that made all of the difference in the world.

In his world, anyway.

"Derek," she said softly. "Life doesn't stand still and wait for us to grow up."

"I just needed a few breaks," he said lamely. "That's all I needed. Just a few lousy breaks."

He had trouble looking at her. Dammit, the whole world seemed like a dark and angry place. The faces around him. People walking past in a slow-motion haze, eating frozen lemonade and cotton candy. It seemed to him that every single one of them knew who he was, what he felt. Knew. *Knew.*

Everyone knew what he felt, except him. He was growing numb. He didn't want to know what was inside that numbness. It would eventually emerge. He wanted to be alone when it did.

There was so much noise. He fought to clear his head, and as he did, noticed three men watching him. Large cop types. Probably L.A. Zoo security. So the zoo was on half days, and they were watching to see if someone would set fire to the tiger cage. Thank you very much.

"You're thirty-three, Derek. You haven't figured out that it's not *fun* to live on pretzels and Pepsi anymore. What do we have in common?"

Before he could reply, a tiny seventyish lady with fashionably blue hair approached them, clasping Dee's hand. They chatted away like old friends. "Excuse me," the lady said in an unexpectedly youthful voice. "But is this your beautiful child?"

Derek and Rachel answered simultaneously. "Yes."

"See, I told you," Dee said cheerfully.

"She says that her birthday was two days ago. Is that correct?"

"She's seven," Rachel said.

"Yep," Dee verified. "Seven big ones."

The lady twinkled. "May I buy her a scoop of ice cream?"

"She'll follow you home," Derek cautioned.

"I can think of worse things," the lady said. "My name is Katie."

"Thank you very much, Katie," Rachel smiled. "You're very kind."

"Not at all: It's pure selfishness. I get to borrow her eyes and heart for a few minutes, and all it costs me is fifty cents."

Rachel bent down. "What do you say to Katie, hon?"

"Yippee!" she crowed, and led her new friend away to the confection stand.

Derek used the respite to collect his thoughts. Rachel turned back to him, still smiling warmly at a stranger's kindness, when Derek took off again.

"More than anyone in the world, Rachel, you know what happened to me. If I'd been white—"

Rachel snorted, the good mood shattered. "But you're not, and the world doesn't much care what you think or feel about it. Will you please grow up? Dammit, Derek, the head of your precious Advanced Graphics is black. The Chairman of the Joint Chiefs of Staff is black. *I'm* black, and *I* never had to steal—"

"It wasn't stealing," he said quietly.

Rachel wasn't listening. "—every time you hide behind that label you get a little smaller, Derek—"

Dee walked back toward her parents, scooping little troughs in the ice cream with the tip of her tongue. She reveled in the butter-rich sweetness, savoring the chill as it hit the back of her throat.

This was so much better than the ice milk her mom bought. Let alone *yogurt,* for gosh sakes. Yech. She loved the rich taste of real ice cream. In fact, what she really liked was just basic vanilla ice cream. Maybe vanilla bean. Without any of the other flavorings or additives, you could just taste the ice creaminess, undisguised. Let her taste a brand's vanilla, and then maybe she would try their other flavors. . . .

Dee suddenly felt hot. The contrast of the ice cream on her tongue became almost unendurable, and she stopped. She blinked. Something was terribly wrong. Again. The world flashed around her like a strobe, bleaching colors into gray-tone outlines.

Sounds faded away to nothing.

The world became a hollow, empty place, an infinite, silent white plain.

Then new outlines and textures appeared. New sounds, new colors.

Dee looked down, and didn't recognize the clothes she was wearing, or the body she was in. She had a woman's breasts and hips. Her dress looked like something out of an old movie, or *Little House on the Prairie*. She glanced back up. The zoo had disappeared.

She stood in the middle of a cabin made of old logs. Two black men held her arms, one on either side.

This wasn't happening. This wasn't happening. She shook her head, hard. Held her breath. Sometimes either of those was enough to take her out of a nightmare. This was a dream. In fact, she remembered that she had had this dream before. The worst part was that she already knew how it ended.

Desperately, she clung to the knowledge that she had to be asleep. They had never come to the zoo. She would wake up any minute, and Daddy would say, "Dee, it's time for us to head out."

A man stood in front of her, a tall, ruddy man with flaming red hair. His breath stank of whiskey. His eyes were fever bright.

She felt her mouth open, and heard herself speak, not knowing where the words came from. The voice wasn't hers. It was a woman's voice, and she was shocked to hear that it sounded like her own mother's.

"Please," her mouth said. "Please don't kill my babies."

The man reached out and slapped her. Hard. And said, in the angriest voice she had ever heard, "Did you think you could get away from me, *bitch?*"

THE JOURNAL OF DAHLIA CHILDE

September 24, 1877
Last Entry

I write these words 'cause I think Grandmama would have wanted me to. For *someone* to. She always told me about the books she wrote, and what she was writing in them. We knew the master might find us one day. We hoped that he and the African was dead, but they wasn't.

Buried Grandmama yesterday. Gray day. Smoke over the mountains. The sun didn't want to come out to see what was happening, neither. Didn't want to look at Grandmama. Didn't want to see what master done to her.

How he done it, don't know. Got into the house while we was working the fields. Got Grandmama. We found her split open like a hog, and there were pieces of chickens and goats around her, spread out to make some kinds of hoodoo signs.

Bad signs. Made me sick to look at 'em.

Old cousin Victor was there, and Bubba, and Kelly Jean Childe, and all the rest. Ten year since the War. Ten year since we been free, but that don't stop master from reaching back out.

Seem sometimes that there ain't enough pain in the world. God feel like He gotta reach out and make a little more, just to keep us knowing that He in control of it, all of it.

Sometime it just ain't fair.

But I know what Grandmama would say about that. She'd say, "You believe, because we have to believe. We have to hold on, boy. There's a power out there, and it watches over us. And it is good. And it holds the other power back, and you should pray, and never stop praying, because the day it stops holding the other power back is the last day for any of us. I seen it. I seen it so close, so terribly close that I'm ashamed. Ashamed of the things I seen, and done. So believe, child. Believe, and pray."

She say that, only she say it pretty, because she always talk pretty, and try to get us to talk pretty, only I never got that kind of talking too good. She also used to say the other thing, the thing she say to all of us, what she tell us to tell our children. "You special, child. Not like other folks. You have special worries."

Then she lower her voice. *"Soul and skin are linked: Soul can lead skin. Skin can call soul. Soul and skin can be stolen or torn apart. Shun the man who tears skin—for he's an evil, evil man. But fear the man who steals souls, for that man can steal the stars from the sky."*

And she used to hold me close, so close.

And now she gone.

One more thing afore I stop. We ran back to the cabin, but wasn't nothing there but blood, and Grandmama. Nothing there. But the thing that made us run was the scream. Lord, ain't never heard a scream like that. Don't never want to hear it again.

Little Joe, he was sleeping at the side of the house, hiding from his chores. He say he heard everything. He say he heard a man's voice, and the man call Grandmama something terrible. Say he was mad as he ever heard a man be. Say Grandmama betrayed him, and he coming after us, all of her family, until hell eat heaven. That's what he say.

Little Joe say he could see through a crack in the wall that there be two men. That one be tall, as white and handsome as the devil. Bright red hair, like a fire burning at midnight. That the other one be a black man, big man. He take off his shirt, and he covered in scars that look like signs, like the ones on the floor. And that he tell Grandmama he gonna take her soul. Grandmama, she say, "Don't kill my babies," then the white man kill her with a knife, and do the things I won't write about.

Little Joe, he not move or make a sound. Little Joe ain't slept since then, four day ago. He got the fever bad.

I know he seen master, and the African. Master should have died in the War, ten year ago. African should have died long time before that. But master ain't no man no more, and maybe African never was, Grandmama say.

She say she don't know what they is.

Good-bye, Grandmama. Hope I wrote down what you wanted. Hope it's good enough. Hope it do someone some good, somewhere, someday.

I hope they don't get your soul.

8

"—if you'd used your balls," Mommy was saying. She and Daddy were fighting. Dee tried not to listen to them when they fought. She didn't like to listen, often retreated into her mind, into whatever fantasy was available to take her out of the world while they argued. But although she didn't quite remember where she had just been, something told her that even the pain of watching her parents hiss at each other was preferable to going back *there*.

"My balls?" Daddy asked caustically. "Was anything left after you finished busting them?"

Dee still felt as if she were drifting, somehow not quite setting one foot in front of another. She felt feverish, that odd sensation that her body didn't belong to her anymore, that it was all slipping away.

There was something terribly wrong. She looked back over her shoulder at the gate. People ambled out. Nothing unusual or strange about that. There were two men close behind Troy. On a TV show, they would have been pretending not to look at him, pretending to look at newspapers or something. But they were watching Troy fixedly.

Waiting.

Suddenly, her mother's cool, soft hand touched her forehead. "Baby?" Rachel said. "Is something wrong?" Her mother's hand felt cool. Cold. Dee felt strange. Hot. Her tongue lay thick in her mouth.

Derek," Rachel said. "What have you been feeding this child? She's running a temperature."

"It's always my fault," he muttered, but bent to take a closer look. She *did* look a little warm.

"If you were more interested in being their father than their playmate . . ."

"Somebody's got to remember that they're just kids. They need to have fun sometimes."

Neither of them noticed the car as it pulled up next to Troy. It was gunmetal gray, a nondescript Ford sedan.

A big pale man gripped the steering wheel. A second man perched in the passenger seat, a dark hard man with a flat face and eyes that barely moved. His hand rested on the door.

Troy was still buried in the souvenir book. He didn't see the two men coming in behind him, and remained completely oblivious even as they reached toward him—

Dee screamed. It was a soul scream, throat rending, ear tearing, sheer terror and pain and rage melding into a sound that should never have originated in a seven-year-old throat.

Derek and Rachel actually stepped back, staring. Derek blinked, hard, trying to adjust his contact lenses. It must have been some trick of the light, but suddenly, the air around Dee *shimmered,* as if the sun were rising behind her. Her hands flew to her hair, gripped, and pulled as if she were trying to pull it away from her scalp.

Smoke.

It couldn't have been. But wisps of smoke rose from her scalp, wafting into the air, as if she were about to burst into flame.

The crowd was turning, people pointing, gawking at the screaming little girl.

The two men behind Troy hesitated, looked at each other and at Dee, then made their move anyway. Troy screamed as they pinned his arms from behind.

His feet dangled off the ground, but the men were momentarily frozen—the car wasn't in quite the right position. Timing had been thrown off by Dee's scream. Troy struggled with all of the wiry strength in his thirteen-year-old body.

A husky blond kid wearing a USC varsity jacket said, "Hey!" and grabbed a kidnapper's shoulder. Without a word the man spun and drove his fist precisely into the cleft of his ribs. Green and gagging, the young man fell to his knees.

Troy was half in and half out of the car now.

Before conscious thought could catch up with him, Derek

charged. He body-blocked the door, slamming it on the man in the passenger seat. The kidnapper screamed, and Troy eeled away.

At that point, everything melded into a confused blur. Derek was aware of many things at the same instant, as if bandwidth of his senses had suddenly broadened without an accompanying increase in clarity.

A man grabbed Rachel from behind. She spun, and a leg lashed out with an Aerobicize-trained kick. It had power, speed, passion—everything but aim or effect. Her foot glanced off his thigh, and the back of his hand cracked across her cheekbone.

She spun, and fell. The contents of her purse scattered across the ground.

Someone clubbed Derek very hard behind the ear. His senses exploded, collapsed, scrambled. He fell to the ground, struggling to breathe, trying to think, unable to do either effectively.

Troy screamed "Dad!" as his father flopped on the pavement. Worry warred with self-preservation. He took a step forward, and then a step back, and turned to run. One of the men grabbed at him, caught a handful of T-shirt.

"Son of a bitch!" The angry voice belonged to Dee's elderly friend Katie. The kidnapper glanced up just in time to receive a full aerosol blast of pepper spray directly in the face. He howled, and his fingers clutched at his seared eyes.

Another bystander ran to join the fray, but a tall, wiry uniformed policeman appeared suddenly, blocking his approach. "Please stand back. Officers on the way." The officer's face was narrow, with a sharply prominent nose. He looked like an Indian. "This situation *will* be resolved. Please do not interfere, there is risk of injury—"

Derek blinked, tried to orient himself. The world whirled. But the kidnappers appeared just as confused. They'd depended on a split second of hesitation, a moment of confusion to make good their escape. The moment was gone. They piled into the car, and sped away.

Derek watched the uniformed police officer slip away into the crowd. He levered himself to hands and knees, and then up. Dee was still screaming, but that odd smoking-hair illusion was gone. Several bystanders still watched, stunned, looking after the car as it sped out of the parking lot. The entire affair couldn't have taken more than twenty or thirty seconds.

Rachel held Troy, who clung to his mother. Over her shoulder he stared at Derek, eyes glassy with confusion and swelling fear. Her blouse was smeared with dirt, and a single smear of blood darkened a torn right elbow. She ignored it. "Troy? Baby? Darling? Are you all right? Baby? Oh, God . . ."

Derek swept Dee into his arms, and gripped her with all his strength.

If she hadn't screamed . . .

Derek held Dee, afraid that if he let her go, for even a moment, his family might simply disappear. All that Derek could hear was his own heartbeat, and Dee's shallow breathing, and the distant wail of sirens as police cars began to arrive.

9

The sounds of the police station unnerved Derek, reminded him of another time, only a couple of years before. Even though the polite, intelligent young man in front of him was trying to be helpful, he couldn't help but remember another time, a time of humiliation and dishonor, when similar men had ripped his world apart.

The room was busy and noisy. Derek could smell the stale coffee and taste old cigarette smoke. For the past two hours the Waites clan had huddled in one of a dozen cubicles, telling their story over and over again to the man whose name tag read "Detective Wally Hicks." He was pleasant and freckled and slightly plump, and should have been raking autumn leaves in a Norman Rockwell painting. Hicks looked like a Wally. Derek wondered where the Beaver was.

"And what do you believe they were after?" Wally asked patiently.

"Probably my wallet. My wife's purse." The entire thing was so confused. He had a hard time putting his memories in their proper order.

"Ex-wife," Rachel corrected automatically, looking sheepish the moment she said it. "Sorry."

Dee sat in Derek's lap. Most of the time she kept her arms around his neck, but now she turned around and addressed the officer. "Troy," she said. "They wanted Troy."

"Excuse me?" Wally asked.

"They wanted Troy."

Wally scribbled something on a yellow legal pad. "And why do you think they were after your brother? In fact," he said, "why did you start screaming in the first place? Apparently you began to scream *before* any of this happened. Is that correct?"

She nodded. "I didn't scream. Dahlia screamed."

Wally blinked. "Excuse me?"

Rachel laughed apologetically. "Dahlia is her full name. We just call her Dee. She's a little confused by all of this."

Wally Hicks smiled empathetically. He looked tired, but concerned. Considering what kind of hell his department had been through for the past four days, it was amazing he could be so polite. "I can certainly understand that."

"No," Dee asserted. "Not me. Great-grandmama Dahlia."

Troy rolled his eyes. A couple of hours and three Mountain Dews had done wonders for his self-confidence. "Give me a break, okay?"

Dee stuck her tongue out at him, then turned to look back over her shoulder. Derek felt her suddenly stiffen.

He looked back, and saw a tall, golden-haired man, his light blue Armani suit the very picture of tailored elegance.

Several of the officers turned to look at him, wondering where they'd seen him before. Trying to remember his name.

The reason they recognized Medford Downs was that, for eight seasons, he had been the most popular detective on television. Every Saturday night, millions of people had tuned in to watch Truman Bach, millionaire playboy turned globe-trotting soldier of fortune. But a series of drug-related arrests, and reports of erratic behavior on the set had hurt his image and derailed his career. Ratings plummeted, and the Nielsen families had done what an army of Mafia hit men and CIA black-baggers had failed to do: kill Truman Bach.

Medford was now in his mid-fifties, still extremely good-looking, lean and swim-fit, with that slight Mediterranean flavor that took a tan so well. Derek felt his hackles raise.

Rachel was just beginning her career at CBC when *Truman Bach* started its run. As his star waned, hers was rising. Initial attraction to Rachel had blossomed into office romance. Only a cad would imply that Medford, or her considerable physical assets, had been responsible for her success.

And Derek wasn't a cad. He kept reminding himself of that.

Rachel stood and gave Medford a swift, warm kiss.

Medford looked over at the kids, saying, "Rachel—are you all right? The kids? Are they—?"

Troy waved at him. Troy liked Medford but demonstrated restraint when Derek was present. Dee liked him just fine, but still seemed distracted.

"God," Rachel murmured. "Am I ever glad to see you!"

Derek set Dee down, and rose. "Hello, Medford," he said, and they gripped palms. It was brief but intense. Their handshakes were always little contests. Nothing impolite or obvious, but enough to keep Derek working out with the little spring-loaded grip thingies during odd moments.

"Derek." Medford displayed depressingly perfect teeth.

Medford sat next to Rachel.

Wally Hicks looked at his report. "And are you Mr. Downs, Ms. Childe's fiancé?"

"Yes, I am." Medford rested a proprietary hand along her forearm.

"Ahhah." Wally scribbled something. "I've seen your show." He scratched his head. "Did they ever film the second half of the cliff-hanger? You know, the last episode?"

"Off the brink and into the drink." Medford laughed. "We were sure that the network wouldn't renew us, but we teased them with the possibility of saving poor old Bach from a watery grave."

"It didn't work?"

"No, it didn't."

"Still liked the show," Wally said. "Anyway. Ms. Childe," he continued, "I assume you would consider yourself a wealthy woman?"

She considered the question. "I've been with the network for thirteen years. After stock options, I suppose some people would consider me wealthy, yes."

Hicks scribbled. "I see. Then kidnapping is a possibility."

"I suppose so, yes."

"All right. We will continue to follow up on our leads."

"And exactly which leads are these?" Medford asked curiously. "Exactly what is being done?" He spoke in an I-pay-your-wages voice, a man who was used to having things done, and quickly, and no bullshit about it.

Wally was briskly polite. "A license plate. Some descriptions. We have confidence in finding these men. We're still running behind. The zoo probably shouldn't have been open. There are a lot of bad feelings—but I think that we'll get things sorted out."

Dee was staring back into the office—at something. Derek craned his head around, feeling the flesh at the back of his neck prickle. He saw a tall, thin officer in his mid-forties. And he had seen this man somewhere before. Hair a black widow's peak. Pale skin, but cheekbones like an Indian's. Weight lifter's chest, runner's waist. Broad, flat, corded hands. It took a moment for Derek to place him.

The parking lot. The kidnap attempt. *"Please stand back. We have officers on the way."*

A cold wave of nausea swept over him. Suddenly everything in the station looked and sounded different. Hell, the smell of the *coffee* was suddenly different.

He looked at Wally Hicks, ashamed, and afraid to admit that he now saw a thousand alternative explanations for every little shift of the man's face, every little intonation, every word.

Derek felt Dee tremble, and then realized that that was *him* shaking. Instead of a place of refuge, the police station had suddenly become . . . something else.

Maybe only the one Indian-looking cop was involved in whatever had happened at the zoo. Maybe. But what if he was wrong? What if the police, all of them, were part of a vast and malevolent charade? And perhaps the charade would continue only so long as the unknown puppet masters believed the Waites clan to be unaware of the danger. At the very least, Derek needed time to think. Then, maybe tomorrow, he would talk to Hicks privately, and tell him about the Indian.

Maybe their only hope was to act stupid. At the moment, Derek didn't consider it much of an act. Derek felt afraid. He composed himself, and tuned back into the conversation. Hicks had commenced his peroration.

"Well," Derek interjected, "I'm sure that you have everything in hand." He tried to make his voice light and unchallenging, as confident as possible.

Rachel composed herself. "I'd like to get the children home," she said. "They've had a very stressful day. Thank you for your help, Mr. Hicks."

Wally Hicks rose from behind his desk, smile still open and very friendly. "We'll be in touch," he said.

Struggling to remain calm and centered, Waites escorted his children out of the station. He was walking a little too quickly. He wondered what Hicks would make of that. Out of the corner of his eye, he saw the other officer. The Indian. The Indian wasn't watching them. But Derek knew he was aware that they were leaving.

Behind them, Detective Hicks scratched his face thoughtfully.

10

The Grenada condo complex sits near the corner of Chosen Drive and Sunset, just north of the Divide. South of Sunset, properties with exactly the same frontage and footage sell or lease for approximately 70 percent of the price accorded properties north of that same line. To the untutored eye Sunset seems a mere traffic artery. It is actually one of the invisible power markers crisscrossing the Greater Los Angeles metropolitan area. On the map, they look like streets, freeways, aqueducts, railroad tracks. Socially, they loom as large as the Great Wall of China.

A small, tidy motorcade proceeded west on Sunset: Medford's Mercedes in front, then Rachel's Jag, and Derek's Tercel behind. The streets were busy but not crowded. The residential section of Beverly Hills simmered into quiescence long before the major arteries died down. This was a time for dinner and wine and relaxation, and sharing brutal stories of life-and-death combat in the financial front lines along Melrose and La Cienega.

The Grenada was two acres and nine stories of exclusive condos, with six tennis courts, three pools and three weight rooms, maid service, and all of the amenities you can't get at home anymore. The gate to the northeast underground parking garage swung up and open. Mercedes and Jag slid into the depths. The gate swung closed behind them.

Derek found a parking place on the street. A yellow sign declared that only permit parking was allowed, but Rachel had obtained a sticker for him not long after she moved in with Medford, eight months before. Thanks, Rache.

That was right after the sale of their house in Santa Monica. After the separation. After his mother died, and Derek moved back to the house of his youth. After he got out of jail.

Shit. His thoughts always seemed to wander back to that, like masochistic pigeons homing to a toxic waste dump.

He hustled the kids out of the car, Dee more asleep than awake. He hoisted her onto a shoulder, felt his back grumble protest. For the hundredth time he resolved to get Dee hormone treatments to stop this damned growing up. He feared the time when he would no longer be able to pick her up, to feel her sweet breath against his cheek, no longer be able to cradle her in his arms. Maybe he should lift weights or something, just to postpone the inevitable by a year or two. Just hold on to her a little longer. As long as she could snuggle against him, and sleep in his arms, he would remain Daddy, just Daddy, the one who could do no wrong. No questions. Just Daddy.

Medford and Rachel appeared from the residents' door in

the center of the building, and motioned to them. Troy ran inside, carrying their luggage. Derek carried Dee. The little girl wrapped her small warm arms around his neck, and purred contentedly.

Medford pushed the elevator button, and it sighed open almost instantly. They entered, and pushed the button for the seventh floor.

"I recognized one of the policemen at the station," Derek said, almost offhandedly. He watched the numbers climb.

Rachel took Dee from around his neck, held her. He knew that he was stronger than Rachel, but somehow, it always seemed that she could hold Dee longer. "What do you mean?" she murmured, stroking Dee's cheek.

"Tall, thin man. In his forties. He looked like an Indian. He was at the zoo, helping the kidnappers, I think."

"You *think?*"

Medford stared. "Aren't we being a little paranoid?"

Before Derek could formulate an answer, Dee murmured sleepily: "I saw him, too, Mommy."

Rachel looked back and forth between them, wondering if there were some kind of conspiracy between father and daughter to make her life miserable.

The elevator sighed to a stop on the seventh floor. The door slid open, admitting them to a lobby with a single door at the far end.

Rachel's condo always made Derek feel a little insignificant. The furnishings in any one room were worth more than everything in his house. He couldn't name most of the designers or brands, but knew that they were so far out of his league it was painful even to contemplate it. Once upon a time, he had begun learning about such things, trying to follow Rachel's fascination with beauty and delicacy. Derek's world was one of thought. Tactile sensations and visual impressions rarely mattered as much. To Rachel, they seemed all-important.

Rachel carried Dee into the child's own small, comfortable room. It had once been a utility room of some kind, but she had knocked the wall out and put in a door connecting it with a guest bathroom, and turned it into a tidy, comfortable little corner. Certainly more comfortable than the couch she shared with her brother at Derek's house.

The room was crowded with plush toys. Two mobiles dangled from the ceiling: one with pastel dinosaurs, and the other with little toy musical instruments. A drum, a flute, a cello, counterbalancing one another and spinning slowly as the air currents drifted.

Rachel plopped Dee down on the bed. The girl giggled as her mother pulled her shoes off, pausing to tickle the toes a little. She was about to slip Dee into a flannel nightgown, when the girl protested. "No," she said. "Great-grand-mama's."

Rachel shook her head. "That's an heirloom, honey. It should really be in a museum case."

"Please?"

It had been a bad day. Anything that might calm Dee was worth considering. She opened the girl's small suitcase, and drew out the nightgown. She felt an unreasoning pang of jealousy. Traditionally, the nightgown was passed to Great-great-grandmother Dahlia's namesakes. Her aunt, and her great-grandmother had both been Dahlias. As a girl, Rachel had yearned to own it, but no luck. Now it was in her hands, and all it had cost was naming her only daughter after a woman who had been a slave.

The garment was hand-spun cotton. Black threads were woven into the white, and Rachel wasn't certain whether those threads were imperfections, or something else. She held it against her cheek. It always felt warm and somehow comforting. She slipped it onto Dee.

The child gurgled like a baby, and curled onto her side. Her mouth relaxed into a smile, and she purred.

Derek followed Medford into the kitchen, collapsing into a seat just before his legs gave out. He'd had no awareness of the depths of his own fatigue until that very moment.

Medford was tinkering with some gleaming chrome instrument of destruction that Derek belatedly recognized as an espresso machine. "Caffeine?"

"Set up an IV," Derek answered wearily.

He suddenly realized that part of the fatigue came from scanning the furnishings. A bitter voice in the back of his head whispered that he would never catch up with Medford Downs. That somehow his life had turned down the wrong path. The main caravan was going by. Sometimes he could see their lights, but they were on another road, a higher road, and the road on which he traveled was dark, and thorny, and bumpy, and every time he tried to make a course correction, he ended up further away. And there were no maps.

And he was getting *tired.* More so, every lonely day.

"You know, Derek," Medford was saying, "until this whole thing is cleared up, it might be a good idea for the children to stay here, with us."

Derek had known that was coming. "Yeah, maybe you're right."

What Medford hadn't said was: *I know that you have custody for a week out of the month, but you almost never take it except during summer vacation, and do you really think that the children are as safe with you, down in that neighborhood, as they would be here in my luxury security condo?*

No one needed to ask or answer that question.

"I love them, too, you know," Medford said. Water was gurgling, steaming. "Really, I'm not trying to be Troy's father."

"It's not always a job I'd recommend." A stream of rich brown fluid splashed into the glass receptacle. The air filled with the aroma of Kenyan espresso roast.

Footsteps in the hall. "Rachel!" Derek called. "How's Dee?"

Rachel entered, and plopped down into a chair, exhausted. "Okay, I guess. Just okay. Where's Troy?"

"In his room playing Dungeon Quest," he said. "I got him the new key." He felt a burble of pride at that. Medford, with all of his money, couldn't get a Dungeon Quest key card ten seconds before the general release. *So there.*

"He spends too much time in that game, Derek," she said. Medford watched them both, his eyes hooded. He looked like a referee about to jump between two boxers before they fouled themselves out.

"He helps me test the program. He's even testing the hardware. No other kid will have a machine like that for maybe eight, ten months."

"Let someone else test it. He's hiding in that game, Derek."

"Let's not do this tonight," he asked wearily.

Rachel was gracious in victory. "I'm sorry. You're right."

Medford appeared behind Rachel, and began massaging her shoulders. The entire scene was depressingly domestic. Derek became aware of the distant sound of running water. It might have come from another condo, or another world.

"Was it my imagination," he asked, "or did I see smoke coming from Dee's hair, or dress or something?" It sounded so crazy he was reluctant to mention it.

Instead of laughing, Rachel carefully said, "I saw it, too, I think. But her hair wasn't burnt," she added quickly. "She wasn't hurt in any way. I don't really know what it might have been, no idea at—" She suddenly stopped, seemed to be listening for or to something. The sound of water was louder now. "What's that?" she asked.

A sudden flush of panic stirred him. "Dee's room?" He was out of his chair and heading into the other room almost before he realized what he was doing.

Steam rolled from beneath Dee's door. Within the room, steam was cumulous dense. The bathroom doorknob was warm to the touch. Derek wrenched the door open.

Dee stood in the shower, her eyes open and staring. She was dressed in her nightgown. It was sodden and dark, a darkness so deep it seemed to absorb the light around it, creating a nimbus of shadow. Her eyelashes fluttered, as if pictures were flashing behind them and she were a motion picture projector, her eyelids the shutters. As the water hit the skin of her hands and face, it boiled into steam like water striking a hot plate.

Her lips moved, and the sounds coming from them were impossible. Rachel stood beside Derek, momentarily transfixed. The disorienting thing was that Dee wasn't speaking in her own voice. If he wasn't mistaken, if he hadn't taken complete leave of his senses, Dee was speaking in *her mother's* voice.

The water plastered Dee's hair down against her forehead, so that she looked a little like a drowned dark angel.

"Bobby in Maryland," Dee recited, almost as if she were

reading some kind of scroll. "*October fourteenth, 1954. After the hurricane. Torrance in Minnesota, October fifteenth, 1918, after the fire storm. Larry dead in Florida, September thirteenth, 1928, after the hurricane . . .*"

Rachel's fingers dug into his arm. Then she was past him, and talking almost—but not quite, as if she weren't seeing what was happening right in front of her. "Honey? What's the matter?"

Her fingers touched her daughter. She yelped in surprise and dismay, and jerked her hand back. "She's burning up!"

Waites plunged into the water without taking off his shoes or his shirt. He grabbed Dee, shook her, and roared with pain. Dee's skin was so hot it was like touching a blast furnace. At this close range, the steam was almost scalding.

Dee continued to talk looking straight ahead, without acknowledging her father's presence. "*Malcolm died, February twenty-eighth, 1972, in Virginia. A flood. Floyd died in Florida. September tenth, 1960. Hurricane. Carver died, September eleventh, 1878, Tennessee. Yellow fever.*"

Derek felt nauseated. "Eighteen seventy-eight?"

Rachel wrapped her hands with a towel, then reached into the shower, and grabbed Dee.

Troy appeared in the doorway. "What is this?" he asked, confused.

Neither parent answered him. Dee continued to speak in the eerily altered voice. "*Kip died after the Missouri tornado. May twenty-ninth, 1896.*"

Troy stared, utterly hypnotized by the sights and sounds before him.

Rachel pulled Dee out of the shower, her hands protected by the towel. The instant Dee left the water, her skin sizzled dry, her hair began to smoke, and she *screamed*. Derek tore Dee from her mother's arms, and thrust her back under the water. "Dammit!" he yelled. "She needs the water!"

Dee's voice grew unstable, almost like a distant radio signal breaking up as mountains and electrical wires interposed themselves.

But still, she continued to speak. "*They killed Tony on June thirty-first, 1957. Hurricane Audrey in Louisiana.*"

Her voice was much weaker now. She sagged back against

the wall. Her eyes seemed more aware of the insanity, as if the little girl within her were a witness, not a participant, in the proceedings. Rachel climbed into the tub with her, her six-hundred-dollar Halston pants sopping and probably ruined.

Dee continued to speak. *"My babies,"* she said. *"My babies."* And then paused. *"Troy is next."*

At the door Troy stiffened, his eyes wide. Rachel sobbed as she held her daughter. Finally, Dee lay quiet in her parents' arms. Medford watched and gawked, disbelieving.

The only sound in the bedroom was from Dee's alarm clock. It was battery powered, and hung on the wall. On the hour and half hour, Bugs Bunny and the Tasmanian Devil emerged to chase each other around the clock. It ticked loudly, but the ticks were out of pace with the seconds. It ticked at the seventy-two beats per minute of a mother's heart. The Sharper Image catalog claimed that this beat provided soothing sleep for young children.

Derek prayed it would work.

Rachel was carefully tucking Dee into bed. Troy looked from his mother to his father with concern. "Would it be all right if I stayed in here tonight?"

It was difficult to know what bothered him more—the pronouncement of doom, his sister's condition or the fact that somebody might tell one of his friends that he gave a shit.

Raoul, Dee's calico kitten, jumped up on the bed and curled into a ball next to her hip.

"You can stay," Rachel answered finally. She still looked at her daughter as if expecting Dee to levitate or begin spitting pea soup. "Baby? Why did you say those things?"

"Didn't." Dee said. "Grandmama Dahlia did." Her voice was a drowsy child's, a voice that might topple over into sleep between the next vowel and consonant. She examined the kitten muzzily. "Hello, Raoul."

The kitten looked at her with great sincerity and said, "Raoww?"

Troy flicked its head with his finger. "That's your name," he said. "Don't wear it out."

Dee instantly said, "Ohhh, Mommy. Troy bopped Raoul.

Troy gets . . . a . . . check mark. . . .'' Her voice drained away, and she was asleep. Rachel and Derek kissed Dee's sleeping forehead, then tiptoed out of the room. Troy sat in a chair at the edge of the bed, watching his sister. Holding one of her small hands in his.

Medford awaited them in the kitchen. Lattes steamed in three mugs. Medford poured a healthy slug of bourbon into his. His hands shook.

"Will somebody please give me a score card?" he asked. "Who is this Dahlia?"

Rachel answered but Derek couldn't get the impression out of his mind that she didn't really want to. "Dahlia is Dee's full name."

"So what is she talking about?"

"I don't know, I really don't know," she said, exasperated. "She's just tired. And scared. I'm calling a doctor."

Derek couldn't quite believe what he was hearing. "A doctor? Why not a plumber?"

Rachel stared at him. "What?"

The words burst out in rapid-fire. "Our daughter's a walking water heater. Something damned strange is going on here." He paused, sipping steamed milk and espresso. Damn, it was good. He had a terrible sensation of turning some dark corner of his life. That he would never enjoy things like coffee and zoos and programming in quite the same way again. "Your mother was nuts on Grandmama Dahlia. I can remember at least six different conversations about her. How Dahlia escaped the old Charleston plantation, snuck across Confederate lines. 'She crossed the line of fire.' Brought back Union soldiers. She freed your family, right?"

Rachel's expression was strained. "So?"

"So that wasn't Dee's voice. Grandmama Dahlia made her scream this afternoon. If she hadn't, Troy would have been snatched. Now this. First we saw smoke, and now steam. Something damned strange is going on. Wasn't there a kid named Tony, cousin of yours, kidnapped or something in Louisiana?"

Rachel stiffened. "He went missing after the hurricane. Hurricane Audrey. What about it?"

Something was coiling and twisting in the back of his mind. "She said a lot of names. Are there any other missing relatives I should know about?"

Rachel looked at him strangely. "There've been family tragedies, but no more than any other family."

"Are you sure?"

For an instant, it was as if Medford didn't exist at all, that the only people in the room were Derek and Rachel.

"Her voice was pretty strange, wasn't it." It wasn't a question at all.

Derek nodded.

"Derek. You know how to research things. Could you look into this? For me?"

There was something in her eyes that he hadn't seen in years, and it sent a chill down his spine.

"What's going on here?" Medford asked.

Derek didn't take his eyes away from Rachel. Couldn't. "Probably nothing," he said quietly. "But it doesn't hurt to look."

She nodded slightly, the faintest wan smile on her lips. "Thank you," she said.

Medford's gaze bounced from Rachel to Derek like an observer at a tennis match. Without a word, he offered her the spiked coffee. "It's got a little zip. I think you need it."

"No, thank you," Rachel said, almost automatically. Still, she took the cup from his hand and sipped. Deeply.

"Maybe I should go," Derek said. "I tell you what—I'll call in the morning."

Rachel smiled wearily. "I'd like that."

Derek squeezed Rachel's shoulder and drew his coat on, heading for the door. Medford walked him out, leaving Rachel at the table, bent over her coffee.

"There's no reason I can't stay here for a couple of days." Medford chuckled. "If I thought there was any real danger, we could all go out to Palm Springs. The house can be ready in hours."

Derek nodded appreciatively. "I don't have to like you, Medford—but I know that my children are safe here. That means a lot."

Medford and Derek entered the lobby together. Medford

pressed the elevator button, and stepped aside as Derek entered. The men hadn't shaken hands.

Finally, just before the doors closed, Medford yelled, "Derek!"

Derek held the doors apart. "Yeah?"

"I don't like you either." Medford smiled. "But I sure like your work."

For a moment, Derek was confused. "My work?"

"You made some great kids."

In spite of himself, Derek chuckled. It was strange. The two men loved the same woman, and that drove them apart. But they also loved the same children, and that brought them closer together. In a way, they were part of the same tribe.

The door slid shut.

11

It took Derek thirty minutes to drive home, and another forty to get politely lubricated.

He slammed the beer can on his desktop, unable to erase the terrible images from his mind.

Despite his best intentions, he knew he was on the verge of getting into real trouble. The old feelings were too close to the surface tonight.

Next to the computer on the desk was a list he had begun over at Rachel's condo. He glanced at the dates and places listed, the intimations of violence. Should he do anything about this? It was craziness. Pure insanity.

He took out a pencil, and rolled his eyes back, allowing himself to go into alpha state. It was a trick he had learned in grammar school. There were places in his mind that simply recorded information like a tape recorder or camera. Collating and cross-referencing the data was another thing, requiring far more labor.

He jotted down a few more of Dee's dates and places. Then he sat back and shook his head. "This is crazy," he muttered. "This is crazy, this is so nuts. . . ."

He triggered his auxiliary phone line, and began to type. The computer tone buzzed, and the message "Compunet Information Service" came up. It asked him, "Code Word?"

He always felt a little embarrassed, and he always typed the same thing: "Daffy."

A menu of services appeared, offering a wide variety of computer services—entertainment, news, research, bulletin boards, special interest groups. He typed "National News Morgue," and when the screen prompted him, he typed in "Louisiana, hurricane, June 31, 1957."

The computer hummed for three minutes, and then news stories began to reel back. They told of rescue efforts relating to Hurricane Audrey, which had devastated Cameron, Louisiana, on the twenty-seventh. Derek pondered a moment, and typed in a second date: "October 15, 1918, Minnesota." And the word "Fire." In four minutes he got three articles dealing with corpses still being extracted from smouldering wreckage in Duluth. The fire storm had occurred on the twelfth.

So. The dates related to disasters of some kind—but followed them.

He typed in those first two dates, and then the command "Cross-reference," and the words "Murder" and "Kidnap."

The computer hummed, the screen temporarily frozen as it began to work. Nothing to do now but wait.

Derek rose and stretched, listening to his joints popping as he did. He felt old and tired. Newspaper images flew across the screen. He wasn't ready for sleep. He got another beer from the kitchen, and sat in a chair by the window, sipping. A police helicopter's searchlight floated through the street like a glowing, malevolent butterfly.

Derek awoke from dreams of pursuit through a dark, damp tunnel. The computer beeped at him patiently. The screen read "Search String Completed." The screen displayed four names, and one of them caught his attention: Tony Childe.

"I'll be damned," he said quietly. "How in the hell would Dee know about this?" He clicked on the name, and the modem blinked as instructions flew back and forth. An article appeared.

"Tony Childe missing and presumed murdered following his abduction and the death of his father—"

Oh, so Tony's father was killed trying to protect him. Perhaps from looters following that hurricane? Whatever the facts, Tony himself was merely missing. Out of curiosity, Derek put in a search string for Tony, and pulled up three more articles.

"Not much news that week," he murmured. One of the articles was concerned that Tony was still missing, and another was a plea from his family, a request for mercy to a small, helpless child.

The last article chilled him.

Four days after his abduction from his New Orleans home, the body of thirteen-year-old Tony Childe was found near the southern train yards, apparently burned to death. Police have yet to establish a time of death, or specific cause, but the search for the kidnappers has intensified. Police are following several leads.

While an official statement has not yet been forthcoming, sources in the police department state that the boy's entire body was covered with fourth-degree burns, so that identification was difficult even with dental records. "It is hard to imagine a killer savage enough to do something like this to a child of this age. We will find him, we will convict him. . . ."

Waites felt the world lurch sideways. It was too easy to recall the image of his daughter in the shower, steam rising from her body, water boiling. He wonder what might have happened had there not been water to cool her.

Then something hit him, hard. The hurricane was in someplace called Cameron. Tony lived in *New Orleans*. What the hell was this?

He searched a while longer, found a few more articles, which grew increasingly plaintive and discouraged. There were no witnesses. No clues. A plea to the community for help. A couple of dead-end leads. And finally, nothing.

Waites leaned back away from the screen, as if trying to find enough room to breathe. He needed to stand up, walk around the office, clear his head.

A thirteen-year-old boy. Burned to death. The killers never found.

Jesus Christ.

After a few minutes he sat down again, and brooded at the screen. He needed a way to speed this up, automate it. Staring at the screen, waiting for another grim story to surface, was going to kill him.

He called up a completely different file, from a different program: "Waites Family Genealogy." This was a project he had begun at his mother's request, years before. She had been a bear on the subject, and while he had never picked up the bug, he indulged her and wrote a little program integrating text and graphics. If she had lived to push him further, he would eventually have scanned in photographs, birth and death certificates, awards and citations, and anything else of interest. He could have cross-referenced it, and created a central library for the family. With her death . . .

He had to pause again. His mother died while he was in prison. He had not seen her during those volatile last few days after the stroke. She had called for him, and he hadn't been there. More damage. Just more damage. One of these days he might be able to look at it, and come to some kind of understanding about what it all meant.

Right now he just *couldn't*.

After her death the project languished, except for occasional updates on the birth of a cousin, or the death of a great-uncle.

But what began as a vanity project for his mother, chronicling births, deaths, marriages and the like, could turn into a genuine asset now. He hoped.

He opened the main menu, currently set to his last entry. He clicked the first tag, and produced schematics of two different family trees: one for Derek Waites, the other for Rachel Childe. Tiny branches from their union suggested two children, Troy (born 1979), and Dahlia (Dee, born 1986). He clicked on the box around Rachel's name, and the screen expanded into a new network of aunts, uncles, grandparents

... some of them carried the name Childe, and others with various other surnames.

Derek created a split screen, and compared the two lists—one from the newspapers, and the other from the genealogy chart. He let his gaze slide down the chart until he found a name that matched his memory: Torrance Washington. He clicked on the name.

The news story unfolded. "Saint Paul, Minnesota, October 20, 1918. Torrance Washington's burned and mutilated body was found after a six-day search. . . ."

October twentieth? Dee had said October fifteenth. And the fire storm had taken place even earlier, on the twelfth. . . .

In *Duluth.*

His head hurt. Derek rubbed his knuckles against his temples, and resolved to start over again.

All right. Suppose there was a natural disaster, followed by a kidnap and a murder in a nearby town. The body wasn't discovered for several days. But why take Torrance? Why not snatch someone local?

Because there was something special about Torrance. And Tony. And the other relatives on the list.

Well, then, why snatch them after a disaster in another town, when that disaster certainly wouldn't cover the disappearance? It didn't make sense.

But a voice in the back of his mind said: *Doesn't it? Doesn't it, Derek? If it doesn't cover the disappearance and murder of one small colored boy, what might it cover?*

"I don't know," he whispered.

Yeah, but if you did know, what would you say?

"I'd say it covered the disappearance and death of other people. Maybe a *lot* of other people."

He scanned down his scribbled list. *Two instances isn't a pattern. I need more.*

But that was his mind talking. His stomach wanted to heave, his heart to die.

What he needed was a method to search further, and faster.

Derek typed in: "New Search String: Disappearances, Murders, Burning." Then he highlighted the entire genealogical charts, every one of the more than six hundred names, and copied them to the search file. They appeared there, in ragged array. He adjusted the margins. Then he typed in *"Cross-reference."*

The screen blanked, and for just a fraction of a second, he felt hope. Then hope died. A list scrolled down the screen. Several were linked to the main list by last names, but were the names of children he had missed. Eight names. Dead children. Three Childes, two Washingtons, and then a smattering of other names.

He said something profane, and cleared the screen, beginning to type again. "Change Search. U.S. Dept. of Census. Access City Records Regarding Birth, Death, Marriage."

Most of the necessary records wouldn't be on magnetic media yet. This was even more sickening, because it implied that for every child whose name appeared, there might be several others.

The computer screen warned him that this information required a special access rate of twenty-two dollars an hour, and asked him if he agreed to that. He typed in "Agreed," and it billed his account. The screen clouded again, and disk drives whirled.

He turned his printer on, stood, stretched, and lay down on his couch. This could take a while. In fact, it could take all night.

"That's all right with me," he whispered. "I've got no place better to go."

12

Despite the constant whisper of the air-conditioning overhead, Officer Godfrey Timms was sweating. There would seem to be no good reason for the state. At forty-six, he was in perfect physical condition—weights and running gave him a whipcord body. His lean face and high cheekbones created a Native American profile so marked that his buddies called him Chief.

He had grown up on the streets of Los Angeles. His alcoholic Tex-Mex mother had never even mentioned his father's name. Timms grew into a street-fighting petty thief until a local boxing gym provided an outlet for his raw aggression. He actually dreamed of attending college, but when no boxing scholarships materialized, he abandoned his dreams. Godfrey Timms began a long slide into an increasingly dark, violent and ultimately pointless life.

Then a miracle happened: as if by magic, his mother produced a ten-thousand-dollar college bond. Where had it come from? Her answer, which could be coaxed out of her only after at least a fifth of Seagrams, was that his father had purchased it.

His father. So the mystery man, the bastard Godfrey Timms had never met, had dropped some serious cash on the old lady before disappearing into whatever sewer he had climbed out of.

Fuckin' A.

Timms was far too practical even to think of turning it down, and UCLA opened its doors to him.

Somewhere in his second year of college, Godfrey Timms decided to make a career of law enforcement. He was accepted, and worked harder than he ever had in his life to get through the academy. The physical stuff was easy for him—but then, it always had been. And he actually applied himself sufficiently in his criminology, psychology, tactics and communications classes, as well.

He still remembered his mother's appearance at his graduation. She was a sallow, huddled figure, a wisp of the vibrant and sensual woman she once had been. But tears of pride sparked in her eyes. "Your father would be proud," she said.

But wouldn't say anything more.

As a police officer, Timms was tough, effective, fearless in action, and willing to take risks. One such gamble had ended in the death of a pusher, and the disappearance of a half million dollars in cocaine money. The resulting investigation could have finished him—there was a witness, a junkie named Billie Wang who knew the secret of Timms's positive cash flow.

Wang ended up dead, skinny neck broken, in Las Vegas—

and Timms was off the hook. The day before Wang was discovered, Timms received a Polaroid picture of the corpse, and a slip of paper with a phone number written on it.

Timms called the number, trying hard to keep his voice steady and official. The voice on the other end of the phone was reasonable and polite—and told Timms that the junkie would be found the next day, either with or without Timms's phone number written on the edge of a coke-stained dollar bill.

It all depended on Timms. Timms agreed to a meeting.

The meeting took place at one o'clock in the morning on what the local gay population called Blowjob Boulevard, a back road off Fern Dell in Griffith Park. Timms arrived early, parked his car a quarter mile away, and walked up, uncertain of anything except that he was in deep, deep trouble.

There, in the park, he had waited. The night was cold and moist, and a mild wind blew through the trees. He had almost given up, when a voice behind him said, "Timms."

The cop turned, and for the first time met the man who would become the most important force in his life.

Today, Godfrey Timms felt only a kind of sour, gut-wrenching fear, because he had been given a mission, and he had failed.

One part of his mind was aware of this, aware of how he felt, and what the feelings meant. And then there was another part that watched the surroundings, paid attention to the environment, and that part watched the man next to him, Pinal. Pinal was the new man. Tall, thin, rapier quick, smart, and possessed of a mercurial temper that had proven deadly on more than one occasion. Handsome, in a hawkish way. He was new to the organization, an officer with a talent and record for brutality—just the sort of man who might have gotten caught up in the Rodney King business. In fact, it was the quiet stifling of a bit of truly bad business—this one involving a pregnant teenage prostitute—that brought Pinal to Timms's attention, and to the room in which he presently stood.

"The bitch screamed," Timms said again, his tone modulated carefully. The man he addressed was largely in shadow, sunken back in a plush leather chair. A woman stood beside the seated man, behind him, massaging his shoulders as he listened. Her name, Timms thought, was Daphnia. A thin wisp of fragrant cigarette smoke curled into the air, out of the shadow. Daphnia was an overwhelming amalgam of dark eyes and cascading blond hair, flawless skin and an impossibly lush body. Every gesture, every word, every glance seethed with erotic promise. Everything about her was a clear declaration that she believed, and had good reason to believe, that she would absolutely be the finest fuck Godfrey Timms had ever had.

Until sixteen years ago, Timms hadn't even known that women like Daphnia *existed*. He had seen them on television and in James Bond movies, but on some level assumed that they were grown in hydroponic vats, or something.

"The screams threw everything off. I'm sorry, Mr. DuPris."

If DuPris had a first name, Timms had never tried to learn it. If he had ever heard it, he hadn't bothered to remember it. "Mr. DuPris" was the only thing he ever called his master when others were around, and it would do.

"You have served me well, Timms," DuPris said. Timms almost fainted to hear that there was no anger in the voice. "I know you will do better next time."

"Yes, sir," Timms nodded agreement. "I only tried a public kidnap to avoid patterns. We've used so many different methods." He paused, thinking. "There's going to be a next time?"

There was a momentary pause, during which DuPris took two more deep breaths, and made another thin exhalation. "Yes," his master said finally. "The little girl's name is Dahlia, isn't it?"

"Yes, sir."

"Interesting . . ." he mused. "I wonder . . ." He seemed about to say one thing, but then appeared to change his mind. "We are *exposed*." He gave the word an unmistakable emphasis. "She has to die. They all need to die."

To Timms's surprise, Pinal chose this moment to speak.

"Sir," Pinal said. "The African won't like that, will he?"

There was a genuine question in the words, but something else as well. A rebuke.

The room temperature seemed to drop another thirty degrees. DuPris kissed Daphnia's hands. "Daphnia," he said. "Would you leave us, please?"

Without a word, the woman complied. She hadn't said a single word the entire time, she had stood there behind him, and she didn't speak now. She was just gone.

The door locked behind her. The room was silent. Quietly, without drawing any notice to himself, Timms stepped away from Pinal.

DuPris leaned into the light. He was a large man with blazing red hair, intense eyes and a high, broad forehead. His hands were fleshy and strong looking. Not for the first time, Timms reflected that DuPris had the perfect body for an athlete. If he had chosen to apply his energies in that direction, he could have been—anything.

The expression in DuPris's eyes was as cold and lethal as interstellar vacuum. "*I* pay you," he snapped. "Not that bastard with delusions of empire."

The words carried enough venom for a colony of asps. "You obey *me.*" DuPris slammed his fist down on the desk. The boom reverberated through the room, shook the shelves. Then his voice dropped down to normal conversational levels, save for a deadly undercurrent that was even more disturbing. "Except that you didn't obey me, did you, Pinal? Did you, you fucking imbecile?"

DuPris stood. He was no taller than Pinal, both men rising to about three inches above six feet. He looked soft in comparison to the cop.

Pinal's fingers brushed his jacket, fidgeting above the bulge beneath his left arm.

DuPris glared at him, the challenge crackling in the air. Pinal glared back.

Insane. This was insane. Timms didn't want to watch this, but was hypnotized, unable to turn away.

Finally, Pinal spoke. "You don't scare me, faggot," he said. "And *nobody* talks to me like that."

DuPris's expression was unreadable. "Truly?" he asked softly. "No one?"

Pinal met DuPris's gaze. After a blistering few seconds, Pinal blinked. Timms held his breath. Willed his heart to stop beating. God. It was going to happen. DuPris lifted a warning finger, telling Timms not to interfere. DuPris grinned. God, he was *enjoying* this.

"I'm warning you, asshole—back off," Pinal said. DuPris didn't move.

He did, however, speak. "In ten seconds," he said. "You are going to die. One, two—"

He stepped from around the desk.

Pinal licked his lips. *Something is wrong here,* Pinal's eyes said. He was looking directly into DuPris's face, and he saw no fear, no tricks, no bluff. Beneath his left arm was a police-issue .38, and DuPris had no weapon at all. Pinal was almost certainly wondering if the man was insane.

DuPris took another step forward, halving the distance between them.

Pinal's gaze flickered over to Timms, perhaps wondering if Timms was going to stop the madness. Timms hadn't moved. His face was neutral.

As DuPris took another step, Pinal's hand blurred. It was a motion he had made a thousand times, machine smooth. Almost certainly the fastest draw that Timms had ever seen.

In the confined space, the noise was deafening. DuPris shifted at the moment Pinal squeezed the trigger, a twist sideways, so fast that he blurred like a fan. Pinal's bullet cleaved empty air, but his trigger reflex was set on a pattern: *Two in the body, and one in the head,* a *ta-tap TAP* rhythm that was so automatic that the next shot sounded a quarter-second later. DuPris's left shoulder snapped back, the bullet smashing into bone and cleaving flesh, and he screamed in surprise—

Then Pinal screamed, his own surprise even greater.

Because at the exact moment that the bullet struck DuPris's shoulder, Pinal's shoulder began to bleed. At the moment that DuPris staggered back, clutching fingers to the wound, Pinal's eyes widened, the gun dangled loosely in his hands, and he shrieked, *"I've been shot!"*

He looked at the blood on his hand, and stared at DuPris. DuPris had no gun. He looked at Timms, expecting to see the officer's smoking revolver in hand. Nothing. Timms hadn't moved, although his hawkish face was pale.

Pinal strengthened his grip on the gun. "Who shot me?"

Timms shook his head. Pinal looked back toward DuPris—

Who was no longer there.

There was a sound behind him. Pinal spun, crying out in new pain—

DuPris stood *behind* Pinal.

Pinal stood there, struck dumb, unable to speak. He looked down at his hand, where he had held the gun. His trigger finger was bent at an unnatural angle, broken. He looked again at DuPris. The gun was in his hand.

Even with the bleeding, shattered shoulder, DuPris grinned at him. The shoulder wound oozed blood, but as Timms and Pinal watched, something moved beneath the cloth. The flesh rippled. The cloth puckered as a small flattened lozenge of metal worked its way free.

The bullet. Pinal watched in horror as it worked its way out of DuPris's flesh, followed by a yellowish material, and a thin milky fluid. It was squeezed all of the way out, and fell. DuPris caught it in his left hand. His hand trembled.

"Little man," DuPris said coldly. "Fast little man. It takes more than that. You see that now, don't you."

Pinal stared at him, unable to speak.

"Fast little man. Would you like to see speed? Real speed?" He cocked his head, almost inviting Pinal to say something. Pinal had nothing to say. DuPris moved again, just his arm this time, so quickly that the revolver stabbed into Pinal's wounded shoulder with inhuman, machinelike speed. The barrel and sight emerged from his back. Pinal screamed, babbling prayers, whey-faced with shock. He sagged to his knees, struggling feebly to pull the gun free.

DuPris daubed at his shoulder again, wiping away red. "He was . . . very good," DuPris said, just a bit shakily.

"You're hurt." Timms tried to ignore the man on the floor. Pinal mewed in pain, tugging at the piece of metal buried in his body.

"I can heal myself." DuPris pushed at Pinal's wounded shoulder with his toe. Pinal fell over onto his side, and groaned. "He isn't my Blood. Nor do I have a Purifier—" He looked at Timms, and grinned wolfishly. "Unless you volunteer?"

Timms shook his head a fervent negative.

The grin was feral now, hungry. Starving. He cast his eyes on Pinal, who was just quivering now, shock and blood loss draining the last of the hysterical strength that had sustained him. He moved his arms and legs to spastic effect, reminding Timms of a crushed beetle.

When DuPris spoke again, his voice was heavy with need. "Leave us, then. And tell the others not to come in for at least two hours. But then I will need help. Without a Purifier, I will be sick for a while."

"Yes," Timms said and backed toward the door. DuPris was kneeling, bending toward the wounded man. Pinal whimpered as DuPris's hands touched his head.

"Yes, Father."

DuPris's body arched, and he hissed, his fingers clamped to Pinal's forehead and chest like leeches on a cow's belly. His face suffused with ecstasy and Pinal convulsed, *screaming.* . . .

Timms slammed the door behind him.

Tuesday, May 5

The next three days were a blur for Derek Waites, an endless succession of libraries, telephone conversations and frantic scribblings on sheets of graph paper.

The task was to tease out every piece of information that he could find, or remember, or deduce, and to organize it in both linear and nonlinear fashions. Each approach revealed different aspects of Truth.

Once he began to dig, it wasn't a lack of information that frustrated him. Far to the contrary, he found himself possessed of an embarrassment of riches. What he needed was a means of tracking and collating all of it.

He chose a variety of ways: a general notebook, in which he captured every thought, every fact, every clue, every scrap of information, in the temporal order that it occurred or presented itself to him. Derek used three-by-five cards, and Post-it notes, taking advantage of their inherent nonlinearity. Two white boards were covered with exploded diagrams, Buzan-style mind maps that looked like pieces of fruit with toothpicks stuck into them, or bunches of grapes with multiple stems connecting each little circle to others nearby.

A 360-degree graph-paper diorama encircled his office.

In the center of one sheet the name "Dahlia Childe" was scrawled inside a cube shape. "Born 18?? Died 1867." He believed that was the date. That was what he had been told, anyway. What he needed to do was work his way back to that date. To that end, he had connected Rachel's lineage, and then branched off in other directions, connecting uncles, aunts, nieces, nephews, brothers, sisters, parents, spouses and cousins of every stripe. It didn't take very long for him to realize that regardless of what he tried to do, regardless of any family's best intentions, it is simply impossible to follow all the relational permutations after three generations, let alone eight.

Hundreds and hundreds of little boxes represented all of the names that he could dig out of family, city, state or federal records. Some had pictures next to them, some had question marks. Some had code numbers referring to the file folders piling up around his desk, and filling his shelves.

His fax machine and printer buzzed almost continuously as computers and Internet correspondents around the country fed him data. More came from the libraries, pictures and facts corresponding to the vast network of strange deaths that haunted Rachel's family.

It was no longer possible even to pretend that it wasn't true. He discovered at least sixteen instances of violent death occurring to boys between the ages of eleven and fourteen. Some were hidden within apparent accidents, some were bare-faced kidnap and murder. All followed some natural or man-made disaster by a few days—a week at the most. All were scattered over such a range of time and distance that no one in the family had ever asked the crucial question: *What the hell is going on?*

Across from Dahlia's wall chart was another chart, this one a huge map, three feet by two feet, of the continental United States. It was, at the moment, marked with red and blue pins, sixteen red, forty-four blue. A legend beneath the map read, "Red equals descendant of Dahlia Childe. Blue equals burning deaths in area within ten days of initial disappearance."

While all of the red pins represented blacks, the ancillary deaths were mixed racially and had no relation to the main family line. They were transients, bums, low-level criminal types, homeless. Nobodies. The lost and the lonely.

So.

Every few years, a descendant of Dahlia Childe was snatched off the street and killed. And about the same time, five or six unrelated people, mostly men, also vanished. All were found burned to death within a week or so of the kidnap. That is, when the corpses were found at all.

Even more depressing was the fact that he only had access to computerized files. He knew that if he were to crisscross the country, seeking information in old town halls and libraries, newspaper morgues and hospitals, police files and the memories of long-time residents in the crucial areas . . .

He would uncover more death, more tragedy in an already appalling cascade.

One of the photographs he had scanned out of Rachel's family album intrigued him. It was a woman named Alicia Tucker, a daughter of Dahlia Childe who had married a man named Chilton Tucker, a blacksmith. Alicia was quite light skinned. Mulatto? Sired upon Dahlia by her master, perhaps? She had five sons. So many sons might permit the name Tucker to survive to this day, straight down her blood line.

He performed a search string, and went back to his work of transcribing data from one format to another, searching for patterns.

Three hours later, the fax machine chimed. In response to his query, a database tied into *Soldier of Fortune* magazine had hit pay dirt. The first line read, "Austin Tucker convicted of multiple murder."

Waites watched, curious, as the fax rolled out.

"Austin Tucker, highly decorated Special Forces officer, was convicted today on charges of murder. Crystal and Dahlia Tucker, his wife and daughter, were found murdered in his house—"

The world rocked. The name Dahlia hit him so hard that he couldn't breathe. Tucker had a daughter named Dahlia?

He read on.

"—Tucker's son, Billy, was found three days later, burned to death. After a trial that lasted sixteen weeks, Tucker, who had been in trouble with the law on numerous occasions, was convicted of all three murders, and sentenced to two life sentences, to run consecutively. There was suspicion of involvement with other cases of burning and mutilation, but as yet, no further charges have been brought."

Two life sentences? War hero or not, they nailed this brother to the cross. . . .

The fax machine dinged again and began to move. This time a picture began to roll out. It was of a man in dress uniform, rows of medals across his chest, a neatly trimmed beard framing a strong face. There was something dangerous about the man's eyes. They had seen . . . death. Frequently. And embraced it. That disturbed Derek, almost as much as the fact that Austin Tucker, beyond any shadow of a doubt, was Caucasian.

Derek stared, disbelieving. "He's *white!*"

He stared at the fax printout, intrigued beyond words. For the next few moments, the world stopped moving, ceased making sounds. He lived in a womb of silence and stillness.

Derek shook himself out of that reverie and pulled a thick notebook from one of his shelves. It was filled with computer printouts, some of them decade-old dot matrix, some of them recently laser-printed. The notebook was labeled "Government Access." He typed in a telephone number and switched on the speaker phone.

It purred rhythmically, and when the phone on the other end answered, he heard a loud, abrasive modern tone. His computer picked it up and began to exchange protocols, and data danced across the screen.

It read, "Purchase Office, California State Penal System. Your Vendor Number?"

It was the right door, but he didn't have the key. If he could get past the initial challenge, he could dig deeply into their files.

But first he had to get in. No sense guessing the vendor number. There were probably ten million combinations, with a pause of thirty seconds between each try. So that to have a fifty-fifty chance of guessing it, he would have to guess . . . oh, say, five million times? That would be, say, a hundred and fifty million seconds, or about a quarter-million hours, or about ten thousand days, or maybe thirty years. Not the best approach.

He got up and stalked around the room, thinking. It had been a long time since he had done any serious hacking or cracking. Like any other discipline, it required a certain method of thinking, which was best practiced frequently. In this instance, the key was the human tendency to think rigidly, two-dimensionally.

There was *always* a loophole.

Derek went to his kitchen, and rummaged through the shelves until he found a large can of mashed potatoes, purchased at Smart and Final. The label read "De-Lighta Food Services. Institutional Size."

Institutional. Yes. De-Lighta was one of the largest suppliers of food to government facilities: military bases, public schools, municipal cafeterias . . . and the California State penal system.

Derek grinned like a shark. He had forgotten just how exciting the hunt was. Once upon a time he had *lived* for it.

As Captain Africa he had stalked through the databases and private communications lines of government and industry, never stealing or doing actual damage. . . .

Well, some people called it stealing, but he and his friends didn't. His attitude was that there were public thoroughfares, information highways. If you chose the right route, you were in position to look down through some mighty interesting windows, and if people left their data lying around for anyone to see, well . . .

Of course, sometimes he might take a shortcut *through*

someone's "house," which made it even easier to find that carelessly exposed data, and that wasn't his fault, was it?

And of course, sometimes the doors were locked, but so poorly that he was doing, say, ITT or the Pacific Stock Exchange a favor to point out to them how *easy* it was. A public service.

Heh, heh.

Oh, there were a million ways to justify what he and his friends did, but in the end what it boiled down to was a grand game, a game between him and whoever designed the target system. And whether the suits at Texaco knew it or not, the programmers they hired often left nasty (or congratulatory) messages for those who cracked their systems. So everyone understood the real game, and if it was at the expense of a little humiliation or frustration for some brassheads, who cared? Down the road, the suits would end up paying a hundred fifty thou a year to some young turk who cut his teeth breaking into their accounting files. In that sense, Derek and his friends were merely creating a healthy environment for young minds to grow and thrive.

Yeah, right.

The De-Lighta Foods data system was a relatively benign environment—after all, they encouraged orders from all and sundry. There were a few elementary challenges, but in general, once he got the first menu, welcoming him as a potential customer, it was relatively easy to get to the purchase office.

He browsed until he came upon an order for eight hundred cases of peas, signed by the deputy superintendent of the California State penal system.

At the corner of the screen was a number, "43567." Oh, bloody hell. Only a hundred thousand possible combinations. That would have only taken fifty thousand tries to have a 50 percent chance of breaking in, which would have only taken ... say, twenty-five thousand minutes, or four hundred hours, or about seventeen days.

Hell, he giggled, it was hardly worth it being a hacker anymore.

He dialed back into the California State penal system, whipped past their initial screens to get to the purchasing department, which promptly requested his number. He gave them "43567." The screen hummed, and then cleared.

"Welcome, De-Lighta Foods," it said.

Derek howled, thrusting his fist into the air triumphantly. "Yes!" he yelled. "Captain Africa strikes!"

The screen cleared. Derek found himself in a maze of messages, requests, notices . . . the web of the California State prisons purchasing department. He was *in*, on the far side of the password system, and all that it would require now was time, and patience.

The name "Tucker, Austin" blinked in the center of the screen. Derek's four hours of careful, patient work had borne fruit. The screen cleared again and Tucker's prison record appeared. At the upper right-hand córner of the screen were the words "Remanded to Tehachapi State Prison."

Derek studied the file, and then pulled a map of California from his wall shelf, contemplating times and distances. And then sat back, closing his eyes.

Everything until now had been a world he understood, a world of information—even if some of the information was illegally obtained. What happened next would change everything in his life, forever.

At first he hesitated, and then he remembered the sight of Dee in the shower, water boiling off her golden brown skin, and he lost his reluctance. He picked up the telephone. He had two telephone calls to make.

Derek speed dialed a number in New York, hoping that it wasn't obsolete. After five rings, it clicked.

"Manhattan Electric," a male voice blandly announced.

"Goober? This is the captain," Derek said. "I need some help."

A beat. Then, "Go to channel two."

Derek relaxed. Goober was a friend from back in his phreaking days. Mostly legit now, in the electronics business. But they had had a ton of fun together in the old days, and Derek prayed that Goober hadn't changed too much. He had hooked the scrambler box onto his ·line before making the call. It wouldn't stop anything serious, but then he wasn't doing anything illegal—yet. Discouraging casual eavesdroppers was always a good idea.

"Captain?" Goober said after the static rolled up and then died away. The scrambler was operational. "Been a long time. Heard about the fall."

"If I stick my head up my own ass, I'm man enough not to complain about the view. Listen. I need some induction mikes, standard frequency. Small, set to broadcast FM maybe half a mile. What have you got?"

Pause. "You remember the Las Vegas conference, six years ago? We talked about some of this stuff. We mapped out some little ones on the back of a napkin."

Derek laughed. "I was drunk as hell. Did it work?"

"Let's just say that somebody's uncle uses something real similar, and paid some Ma Bell wiz a fortune to develop it. Yeah, works like a charm. When do you need 'em?"

"What do you have in stock?"

"Maybe six."

"Do you speak FedEx?"

The offices of the Central Broadcasting Company were located at the corner of Fairfax and Sunset, a gigantic black building with a parking lot four times as large. It had been there for thirty years, and the number of stars and newer stars, would-be stars and star fuckers who had paraded in and out of the doors over the decades was beyond meaningful calculation.

The bottom three floors were artists' and executive suites. The building held five stages where game shows, variety shows and situation comedies were filmed and taped. Tourists from around the world filed through every hour, hoping to catch a glimpse of the latest hunk or hunkette.

Behind the building was the gigantic water tank where *Beach Watch,* the most popular show in television history, was filmed. Here, the daring lifeguards at Brisco Beach swam and dived, saved thousands of lives, pried hapless civilians out of submerged vehicles and otherwise moistened their swimming gear sufficiently to reveal areole size and religious affiliation to an estimated billion viewers worldwide.

From the third to the fifth floor were the executive offices, where decisions were made and intrigues played out. Consistent rumors warned the unwary that all elevators, hallways, offices and toilets were bugged for sound, and most of them for video as well.

Just rumor, of course.

The southwest corner office overlooked Sunset Park—definitely preferable to the northeast office, which overlooked the intersection of Sunset and Clover, known for its colorful traffic in prostitution, but less desirable than the southeast corner, which overlooked the aforementioned *Beach Watch* set. It was rumored that several bit players had advanced to *Beach Watch*'s oddly multitudinous special guest star slots because of topless sunbathing sessions beneath the southeast corner offices. Just a rumor, of course.

At any rate, the door of the southwest corner office read Rachel Childe, Vice President in Charge of Children's Programming. It was a beautiful office, almost but not quite ostentatious. At the moment, quite a large portion of it was actually in use. Fifty or sixty large white cardboard sheets were arrayed around the room on metal easels, leather couches and composition plastic chairs.

The drawings on the poster board were professional quality, but somewhat ludicrous. Rachel had to work very hard to maintain the precise mind-set of a seven-year-old child to understand what Dee might see in an episode of the *Potato People*. Dee loved the show. Troy found it an acceptable substitute for syrup of ipecac. Rachel tended to agree with her son, but younger kids loved it. If only she could find the next Muppets, life would be complete. For now, she had to be happy that *Potato People* had a thirty share, and that commercial time went for a hundred and fifty thousand dollars a minute.

Successes like the *Potato People* bought her the clothes she loved to wear, the car she adored driving, the condo she cherished. They bought the sauna and steam room, the private trainer who kept her body perfect, the masseuses and complexion experts who discreetly smoothed away the years.

She studied a picture of a potato. It was garbed in spandex tights and a flowing cape. It lifted an enormous Mack truck over its head while a dozen human beings gawked and applauded. She winced. The rendering would improve by the time they came back from Korea, but overall she thought that in comparison, Barney the Dinosaur had been designed by da Vinci. On poster board after poster board, garishly colored potatoes in superhero outfits leaped around the city, deterring crime, rescuing the helpless.

She sighed. Why was she doing this?

For two hundred and ten thousand a year plus profit sharing, that's why.

The two men waiting to hear her opinion were the most typical nerds she had ever known, undeniably brilliant within their narrow fields of interest. Their names were Don and John, the Boote brothers, of Boote Brothers Animation. They were single-handedly responsible for 17 percent of children's animation on network television. Part of their success was their personal involvement in story conferences like this one.

She finally spoke. "We like 'Spuds in Space,'" she said, considering her words carefully. "And the storyboards for 'The Eyes Have It' look pretty good, Don."

Don's Adam's apple bobbed appreciatively. "Thank you. We're very proud of that." His twin brother mirrored the sentiment.

"There's just one little change," she said.

"Whatever you say," John said. She would have found them almost impossible to tell apart, but John had a scar on his left eyebrow that turned it into little more than an umlaut. Or maybe it was Don who had the scar. Dammit.

She focused again. "It's about the police precinct captain in the third scene," she said.

"What about him?"

"I'd like him to be a woman. And black."

Stone silence in the room. Then Don cleared his throat uncomfortably. "Rachel," he said. "I know I speak for both of us when we say that we love you."

"Both of us," John interjected.

"But the Boote brothers have always prided ourselves on verisimilitude."

"Secret of our success," John said.

"Frankly," Don continued, "there aren't any black female precinct captains in New York City. Right, Johnny?"

"Not a one."

Rachel looked down at her fingernails, and sighed. She met their eyes evenly. One eye for Don, one for John. "And there *are* Potato People?" she asked innocently.

Before they could answer, the intercom beeped. She held up an apologizing finger, and pushed the left-most button. "Yes?"

She was pleased to see that the fabulous Boote brothers were going into a whispering frenzy.

Ina, her wonderful secretary, said, "It's Mr. Waites on line one."

She picked up the phone, feeling a bit of trepidation. "Yes, Derek?"

"Rachel?" he asked, voice a little cautious. He used a voice like that sometimes when asking for money, which he had, several times over the three years since the separation. Oh, he had paid most of it back, but it still was a source of pain between them.

"I need a favor, Rachel," he said. And something about his voice told her that the favor had nothing at all to do with money.

She listened to him, nodding, making occasional notes, and feeling a little surprised. "And what do you need this for, Derek?"

"Just trust me on this one. It's important. I'm not trying to defraud anyone—at least, not for money. I just need information, and it has to do with Dee. Can you help?"

She nodded to herself, as if unaware that Derek couldn't see her. "I have some contacts in the news department, some people who owe me favors. I think that I can swing this."

The relief in his voice was obvious, and somehow, in some way that she couldn't name, lifted her spirits immensely.

"Great. Messenger it over to me," he asked.

"I can do that. I think I can take care of it by . . . say, four o'clock."

"Great," he said. "I love you."

That word, those words hung in the air for a while. When she didn't say anything, he quietly hung up. She looked at the phone, wishing that she had answered him. Said something. Anything.

Dammit, why did she do that? What would it have cost her to admit the truth?

Don and John were waiting for her, almost vibrating with impatience. They seemed to have come to some kind of decision.

She decided to speak first. "I believe that is all, gentlemen?"

John cleared his throat. "What if we made him handicapped instead?" His tone was conciliatory, convinced that he was being not only reasonable, but downright generous.

"A nice eye patch," John chimed in. "Maybe a hook . . ."

They looked at each other and nodded, certain that their vision was profound.

Rachel smiled warmly and leaned back in her chair. "I hear Marvel's putting Spiderman back into production—"

They sat up as if she had jerked twin hooks through their lips. "Fine, fine. We'll do it, you win, Rache."

They assured her that they understood her vision, that she had been right all the time, apologized profusely, and gathered up their storyboards.

She hit the button to the right. "I need Waverly, in News, Ina."

"Yes, Ms. Childe."

Wednesday, May 6

13

Raymond Cross, former football hero, small-time thief, pimp and riot-inspired looter, the man that Derek Waites had almost run over a week before, knew that he was in very serious trouble.

This was hardly the first time this realization had come to him, but Cross had drifted in and out of a drug-induced mental miasma for days. The fog kept him from focusing upon what had happened to him, or what it might possibly mean.

He knew that he was in a concrete cell just a little more than four by six, with enough room to lie down or sit, but not to stand. A heavy steel grate sealed the entrance. There was no light in the cell, and only a little coming from outside. He couldn't see much outside his own prison. There was an empty cell across a narrow aisle. A stark electric light blazed somewhere to his right, and if there had been anyone out and about, he thought he would have been able to see their shadows against the wall.

There was no toilet. Cross was stark naked, and had fouled himself while tossing in delirium, but during his hours of deeper coma, someone had sluiced the cell clean with a hose.

He was always hungry and thirsty when he awakened, and there was always a sandwich and a cup of water waiting for him. It was drugged. He swore, for the tenth time, that he wouldn't touch it.

He wasn't alone, though. There were four or five other prisoners in cells in the immediate vicinity. But he felt too thick tongued to speak most of the time. When he finally managed to force out a few words, he got no answers.

The drugs. They were fucking him up bad, making him weak, confusing his thoughts, but keeping him hungry. Starving. He looked at the sandwich, a chunk of round bread thick with meat and cheese, and made a low, animal sound.

If he ate, or drank, he would soon drift off to sleep again.

He wouldn't eat this time, he swore it.

Consciousness and drugged sleep had swirled together, intermingling freely for days. Weeks, as far as he knew. His sense of time was gone. Sometimes when he woke up he heard men sobbing. Sometimes, the sound of someone being struck.

The air, moving against his naked skin, was warm and damp. And stank.

"Get me the fuck out of here!" he screamed.

No one answered.

"Motherfuckers. Let me . . . out!"

The sandwich lay in front of him, a round roll thick with meat and cheese. And a cup of water. It was drugged. He knew it.

He wouldn't eat it. He wouldn't drink. He would resist the hunger within him, the sensation that burrowed like a rat, chewing at his guts.

He needed food.

He couldn't eat.

True, he had said that before, and every time had suc-
cumbed to the immediacy of his thirst and hunger. But this
time he wouldn't.

Not this time. The sandwich was darkness, and death.

But the water. Maybe just one sip . . .

14

Derek Waites took the San Diego Freeway north through
Sylmar to the Antelope Valley Freeway. Taking it northeast
to the high desert, he transferred to 58. Here the freeway
went into a constant shallow incline, hills tilting steeply to
either side. The hills were mostly brown and green, crested
with a few small distant patches of snow.

The community of Tehachapi is semirural, with enough
industry and sufficient railroad track to give it a cosmopolitan
flavor. They even had their own Jack-in-the-Box restaurant.
Who could ask for anything more?

Derek pulled off the freeway, checking his directions as
he went. He navigated the old-fashioned way: take the Jumbo
Jack exit, turn left at the doughnut shop . . .

And drove up into the foothills, past the residential units,
tiny cracker boxes sealed tight against the cold and wet.

The first pertinent sign he passed read, Tehachapi State
Prison: Do Not Pick Up Hitchhikers.

Tehachapi State Prison had once been a women's institu-
tion, but that was a long time ago. Now it was a "men's
club," a sprawling complex of tan bungalows and internested
fences crested with razor wire.

As he approached the front gate a wave of nausea swept
him. He stopped the car, lowered his head to the steering
wheel, and gulped for air. He'd sworn never to enter one of
these places again. Ever. And here he was.

A wave of nausea overwhelmed him. He opened the car
door, and vomited explosively.

The racking coughs swept his body for almost two minutes, but he managed not to splatter himself with any of the yellowish, curdled bile.

He carefully wiped his mouth with a tissue, and took a swig from the Coke sitting in his cup holder. He spat the resultant broth out into the gutter. Another swig.

He glanced at himself in the rearview mirror. His eyes were bloodshot. A drop of Visine would take care of that. The main thing was that he couldn't afford to project fear. Fear would draw attention to him faster than anything.

He pulled the car toward the gate marked Visitors and Loading Entrance.

To get there he had to glide along a strip of fence topped with a single strand of razor wire. On the far side of it were the residential dwellings, guards quarters, and a bungalow for the warden. Tehachapi was fairly self-contained.

Derek watched a half-dozen men work the grounds. Not guards. Not civilians. They wore blue denim dungarees. They swept the grass, pruned, picked up trash. A squat older man hosed the ground between two buildings. They all seemed to use short, efficient motions. Their eyes stayed low, but there was something . . . something about them. From time to time one of them stopped and peered through the fence at the outside world.

When their eyes met Derek's, even at this distance, he felt the charge.

God. His stomach twisted again, but he managed to control it. He had to remind himself that he was safe. That they were over *there*, and he was over *here*. That between them was a wall, a not-so-damned-invisible wall.

A wall that separated predators from prey.

A wall he was about to breach.

The exercise yard was as large as a football field, fenced not by signs promoting soft drinks or athletic shoes, but razor-wire-tipped cyclone fence. Three rows of fence, separated by dog runs and finally by solid wall.

Austin Tucker sat at the edge of a weight bench at the edge of the exercise yard. His sweaty face was all harsh planes, a broad expanse of forehead and clifflike cheekbones. He was an enormous man, soft in the belly but swollen with muscle elsewhere. Not surprising. There was little to do with his days, his weeks, with his life except to work his body, strain his body, give pain to his body. One of the prison shrinks suggested that he did it more to torture himself than to maintain fitness. That was possible. He didn't know. He didn't think about things like that. What he *did* know was that the pain felt good. *Really* good. And it kept him ready.

Ready for what, he wasn't sure. But by this time in his life, it was too late to be anything other than what he was, or what he had been. Some part of him, one antagonistic to the part that wanted to die, struggled to remind him of his former life.

Around him men played basketball, ran, shadowboxed and hit the heavy bags dangling near the weight piles.

Sometimes Austin Tucker did these things. Usually, he did not. Usually, he came here, to the weight pile, and pushed his body to the limit against the iron that didn't know what he had done, or what he had not done, and didn't care. Weights just sat there, challenging body and will without caring about the outcome.

He lay back down against the bench, and hissed breath. He set his palms against the bar. Two hundred and seventy-five pounds of iron plate awaited him. He straightened his arms so that they were aligned with his shoulders, and hissed hard, pushing. For a moment the weight was unyielding, but then he drove it up a few inches, found the balance, and then locked it all the way. Lowered it. Raised it. Lowered it. Raised it. He did eleven repetitions, the world contracting to pinpoints of light and heat as the weight went up and down, as his arms burned and then numbed, as the thunder in his heart grew so loud that he was certain that this time, this time certainly, it would burst.

He clanged the weight back onto the safety rack, and let his swollen arms drop to his sides. Engorged with blood from a workout, they were immense. Nineteen-inch biceps, a fifty-inch chest, a man of such size that the other prisoners generally avoided him. A man who drove himself to such painful extremes that few had ever offered even the pretense of friendship.

A thunderclap left the air beside him. Tucker wiped his

face with a towel, and turned to see the black, duct-tape-wrapped heavy punching bag swinging back from a seven-o'clock position. Before it could drop back to the perpendicular, Ahmed hit it again.

Ahmed was over six feet, black as Samsonite luggage, with the extreme muscularity and hyper-agility of a professional athlete. He wasn't a professional athlete. He was, variously, a pimp and a pimp's bodyguard. Professional muscle. He beat two men to death in an Encino bar, then put two arresting officers on permanent disability. Once, long ago, Ahmed might have had plans to become a professional fighter, but a love of cocaine had squashed that dream. Besides, breaking heads outside the ring was more fun.

Whatever his past might have been, Ahmed kept himself in fine condition, smashing the bag again and again with kicks that were impressively acrobatic. Round kicks, side kicks, front kicks. A jump-spinning-back kick, one of the most difficult maneuvers in the entire tae kwon do arsenal. Ahmed knew how to do it correctly.

The bag shot up into the ceiling and crashed, resounding thunderously. Ahmed landed light as a bird, turned, and grinned. "Can't touch that."

Tucker said nothing. No, he couldn't have performed that kick. On the other hand, he was pretty certain Ahmed just exposed a critical vulnerability: a need to show off. He figured that if he gave Ahmed the opportunity, he would take it, and in taking it, leave himself open for a critical moment. All that Tucker needed. He wiped his sweating face again.

Ahmed still grinned at him. "You can run, but you can't hide," he said. "It's gonna be me and you, white bread." He paused, waiting for a reaction, and when he got none, continued, "I'm gonna piss on your Aryan Brotherhood grave."

Tucker was inside himself, contracted to a pinpoint. He showed no reaction. If he let anything out, anything at all, it was all going to happen, right then.

And there was a part of him that wanted that, craved that. But not now. Not here.

What he said was, "Big dreams, little man," in a voice

so soft and reasonable that he might have been talking to a dear friend.

The soft answer served only to inflame Ahmed even more. "Then just wake me the fuck up," he said. "Come on. Stop my heart. Come on, Kung Fu. Baby-burning Bruce Lee wannabe. Stop my motherfucking heart." Hatred and menace radiated from him like waves of heat.

"Maybe later," Tucker said, and rose to walk away. Deep within him he felt the animal. Yearning. And the effort it required to keep it in line was severe.

Ahmed clasped a callused hand on Tucker's shoulder.

Where the hand came down, Tucker felt the light blossom inside him, flame to life. Felt the fire pierce down to his core, felt it meet the fire within him, felt the core of magma surge up joyously and—

Suddenly, a black baton pushed down between them. Berger, the duty guard, said, "All right, children. Peckers in your pockets." He stepped back, eyes wary. "Tucker, you have a visitor."

Ahmed's confident grin made it obvious he believed a white guard had interceded to save a white inmate the ass whipping of the century.

Tucker ignored him, and rose, walking with Berger toward the first door leading out of the yard.

Berger was quiet until they were farther away, then said, "The Brotherhood has a shitload riding on this one. Hell. You're sending me to Maui."

"Yeah?" Tucker asked, vaguely interested. Maui. He remembered vacationing there with his men once. Snorkeling, drinking, partying. A lifetime ago.

They reached the first gate, and Berger buzzed it. Up on the wall, in a sealed cubical, a blond woman sat behind thick glass, watching the yard. She recognized Berger. He stepped away from Tucker, raised his baton to show that he was in control and under no threat, and she buzzed him through.

They stepped into a small barred corridor, walked to the end. Guards scrutinized the two of them, buzzed them through the far door. They were in a hallway painted with a series of parallel lines now. Green, blue, red. Signs read, Prisoners Must Keep Hands in View at All Times.

"Spooks need slapping down," Berger said casually. A black guard nodded at them as they passed. Berger grinned warmly at him. "Do it the same way you did the last one." He mimed a palm strike to the chest. "Use that palm thing. No marks that way."

Yes. Tucker remembered that. A knife fighter, a hit man for the Mexican Mafia. Tucker hadn't wanted the fight, but had been pressured into it. He hadn't felt about it one way or the other. It just didn't matter. Most of life was simply a gray haze to him. He would be killed, and out of his agony. Or he would kill and get practice. One day. One day he would find the men who killed his family. He scanned every face that entered Tehachapi. One day he would find one of them, and that day would be the best day of his life.

The Mexican was tough and quick, and his homemade knife scored one on Tucker before Tucker killed him, slamming him in the chest with the corner of his palm, a shot judged perfectly, professionally, sending the heart into fibrillation.

Then the heart just stopped. The man was simply found in his bunk curled up. Dead. Everyone knew what had happened, no one could prove anything. The prison doctor could only scratch his head.

Tucker spent two weeks in solitary.

When he came out, he was ten cartons of Camels and five hundred dollars richer. He also had the memory of the Mexican's eyes as the light left them, as Tucker sent him to hell.

"Good-bye," Tucker had whispered to him, almost lovingly. "Good-bye."

That would be a good trip, spiraling down into darkness. A trip worth taking. He just wanted to kill the men who had killed his family thirteen years ago, and then die. That would be good. Or just to kill. Or failing that, just to die. Any of them would be all right. It felt as if nothing lived inside him anymore except the hate.

He wrenched himself away from that train of thought. "Who's the visitor?" he asked.

Berger shrugged. "News man. Must have pulled some strings. You don't have to talk to him, of course, but I figured you might—it's been a while. Some kind of priority on it. Did you already agree to it?"

Tucker shook his head. "I didn't agree to shit."

"Funny," Berger said. "The record said that you did. Well, you don't have to talk to him."

"Might as well."

"Might as well. It'll look good on your review."

"Who gives a fuck?" Tucker said. "I'm not going anywhere."

They traversed another long, drab corridor, this one painted green. At the end of the corridor was a row of small doors. Berger opened one of them marked *C*, and ushered Tucker inside. The room was small, and well lighted. A wall of steel and transparent plastic divided the room. On the far side of the plastic window sat a black man. Thin. Maybe five ten. He wore a badge reading, "CBC News, Otis Cawthone."

Tucker laughed to himself. Instinctively, he knew that Cawthone was not this man's name. He sat. For a full minute the two men watched each other. Tucker listened to the whisper of the air-conditioning overhead. A trickle of sweat rolled down his back. The walls reverberated with distant, secret sounds. He wanted a cigarette.

Finally, he said, "Well? What do you want?"

"I know something no one else knows."

"What? Where they keep the key?"

Not-Cawthone paused. This man was afraid. And not of him. Despite his irritation, Tucker found his interest piqued.

Not-Cawthone leaned forward. "I know that someone killed your wife, your daughter and your son. I know that you were framed."

Tucker stared. All curiosity died as a door slammed down over his heart.

He took his time plucking a cigarette pack out of his shirt pocket. He shook out a Camel, and rolled it around in his mouth. He liked to get the tip moist before lighting. He lit it carefully, taking a deep drag before exhaling directly at the transparent plate separating them. "Really?" he asked finally. "And why would you believe that?"

"Because the same thing happened to your great-grand-uncle. And to a cousin on your father's side, almost forty years ago. The boy disappeared.''

This was a new one. Tucker received visitors from around the world, hundreds of them, although lately the torrent had diminished to a trickle. Newspaper reporters, prospective book writers, religious fanatics, Lightning Dawn groupies and other right-wing ding-dongs once the Krause story came out. Women who thought him a tragic and romantic figure, informants who swore that they knew something about the men who killed his family, pro bono lawyers salivating to assume his case.

Those were just the ones who had the juice to get through the screens erected by the state of California. Their ranks didn't include the weirdos who scripted a mountain of mail: college students, bored housewives, Soldier-of-Fortune wannabes, and even a few old friends, men that he served with long ago, in another lifetime.

Tucker pegged this little geek as a stringer for some new tabloid show, some video equivalent of *"I Sewed Elvis's Head onto Michael Jackson's Llama."*

He exhaled again. ''You from the *National Enquirer*?''

Not-Cawthone didn't flinch. ''I know that you told the truth, because they tried to take my boy. Three days ago. At the zoo. They tried to kidnap him.''

Tucker bristled. Lying to get a news story is one thing. He could almost—*almost* admire it. But this was too much. Anger boiled within him, and he realized it was lucky this little bastard was sitting on the far side of a plastic pane.

Something still bothered Tucker. Something was not quite right. ''Is the DA still measuring me for the San Diego killings?''

''Listen to me—''

Tucker ground out his cigarette on the plastic plate between them, directly at eye level. ''Fuck you,'' he said. He rose and headed for the door. He wanted to get out of this room, away from the little geek. Maybe he would break a couple of Ahmed's bones, just for the hell of it. Or get a couple of his own broken. It hardly mattered.

He heard Not-Cawthone's voice behind him, desperate now. ''I have a daughter named Dahlia, too. She was scream-

ing.'' The bastard even lied about the girl's name. Shit. Fucking porch monkey—

Not-Cawthone's voice broke. ''She was . . . her hair was
smoking. We almost lost her. Please.''

Tucker's hand was on the door, but he didn't slam his
palm down. He didn't call for the guard. His heart hammered
in his chest. His carefully erected barriers had just cracked.
He didn't want to turn around. He didn't want to stay here,
but he didn't have any choice.

''Who told you that?'' he asked. His voice was low and
hard.

Not-Cawthone seemed genuinely puzzled. ''What? Told
me what?''

''About the *hair,* you bastard.'' He wanted to grab Not-
Cawthone by the collar, drag him through the plastic and
slam him into the wall, reach into his chest, pull out his heart
and squeeze until the bastard stopped lying. How *dare* he?
''About the hair. I didn't even tell my lawyer.''

''She went into the shower,'' Not-Cawthone whispered.
''When the water touched her skin it boiled. Please. Please
help me. You're the only one who can.''

Something in the man, in his face, in his eyes finally
touched Tucker. Just enough. He sat down again.

''Two minutes,'' Tucker said.

Not-Cawthone nodded gratitude. ''There's something going on. It's been happening for at least sixty years, and
maybe for a hundred and sixty. Every three or five years, a
boy about thirteen years old is kidnapped, and found dead a
few days later. Something else strange—I had to hunt for it,
but it looks like five or ten other people are killed at about
the same time. People turn up missing from nearby disaster
areas. And a couple of them have been found, miles away,
bodies burned to a cinder.''

Tucker heard himself say: ''Billy was twelve. He would
have been thirteen in a week.''

Not-Cawthone nodded soberly. ''I know. Maybe one child
is taken a year. Maybe more—I may have only found ten
percent of them. One child, and then five or ten random
adults—transients, homeless people, usually. And usually
covered with some kind of disaster. Fire, flood, hurricane. I

think we're talking about some kind of opportunistic cult or something.''

"What are you babbling about?''

"The children are linked by bloodlines. The dead could total in the thousands. I could . . . give proof to your lawyer.'' He moistened his slightly pinkish mouth with the tip of his tongue. "I could get your case reopened.''

Tucker suddenly started, as if the implication just now truly struck him. "Bloodlines? You're saying I'm *related* to you?''

"To my wife,'' Not-Cawthone corrected. "Maybe. All I know is that the name Dahlia keeps cropping up in both families, and my wife has some relatives named Tucker. I don't know what's going on. Please. Just . . . talk to me.''

Silence. Then: "What do you want?''

"Tell me about that night,'' Not-Cawthone pleaded. "Please.''

Tucker lit another cigarette, inhaled and exhaled twice, making up his mind. Finally, he spoke. "They were your people,'' he said. "Just like you.''

"Black?''

"Is that what you're calling yourselves these days?'' He exhaled slowly. "They killed my wife.'' He felt as if someone were driving a white-hot stake into his guts, but he kept talking. "They killed my daughter. And they took my boy.'' He watched the cigarette in his hand. It was dead steady.

Not-Cawthone followed his gaze to the steady hand. Doubtless he was impressed as hell.

Tucker kept his eyes on the cigarette for a long moment, and then looked up. There must have been something unexpectedly awful in his face, because Not-Cawthone flinched. "You want to know about Dolly?'' he asked. There was something in his voice that he didn't recognize, a quality that belonged to another man. "You want to know about the little girl I taught to walk?''

The phony newsman wound his fingers together, perhaps trying to keep them from shaking. Very quietly, he said, "She burned, didn't she?''

The room around them was silent. "She *screamed.*'' Tucker's voice was out of control, as if something had coiled inside him for over a decade, waiting for any excuse to jump out and sting him in the eye. "She screamed," he repeated, "and *then* she burned. In my arms. Get out of here. Damn you. Damn you!" As he said those words, he realized that for the first time in his life he meant exactly what he said. He actually wished he could send this bastard straight to hell, wished to watch him in torment, drowning in burning slime, devoured by rabid dogs, dismembered by demons, consumed from within by maggots. Damn him, damn him, *damn him.* "Get the fuck *out!*"

Not-Cawthone swallowed, hard. "I can help—"

Tucker screamed now, out of control as he hadn't been for the thirteen years of his incarceration. *"Leave me alone! Guard! Goddamn it! Guard!"*

Tucker slammed his palm against the two-inch plastic hard enough to shiver it in its frame, to boom through the entire room. The little crawling bastard rocked backward in his chair, eyes wide with fear. Good. What Tucker wanted was to be alone with him for a few minutes, to lay hands upon him, to show the little fuckword what terror really was. Make him hurt as *he* had hurt, bring him pain beyond anything—

Behind Tucker the door buzzed. He was up and out in a blur of motion. The pain rose up in a red tide, swept him through the corridors and through the doors. The guards at the various stations glanced at him and allowed him through without the usual bullshit, didn't ask him any questions, just let him back into the depths of the prison. Figuring, perhaps, that as long as he was heading in deeper, into the pit, into the labyrinth, it was fine. They had no objections at all.

He ran out to the exercise yard. The sunlight stung his eyes. He squeezed them half shut and began to run. He stumbled at first, then almost fell, but managed to catch himself.

He had to get control of himself. Some of the other men on the track were running smoothly, freely. They saw him coming and got the hell out of the way. A great bear of a man, he thundered around the track with legs like tree trunks, barrel chest heaving, arms pumping, scarred bearded face reddening. He must have looked like something out of a nightmare. And what might they make of the sounds issuing from his thick mouth? The *ahhh, ahhh,* sounds that originated in a pain so intense that it made death by torture seem a happy alternative? Was that sweat streaming down his face, or tears? He didn't know. He only knew that if he kept moving, moving, maybe he could outrun what was coming behind him.

It was close now. If he looked back over his shoulder, he would see it. It was pictures and sights and sounds and feelings walled up years ago, unexamined to this very day. They were close, so close that as he tired they reached out to tap him, touch him, reach icy fingers into his chest, swallow him and spit him back out into the past. His vision blackened, and his world spun back into the heart of the nightmare he had lived for thirteen years.

He stumbled in the darkness, suddenly carrying a precious, doomed burden in his arms. His daughter. His flesh and blood, the one thing that he loved the most in this world. Sizzling in his arms. Burning. Dying.

Crystal fell. A dart red against the sweet white of her throat, the living darkness where he had murmured so many endearments. Where he had tasted her so often, reveling in the way her sweat actually changed taste as her rhythm quickened, as she held him and met his fire with her own.

God.

Everything was coming back now. Billy. Down. Dolly. Boiling in the bathtub. The steam cascaded from her like vapor boiling off dry ice. Then he remembered the fight. Three men. He laughed wildly, hopelessly. He killed two of them, gravely wounded another. But there was a fourth man. They shot him full of darts, and he fell into a hole deep enough to swallow the universe.

Blackness.

Thirteen years ago . . .

Slowly, sickly, a return to consciousness. Tucker rolled from his stomach onto his back, gasped for breath. Fatigue and alcohol and the dart-conveyed sedatives all worked together to calamitous effect. His head pounded like the drums signaling Armageddon.

Colors devolved to primaries, without subtlety or shading.

He levered up to hands and knees. He shook his head and blinked hard.

He crawled out into the hall, eyes still not focusing. He stood, and opened them wide, praying, hoping against hope that he was merely insane, had merely slipped into total delirium. He would rather be insane than accept the evidence of his senses.

Crystal sat against the wall, her hands at her crimsoned waist. Her eyes were still open, face a mask of shock and fear, as if still attempting to shovel her intestines back into her body.

He wrenched his eyes away from Crystal's twisted, violated corpse. He gulped, struggled for air, trying to stop the blood thundering in his ears, to slow it, end it. The walls were splashed with blood and bits of flesh. The words "Love Satan" were scrawled in brownish red.

He staggered to the bathroom, plucked up the charred, sodden mass floating in the murk. Ash seeped from the nightgown in a muddy black stream. There was just nothing left. Nothing at all.

He remembered standing there in the middle of the floor, cradling his daughter's empty clothing in his arms, screaming as if the screams would never stop coming, as if there were nothing inside him but screams, until the red lights began flashing outside of his house, and uniformed men with guns pried his daughter's body out of his arms and forced him to the ground.

He lay there, hands cuffed behind his back, staring at his wife, at Crystal, remembering the day they met in band practice, of the times he had kissed her and touched her. Remembering the things they had said to each other over the last few years while their marriage was falling apart. And knew that he had failed her, failed his children, failed himself deeply and utterly and ultimately. Eternal damnation would have seemed a bargain, if in exchange for his soul he could buy a chance to live those critical seconds one more time.

God. Just give him another chance.

Derek clutched his briefcase, still shaking. He felt as if he were breathing wet cotton. The tall muscular guard escorting him out watched him sympathetically. "Problem?"

"Little claustrophobia," Derek said. "This place gets to me."

The guard clucked sympathetically.

"Excuse me," Derek said. "Can I use the rest room, please?"

"Sure. Catch me on the desk on your way out."

Derek bulled through the doors, made it to the toilet before he threw up. He washed his hands, his face, looked at himself in the mirror, frightened by the yellowish, sweaty image before him. He hurriedly opened his briefcase, and pulled out a small cassette recorder. Thankfully, no one had asked to play it.

He pulled a strip of epoxy tape out of a pocket. It was a thin strip of clay, half yellow, half blue. He stripped off the protective plastic layer, and twisted the two together. It turned into a tacky green substance that would set hard in minutes. Derek wedged a glob of it onto the cassette recorder, and stuck the whole thing underneath the sink.

The cassette recorder wasn't a recorder at all. It was an FM booster, receiving signals from the little bugs he had planted on the way in, and sending them back out. The little induction bugs were the size of a quarter, and broadcast about a thousand feet. The booster was better, its signal reached almost a mile.

A second booster to receive that signal was already planted outside, and that one was good for three miles.

The little bugs, four of them, were planted on every telephone he had been able to reach—an office phone, a pay phone, an inter-office intercom and a fax machine. It was the best he could do, and he hoped it was all unnecessary.

Prayed it was. Still, all fingerprints had been removed, and the stuff came out of Goober's private stash—no ID codes.

It never hurt to be prepared.

Tucker leaned against the wall, gasping for air. Around him, prison sounds grew louder, began to intrude into his misery. He coughed and tried to spit, but felt the phlegm catch in his throat. He ground his callused knuckles against his eyes.

He felt as if he had vomited his heart into his throat, as if someone ripped his flesh open to expose the world's deepest, rawest wound.

Something in Tucker's universe had changed. It had been an endless stream of gray days, of black-and-white decisions. There was a spot of color in the grayness now.

The color was red.

And it pulsed.

15

Four police cars pulled quietly up to the street corners near Chosen Drive. The men who exited the cars wore LAPD blue uniforms, they stood professionally while the drivers blocked the street and set up flares. A blue truck with LAPD emblazoned on the side pulled up, and yellow striped sawhorses were carried out of the back of the trucks, and erected to block the streets.

Men dispersed, and went about their several tasks with efficiency.

The man directing them was tall and lean, with high cheekbones, eyes as black as death, and a nose like a sharp chunk of granite.

Quietly, efficiently, they went about their business of sealing off the 2300 block of Chosen Drive.

Troy Waites fluttered his thumb on the trigger of the GameMaster joystick. In response, a sword swung at a diagonal, slicing the tendons of a troll, who perished with satisfying gruesomeness.

He enjoyed beta testing Dungeon Quest because it was fast, and challenged his excellent reflexes, reflexes that had won him a dozen sports trophies, including four for basketball and two for soccer. He enjoyed it because it was a delight to the eyes and the ears, and a never-ending source of wonder. Beta testing was also neat because he got the loan of a special Advanced Graphics machine, a big silver box that plugged into a phone outlet on one side, and his 386 on the other. It made his Packard Bell machine perform *way* above spec, in fact, he suspected that the 386 wasn't really doing much except providing a keyboard and a CRT.

But what he enjoyed most was the *reason* that he was a beta tester. He enjoyed it because his father was one of the programmers, and so in a sense when he played with it, he was playing with his father. Playing with Dad. And that, he liked a hell of a lot.

Troy's room was a fairly typical twelve-year-old's room. There were posters from *Who Framed Roger Rabbit?* (a current video favorite), his trophies, a stuffed and mounted piranha. (He wanted to get a real one but his mother insisted that this would not happen even over her dead and dismembered body. He had replied that if she were ever dead and dismembered, a few piranha might come in handy. This line of argument had not impressed her.)

There was also a chart on the wall, known loosely as the "check mark chart." On it, various offenses were noted, to be tallied with check marks when violations were noticed. Every ten check marks led to a punishment of one kind or another: cuts in allowance, grounding, extra household duties, etc.

Most of the offenses ("swearing," "not doing homework," "not washing dishes") had one or two check marks beside them, as the check marks were tallied and erased on a weekly basis. One offense had seven: the category "teasing Dee." Not all of these were in official black marker. Several were in crayon, and would be taken less seriously by Mom, since Dee was likely to see a prospective check mark in everything from a lifted eyebrow to a misplaced Barbie doll.

On the computer screen, an animated version of Troy (one of the very best things about Dungeon Quest was the fact that it would employ the digitized images of its subscribers rather than stock library figures. It made the fantasy that much easier to buy into) crept down the corridor. He yanked the control, and the cartoon Troy pivoted. The entire perspective of the game shifted. Cartoon Troy zapped a big hairy something, reacting on the basis of a shadow alone.

"All right!" he yelled delightedly, thrusting his fist into the air. "We're kicking some serious butt tonight!"

Behind him, his mother said, "And it's time for some serious sleep."

"Aww, Mom . . ."

She was in full-tilt Mommy mode, brooking no argument. "Come on, it's almost ten o'clock."

She made a move as if to turn the set off, but he held up a protesting hand. A man has to shoot his own dog. Troy punched a button. The screen froze, and asked him if he really wanted to quit. He maneuvered the mouse around until a little star was superimposed over the "Yes" response. The video images winked away, leaving only the blue screen of the television set switched to the game mode. Troy pointed a threatening finger at the set. In his very best Terminator voice, Troy said, "I'll be back."

And trudged into the bathroom that connected his bedroom to Dee's, ready to perform his evening's ablutions.

Rachel plopped herself into a chair in the living room, feeling all of the zest and energy of a sack of wet oatmeal. Medford appeared next to her and handed her a drink. She nodded gratefully, and sipped.

He plopped down on the couch, close enough to take her hand. His fingers were long and cool, and pressed hers firmly enough to give warmth.

"So," he asked, "what do you make of all of this?"

She shook her head. "Do you want to know what the strangest thing is?"

"What?" he asked.

"I stood there. I watched the water hit her skin, watched the steam boiling off of my child, knew in my heart that this was utter, raving madness, insanity. . . ." Her voice trailed off.

For the next few moments, there was just the quiet of the night. Medford didn't interrupt her, as if he realized how difficult it was for her to say these things, fearing that any interruption might stop the flow of information altogether.

After a while, she started again. "I know I experienced something crazy. Something that I can't understand. And yet, not three days later, I'm already telling myself that it didn't happen. I'm trying to tell myself that I didn't see what I saw.

That the water was already hot when it came out of the tap, that it just splashed off.''

"What's so strange about that?"

"Don't you see? My daughter's life depends upon my ability to sort the facts, and rearrange the evidence until I get some answers. But my mind doesn't want to answer these questions. It wants to come up with new questions, to which there are easy answers. Or logical answers, anyway. Do you see what I'm talking about?"

He nodded, slowly. "I think so." He smiled, a smile that had once flashed across millions of television sets every week. "You know, in my last two seasons as Truman Bach, we started doing strange shows, bending the formula a little."

"I remember." She smiled. "I think that those were some of your best."

"I wish the audience had agreed. Anyway, we brought in some borderline supernatural things. An immortal Sawney Beane, a vampire who had slaughtered Hitler and the Nazi crew in that bunker, a shape-shifting Cherokee hooker stalked by her shaman pimp . . ." He laughed again. "What I remember is one thing that turned up in dialogue quite a bit. Truman used to say that sometimes you cling to rationality, even when rationality doesn't fit. That our ordinary way of looking at the world has a tendency to protect itself." He shrugged. "Run smack into the irrational, and you believe in miracles for about five minutes—then your ordinary worldview heals right back up again, and you question your experience."

"Good old Truman. I miss him."

"Well, Spelling is still talking reunion movie. Don't count Bach out just yet."

She let him pull her out of the chair and into his lap. Her arms went around his neck, and they kissed. His lips were so soft and gentle. She thought that was probably the most wonderful thing about him. Well, the second most wonderful thing, anyway.

She pulled back, and laid her head on his shoulder. "I don't know, I really don't. Dahlia was a great woman."

"Dahlia Childe?"

She nodded. "Hearing about her made me believe I could do anything. The whole thing about her rescuing the slaves, sneaking out across the Confederate lines." An odd light came into her eyes. She seemed illumined, inspired from within. Then the light faded, and was replaced by another, more somber expression. "But there were other stories."

"What kind of stories?" Medford asked.

"Ghost stories. Scary stuff my grandmother whispered about. Mom didn't want me to listen to that part." She clutched at him with desperate strength. "Medford. We can't keep them out of school forever. What are we going to do?"

Before he could answer, Dee shuffled into the room, half-asleep. One hand clutched at Grandmama Lulu's nightgown, the heirloom Rachel should have boxed back into the cedar chest. Unfortunately it was the only way to get Dee to sleep.

Dee's little brown eyes were utterly guileless.

"They're coming," she said in a flat voice.

Rachel cocked her head to the side. "Who's coming?"

Dee repeated her words patiently, only careful observation detecting the edge of fear underneath the words. "They're coming."

She stood there as if she had said enough, as if somehow they should completely understand her words, and what they meant for all of them.

Uneasily, Medford rose and walked over to the window overlooking the street. It filled half the wall, with a sliding panel opening onto a balcony. He slid the panel back, and looked out on the empty street. The cool night air ruffled the hair on his neck. He thought that he heard a television set somewhere in the building. A radio crackled in the distance. There was something vaguely familiar about the radio sound, something that made him a little uncomfortable, but he couldn't bring it fully to consciousness.

"There's nothing out here, honey," he said finally. "Why don't you go back to bed?"

Dahlia repeated the same words again, and this time there was an unmistakable edge of fear. "They're coming," she repeated.

"There's no traffic." He leaned out and looked up the

street. He could see up about two thirds of a block. In the other direction, after half a block his view was obstructed by vines. Nothing. Distantly, voices murmured. A sound like someone arguing. Maybe another voice answering calmly. He wasn't certain—the night generated its own sounds. It might have been nothing but the wind rippling through the trees. Perhaps. "It's really damned quiet."

Rachel knelt by Dahlia, testing her temperature with the back of a hand to the forehead. "No fever," she said in relief. "A little warmish, maybe."

She looked up, concern creasing her brow. "I wonder if Derek is home yet. He should be home by now."

There was an expression on her face that Medford hadn't seen before, one that twisted his gut a little. Was that a touch of jealousy he felt?

Rachel picked up the closest telephone. She raised the earpiece to her head, and jiggled the receiver with a finger. A look more puzzlement than fear crossed her face, but he knew that the fear was there—and growing. "The phone's dead," she said.

Medford crossed the living room with a brisk, purposeful stride, hand outstretched to open the front door. Just before his hand closed upon the knob, it stopped, as if wary to make contact. Then he smiled ruefully, and opened the door.

The hall was quiet. The orange carpet of their foyer bore no recent footprints, no sign of life or trespassers. He was about to close the door when he heard the humming sound. Above the elevator was a green strip of plastic, etched with numbers. A light moved slowly behind them. The elevator noise filled the foyer. A tight sound, like vibration inside a sealed drum.

They had visitors.

Rachel leaned out over the balcony. The night air smelled of magnolias and jacaranda and pine. She braced herself, and leaned far enough out that it was actually a bit dangerous—and saw a hint of light. A regular pulse of red light. *Blink, blink.* Like a fire engine, or an ambulance. Or a police flasher. Distantly, a police-band radio squabbled in the night.

The evening seemed suddenly chillier to her, and her hand brushed her throat lightly.

And suddenly, unaccountably, she felt very much afraid.

The elevator door slid open. Two men stood there, police officers dressed in blue uniforms, badges displayed prominently upon their chests. Revolvers at their hips.

Medford felt something that he had never felt before in his entire life. All of his life, the appearance of a police officer had triggered sensations of security in him. They were symbols of order.

But now, for the first time, he felt a flash of an attitude he had always despised in Derek: fear of the police. It was irrational, it was unreasonable, but there it was.

They seemed to be moving in slow motion as they approached him. There was so much time between their steps that it seemed he had forever to count the thunderous explosions of his own heart. Walking, walking as if they had all of the time in the world, but somehow covering more than an ordinary amount of distance in each stride.

But their smiling faces were open and honest. They were public servants. They were the friends of the law-abiding. They existed to Protect and to Serve.

They were Death itself.

The first one was younger, with a military haircut, his cap tucked under his arm. Little smile lines crinkled out from the sides of his mouth. "Hi," he said. "You must be Mr. Downs."

Medford nodded. "Yes," he said. "And what can I do for you?"

The second cop was taller, more fully muscled. He was lean, and his profile reminded Medford of an Indian. His body language was all business, and his sense of purpose created a moving wall of energy. "I'd ask for an autograph, sir, but we're on business."

Ha ha. They laughed at the calculated icebreaker, but their eyes remained cold. The taller cop continued. "You have a Troy Waites living with you?"

Medford nodded.

The cop smiled, one of those just-between-us-men smiles,

intended to put him at ease. It reminded him of a dolphin's smile. Just the curve of the mouth. Meaningless. "You are probably aware that he's a material witness in an assault. We need to see him."

Medford smiled back just as meaninglessly. "Ah . . . just a minute, all right? I'll be right back."

He eased the door closed.

His heart wanted to explode out of his chest.

Rachel appeared in the living room. Troy was with her, rubbing sleep out of his eyes. She struggled to dress and awaken him at the same time.

Dee watched all of their actions with that same unearthly calmness. She yawned, a very little-girl yawn. "They're going to kill him," she informed them somberly.

Medford's mind spun with a dozen different problems and possible solutions at the same time. "The fire ladder," he said finally. "Get the hell out of here."

Rachel looked at him as if he were crazy for a minute, but then turned to Troy. "All right," she said very calmly. "You know the drill."

From the hall closet, she extracted a rope ladder, with eyelets at the end. She pivoted and handed them to Troy. Troy didn't hesitate. He ran to the terrace and with nimble, practiced fingers anchored the eyelets onto hooks set in the balcony rail. He lowered the ladder over the side.

On the other side of the door, the cop said patiently, "Mr. Downs? We just want to talk with the boy."

Medford spoke back, just as much patience forced into his voice. "They've gone to bed," he said. "Are you sure this can't wait until morning?"

The taller cop spoke again. "We can hold the suspect if we have an identification. We need your help, sir."

Rachel kissed Troy's forehead. His skin was salty with sleep. She hurried him down the ladder.

Troy was strong and nimble, but he was also afraid. If he slipped . . .

He held the ladder tightly, twisting in the night breeze, and stared at the ground beneath him. If he fell, they'd have to scrape him up, and they wouldn't need any bad cops to kill him. Shit.

He took another rung, and then another, driven by the need for speed as well as the desire for silence. His hands almost slipped once, and looking up at his mother, he saw her face shift from concern to panic. He caught his balance, and scurried down the rest of the ladder until he was on the sixth-floor balcony.

Only then did he realized he had forgotten to breathe.

Jesus.

Rachel hauled the ladder back up. She had pondered this moment. There was no way that she could trust Dee to climb down the ladder alone. It was just too much of a risk. Rachel would gladly carry Dee herself, but she would need someone to tie Dee to her back. No time for that. But there was another option.

She used her own belt to lash Dee securely to the ladder, giving her enough play to set her feet and hands securely around rungs. Knotting her on strongly enough to carry her weight, plus having her hang on, and then lowering her down on the ladder . . .

It just might work.

She pulled her daughter's face close. "Hang on tight, honey," she said, smoothing the troubled brow. "Troy will get you, all right?"

Dee nodded. "I'm not scared," she said. Somehow, Rachel made herself believe it.

She very carefully began to lower Dee down over the edge of the balcony. An inch at a time, her daughter's round, loving face disappeared over the edge.

The night was chill, but Dee hung on, her mind a little dazed. The Other who lived in her mind sometimes began to retreat a little, almost as if it knew that it couldn't help now. She needed to be alert, and needed to trust. Below her, her brother leaned backward over the balcony. He smiled up to her, holding his hands in catcher position. She thought that he was smiling, a warm, trustworthy smile, but she wasn't entirely certain.

Her hands were tired, and she thought that maybe she should trust her mother's knots a little.

She wiped her hands on her nightgown, for a moment trusting the weight to the knot. She felt herself slip—the knot held, but the leather loop around her body wasn't tight enough. She began to slide through. She grabbed for a rung, and her hands slipped. She looked down at the ground below her, and felt her little heart galloping in her chest. She slid down a half a foot, and then another few inches, but then caught herself, barely.

She didn't make a sound. She looked up at her mother's face, a shadowy oval above her. The ladder rungs bit into her fingers, but she held on.

Dee closed her eyes. She felt her body against the belt, the weight pulling at the knot. She opened her eyes. The knot was a granny, unraveling even as she watched. She wanted to scream but if she did, all was lost.

Even if she fell, she wouldn't scream. She wouldn't disappoint the Other. She would just drift to the ground like a snowflake, like a leaf—

The knot popped loose, and Dee was dangling now, holding on, her feet not quite able to make the rung and her fingers, slipping with perspiration or night dew, were sliding, one at a time coming undone from their purchase—

And she fell. Directly into Troy's arms. He pulled her back over the lip of the lower balcony, hugging her so tightly she thought he would crack her ribs. He was biting his upper lip hard enough to draw blood.

Dee's eyes shone with love, hugging him back. "Free check marks for a *week*," she said.

Up above, Rachel breathed a deep sigh of relief, and felt one of the knots in her chest begin to unravel. Dee was safe. She turned back to Medford, who stood at the door. "Come on—" Her feeling of relief turned to one of alarm. He held a .22 target rifle in his hands, and was fumbling with the bolt, trying to load it. Absurdly, she told herself that this was wrong, that she had seen him effortlessly wielding a pistol, a rifle, a knife many times. . . .

But that was on television, and her stress-racked mind had

just blipped on her a little. She had to focus and fast. She stuck a fist against her mouth. "Medford?"

His face was ashen, as if something inside him had died, as if life had suddenly disclosed some mortal secret, the essence of which he now struggled to comprehend.

Through the door came the first cop's voice. Still reasonable, but becoming irritated. "Sir. Sir, please open the door *now*, sir—"

Medford jerked his head urgently toward the balcony. He looked directly at her, and at that moment she felt as if she could have fallen into his eyes. "Take care of Dee," he whispered.

She mouthed the words "I love you," but knew that she was saying something else, something far more final. She pulled the drapes closed behind her, and climbed down the ladder.

Medford leveled the rifle at the door, braced the stock against his hip. He shook. The taste of fear was a coppery thing in his mouth. He fought to keep the tremor from his voice when he spoke the next sentence. "The kids are asleep," he said. "Come back tom—"

He never had the chance to finish. Three small holes appeared in the door, one after another. He heard nothing, but the last thing he felt was a smashing pressure against his chest, the sensation of an enormous hand sweeping him up and flinging him across the room, a silent wall of blazing white light.

The two cops stepped through the smoking doorway. Timms balanced a silenced automatic easily in his right hand. The tip of the obscenely distended barrel still oozed smoke.

He silently motioned to the other cop: *search the hall.*

Timms paused only a moment to examine the bloodied body of Medford Downs. Downs had been shot several times in his eight seasons as Truman Bach—three times in the shoulder, twice in the leg, once a grazing shot above the ear, triggering a three-part episode where an amnesia-plagued Bach believed himself to be a mob hit man.

Never had Downs's televised alter ego's lungs filled with

blood. Never had his eyes stared, unable to focus, uncomprehending.

Medford Downs would be dead in a few seconds.

"Always hated your fucking show." Timms smiled.

Medford's fingers slowly uncurled from the trigger guard of the Remington .22, the inadequate weapon with which he had tried to protect the life of the woman he loved, and the children he cherished. He tried to raise it, but Timms just hummed and kicked the barrel to the side.

"Not like Hollywood, is it?" Timms said.

Medford lived just long enough to see beyond the pain, to feel beyond the fear. He tried to whisper a prayer, one blotted out by a sluglike gout of blood that raced from his lips and puddled onto the flood beneath his head as he died.

On the level beneath them, Rachel froze. What had she just heard? The door above smashed open? The sound of a heavy mass hitting the wall or the floor?

No. She couldn't allow herself to think that way. She went into a kind of cold overdrive, shutting all of her feelings away. Something so large and so frightening hammered against the walls of her resolve that if she stopped to consider, if she stopped to think about it for a moment, she would lose all control, all resolution.

The sliding glass door opened easily. Only the last couple of inches made any sounds at all. She ushered her children into an apartment laid out much like their own. The only problem, of course, was that it was decorated differently. Troy bumped into a table. A muffled "Shit" escaped his lips. Dee was kind enough not to charge him a check mark for this, but her face twisted with disapproval.

Rachel held a shushing finger to her lips, and hurried on to the front door as a stork-thin, elderly man emerged sleepily from his bedroom. He peered at them through the gloom.

Her mind raced, trying to place him. Certainly she had seen him in the lobby of the apartment! Mr. Bones? Ichabod? Damn. This was no time for pleasantries.

"Hey! Hey!" he said eloquently.

"Wrong room," she said, and slipped out of the door, leaving him pointing after them.

They were out of the front door and gone before he could question them.

There couldn't be much time, that she knew. What had anyone heard? Were there any resources available to her at all? Anyone she could count on in any way? She had to get the hell out, and trust that her next idea, the next piece of information, would come in its own time.

She opened the heavy fire door carefully, listening, and then peered down the stairwell. Nothing. She entered first, pulling her children behind her, and as soon as the door closed behind them charged down the stairs.

She rounded the third landing as she heard a door open. Rachel halted her children with an outstretched arm. Leather shoes scuffled against metal steps. The sound of her own breathing was oppressively loud. She couldn't stop herself from trembling. The footsteps drew closer and closer. She felt herself coiling like a spring. When the cop turned the corner she charged, smashing into him with all of her strength. They tumbled down the stairwell together.

She desperately clung to him, knowing that he was bigger, stronger, better trained, knowing that the only marginal advantage she had was raw fear and adrenaline. If she lost that advantage, she and her children were dead. The world whirled, stairs, floor, ceiling exchanging places so rapidly she felt as if she had awakened inside a clothes dryer. She cracked her shoulder against the stair as he rolled over her, and she grunted with pain. His breath was hot and foul in her face, but only for a moment, because then he had rolled over her. His head smashed into the wall hard enough to dent plaster. He collapsed atop her.

Sobbing, she pushed out from beneath him and tried to pull herself free. Her impact-traumatized shoulder screamed at her.

Dee and Troy helped pull the man off her, and she fought off the urge just to hug them to her. She rose and stumbled down the stairs to the parking garage. Over and over again, Dee murmured "Mommy . . . Mommy . . ."

Rachel didn't have the time to comfort her girl child. They had to keep moving, moving, moving, or all was lost.

Gingerly she opened the door to the underground parking

garage. It was deserted, but at the far end, at the bend of the exit ramp, a red flashing light was reflected against the pale brick wall.

No escape that way.

She held her car keys in her hands, looking at the seductive profile of her Jag. So close, so far away, an impossible dream. What now?

Suddenly she heard a distant, silly, wonderful sound—the sound of the *Mission: Impossible* theme song played through the car horn system.

"Daddy!" Troy whispered. Rachel choked back a sob of relief.

The rear exit door led to the trash Dumpsters. She opened the door and peered out carefully. A faintly sweetish scent of garbage wafted through the air, and she ushered the kids out. Distantly, she heard police loud-hailer split the night.

"Please remain indoors," it said. *"We have the situation under control, but there remains an element of risk. Please remain indoors. . . ."*

She bit her lip to keep whimpering sounds from escaping her throat, and helped to boost Troy over the fence. He paused at the top, and then scrambled and dropped down. Her heart nearly stopped beating as she waited for him to give the all-clear sign. He put his mouth close to the fence, and stage-whispered, "Okay."

She lifted Dee up onto her shoulders, then boosted her over. Dee climbed up and then disappeared. Rachel didn't much care what happened on the far side of the fence. Even a twisted or broken ankle was preferable to the men who stalked them.

Rachel jumped up and grabbed the top of the fence, wincing as her injured shoulder screamed protest.

She bit down and ignored her pain.

She was suddenly very glad for the evenings in the Nautilus gym. She closed her eyes and imagined her personal trainer urging her on. Her shoulder was injured, so she didn't pull with her shoulder. She pulled with her lat muscles, and hoisted herself up, thinking *Isolation, isolation, isolation,* almost like a mantra.

Her toes scrabbled at the wooden fence, gained purchase,

levered her sideways and up, swinging until her foot was at the top of the fence, and then she was hugging the rim. There were footsteps behind her, coming closer, and a quiet voice. A surge of adrenaline completed the effort needed to clear the fence, and she dropped down onto a flower bed on the other side in a clumsy crouch.

Slowly and carefully, she picked her way through the darkened backyard of one of their neighbors, and out into the street. Just before they emerged, they heard the *Mission: Impossible* theme again. She ran out, and the sight of Derek in his little red Tercel was very nearly the most wonderful sight she had ever seen in her life. The rear door popped open. They piled in. She slammed the door behind them, and they roared away.

Derek's hands were tight on the controls. His face was strained and haggard and worried. And wonderful.

As they accelerated, she felt the tension and stress actually increase, or at least her awareness of them, as if they had been hiding from her. "I couldn't get through on the phone," he said quietly, as if that explained everything. Then added, "I saw the police."

She met his eyes in the rearview mirror. "Medford," she said numbly. "I think—I heard shots."

Rachel leaned over and wept on Troy's shoulder, feeling utterly lost.

Derek accelerated, losing himself in traffic, leaving the flashing red lights behind them.

16

Derek's car pulled off the Harbor Freeway at the Century Boulevard off-ramp. He drove through a tattered neighborhood, yellowish street lights casting skeletal shadows through dying trees. Few people walked the street this time of night, just the usual assortment of busy straights hurrying toward night jobs or away from day jobs, a few shoppers walking briskly home pulling carts of groceries obtained at the less expensive, more opulently supplied supermarkets up-town. And the dregs: sparsely bearded men in soiled over-coats, a few desperate hookers still trying to make the week's rent at sleazy cold-water walk-ups.

And then, most disturbing, were the children. A few youngsters wandered the street, even at this hour. Their eyes seemed dark hollows, staring at the car.

Several dark-skinned women in pumps and hot pants watched them as Derek pulled into the driveway of the Laz-E-Boy Motel.

Derek watched them watch him, nervously counting the number of people who saw their faces, and therefore might remember them. It was impossible to say how much time he had before the people looking for his son caught up with them, but at least here in the heart of Los Angeles's black community, it might be a little easier to blend in.

He left Rachel to take care of the kids while he went to the front office. The desk clerk was a dark little potato of a man. His thin eyebrows arched at the notion that an entire family actually wished to stay the night at the Laz-E-Boy. Two adults, two children. The clerk would probably peer out from behind the desk to see if video equipment and perhaps a donkey or dwarf lurked among their luggage.

The rust-speckled room key was numbered 226. Derek carried Dee up the stairs, followed closely by Troy. The room seemed to have been decorated out of back issues of *Players* magazine, with a certain tacky elegance that almost brought a smile to his strained face. "Just the place for a second honeymoon," Derek said as he locked the door behind Rachel.

Rachel looked numb, almost pole axed. The corners of her mouth tried to twitch up in a smile, and failed.

He laid Dee down on the bed, and examined the faux velvet lampshades, the king-sized bed's black sheets, the gold-veined mirror on the ceiling, the quarter-fed vibrator unit in the bed itself, and the bathroom dispenser of unguents and latex novelties. "All the comforts of home."

He heard a click, and Troy said "Wow." Synthesized mu-sic and heavy breathing filled the room. Derek turned in time to see Troy's enraptured face glued to the television. A title

wobbled unsteadily on the screen, yellow letters that read
"Lickety Split."

"Wow, Dad, will you look at—"

Click.

"None of that, young man," Rachel said sternly.

"Oh, Mom—"

He smiled to himself, noting the attempt to generate some
kind of normalcy, to find within their circumstance some
sense of family. Because whether she loved him or not, this
was all they had right now. They belonged to each other.

Till death do us part.

Troy sat at the edge of the bed, staring at the blank television screen. Dee was curled up asleep next to him.

"You paid cash," Rachel said quietly. "That should help,
for a while."

Troy spoke. "What's going on?" He looked up. "Dad?
Why does someone want to hurt me?"

Derek's heart felt like a stone. "No one is going to hurt
you," he said, trying to put enough spine into his voice to
convince himself. "I promise. I've got some clues. There's
a man named Tucker. Austin Tucker—"

Something happened at that moment. At the mention
of Tucker's name, Dee's eyes flew open. She said,
"Tucker—"

But the voice wasn't hers.

"Get help," she said.

Rachel felt Dee's forehead. "She's burning up."

"Come on," Derek said. "Let's get her into the shower."
He gathered his daughter into his arms. The heat was strong,
but not yet unpleasant.

Troy took her hand, and held it tight. "Dee? What kind
of help?"

"Derek," Dee said.

The hair on the back of Derek's neck stood up. His daughter never called him Derek.

He set Dee into the shower and ran the water against her
nightgown. *"Derek,"* she said again, in that altered voice.
"Get the Warrior."

He was genuinely confused. "Who?"

"Tucker. Get Tucker. Get the Warrior, or your family will die. Help them."

Derek wanted to ask "who" and "what" again, but he knew, he *knew* what she was asking for, and he felt panic such as he had never known. This was madness. This was death. It was utter insanity. Suddenly, he was convinced that the entire thing had been some kind of dreadful mistake, all coincidences. That Medford was still alive, and worried sick about them, that the police were merely looking for them in connection with the kidnapping, and that all of his computer work was nothing but a series of bizarre coincidences.

After all, he had never looked into the history of another, randomly chosen family. Who knew how often such strings of murders or disappearances occurred? He would have to run a statistical check to see if there was really an anomaly, and even if there were, what the hell would that mean?

She looked straight at him, through him, into him, as if she knew exactly what he was thinking. *"Get the Warrior, or your family will die. Help them."*

Derek's head spun. "You don't know what you're asking."

"Derek? What is she saying, what is this? Who is the Warrior?"

For the moment, he ignored Rachel.

"Dee." He knelt in front of her. "I can't do it. I just *can't.*" But he knew he was lying. Another voice inside him whispered, *If you didn't know this was coming, why did you take those little precautions at Tehachapi, hmmm?*

The voice from Dee, the voice that sounded so much like Rachel, only not Rachel, rang out at him. *"I have waited a hundred years for men like you, and Tucker. Together, you can end it. Only together."*

Troy looked at her, and looked as if he wanted to shake his sister, put some sense back into her. "Dee?" he asked.

She turned her face to him. He was almost knocked backward by the force of her new, strange personality. *"Not Dee,"* she said calmly, still in her mother's voice. *"Dahlia."*

Troy looked back and forth between his mother and Dee. "She sounds just like you, Mom."

"Dahlia?" Derek asked. "*Your* Dahlia, Rachel?"

Rachel shook her head, a helpless expression. She hugged her soaking wet daughter to her. Dee was a tiny eight-year-old girl but at the moment she seemed infinitely wise, strangely sober and intractable, asking and expecting the impossible from him.

"You know who I am," she said in Rachel's voice. *"I tried, and failed, to free you. To free my family."*

"Failed?" Rachel asked, and her face showed that she had, for the moment, accepted the impossible: that it wasn't her daughter speaking, but a woman dead for over a hundred and thirty years. "You *did* free us."

"No," she said. *"I damned you. It is your turn now. Free the Warrior. Save your family."*

The power and authority in those words were unmistakable. As was the stark desperation. This was an old, old woman, of incalculable strength, but still bowed beneath the guilt of ages.

And just as incredibly, Derek found himself speaking not to his daughter, but to the voice, the voice that was not-Rachel, the voice that said it was Dahlia, Rachel's great-great-grandmother.

"You want me to break Tucker out of prison?"

Dee nodded soberly.

Derek bit his lip. "How can I believe this? How can I know that any of this is real? Any of it at all?"

Dee nodded as if this were a completely reasonable request. Then she screwed up her little face. The face she made was the one she used to make at the age of two or three, struggling on the pot. Somehow, perversely, at the moment an inexpressibly dear memory.

There was a sizzling sound. The water striking his daughter's skin began to boil. Steam filled the bathroom, but through the steam, through the wave of heat that suddenly seemed to twist the air around her face, he saw Dee's face *change.*

It flowed like lava. The contours shifted and corrected themselves, churning and then swirling back together, swirling until—

Rachel stumbled away, pressing the back of her hand to her mouth. "Oh, my God."

The face in the steam was a bit younger than her own, but still nearly identical to hers.

Then that bizarre *flowing* again, this time in reverse. Dee collapsed against the tile, weeping.

"Jesus Christ," Derek said fervently.

Troy backed away from the tub. "This isn't real," he said, raw fear in his voice.

Dee sobbed. "It hurts," she moaned. "It hurts . . ."

Rachel held her daughter. "Dee. Darling," she murmured, and the condensation of the steam was indistinguishable from the tears on her cheeks. "Hold on, sweetheart. Please. Please." She looked up, almost as if addressing the ceiling. "Dahlia? Don't hurt my baby anymore."

The voice, Dahlia's voice, for surely that was what it was, spoke through Dee's mouth again. *"Do you believe now?"* she asked.

"Yes," Rachel said. Rachel looked at Derek, the impossible request in her eyes. "Derek? What she's asking you to do. Do you understand it? Is there any way at all?"

Something lived in her eyes, something that he hadn't seen in years. Something beyond fear, and her concern for her child. Something he hadn't seen since their first days together. Trust. Belief.

His son and his daughter, and the woman who had been his lover studied him, and whether he could understand or not, there was no way that he could say no. He couldn't say yes, not yet. But he couldn't say no, either.

He had to buy time. "Let me think," he said. All confusion fell away and he experienced a clarity so absolute it was almost eerie. Damn. It felt as if he could reach all the way back up inside himself. Doubt and fear were both dissolving. He was somewhere beyond them both, in someplace where he simply *had to do it,* or die trying.

And that clarity was something he had sought his entire life.

"All right," he said. "If I tried. If I even *tried* to do this, Tucker would have to know that I was coming for him. He would have to know to try to escape. I don't think that I can get that kind of message to him. Can *you,* Dahlia? Can you reach him?"

A pause. Then the altered voice again, but this time the voice was softer, less forced, as if tired.

"Yes," Dahlia Childe said. "I can reach him. Through this child. But first, we must both rest."

Dee seemed to fold in on herself. Rachel held her daughter tightly against her chest, as if releasing her would consign Dee to the deepest pits of hell.

And Rachel wept.

There was silence in the room for a long moment.

Finally Troy said, "Dad?"

Derek thought his son had never looked smaller or frailer, not even as an infant. The thought of forces beyond his understanding grouping to tear him screaming from this world were weighing upon him, giving him an odd translucency.

"Dad," he repeated, and Derek realized that he had been so hypnotized by his thoughts that he hadn't answered his son's first call.

"Yes?" he said, already knowing what the question was, and welcoming its impossibility, its awesome, terrifying clarity.

"Dad?" he said for the third time, and Derek knew how very close his son was to breaking completely. "What are you going to do, Dad?"

Derek Waites listened to his own voice, as if it came from somewhere far away. He took his son's hand, and gripped it so tightly that he was certain it must have hurt. But there was something there that he was fighting to communicate. To his son. To himself. "What am I going to do?" he asked. "I'll tell you what I'm going to do. Whatever it takes."

17

The guards came for Tucker at the appointed time. He was warmed up. That warming-up process was more mental than physical.

The technique was something he had learned from Miles Tucker, his father. Miles Tucker was a strong quiet auto mechanic from Florida who had supported his wife and child with thirteen-hour work days and an unfailing faith in Jesus.

He learned it on a warm September twenty-second, his thirteenth birthday. Miles told his wife that he was taking the boy out to play a little catch, and walked, with ball and glove, out to the auto shop behind the house.

The shop was a good place, with gasoline and oil smells, tools arrayed neatly in their racks, and, invariably, pieces of the neighbors' cars scattered about awaiting discount repairs.

His father sat him down.

Miles, a tall, broad man with sunburned freckled face and thick hands that felt like leather, asked him if he wanted a beer. Austin said yes. Miles handed him a Coors, and grinned as his son chugged it down.

"I'm supposed to tell you something," Miles said.

"Like what, Dad?"

"Well, when I was thirteen, my daddy had this conversation with me. He told me his daddy had had it with him, and I was supposed to have it with my kid."

Austin waited.

"I been noticing that you been sneaking your sheets into the laundry, not waiting for your ma to take 'em off. Is that what I think it is?"

Austin burned with shame, but his father laughed warmly.

"Nothing to worry about. You're just becoming a man, that's all. And that's what I'm supposed to tell you about."

"Is this the birds and the bees? You already told me about those. . . ." he started, but knew that that wasn't where his father was going at all.

"No. Sex isn't it. It's something else. Something that you need to find out about yourself. All I know is that the men in our family are a little special. What I want you to do is to close your eyes."

Austin coughed nervously. "Why, Dad?"

"Just do it, boy. I ain't sure this is Christian, and if I hadn't promised to teach you, I wouldn't. I don't know what it is. It just works, that's all. Close your eyes."

The boy did.

"Now—imagine a ball. Size of a baseball. Down in your belly. Can you see that? Good. Now. Make it blue."

Much to Austin's surprise, it was not only easy, it was vivid. He had always dreamed in color, but this was something else.

"All right. Now. Imagine a second one, right at your heart. Make it yellow-gold. All right?"

Austin nodded. The light in his chest was a nugget of stolen sunlight.

"And last, imagine that you've got a red ball right where your head is. Like a big red diamond. Like a ruby. Can you see it?"

Again, somewhat to his surprise, he could—and clearly.

"All right, boy. Now. Float up above yourself, like you're looking down on yourself from over your own head."

"Floating like a balloon?"

"Yes, up over your own head. Are you doing that?"

He nodded.

"Now—are they all in a straight line?"

He looked. No, the blue ball was a little to the left, and the gold was to the right. And the blue one was a little bigger. He told his father these things, the way things looked when he closed his eyes. He thought his father might be mad, but instead he just made a clucking sound.

"That's because you play football more than you do your homework. What I want you to do is to see all three being the same size. And in line with each other. Can you do that?"

He watched, and the three balls lined up perfectly so that he could only see the top, red sphere, and it looked like a big circle.

The circle suddenly *flashed,* and white light surged up in his mind, flooding everything. Filling his limbs, making him feel as light as air. It felt wonderful.

"Doesn't work like this for most folks," his father said. "I don't know how it will work for you—works different for different members of the family. Daddy said it was dying out. But you practice that, and you'll learn some things. You got gifts."

Austin Tucker watched the light, and felt the light, flooding through him. "Grandpa taught you this?"

"Yeah. He said that there used to be more. That it wasn't

Christian, some of it, so he'd have no part of teaching it. Nothing I could do would get more of it out of him."

"Here," his father said, and threw the baseball to him.

But the baseball seemed to take forever. He could count the stitches on the ball as it spun toward him, and thirteen-year-old Austin Tucker knew that he had found the key to his life.

Mastering any sport was simplicity itself. Austin Tucker just saw *faster* than other people. He learned to manipulate the colors in his mind, and his senses opened in ways that he couldn't explain to *anyone,* not even his own wife. He simply experienced life more completely.

Tucker had only one male cousin on his father's side, a big rawboned boy named Rudy. Staying over at Rudy's house, he asked him about the Gift. Rudy was seventeen, and looked at Austin as if he were crazy. Miles Tucker explained that Rudy's dad was Baptist, and hadn't taught the secret. And now Rudy was too old. It was just too late.

As Tucker grew older, and used his secret to excel at sports, to survive a war, to develop his body in ways that others couldn't dream, he promised himself he would teach the secret to his son, which he had begun to do.

But all of those dreams had ended on a terrible Thanksgiving night, years ago. A night that had shattered his dreams, his life, and very nearly his sanity.

Sitting in his cell, Austin Tucker prepared for his match.

Once the white light flooded him, he slipped inside himself, and listened to his heartbeat, making it louder and stronger. Then slower. And slower. Once upon a time he had wondered if he was literally slowing his heartbeat down, but now he knew better.

To answer the question, he had hooked himself up to a biofeedback machine, and let it record his brain waves and vital signs as he did his trick. Whereas he was generating an abnormal number of delta waves for a person fully conscious, and his heartbeat slowed to about forty per minute, that didn't explain the enormous subjective difference. It seemed his entire world fell silent between the thundering, glacial pulses of his heart.

He could read whole chunks of the *Encyclopedia Britannica* between beats.

Traces of that illusory perception persisted even during motion. It was something that he never discussed with anyone. In survival situations, it was his edge.

So he sat, staring at the wall when the two guards came for him. One was Berger, the other, with the pale fringe of beard, was named Quest.

"You ready?" Quest asked.

"Born ready," Tucker grunted. That was the kind of macho bullshit answer they were looking for. As little as he wished to admit it, he needed their fear and respect. He once swore to himself that he wouldn't, but over the years his world had contracted to the walls and rhythms of this prison, and within that kingdom, he needed some sense of power, of acceptance.

You take what you can get.

They led him out of the cell down the cell block. It was mostly deserted, although there were a few sullen inmates sitting in them, those who didn't want to go down and watch what was about to happen. Some had seen it before, and decided they had no taste for blood.

Quest and Berger led Tucker down a narrow flight of stairs, through darkness, until they emerged once again into light.

As he came through the door a robe was draped over his shoulders, something designed to emphasize the pomp of the circumstance. The gym was packed with inmates, perhaps three hundred on bleachers set up for the monthly boxing exhibitions. Guards ringed the rooms, not so much to keep order as to treat themselves to the show.

The room was divided racially. The blacks on one side, almost as numerous as the whites. Their eyes were hungry, shining out pale and sullen from their dark faces, their lips parted. They hoped that the day would bring victory, vindication.

On the far side of the room, the whites mirrored their hunger.

As he climbed up onto the raised canvas surface of the ring and shook his robe off, raised his great muscular arms above his head and received the adulation of the white prisoners, he was chagrined by how *good* it felt. How much he needed to hear that. Something was slipping away from him, something he couldn't quite identify.

Perhaps, just perhaps, its name was Honor.

A white inmate with a swastika riding his biceps checked Tucker's hand wrappings.

Berger looked at him carefully. "What's the matter, Tuck? You feeling solid?"

There was an automatic reply on his lips, but before he could speak, he had that feeling again, the one that first came to him in the cell. It boomed to life like a dull pressure behind his heart.

It was the third time that he'd heard the voice in his head, and it was even more disturbing this time. If there was anything in his world that he counted on, it was his sanity. After all, it was only confidence in his own sanity that allowed him to refute what the prosecution said about him. What the forensic evidence said about him. He had to trust himself, his memory, his sanity, because in the final analysis they were all that he had.

But still, there remained that voice, returning to him again, and again. And this time it said, very clearly, *"Tomorrow, Tucker. You will be free tomorrow. You will avenge your family. Be ready, Tucker. You will only have one chance. . . ."*

He whipped his head about. "What the fuck—?"

In a motel room two hundred miles away, a small black girl was packed in ice. The ice melted into water, and steamed in the tub about her. Boils erupted on her skin, which reddened and split. Her eyes rolled to the whites; and she arched and screamed so loudly that a man in the next room hammered on the wall and yelled, *"Goddamn it, shut that bitch up or share her!"*

Troy stood in the doorway, eyes wide and frightened, watching.

Rachel turned to him and spoke with her voice low and deadly calm. "Get more ice, dammit."

Behind them in the middle of the living room sat an immense pile of ice, ice in plastic sacks, in buckets. Ice that might keep Dee alive long enough for whatever it was that Dahlia had in mind.

Derek tore the ice bag from his son's hands, and heaped it over Dee's quaking body. It tore his heart out, destroyed him to see his daughter in such pain, but he just didn't know what else to do.

The ice sizzled when it touched her skin, as if there were a layer of fire just above the precious flesh, one that required continual cooling.

"More ice," he whispered.

A black angel, a shatteringly beautiful, shimmering mirage of a woman appeared before Tucker's eyes. She was dressed in rude, coarse cloth, but a mummy's shroud couldn't have concealed the richness of her body. Nor could her raggedly cut hair disguise the intelligence burning in her eyes.

Tucker stared, feeling something bordering on supernatural awe. The image shimmered magically. He felt, somewhere deep within him, that he knew this woman. He fought to find the memory. The woman spoke to him. *"Tomorrow, Tucker. You will have one chance. You failed your family before. Don't fail them again."*

The words reverberated in his head, chilled him. It was so real that he wanted to speak to her. There was something—dammit, something fierce, but *calm* in that visage. Something that he longed to touch. He couldn't be certain, but he thought that he heard a sob escape from his own lips.

She spoke again. *"Tomorrow, Tucker,"* she said. *"One chance. Don't fail them again. . . ."*

The image faded. Across the ring, the phenomenally muscular Ahmed stretched and leaped, displaying an impressively athletic array of lethal kicks. Tucker didn't believe for a minute that Ahmed would actually use such absurd tactics once the fight began. This was pure intimidation.

Ahmed dropped into a full split, grinning. He pointed

across the ring. "Hey, white boy!" he yelled. "Gonna stop my heart, big man?"

Tucker ignored him, torn between the vision in his head, and the need to recenter himself. Quest leaned close, a strong smell of baloney on his breath. His voice had a Texas twang. "Put some kittycombotty on his head," the guard said confidently. "You'll be in the hole a week, tops. Upside, there'll be some kick-ass perks."

Tucker listened to the words as if he had never heard them before. "In . . . the hole." A solitary confinement box not long enough to lie down in, not tall enough to stand up in. Tucker could sleep sitting and wake up without being stiff. The hole held no terrors for him. But there was something . . .

"In the hole?"

"Just for maybe a week. Two, tops. Accidental death. Hell, the guards will vouch for you, Warden Treiger will look the other way. You know that."

Tucker remembered the woman's voice. Remembered the calm in her face. The calm that promised something beyond the frozen hell of his empty nights. He was insane, he had to be. But that damned pseudonewsman had opened something in him, a box called Hope. And even if it turned out that there was nothing inside it, he had to play out the game.

"I can't go in the hole," he said, more to himself than to Baloney-breath.

Berger looked at him with a hint of irritation. "Hey," he said. "You been there before, and you didn't bitch. What's the big thing?"

Tucker tried to answer, but the woman's voice filled his head. Reverberated in his head, rang back and forth until he had no sense of himself, of who or where he was. Until there was nothing in the world except that voice. He looked around desperately, his eyes wide and wild.

He heard his voice before he realized that he was speaking. "I can't," he murmured. "I can't do it. I just *can't.*"

He said it louder and louder, the two words becoming a litany, a prayer, a shout, a roar, a thunder breaking from his throat, until the entire room stopped in shock, silenced, everyone staring at him.

Victor of a hundred battles, fearless, physically awesome.

Now there was something cornered and small about him, like a child confronted by an angry parent.

Tucker clapped his hands to his head. He stood, shaking off the grasping hands of his handlers. He turned, and ran.

For a long moment after he left the room, there was no reaction save stunned silence.

The giant Ahmed was shocked, and still. The sweat glistened on his chest, his breathing rose and fell somehow out of tempo with the emotions which filled the room.

Finally Ahmed spoke. "Godzilla motherfuck," he said in astonishment. "He's a *punk!*"

The motel room was silent, or nearly so. Waites tucked Dahlia into her bed. The small child was blistered, but alive. Troy stood on the other side of the bed, goggle-eyed as he looked at his sister.

He shook his head. "Dad?" he asked. "Has she always been able to do that?"

Troy was trying to take something of unimaginable impact and put it into a safe, small box where he could deal with it. "I don't know," Derek said shakily. "Why?"

Troy smiled, a fragile thing that Derek was inordinately happy to see. "I mean, if she can do that whenever she wants—I mean melt ice into steam—I could use her for a science project next semester."

Derek wanted to laugh and cry. Thank God for Troy. "You're very sick," he said seriously. "I think that that's a check mark."

"Nope," Dee said, not quite as asleep as they had supposed. "Not this week. No check marks for Troy this week."

Derek tousled her hair. Her scalp felt warm, but not hot. The hair felt a little crispy, as if it had lost some of the oils. Aside from that, there was no evidence of what had just happened.

Dee struggled to sit up. "I'm *really* hungry," she said. "I feel like there's a big hole inside me." At first she said it playfully, but then her smile crinkled into a frown. "I'm really hungry, Mommy."

"I'll bet she is," Derek said. Her face looked gaunt. "I

don't know what happened here, but she probably burned up five or six pounds of fat. And she didn't really have it to spare."

"What do you want?" Rachel asked.

"About a dozen cheeseburgers, and a couple of malts," Dee said.

Troy protested. "Hey!"

Derek could let them sort that out. He opened his computer case and stared at the machine. He knew what he had to do, and what it would take to do it. He just couldn't believe he was actually considering it.

Rachel put a soft, warm hand on his shoulder. "You have to do this?"

He put on his bravest face as he smiled up at her. "Don't worry," he said. " 'Captain Africa strikes,' remember?"

The words very nearly stuck in his throat. It was too easy to remember the pain that his hacking and cracking had caused his family. Rachel buried her head against his shoulder.

"Please," she said. "I can't . . . I can't lose you, too."

"Maybe he isn't dead."

Her eyes were cold.

There were so many things that he wanted to hear from her, so many things that he needed to say. But what it came down to, in the final analysis, was Derek smiling bravely, despite the vast mantle of fatigue that settled over him. He folded her into his arms, and pillowed her head against his chest. God, it felt wonderful, and the scent of her hair was so fine. He ran over and through its softness, warming his fingers.

She still loved him. But she was *in* love with Medford Downs. Even if Medford had died, he still had her heart.

Derek felt her breath against his chest. Could feel the dampness of her tears, sudden and hot and streaming.

She leaned up and kissed him lightly, a warm moment as their lips touched, a touch containing all of the hope and fear of a shattered world. When the world collapsed upon them both, there was one thing that remained. They were family. Their troubles were family troubles, and in some way that would have seemed sick to someone who didn't understand, who had never been through it, even the pain, the hurt, the anger, the arguments, all of that somehow just reinforced it. Somehow all of that brought them closer together. It shouldn't have, but it did.

His son's small fists were clutched together tightly. "Troy?" he asked. The boy flinched slightly, almost as if he had been struck. "Take care of your mother. I'll be back in a day. Two at the most."

Troy nodded. "You'd better," he said.

Dee half opened her eyes. "Or check mark for Daddy," she said.

Stumbling as if he were half-asleep, Troy crossed to him, and hugged him. Troy and Rachel and Derek stood by the side of the bed holding on to one another as if letting go would drop them off the edge of the world. Dee watched them, a small sleepy smile on her face, and flipped herself over onto her stomach and crawled across the bed toward them, joining in the group hug.

Derek closed his eyes and let it in, felt a doorway in his heart open. The feelings became almost too intense, and as he let it in he felt one doorway after another slam open in his heart like a succession of sealed mirror portals.

No. Not now. There was too much to do. He had to lock those feelings, those memories tightly inside his chest, where they could nurture him, but wouldn't get in his way. Where he had to go, thoughts of softness, of his wife and children, simply couldn't follow.

Thursday, May 7

Derek pulled into his driveway, quietly, checking the clock on the dashboard. Almost four o'clock in the morning. He wanted to take a shower, and sleep, but knew he didn't have time for that yet. First, he needed to get some equipment.

He had circled the block twice before parking. The streets, and the houses on either side were quiet. The traffic up on

Washington Boulevard was still minimal. True, some early commuters were on the Santa Monica Freeway, but that artery was busy at any hour of the day or night. Hadn't he heard that it was one of the most heavily traveled stretches of concrete in the world?

The front door opened to his key, and he stepped into the living room, pausing to listen. Water dripped from a kitchen faucet. A clock hummed. Nothing else. He had to focus his thoughts now. He went to the closet, and began to dig. He needed to pack a few things. He had an outline of the plan, a ghost of an idea, but it would require specific equipment, equipment that had been in storage for over a year. Stuff from his Captain Africa days. Even after completing parole it seemed smart to leave it in the cubicle at Culver City Storage.

One of the three electrical outlets in his office was a phony, and a minute with a screwdriver was all it took to undo it and remove the tiny lock box. All it contained was a key, but that was enough.

He stood and—

Stars exploded in his eyes, and he never even felt the pain that caused the shock. He tried to turn, but a savage blow to the kidneys drove him back to his knees. Then a horribly strong hand at the collar of his jacket hauled him to his feet and spun him, and he caught a glimpse of the Indian-faced cop an instant before a fist drove so deeply into his stomach he hoped he would die.

To his horror, he didn't. Another blow, and another. He had forgotten what such thunderous body blows did. No— that wasn't true. He had never known blows like these, punches that drove the air from his lungs, squirted bile into his nose, pushed all rational thought from his mind. Jesus, Jesus, one more, harder than the rest, and he collapsed onto hands and knees, and then was hauled up again.

"Funny man," the Indian said. "Funny man with the funny car horn. I'm going to give you one chance, and just one."

The cop's face was very, very close in the darkness. His teeth gleamed. "One chance. Where is your family now?"

Derek desperately needed a second to think. His breath rasped in his throat. "Why?"

The Indian drove his fist into Derek's gut again. "Wrong answer." Derek sagged, trying not to throw up. He tried to find the strength to fight back, but as he tried to gather himself, the Indian drove a knee into his crotch, and what little strength remained drained there, exploded back up in a volcanic surge of agony, left him nerveless and empty and spiraling on the edge of unconsciousness.

"I . . . I don't know—"

The fist went back, came down, and struck Derek under the eye. Skin tore. "I don't know," he whispered desperately, "but I can find out."

The fist stopped. Derek tasted blood. The whole side of his face throbbed.

"What the hell are you talking about?"

"I told her. Told her to go to her cousin's house in San Diego. I don't know the address, but it's on the computer."

The Indian shook his head. Grinned. His teeth were very white. "Big computer hero, huh?" He pushed Derek over to the desk. "Go ahead."

His hands were shaking. Blood was running into his right eye. A dull ringing filled in his ears. He reached out for the light switch, then looked nervously at his tormentor. Jesus, the bastard was big. "May I?"

"Sure."

He turned on the light, and squinted against the glare. So did the Indian. He saw the man more clearly now. Over six feet tall. Lean, and strong. He was out of uniform, but the pale leather jacket didn't conceal the bulge of his shoulder holster.

"Don't try anything," the Indian whispered. "I already killed a TV star tonight. Don't think I won't do you."

The Indian slid the gun out, and rested it on his thigh, the tips of his fingers lightly stroking the barrel, an obscene threat.

And you wouldn't have told me that if there was any chance at all you were going to let me live, Derek thought.

Derek said, "Do you want a printout?"

The Indian said, "Sure."

Derek nodded and turned on his laser printer. Then his computer. And the removable cartridge drive.

The computer beeped, and the screen began to flicker. "Dirty screen," Derek said, in his very best computer nerd voice. Another wave of agony from his crotch washed through him. Something in there might be ruptured, damaged. Not that it would matter. He would probably be dead in about two minutes.

Derek used a Windex bottle to squirt a little mist on the monitor screen. He wiped it with a tissue, being very anal about specks of dust.

Behind him, the Indian chuckled darkly. "Machines are the friend of man," the Indian said.

Derek smacked his forehead with his palm. "Oh, shit—I need to use this printer," he said, and reached for the fax machine. He stretched his arm around behind it, and switched it on—

And the awful, blessed, ancient electrical wiring blew.

The room was plunged back into darkness. In that instant Derek's hands grasped the Windex bottle filled with his custom glass cleaner, a mixture of isopropyl alcohol and ammonia, and pumped five blasts directly into the Indian's face.

The Indian roared, grabbing his eyes and raising his gun. It went off in the next moment. The flash and the roar filled the world.

Derek felt something burn his side, but didn't care, because he had snatched the coffee pot from the table beside his desk and smashed the glass receptacle into what he hoped was the Indian's face.

Neither of them could see in the sudden dark, but he knew that the man had shifted sideways, that the glass bulb had smashed on his cheek. Stale coffee splashed in all directions. There was a sudden gush of curses, and a satisfying moan of pain and distress.

Derek kicked and kicked, and felt his foot strike something . . . maybe a cheek, maybe a stomach, and then he was free, and running like hell for the door.

The darkness was worse for the Indian than it was for him. The Indian didn't know the layout of the house. Derek heard a satisfying thump as something—he sincerely hoped it was the bastard's head—thumped into the corner of a door. Then Derek was out the front door and into his car.

An answer to his prayers, his engine started without a hitch, and he slewed out of the driveway, made a three-point turn in the street, and was halfway up the hill before the Indian emerged from the house.

Officer Godfrey Timms was beyond anger. The left side of his handsome face was a ruin. People were waking up, and he knew that from behind blinds and curtains, they were peeking out at him. Shit. *Shit.* He had missed, and his face was hamburger. Maybe ex-star Medford Downs was a drug arrest gone sour—but there was no way in hell to keep the lid on *now.* Best for him to get the hell out of California— his father had other places he could work, in fact, a network across the country.

That network had existed for over a century. A few trusted agents keeping eyes on the cattle, watching the local newspapers. And when a disaster occurred near an appropriately aged Purifier, a boy of thirteen or fourteen, the machinery went into effect. Winos or hookers or homeless were snatched near the disaster site, and then the boy. . . .

And then magic happened.

Yes, there would be other uses for his skills.

But first, first he was going to find this little bastard and his family. First he was going to kill the wife, and the daughter. And then cut the father's eyelids off and make him watch his son die.

Then he was going to take his time about showing the little punk exactly what pain really was.

18

Derek Waites was exhausted, but satisfied. For two days he had holed up in Tehachapi's Motel Six, listening to the microphones planted on the prison phone system.

With the help of the equipment claimed from his Culver

City locker, he had learned a variety of things. He had sorted his way through their lines, and mapped out a large percentage of the communications network that linked the prison together. Dummy calls and faxes to the various departments gave him more information, and a full day researching the electrical contractors and original telephone company specs gave him even greater detail.

Dozens of purchase orders for the various departments were found in various low-security files, and the most interesting one was for something called an ITT Securelink.

A back issue of an on-line magazine called *COMMworld* gave him more information about this fascinating device, and e-mail messages to six friends led to twenty other people, two of whom had pertinent data, and one of whom had actually installed the Securelink system in a Detroit stock broker's office. She was happy to talk about it, despite her nondisclosure agreement.

Derek felt as if his eyes were full of sand, his joints packed with concrete. He was still sore from the beating the Indian had given him. But he finally felt ready. He had to be ready. He was running out of time.

19

It was raining in Tehachapi, a freezing, depressing, sleeting kind of rain that stole heat from the body faster than a thermal jacket or space heater could replenish it.

The lights at the prison's visitor gate were dimmed. There were no visitors or deliveries expected this night. It was almost nine o'clock, and Morris Freeman was looking forward to a quiet night, a relief guard at ten o'clock, a beer at home with his new live-in girlfriend, and then maybe a little of the old horizontal bop, just to put an edge on things for the night.

She was a good lady, and he took a lot of pleasure in remembering their first night together, two days after meeting her at the Victory Lounge in Pasadena, where he had gone for prime rib, and had been stunned by a brunette sitting at the bar with a girlfriend, obviously entirely involved in her conversation. Not there to meet or pick up a guy, she was nonetheless a stunning piece of work with a dress that could be accurately described as either tight clothing or loose paint. He sent her over a drink, and she had ignored him, but after fifteen minutes their eyes kept meeting in the mirror, and—

Morris broke off the pleasant ruminations as a huge supply truck rumbled through the slush up the narrow drive. Morris consulted his clipboard, and frowned. There was nothing on the slate tonight, and that was a pain, because it meant more paperwork for somebody—hopefully not him.

A sign on the side of the truck read De-Lighta Foods. This was an additional pain. De-Lighta was a major supplier, and sometimes got their orders scrambled. He was feeling more than a little irritation until he got a better look at the driver.

It was Trish Campbell, the prettiest truck driver in the state, and Morris's mood immediately lightened. He had never managed to score with Trish, and as far as he knew neither had any of the other guards, but it had sure as hell been given the old college try. She was about five nine, slender but wiry as hell. She could have been drop-dead gorgeous if she had ever bothered with makeup.

Trish was a widow. Her husband had been a teamster and owned his own truck, an independent operator. She had been out of the workforce for at least ten years when he died of a stroke, and with three kids to feed and few assets except that monster truck, she had called in favors at the union, gone to one of those big-rig driving schools that promised to train the unhappy laborer to "drive the big rigs and bring home the bacon!" and with a little help from her friends, gotten her CDL. She worked hard, had a smile for everyone, and was a joy.

He hoped for her sake that everything with the night's deliveries was jake. He wasn't certain, but he had a feeling that truckers were only paid for deliveries completed, and attempts didn't count for much.

He put a genuinely regretful expression on his face. "No delivery scheduled tonight, Trish."

Her bright little smile faded, then bounced back. She shook her head, one of those *I-knew-it-was-going-to-be-one-*

of-those-days-when-I-woke-up-this-morning smiles. "This is great," she said. "Just great. Listen, Morris—this is some kind of special order. It came over the fax. Can't you give me a break here?"

He wanted to. Boy, did he want to give her a break. Say about a twenty-minute break in the back of her truck. He assumed that there was a mattress back there somewhere. He wasn't certain, but he always saw these truckers pulled over at the side of the road, and he bet they weren't reading *The Wall Street Journal.* "Listen," he said. "Pull around, park outside. Use my phone. We'll straighten this out at the top. There's probably an answer."

"The answer is that life sucks," she said philosophically.

She pulled past him into the circular drive, bringing the truck around in a great arc, near the service bungalows. Beyond them were the residential units.

As she circled, what she didn't see, what Morris didn't see, was the form of Derek Waites clinging to the top of the truck. He and his portable computer were both covered with a metallic "space blanket," a light, flexible, semimetallic material the same shade of silver as the top of the De-Lighta truck. The metal was so cold he thought he would die, even wrapped in heat-reflective sheeting as he was.

He was afraid that when the time finally came for him to move he wouldn't be able to. That his aching body wouldn't be able to respond—but it did. He chose the moment when the truck itself blocked the view from the guardhouse. He hit the mud hard, nearly twisting his ankle, and rolled off into the bushes.

His arm covered his eyes, but he felt branches poking at him, tearing at him, and the worst thing was that he couldn't give himself time to react to the pain. He had to keep going, keep rolling over until he made it out of the light and into the shadows, taking his computer case with him. He hid there, breathing heavily, but safe and inside the main perimeter now.

He waited another few moments, getting his bearings. He watched the guard talking with the truck driver.

This was good—Trish Campbell had been a good choice. He had spent a long time looking through the personnel files, finding a female truck driver who would be on call, making certain that she got the assignment, making certain that she was attractive.

Whether the guard on the gate was male or female, an attractive woman was far less likely to cause suspicion.

The outer area was minimum security, and contained a number of residence bungalows. These were neat, small cottages, some of them with flower beds that might have held azaleas or carnations in the summer, but here in the first weeks of a chilly spring were barren of anything recognizable as flowers. Bare stems twisted up from the earth.

He crept from shadow to shadow, pulling back into darkness whenever the glare of headlights passed. His heart pounded in his chest. It was too late to turn back now, but if he turned himself in, there would be no charge save trespassing on state property—he hoped.

But Jesus, he had been a convicted felon. No, if they caught him, it was terribly unlikely that they would assume that he was here to sell Girl Scout cookies. He clamped his mind down on the thoughts that followed. There was no time or place for them right now, and they were as counterproductive as hell.

The largest bungalow bore a sign reading WARDEN JAMES TREIGER beneath the mail box. A low gated fence surrounded the house. After a visual inspection and a quick prayer, Derek found a dark spot to clamber across, and once again enter into shadow, flush against the side of the house, listening to his heartbeat.

Someone inside the house was talking. Derek came up close enough to a window to take a stealthy peak through it, and saw a white-haired man in his early sixties, still strong and erect, talking to a woman perhaps ten years his junior. The shelves around them were filled tightly with leatherbound volumes. A quiet evening at home, two hundred yards from the most complete collection of vicious criminals in the state.

Derek skulked about the edge of the house until he found what he was looking for, a telephone connector box. Its metal seal took only a moment to break.

Within the box was the usual warren of wiring and connector poles, but he was looking for something more. When he found it he whistled softly. There, snuggled within the forest of wiring, was a little box half the size of a package of cigarettes. He ran his fingers along it and felt the raised lettering. He cautiously shone his flashlight inside, and read the black letters: *"ITT Securelink: Restricted Usage."*

"Captain Africa strikes!" he murmured.

The Securelink was one of the security innovations on the prison computer net. It allowed Treiger to receive and transmit secure communications from his home, and theoretically, at least, such coded transmissions could only be broken by someone with an identical scrambler on the opposite end. That plus the caller ID signal made for a supposedly impenetrable system.

Derek's entire gamble depended on how complacent the staff had become concerning fax transmissions, and how long it took for a prisoner like Tucker to seem like a member of the general population. If the notoriety had died down, if people were sufficiently used to secure communications not to demand or need a face-to-face interaction, or the sound of the warden's voice . . .

If, if, if. Jesus. There were a million things that could go wrong, and only one that could go right.

Great. He loved odds like that. As carefully as he had ever done anything in his life, with the highest level of expertise that he could muster, he draped plastic over his computer to protect it from the rain, and began to run wires into the phone box. The next step was attaching them to the modem port on his computer.

A pair of headlights slid by. Derek froze as a truck roared past. Then he booted up the computer, and said a silent prayer.

From the menu he selected the communications program, waited until it had loaded, selected the file marked "Tucker" and typed "Send."

If this worked, a message would run from the computer into the phone line, passing into the ITT Securelink box as if it had originated on the warden's fax machine, carry the proper caller ID number into the computer, and be accepted.

He had seen computer files of two such faxes, and he had formatted his own to look exactly the same.

All he could do now was pray.

In the Special Services office of Tehachapi State Prison, there was a fax machine wired to a box identical to that at the warden's residence. A tiny red light atop the box flashed on, and the fax made a dinging sound. A liquid crystal display atop it read, "Receiving priority fax. Security verifying caller ID"—and here, it gave Warden James Treiger's telephone number—"exchanging security protocol."

There was a pause of a few moments. The night secretary looked at the machine, not terribly worried or impressed. She had been over all of this before, many times. The warden was likely to do as much work from home as he could, was a little less compulsive about getting in to work early in the morning. It had become more noticeable just over the last couple of years. Slowing down. We all do that eventually, she mused.

On the other hand, he had a great love of paperwork and occasionally still burned the midnight oil.

So tonight's late fax was no real surprise.

A moment later, the second light shone. "Security protocol completed. Receiving transmission . . ."

Another pause, and a sheet of fax paper began to roll out of the top of the machine. She looked at the first few lines: "Request Prisoner 34891 Austin Tucker transport to California City PD 4/24/92 for questioning in recently unearthed homicide. . . ."

She read the rest of it. Tucker. People were really interested in him, once upon a time. It was surprising that anyone still cared. He seemed pretty much a broke dick at this stage of his life. But another corpse might give the tabloids something to feed on. You never knew. It was distasteful, but she supposed that everyone had to make a living, one way or the other.

She picked up the telephone. "I'd like to arrange security transport for the front gate in twenty minutes. . . ."

20

The rain was heavier now, streaming down in sheets that seemed to slice the night in half, pouring down from the sky more and more heavily, thick enough to dim the streetlights.

The cars parked along the street were dark and deserted, their owners turned in for the evening, snuggled comfortably in their beds, watching Arsenio, or the late movies, or *Star Trek* reruns.

They were thinking about jobs, or family, or weather. Few if any of them were thinking about their cars.

Their cars.

For instance: a red-and-black Pontiac Grand Prix, parked in front of a two-story brick house, shaded by a weeping willow tree. It was barely visible from the house, and the man who carefully and gingerly tried its door handle couldn't be seen at all.

A half a block away, a Mercury Montego's door opened, and the man searched swiftly for a key. And found nothing.

The shadowy form slid along the street, seeking another car. A Ford. Its door was locked. Next he tried a Jeep. The door was unlocked, but a swift search found nothing. He tried three more, with no results, but on the fourth try the car door was open, and the keys were under the seat.

He threw a bag of equipment into the car, started the engine, and drove away. As he drove, he extracted a police-band radio from the bag and propped it on the seat next to him. And turned it on, listening carefully to the chatter.

21

When they came for him, Austin Tucker was curled on his side on his bunk, staring into the wall. His mind was going. Gone. What had that voice been? And the image of the black woman. It seemed so real, so real.

Two guards were coming for him. He recognized their footsteps before he saw them, or even heard their voices.

Berger stopped outside the cell and laughed unpleasantly. "This is your big day, hero." There was something unspeakably nasty in Berger's voice. "Looks like they unearthed another of your little artworks."

Shit. He hoped that all of that was over, the tabloids and the police questioners, trying to link him to every unsolved crime in the state. There was no end to the interrogation sessions and ultimately he had ceased cooperating.

What more could they take from him?

He had thought it was everything. But it wasn't, of course. There was always more. There are always petty hells they could drag him through, and he had had enough of those, and just wanted to pass his days with as little pain as possible. With as much sanity as possible. Because . . .

There was always the chance. Just the chance that one day he would have an opportunity to meet the men who destroyed him, who killed his wife and daughter. Who burned his son to death. He clung to the thought that maybe, just maybe he would have an opportunity to meet them. That wonderful, glorious thought had kept him sane over the years.

So he cooperated. And they learned nothing from him, but had the dubious pleasure of forcing him to talk about the terrible things that had happened, over and over and over again, ad nauseam.

And now, years after the last time, someone had found another corpse, something else to hurt him with. "Where?" he asked.

"California City, asshole. Move it."

"What?"

"You're going out there. Don't ask me what it's all about."

Tucker shambled out of bed, his mind slowly gripping the facts as they were presented to him. They were taking him out of the prison? To California City.

He thought about a number of things and as he thought about them he was very careful not to let his emotions touch his face.

The woman said to be ready, that he would have a chance to avenge his family. To be ready when the opportunity came.

And here he was being taken out of the prison.

He held his breath. Could this really be happening?

They opened the door and cuffed him and then pushed him out of the cell, more roughly than was actually necessary. They led him down the block.

The other prisoners tossed piss sodden wads of toilet paper at him and jeered.

"Yellow-bellied fuck!"

"Get those tiny little balls out of here, baby killer!"

They took him down the corridors, and through the portals, and down the stairways, at each of the security checkpoints giving and receiving the proper protocols.

And then he was outside the main building, in a courtyard dominated by a police transport van, a big squarish thing resembling an armored bread truck.

The prison lights reflected off the rain-swept tarmac in a nightmarish glare of color. They pushed him inside.

The front gates opened, and the van roared out.

Tucker sat with his hands chained in front of him, hunched slightly as if on the verge of implosion. The connecting door to the driver's compartment opened and Quest entered.

The two officers grinned at each other, and then even more savagely at him. They chained Tucker's legs to a brace below the seat, trapping him effectively.

Quest and Berger might have had smiles on their faces, but both men were murderously angry.

Berger sneered. "Thought you were pretty cute, didn't you?"

Quest leaned forward. Shadow slid across his face as he did, transforming it into a primal mask of rage. "Cost me a thousand bucks, asshole."

He waited, expecting some kind of an answer: an explanation, an excuse, perhaps a curse. Tucker said nothing.

Quest laughed nastily. "I think this van is going to have some trouble along the way. Maybe break down. Radio trouble. Be out of communication for a few minutes." He looked at his friend. "Think Tucker will ever make it to California City?"

A slow shake of the head. "No chance." Tucker could smell Berger's breath from across the van. Bad teeth. "What do you think the report will say?"

Berger's eyes were small ugly holes. Excited eyes. Tucker felt himself pulling back into his mind. Within him, colors swelled, began to align. The world began to slow down.

He wasn't in himself. He was watching himself, and the movie on the screen was slowing down. Slowing and slowing, until Berger and Quest were figures in a dream, not real human beings at all. Each ponderous beat of Tucker's heart seemed to take an eternity. Time to think, and plan and feel. Time enough for men to die.

Berger repeated Quest's question. "What do I think the report will say? How about 'strangled while trying to escape'?"

They laughed uproariously at this, as if they have never heard a joke in their lives.

"What do you say to that, Tucker?"

Once again, trying to get a response. He stared at them. The sense of an impending *something* was almost overpowering, like an express train thundering down upon them. The guards felt it, too. Something was wrong. Out of control. They probably thought it was their own tempers, their own anger, their own drive for revenge.

"You cost me a fucking trip to Hawaii," Quest said, as if that justified what he was about to do.

He fingered his baton. The mood shifted again. It was about to begin.

Then—

A blinding glare of auto headlights filled the cab, and Tucker heard the driver scream, *"What the fuck—?"*

The half door to the driver's section swung open. Tucker saw a car barreling out of the darkness, high beams blazing, and coming at them at top speed and at an angle barely sufficient to avoid a head-on collision.

He saw something else—a man clumsily throwing himself clear of the car. Just a shadow outline, because nothing could really be distinguished in that glare. Then the car smashed into the prison van, and the entire world inverted.

For one crazy instant the van hovered in the air, then jolted down. It careened on two wheels, then crashed and skid onto its side, engine still whining.

Darkness.

In the darkness, something within Austin Tucker was completely alive for the first time in a decade.

The three colored spheres aligned instantly, and his mind flashed, suddenly swollen with light. And dancing in the light was a snarling beast.

It was strange, almost as if there were deeper emotional sections of him analogous to the inner lights. For years they'd been out of alignment, like pools of glare from a searchlight, bright and only partially overlapping.

And in that fragmented way he had suffered his incarceration, removed from himself, forgetting who and what it was that he had once been. Forgetting that there was a time that people considered him to be something . . .

Special. Yes. .

But now, entirely unbidden by him, something clicked inside his heart and mind and body, and that light became an enveloping thing, lifting and carrying him into an odd clarity, into a place so pure and crystalline that the entire universe seemed suspended in time.

Yes.

Quest and Berger. The two guards. They would kill him.
Really?

Something within Tucker bared its teeth.

* * *

Quest came to awareness, groaned, rolled over on his side, mildly surprised to find that he was still alive. What the hell—accident?

Something moved in the dark. Suddenly, Quest realized, remembered, that Tucker was there. That in the moments just before the collision, they had taunted Tucker with death threats.

"Mike?" He whispered. "Mike?" Only a groan in return.

He reached into his holster, found the reassuring shape and heft of the revolver. He shouldn't have had it with him. It was against all regulations to carry a pistol while traveling in a confined space with a prisoner. But regulations be damned—he wasn't going to be in a confined space with someone like Tucker without a fucking piece.

His eyes were beginning to adjust to the light·when he heard a muffled scream. The sound of someone suddenly, horrifically stressed. Then a gasp. It was the timbre of that gasp that horrified him. It was a tortured wheeze that went beyond ordinary human endurance into the realm of sudden pain, sudden fearful effort. Then a sound like a sob. Then a crunch. Then silence.

"*Mike?*" he shouted, and something was moving toward him in the darkness. He fired twice. The sudden flare of the revolver blinded him, but in the brief light he saw Mike Berger inching toward him in the topsy-turvey space, Mike's head lolling on a broken neck, his mouth smeared with blood, his eyes open and staring at nothing, nothing at all.

Quest's nerve broke and he fired again and again, seeing only Mike's body twitching as the heavy slugs tore into him at point-blank range, seeing only the charring cloth and torn flesh, smelling cordite and burnt meat and the coppery taste of his own fear as the corpse came closer and closer. Then the man behind the corpse reached out with arms that were impossibly quick and strong, and grabbed his gun hand and wrenched, breaking fingers, tearing the weapon away and then backhanding it butt first into the bridge of his nose, smashing cartilage and bone, sending blood and savage, white-hot pain into his eyes.

And then he heard Tucker inhale sharply, and saw the palm strike coming. Even in the confined space saw Tucker twist his body into it, had time to note that there was a beauty, a grace to the strike even in the midst of the chaos, looked down in time to see it smash into his breastbone.

He felt as if he had swallowed an inflatable raft, and the carbon dioxide cartridge had suddenly, massively triggered. Just an overwhelming jolt of shock and pressure, but no pain, none at all. A wave of percussive force washed through him, canceled itself out, and then there was nothing. Silence. He couldn't breathe. But he could still think, clearly. Strange. His heart had stopped. It was an odd, total silence, a quiet he had never known. Almost peaceful. No pain.

It was nothing. Nothing at all.

22

Derek Waites stood beside his car, the rain slicking his eyes and face, running a hand over it. His head felt packed with cotton. He just didn't know what to do next.

He heard four rain-muffled gunshots. He felt paralyzed, fascinated, and wondered what in the hell was happening in that truck. Surely the man was dead. Surely Austin Tucker had been killed. The crash, the shots, two or three guards. Certainly—

Then the rear door of the van opened, and a giant emerged.

Somehow, in the rain, Austin Tucker seemed immensely larger than he had in the visitors' room. Somehow, pushing aside the door and emerging into the wet and the night and the dark, water plastering his beard to his face, plastering his hair to the sides of his head, he looked like some creature of myth. A golem, not a human being with human weaknesses, and hopes and dreams. He moved so the great head swept around and the burning eyes found him.

Seeing a lion in a cage, or behind the bars and trenches of a zoo is a distinct experience. There, the creature is one of power and ferocity, but you are safe. You can imagine what it might be like to face such a thing, but it is all imagination, because you are safe. You don't really have to deal with the emotional impact of such a confrontation because of the bars and pits and fences.

But when those artificial boundaries are removed, what remains is the reality of the creature itself.

It was the way Tucker moved. For all of his bulk, he moved out of that truck like a python with legs. The way his eyes snap-locked onto Derek's. Although he was thirty feet away, Tucker seemed to cross the intervening distance in three strides.

Lightning flashed. Waites saw Tucker through a filter of red. He wondered if it was his own fear, something inside him telling him to run, to get the living hell away.

Then he wiped a hand over his own face, and realized that the red in his eyes was blood from a torn scalp. He was hurt in the roll from the car. In watching the drama playing out before him, he had missed the fact of his own injuries. His leg throbbed. It should have been enough to distract him, but wasn't. He barely even heard the sound of police sirens. Distant now, but growing closer.

Tucker was in front of him. Derek hadn't even seen the man move the last few feet. "Keys," Tucker said.

For a beat, Derek didn't move. The police sirens grew closer. Derek made his decision, the only decision he could make, and threw Tucker the keys.

He ran around to the passenger door as Tucker slid his bulk behind the wheel and gunned the engine. The wheels were spinning even before Derek could get in, and if he hadn't managed to get his leg into the car, the door would have broken it.

Through the mist, police flashers could be seen, converging now. *Shit, shit, shit.* They were doomed.

But that just wasn't true. In Tucker's hands, the car came to life, revealed strengths Derek had never imagined.

Tucker headed directly for one of the police cars, playing chicken. A second car was directly behind them. Derek clutched his seat and held his breath, not daring to speak or scream, although he felt like a boiler edging into the red. As the police cars grew closer and closer, their headlights filled his vision. That scream finally emerged unbidden, fully formed, a scream for life lost and this lunatic who cared nothing for his own safety. The man was insane, insane, and oh, my God, it had all been a mistake, Derek had killed his family, and—

It shouldn't have been possible, but Tucker seemed to know which way the patrol car's driver would swerve an instant before the driver himself did. Tucker went to the left, not the right that Derek would have expected. They missed the police car by a hairbreadth. The wheels spun and slid just a little on the wet pavement. The car fishtailed, but then Tucker was back in control.

Metal howled and screamed. Derek turned back and saw two of the police cars smashing right headlights.

A third car coming in behind them was blocked for a crucial instant by the two damaged cars, and was forced to slew sideways to avoid the pile-up.

And in that moment of indecision and blindness and pain and confusion, Tucker slipped into the night and the rain, and was gone.

23

The rain was driving hard, and Tucker drove harder. They were almost eighty miles away, traveling along side roads that Derek had never seen. Tucker pulled over beneath a stand of magnolias, and dimmed the headlights. For the past hour he had said nothing, just driving with an air of complete, cold concentration.

For almost four minutes they sat there, while Tucker peered out into the rain. Derek watched him, not daring to speak. Wet, the man smelled like some kind of animal—a clean animal, but an animal nonetheless. The barrel chest rose and fell slowly. Derek could see nothing out in that downpour. He had the odd notion that Tucker could see everything.

Although unable to hear them distinctly, Derek had the feeling that police sirens droned distantly, bleating. The police-band radio crackled plaintively on the seat behind them, directing the sweep of men and machines.

Derek listened to the radio, then turned back to Tucker.

Tucker stared at him as if he were some variety of paramecium. "Give me one reason not to throw your black ass into the rain," he said.

For just an instant, so intense were the glaring blue eyes, that not only could Derek think of no reason Tucker shouldn't throw him, but also no reason that he shouldn't *go*. Go anywhere. Get away from this man. Jesus, he knew that smell. It was a locker-room smell, a testosterone and sweat smell.

There was something about this human being so utterly male, so utterly masculine, that Derek felt almost feminized in his presence. He felt as if he were going to *wilt*. He couldn't let that happen. He knew that unless he kept control of the situation, his family would die. Horribly. And Tucker certainly wouldn't give a good goddamn.

"I know who killed your family," Derek said.

Tucker blinked once, slowly, like a lizard. When he spoke again, his voice was totally without inflection. "Name," he said.

Waites swallowed hard. "We can help each other," he said.

He didn't see Tucker's hand move, but suddenly the man's hand was at his throat.

The words "viselike grip" are an utter cliché. But the sudden, awful pain, the absolute constriction of the air passages, the dizzying reduction of blood to the brain, all of those suddenly made Derek aware of what that term *meant*. The fingers dug in cruelly, and Derek was hissing, trying to breathe, pitifully grateful when the fingers let up for a moment. Fear and corrosive anger flooded through him. His heart hammered in his chest. What kind of human being was this? He had never known physical power like this existed, let alone dreamed that he would ever be close enough to it for it to reach out and savage him.

"Name," Tucker repeated, and then relaxed his grip a little.

Derek had barely enough oxygen to speak. "Kill me," he frog-whispered, "and you'll never know."

Tucker looked at him as if Derek were a piece of mud he had somehow managed to smear on his hand. Something to be dealt with at a future time, something of temporary importance. He leaned his head very slowly to the side, evaluating. Derek could almost hear the gears turning in the man's head.

"If I had one hour," Tucker said, "I'd get the name, your fucking Swiss bank account, and the last time your mother gave head."

Faintly, sirens wailed in the distance. The hand squeezed his throat again, then relaxed a little, allowing him to speak again. When he spoke, he barely recognized his own voice. "My mother's *dead,* asshole. And you don't have an hour."

Tucker almost smiled. Almost, but not quite. As if back in the depths of that unfathomable mind, Derek's answer made sense, and even more, gained Derek an iota of desperately needed respect.

Slowly, Tucker shook his head. "No," he agreed. "I don't."

Then he released Derek's throat and started the engine. He waited another moment, then drove out into the rain and the night.

On the seat behind them, the police radio continued to crackle."—the search area for escaped convict Austin Tucker. Two guards dead, one wounded. Tucker is to be considered extremely dangerous. He is responsible for at least seven deaths, including his wife, and two children—"

Derek stole a glance at Tucker. The man drove without any emotional reaction to the words on the radio. As if they related to another man altogether. Or as if he was no longer a thing of blood, and bone, and heart.

At three o'clock in the morning, they pulled into the parking lot of the Laz-E-Boy Motel. It was still raining, but down here, in the heart of Los Angeles, the rain was a thinner gruel. "Wait here," Derek said to Tucker, and ran up the stairs to room 226. Tucker sat behind the wheel, engine idling.

Derek fumbled for his keys. He knew, for the last few miles he had absolutely *known* that in his absence death had reached out for his family. That when he returned to the room he would open the door to breathe the stench of burnt flesh, to stare into the lidless eyes of his wife and immolated daughter. That his son would be gone, leaving only a smear of blood around the room to suggest he had ever existed at all.

His hands shook as he fought to fit his keys into the lock, and he cursed under his breath, trying to steady himself, knowing that when he saw the carnage, when he saw the destruction, the death of the only human beings in the world who mattered to him, that he would find the strength to go on. That in the car behind him, there was a weapon of unimaginable violence, and that he would find the strength to use that weapon, and find the men or creatures who had brought death—

He opened the door, and a wedge of light fell into the room.

Rachel lay across the bed. Troy and Dee were curled, asleep beside her. When the light crossed her face she stirred. She shielded her eyes against the light, sudden fear taunting her beautiful face.

"Derek?" she asked, and in that one word, he knew the dreams that had plagued her nights. They must have been hellish.

He hugged her head against his waist, saw in her face the tears that had taken her into sleep.

"Medford's dead," she whispered. "I heard it on the radio. It's being played like some kind of a drug thing." He wanted to say something about the Indian, about the man who had said, *"I killed a TV star already today. . . ."*

But couldn't.

"Come on," he said quietly. "We have to go."

She nodded, without asking any more questions, and woke and dressed the children. Dee was never more than half-conscious, and Troy stumbled through the process, asking questions that Derek didn't answer.

There was nothing to pack, so they were up and out of the room within five minutes. Tucker idled the car. The rain had stopped, but the motel lights still glistened off the wet black concrete. Condensation from the car exhaust puffed like morning breath in winter.

Derek opened the rear door of the car and Troy tumbled in. For a moment he was still sleepy and unfocused. But as he came to fully realize that a stranger drove their car he became more alive, gave Tucker his full attention, seemed to draw conclusions rapidly despite the hour and his own sleepiness. His entire expression suddenly changed. He raised a thin finger. "You," he said, voice shaking. "I've seen you on TV! You're the serial killer. You're the Mad Dog dude on TV!" He paused, and Derek wasn't certain what his son was experiencing. Fear, terror, panic. Certainly. Disgust, rage, betrayal.

He turned to his father and raised his hand. Reflexively, almost without knowing what he was doing, Derek raised his own, and Troy high-fived him. "You did it!" Troy crowed. "Word up, Dad!"

Rachel, Dee asleep on her shoulder, had blanched. She was examining her ex-husband with a mixture of admiration and horror. And to Derek's surprise, Tucker was looking at Rachel with the first flush of genuine emotion that Derek had seen on the big man's face: fear and surprise.

"You actually did it," Rachel whispered. "My God."

She paused, and then, as if forced to compel her limbs to move against their will, she entered the car.

Derek slid into the front passenger seat and closed the door. Tucker backed them up, and pulled out of the parking lot. Water splashed up from the tires as they rolled through the gutter.

Tucker drove silently. They pulled out into the traffic. He put his head down slightly as a police car roared past, siren blaring.

Dee finally woke up, perhaps at the sound of the passing police car. She snuggled against her mommy, and then looked at the man in the driver's seat. She studied him hard, tensing at first, and then relaxed.

"You look like the other man," she said.

"What other man, honey?" Rachel asked.

"The man in my dream," Dee said. She seemed balanced

between dream and wakefulness, with most of her toes dangling into dream. For a minute Derek thought that she was finished speaking. Then she continued, "But you're not him. Grandmama says you're a good man. Where are you taking us, Mr. Warrior, sir?"

"He says it's somewhere safe," Derek said hurriedly. "Where we can think."

They turned onto the on-ramp, heading north toward the Santa Monica Freeway.

Rachel leaned forward across the seat. "But where?" she asked.

Derek turned to look at Tucker. So far, the man had been decidedly tight-lipped. But now, his bearded lips curled in response to some private joke.

"Where?" he asked. "That would be telling. But you're gonna love it."

24

They traveled the Santa Monica Freeway east to Ontario, where they took 15 north through towns with names like Wrightwood and Cajon Junction. Near Victorville they turned onto a network of back roads that Derek couldn't have found again if he had videotaped the entire procedure.

Derek drifted in and out of dream, but whenever he awakened, Tucker was at the wheel, driving in a steady, hyperalert trance state.

Once Derek awakened, and found that they had stopped at an all-night minimart with a single pump and a Confederate flag in the window. Tucker came out waving, wearing a new shirt, a baseball cap and a pair of sunglasses.

He got back into the car without a word, and started them off again.

At around three o'clock in the morning they came out onto a stretch of highway called 395, and motored north. Derek floated off again.

When he awoke, they were in mountains, and the sun was

rising behind them, its pink flush along the crests of the ridge.

Derek realized what had awakened him. They had taken a sudden turn onto an unpaved dirt road winding up into the mountains. The Tercel's springs could provide only marginal comfort. Rachel slept on, her arm nestled around the children. Her face was unusually peaceful. Derek's heart ached. It would be too easy to imagine that the Waites clan was headed to a beach or picnic, far away from anything more threatening than sunburn.

"Where are we?" he asked, and got no answer at all. A barbed-wire crested security gate loomed ahead of them. Two cameras rotated atop posts set twenty feet apart. From side to side, each unceasing sweep took about five seconds. When it passed them the third time it slowed, and locked as their car pulled up.

A three-inch speaker was set in a small, recessed black box atop a pole on the gravel drive. It crackled with static, and then a male voice asked, "Who the fuck are you?"

Tucker leaned out of the car on one massive elbow. "Tell Krause it's Tuck," he said.

They waited. Ten seconds, twenty. A minute, two. Five. Despite the cold, sweat drooled down the small of Derek's back.

Then, with the hum of a hidden electric motor, the gate clicked and swung slowly open.

Tucker drove up an uneven gravel road. As the car jounced, the children rubbed their eyes and took note of their surroundings, yawning. The gate swung slowly closed behind them.

The road was lined with pines on both sides. Derek thought he saw movement in the woods, signs of human activity. Signs of human habitation should have been comforting, but weren't. Men headed straight toward the car. Most wore black cloth armbands displaying crossed lightning bolts. He shuddered.

A twenty-foot guard tower ahead rose above the road, an even larger lightning bolt symbol was emblazoned on the side. Derek's stomach contracted to a sour knot.

Every face was white. Very.

Many of them carried small machine-guns, which he recognized as Uzis.

"Why would neo-Nazis carry Israeli weapons?" he said.

"They're not Nazis."

"What are they, then?"

The men looked very alert—hyperalert, in fact. Intelligent, but somehow out of focus, as if they were late to a party that had ended long ago, dancing to music that no longer played.

A few wan and pale-looking women were up at this hour, performing various chores and watching the car's progress with detached interest.

A few small children played games in the dirt: Soldier. Dodge ball. Cowboys and Indians. They looked dirty and tired.

"What is this place?" Derek asked warily.

Tucker chuckled, the first sign of mirth he had seen from the man. "Welcome to the Lightning Dawn, the California militia."

"If not Nazis, then what?"

"Patriots. OA's."

"OA?"

"Original Americans. Good, God-fearing folk. Hell, Waites—they're gonna *love* you!"

A hairy behemoth approached them. He wore black fatigues, with flared pants tucked into spit-shined army boots. His belly was enormous but looked hard, and hung over his belt like an awning. His beard was red, and for some reason Derek thought of Thor, the god of thunder. He bent down and stared at Tucker.

"You're Tucker, all right. Heard you'd busted out." He looked at Derek with a thin curiosity, and then at the three in the backseat. "What are *these* doing here?"

Tucker turned the engine off, and got out of the car. When he stood, Derek saw that his first impression was correct: Tucker was the smaller of the two men. But it was the guard who took the step back.

"What's your name?" he asked.

"Maddox," the man said. "Chip Maddox." Tucker shook his hand, with what looked like crushing strength.

"Well, yeah—for right now, I need their help." Tucker

said simply. "I don't want anybody fucking with them."

Derek felt the oddest, most confusing combination of emotions he had ever experienced. Sulfurous anger. Insult. Shame. And most unsettling of all, gratitude. Looking at the machine-guns, and the paramilitary hardware, he realized that they were in one of the survivalist encampments he had read about, and knew that Tucker was correct—as long as they were under his protection, the Waites family was safe. A small crowd had gathered. He estimated that there were two or three hundred people in the camp, counting women and children.

A crescent of bungalows bristled along a shallow slope of dusty hill. Twin flagpoles rose above the central quad. One carried the American flag, and the other its LD counterpart. Some of the territory behind the buildings was still shadowed, but Derek heard the staccato crackle of gunfire from somewhere out there. A firing range, and maybe an obstacle course. Someone getting his RDA of target practice before a hard afternoon's Jew-baiting. Afterward, curling up with a nice fire, cocoa and cookies and the Classics Illustrated edition of *Mein Kampf.*

The men were fit and hale, but seemed puffed up on their own egos. The women, more than half of them blond, looked weary and bedraggled, although some of them were attractive in an anemic way. They seemed like spiritual anorexics.

He was most frightened for the children.

The children knew only the world that the adults had made for them. Input only the data their parents had selected. The seven- and eight-year-olds stared at the Waites family with curiosity. The younger teenagers evaluated Troy as if wondering what kind of center fielder he might make. But the older teens, and their parents—

Displayed contempt. A searing hatred, shuttling young ones off, whispering to them, warning them. *"Let me tell you about those people. . . ."*

He had the feeling that the parents wanted to string them up as piñatas for bayonet practice.

Tucker leaned close to him. "Don't say a fucking word."

"What if someone speaks to me first?"

"I'm sure you know how to kiss ass. Can't be the first time."

Waites looked back at his son and daughter, and tried to weigh his choices. He didn't like any of them.

A tall, wiry man with wolfish good looks stepped yawning out of the center house. In contrast to the military crewcuts worn by most of the other men, he had a Jesus mane of brown hair that flowed almost to his shoulders. Derek guessed he was looking at Krause.

A voluptuous blonde wrapped in a nightgown emerged behind him. She swept her eyes from Krause to Tucker to the Waites children, to Rachel and Derek and back again. Her eyes narrowed as they locked onto Tucker. Somehow, in some manner that Derek couldn't completely understand, the situation had just changed. Derek doubted that Krause would have been thrilled to see the heat in her eyes as she regarded his old pal "Tuck."

Krause was busy giving Tucker a bone-crunching hug. "You god-damned goat-fucking son of a bitch!"

They pounded on each other in a few seconds of testosterone overload, then Krause turned. "Everybody!" he yelled. "This is Tucker!" He said that as if he had told the story many, many times before. "Saved my ass in the slam, I'll tell you!" He hawked noisily and spit in the dirt. What a stud. "We whipped the shit out of five of the biggest, blackest jungle bunnies you ever saw."

Yahoo. Derek guessed that Tucker had taken four and a half of them.

"We all make mistakes, Krause." Tucker's smile took the edge off the words. "Hello, Tonya," he said as the blonde came up behind Krause. "Thanks for the cookies."

"Pleasure," she said.

So. Tucker had saved Krause's ass in prison. Probably literally. Krause got out first, but maintained contact with Tucker. Tonya was the go-between, bringing a few goodies, along with messages, perhaps? He wondered if California allowed conjugal visits, and whether Krause had intended for their contacts to become as seriously smoky as they obviously had.

Oh, boy. We're having some fun now, aren't we? He felt

as if he had fallen all the way down the rabbit hole, perhaps into the George Lincoln Rockwell memorial edition of *Winnie the Pooh*. He saw his face superimposed on a fluffly little stuffed feline. *''Hi! I'm a Nigger! N-I-Double-Guh-ER! And the wonderful thing about Niggers—''*

Tucker didn't exactly ignore her glance, but acknowledgment of its subliminal content passed so swiftly that it was almost a microburst. ''You owe me sanctuary, Krause,'' he said. ''These . . . people are going to point me at the . . . people who killed my son.'' He seemed torn by conflicting emotions. Derek wasn't certain, but he had the impression that Tucker didn't completely like Krause. ''They need protection.''

Krause scratched his ear and laughed. ''Life is sure strange as shit. Strange as shit,'' he said. ''Okay. They can have the horse stall.''

Derek felt a wave of heat pass through him, but managed to control it. Humiliating or not, he needed these people.

Behind him, Troy said clearly, ''Horse stall?'' His adolescent indignation caused his voice to break. ''Son of a bitch!''

Derek turned and saw Rachel's strained face. ''Quiet.'' She was close to panic.

There was a general rustle. Derek had the impression that itchy fingers were a little closer to trigger guards.

But Tucker was also looking back at the car, and when he did, his eyes met Dee's. Dee sat, unnaturally calm for a little girl of her age. Despite the setting, although surrounded by hatred and threat, her little heart-shaped face shone with love. Oddly, that love seemed focused on Tucker. Derek watched it, watched the big man. Tucker's eyes softened, and the web of wrinkles spreading out from their corners relaxed.

Then the shell hardened again, and he was the same hulk who had climbed from the wrecked armored transport.

Tucker spoke quietly, looking at Dee. ''There's a little girl. Age of my daughter. She doesn't sleep in horse shit.'' He spat into the dust. ''They can stay with me.''

The words startled Derek. Something had happened there, and he wasn't at all certain what it was.

Krause was just as startled. His eyes narrowed, the feral

mind behind them searching for an answer that he could understand. His eyes fell upon Rachel.

Krause smiled nastily. "A debt is a debt, right? All right, you and your entourage can take cabin six." He indicated a shanty near the top of the hill, sweeping his arm to point it out as if he were a uniformed concierge welcoming them to the finest accommodations in the Ritz.

"Maddox," he said. "Help these *good people* to their room." Maddox wrenched the car door open.

"Out," he said to Rachel and Dee. They slid out past them.

A couple of soldiers opened the trunk, found nothing, and slammed it back down. Derek kept his family close beside him, and they trudged up the hill toward the cabin where he and his family would begin the process of saving their lives.

25

Through the back window, Derek watched some kind of night drill in progress. Men in light commando gear, camos and StarVision goggles moved through the woods in teams, firing at dummies dressed as rabbis, Arabs, and blacks with thick lips and coarse features. As they did, they didn't bother to maintain any kind of auditory discipline. There were snide comments, whoops of mirth, and a general impression of merrymaking. He had the distinct impression that their comments were louder than normal or necessary.

A nasty laugh followed by the promise, "We're comin' for you next, boy!" followed by a chattering burst of machine-gun fire, and some more unpleasant chortling.

Derek turned away from the window. Rachel sat in a corner of the cabin on a vinyl couch, holding both of her children close.

The cabin was relatively spacious, but sparsely decorated. The couch was a surprising luxury. A kitchenette took up one corner of the living room, and the single bedroom was to the left of the main door, the toilet—again something of a surprise given the rude conditions—to the right.

A large rectangular window in the front wall gave them a wonderful view of the main camp, the quad with the twin flagpoles, and other buildings.

Tucker had been gone for much of the day, telling Derek to stay put in the cabin. He had needed no urging. The last thing in the world he wanted to do was to wander around this camp full of lethally armed bigots. He might end up as a target dummy. Maybe his lips weren't thick enough, and features weren't as coarse and vacuous as those of the dummies currently in residence, but he was quite certain that his hosts were flexible enough to make do with the new and warm-blooded resources that had been delivered unto them.

Tucker walked into the cabin, followed closely by Tonya, who was doing a fairly decent job of remaining neutral. Only fairly decent, though. Derek was too damned aware of the energy between them. Tonya handed the blankets to Tucker at the doorway, as if afraid to step into the cabin. Perhaps it was distaste for the Waites clan—or something else.

The distaste was definitely there. He could imagine Lightning Dawn disinfecting the cabin with steam hoses and peroxide. Or maybe burning it to the earth, sowing the ground with salt, surrounding it with barbed wire and setting up skull-and-crossbones signs. He had a morbid fantasy about some poor fool, generations hence, after the Great Race War, accidentally planting crops on this tainted ground. And the squashes and pumpkins would come up looking precarved for Halloween, only with thick lips and nappy vines growing from the tops—

He shook his head. That way lay madness. Amusement, he admitted, but madness as well.

''Something to keep you warm,'' Tonya was saying.

Tucker took the blankets and leaned back against the wall, smiling almost to himself as he scanned her. ''You look a lot prettier without the glass wall,'' he said.

Tonya grinned. ''It gets better.''

She turned as one of the guards approached and threw a pair of sleeping bags into the room. They were rough, and smelled well used, but from Krause and this company, it was a remarkable concession.

"These are for you," Tucker said. "And now it's time to show me what the hell you can do." His heavy brows beetled together. "And you had better deliver."

There was no need to spell out the threat behind *that* comment. He understood full well what was at stake here. And if Derek forgot, even for a moment, he had only to look over at his family on the couch to remember what the cost for failure would be.

Tucker and Derek were bent over the laptop computer. They had set it up on a folding table, and at Tucker's request hooked its modem into Krause's cellular telephone. Tucker watched the play of names and numbers on it with increasing consternation. "Jesus Christ," he breathed. "What in the hell are you saying?"

Waites was patient, but growing more and more exasperated. "Look at the dates," he said. "In every case, disappearances of family members coincide with national disasters."

Tucker looked at him blankly. Derek remembered something one of his teachers had told him once: "Treat a student as if he is as intelligent as you—but just needs things explained."

"All right," he said, starting over at the beginning. "Look at this one. May second, 1917. We have a major tornado in Missouri. Five days later, Rachel's great-grand-uncle disappeared. And here. October twelve, 1954, Hurricane Hazel hit Washington, D.C. Three days *after* that, your cousin disappeared from Wheeling, West Virginia."

"Three days later . . ." Tucker's expression grew darker. "So you're saying that someone steals children after a disaster."

"Exactly. I think the disaster covers a snatch of indigents and petty criminals, anyone who won't be missed. Then they steal a member of Rachel's family. Your family."

"Why?"

"I don't know. I know that a lot of people disappeared from my family, and from yours. And a few days before each occurrence somewhere, within a few hundred miles, there was a major disaster. Earthquakes. Flood. Fire."

"And this has been going on for—?"

Derek shrugged. "The records aren't good enough. Since the Reconstruction, probably. Probably even earlier."

Tucker paced. "What about me?" he said. "November twenty-seventh, 1980. There wasn't any national disaster. No earthquakes, tornadoes, typhoons or anything."

His expression was a direct challenge.

Waites was unperturbed, prepared. "November twenty-first," he said. "MGM Grand Hotel fire in Las Vegas."

The thoughtful, and then shocked, expression on Tucker's face said that the impact had soaked in instantly. Good, good. Tucker wasn't just an animal. There was a mind in there somewhere, and it was possible to reach it. "Eighty-four dead. At least."

Tucker seemed stunned, but thoughtful. "This can't be real," he said, but Derek could tell that he was no longer fighting.

Outside, someone fired a machine-gun. The burst was a sharp, vicious staccato, a sting of rapid dull pops. Derek felt sick. He turned to watch Rachel, who stared out of the window.

For a long moment she didn't see him. She stood, in profile, watching the rehearsals of death and destruction, the preparation for genetic Armageddon. She looked at Tucker, and shook her head. She smiled weakly at Derek, arms crossed, head bowed slightly.

"Rache?" he asked. "You okay?"

She shook her head silently, honestly.

The front door opened. Maddox, the gigantic Viking guard, entered, pushing a wheelbarrow filled with crushed ice. Forgetting where he was, Derek said almost casually, "Take it to the bathtub, please."

The Lightning Dawn guard ignored him. He looked at Tucker with respect. "What'chu want me to do with this, Tucker?"

Tucker jerked his thumb toward the bathroom. "The tub, asshole," he said good-naturedly.

"You got it," Maddox rumbled, and trundled his load in.

Tucker grinned at Derek mirthlessly.

Derek shrugged. "Must be my manners," he said.

The ice was dumped in the tub with a crunch. Maddox thumped the wheelbarrow back down on the ground, and trundled it back out. Dee, who had been reading a copy of *Boy's Life* magazine detailing the adventures of Goofus and Gallant put it soberly aside and came to her father, burying her head against his waist.

He stroked her head, trying not to think about the next few hours. "Scared, baby? You don't have to do this."

"Yes," she said. "I do. They'll kill Troy if I don't. It's all right. She's a nice lady. She doesn't mean to hurt me. Or burn me up."

Tucker's eyes narrowed, and Derek felt the energy in the room shift again, as the big man's interest re-engaged. "Why? Why the burning, Dee?"

"Two souls can't fit into a single body," she said. "Grandmama needs to come into me to talk. She's been trying for a long time. A hundred years. And she gets a little better at it every time. But she's hurt a lot of her children learning. She knows more about it now." She stopped, considering. "At least, I hope she does." She paused, then said to her mother, "I need Mommy Lula's nightgown."

Like a little old woman, Dee walked into the bathroom and stripped down to her underwear.

Rachel helped her off with her things carefully, her own hands shaking. Derek thought that she looked something like a woman preparing her daughter for burial. Dee kissed her mother's lips gently, then climbed into the tub.

The ice crunched beneath her bare feet. Rachel slipped the nightgown over her daughter's head and shoulders, and held her hand as she lay down in the ice. She gave no sign of discomfort, which Derek found most disturbing of all.

She lay there for almost a full minute, eyes closed, her breath rising and falling slowly. Her eyelids fluttered.

"She's coming," Dee murmured.

Tucker seemed withdrawn, but watchful, and uncertain of himself.

"It's happening now," Derek said to him.

The big man seemed to be on the edge of real emotional distress. "How long?"

"Don't know. This is new to us, too."

He was about to say more when Dee's eyes flew open. When Dee's lips moved, the voice that passed them was an older woman's.

"I made a deal," she said. *"A deal to protect my family."* A pause, a very painful pause. *"I was so wrong."* A single tear rolled from the corner of Dee's left eye.

Tucker seemed to have drawn up inside himself. "That's the same voice my baby used." He sounded as if something inside him had just broken. Seeing Dee in the ice, hearing the voice that had come from his own daughter's mouth, he was undergoing some kind of terrible epiphany, some inner opening of trap doors leading down to some private, personal hell, some dark emotional battery that had sustained him for long prison years.

"That's the same voice my baby used." He looked pale.

Rachel ignored him. "What do they want?" she asked.

The vocal change was even more noticeable now. Dee's face was contorting, suggesting an older, more mature and tortured woman.

"African," Dee said, still in the other woman's voice. *"African wants his kingdom back. Master just wants to live forever. Got the soldiers, brought them back. He caught me."*

Derek leaned forward, desperate to catch every word. "Who? Who caught you?"

Dee started crying again. *"DuPris. He killed me."*

For several minutes there were no more words, just tears. The small, ice-damp body was wracked with convulsions. Rachel swabbed Dee's forehead.

Derek fished his hand down into the tub. Where the ice met her skin, it melted.

Dee began crying again. Rachel swabbed her head gently, wiping sweat and condensation away.

Derek touched his daughter's hand. It was fever hot, but no worse. The rest of the heat seemed to have been bled off into the ice. Tucker watched them.

"Ice," Tucker said. There was something wounded in his face. "We didn't have the time to get ice," he said.

Derek nodded. "You didn't know," he said.

Dee swallowed hard, and then spoke again. *"I can't help*

you more," she said apologetically. *"Even with the night-gown, I'd kill this body."*

"The nightgown?" Derek touched the fabric. The garment, so beautiful just days ago, was starting to look worn and ratty.

"My hair is woven into it," she said. *"My spirit can touch hers. It helps. But her body is so small. . . ."*

"Could I put it on?" Rachel asked. "I mean—could I put it next to my skin? Would that help?"

"No. Children are magic. The cloth is magic. The name is magic. The three together create a doorway."

"But we don't know enough. Is there anything—anything at all that you can do to help us?"

She paused, considering. *"There is a book. I wrote everything in ink mixed with my own blood. And there is another Dahlia,"* she said. *"I need another Dahlia. Bring the two Dahlias together, and the book. Between the three of them, I can come more fully into your world. Then, perhaps, we can find a way. Bring the three together. Spread out the hurt."*

Tucker spoke. Something in his voice told Derek that the man needed a plan. He was mission oriented, and without a clear idea of what to do next, he was almost lost. "Where is she? Where is the book?" he asked.

Dee spoke again in the older woman's voice. *"My people left the plantation. Went north. Settled north. Dahlia . . ."*

"Where?" Tucker asked urgently.

The girl's voice was weaker now. *"Chicago. Ask for the wedding chest."*

Dee's exhausted head fell forward onto her chest, and she made a soft snoring sound. With infinite care Derek and Rachel lifted their daughter up out of the ice, peeled off the wet nightgown and toweled her dry. Rachel slipped Dee into her pajamas and took her to her sleeping bag.

Dee didn't stir when her parents kissed her goodnight.

Tucker shook a cigarette out of its pack and lit it, taking a long, slow draw, staring into the air at nothing in particular. Then he looked at Derek. "What now?" he asked.

"Now I get to work," he said. "I've got my genealogical

program, and the rest is research.'' He took on a similar, detached expression.

''Why couldn't she have just told us?'' Troy asked.

''She came pretty close. The more time she spends in Dee, the more it hurts. But she gave us enough.''

''You'll get on it now,'' Tucker said. It wasn't a question.

''I'll need some coffee,'' Derek said. ''It's going to be a long night.''

''Coffee is doable.'' Tucker started toward the door. ''You can really do this?'' he asked. For the first time there was a hint of uncertainty, the need for reassurance.

For the first time Derek saw not the Green Beret, not the lethal killing machine, not the convicted murderer of his own family, not even a man who, for whatever reasons, saved a murderous loon named Krause. He saw a man sustaining himself on sheer emotional energy, and the only energy strong enough to sustain him through the long and lonely years was hatred. Now, for the first time in a decade, Tucker was allowing himself to feel something else, and he was afraid of the new feelings. Hope. Hope that there might be justice in the world. Hope that he might come face-to-face with the men who had destroyed his life. Hope.

Hope could kill.

Derek met his eye. ''This is what I do, Tucker. You keep my family safe. I'll get you to the men who destroyed yours. That's our deal, right?''

Tucker nodded. ''That's our deal.''

And he left.

Derek sat down and unbuckled his computer case. As it booted up, it sang the *Mission: Impossible* theme song to him. He sighed, remembering when he had added those sounds to the system folder, customizing it. That had been a happy day. There hadn't been that many happy days since then. But if he could do it, if the old skills were still there . . .

Hell—finding a woman named Dahlia Something who lived in Chicago, who was descended from the original Dahlia Childe, *had* to be easier than breaking a convicted multiple murderer out of a state prison.

Didn't it?

26

Troy Waites was the first to wake. He rolled in his sleeping bag, scratching lazily. He yawned in the chill morning air, and for a perfect moment didn't remember where he was.

The only time he could remember these smells and sounds and feelings was summer camp. Someplace called Round Meadow, a YMCA camp where his parents had sent him, and where he had spent one of the most wonderful weeks of his life. But that memory swiftly fled, and he was left with the memory of where he was. The Lightning Dawn camp was no benevolent association's gift to inner-city kids.

He sat up in the sleeping bag, still cocooned like a butterfly half emerged from its chrysalis, and looked around. Everyone was asleep—but not everyone was in his sleeping bag.

Derek Waites sagged over the portable computer. Against a black screen a cartoon kitten chased a bouncing ball around from side to side and back and forth.

Troy knew that his father must have worked all night long, trying to find information, searching for any clue that might mean life for the ones he loved. Troy pulled Derek's coat, up over his shoulders.

Outside of a window over to the right, men drilled in orderly formations. Someone barked orders in a loud, crude voice. He peeked out the window. Two men thrust bayonets into Afro-wigged dummies. They twisted the rifles before retracting, and Troy's stomach knotted.

This was worse than horrible. He had to find a way to cope with the fear, or it was going to destroy him.

27

Tucker worked at a metal lathe, grinding and polishing a twelve-inch length of flattened steel. It was unusually crafted, with a curved hand grip and an indentation to fit his thumb. The backside of the knife was a half-moon indentation. Eight inches of blade curved with deceptive gentleness to a point that was almost blunt.

This was a slicing weapon, not merely a stabbing one, and as he ground and polished, putting the edge into place, as he looked at the two pieces of synethetic bone that would form the grip, a sensation of warmth spread through him.

It was just too long since he held something like this in his hands, too long since he felt complete.

It was odd. All of the time in prison, he had felt like ice. Now, emerging into the outside world, even on this one mission of vengeance, made him feel incredibly alive. He whistled as he polished and honed.

He spun the knife in his hand, flipped it and let it settle in. It became an extension of his bones and muscles. His balance extended outward into it, and Tucker felt another rush of emotion, one swiftly embraced. He slashed the air, reversed the path of the knife, flowed with fire, felt the old memories, the old sensations racing back into him. God, *this* was right. This was who he had been, once, a long time before. Was it really that easy to forget who and what you are? Had the death of his family really done that to him?

The knife spun, a needle of glittering steel, flowing, fluttering almost like a living thing, passing from hand to hand with ever-growing fluidity. He visualized the three spheres of light, aligned them, and groaned with pleasure as the core of his body became luminous.

Yes, yes, yes. The glow spread from his central body out through his nerves and into his muscles.

God, it was so good. He moved, feinted, drew, swept, kicked low, slashed, stabbed. He caught imaginary wrists on the indentation on the back of his knife, and drew the knife across an imaginary throat, spun his enemy and took the throat again, kicked the body away and spun, dancing now, the knife alive in his hand—

There was a radio on behind him, and as he danced, feeling the years falling away, feeling the cocoon of pain and guilt dissolve some distant part of him heard "—and the manhunt for escaped killer Austin Tucker expanded through five counties—"

The radio suddenly clicked off. Tucker spun so quickly and fluidly that he almost seemed to flow through himself. He changed the grip on the knife from a fighting to a throwing position, shuffling to hold it by the blade so swiftly that it must have appeared magical.

Krause stood there, his mouth open, eyes wide and astonished. "I see you haven't lost it," he finally said.

Tucker froze there for a second, then flipped the knife over in his hand, and sat back at the polishing wheel, completing his edge.

Krause approached him carefully. "You know," he said, almost too casually, "I heard about the freak show last night."

"Freak show?" Tucker asked.

"The little bitch. The ice. Pretty fucking strange."

"Pretty strange," Tucker agreed. The wheel whined.

Krause went around to the other side of the table to watch the process. "My people are good God-fearin' folks," he said without a trace of irony. "This Mogambo bullshit seems kinda un-Christian to me."

Tucker didn't look up. "Me, too," he said. He flipped the knife into the air, caught it, juggled it with effortless dexterity.

Krause was riveted. He shook his long brown hair. "Jesus," he whispered. Then Tucker caught the knife and returned it to its sheath.

Krause shook his head. "Are you sure you can't teach my boys some of that?"

Tucker ignored the question. "I need to get to Chicago," he said.

"Sure, big man. Whatever you want."

Tucker grunted, and left the room. Krause rubbed his chin, playing with the straggly growths of hair, thinking his own dark thoughts.

28

Derek awoke in the morning to find the coat around his shoulders. Troy sat watching him, quiet, thoughtful.

He smiled at his son, nodding acknowledgment of the gesture, then washed up and went in search of breakfast.

The reactions that met his request for food were mixed. There was hatred, and suspicion, and contempt. And an edge of fear. Only a part of that was the fact that they were under Tucker's protection. Someone knew what had happened last night. The ice. The voice change. Word had gotten around, and Lightning Dawn wanted as little to do with him as possible.

After the Waites family ate a meager breakfast in their cabin, they explored the camp a little, keeping to themselves. They attracted stares and derisive laughter.

Derek stayed with Troy, and felt the boy's anger flare over and over again at every real or imagined slight. He hoped and prayed for all of their sakes that Troy would be able to keep it under control a while longer. They needed this sanctuary. A little derision wouldn't kill them.

On the other hand, he also shared Troy's frustration. Not only with their situation, but with his own impotence.

On an outdoor asphalt court, some of the LD men were playing a rough game of basketball. They pushed and shoved good-naturedly, driving each other hard. The mountain air was bracingly cold, but dark damp patches stained the chests and backs of their jerseys.

Tucker approached, cigarette in his mouth. He nodded to the men on the court when they hailed him, but addressed Derek. "We're working on transport. You're sure about the address in Chicago?"

"Talked to her on the phone," Derek said. "She'll be there."

"And this wedding chest?"

"I offered her a hundred dollars for a look at it. She said it was in storage, but she'd find it."

Tucker was taken a bit aback. "What did you tell her?"

"Not the truth, that's for goddamn sure. Got her interest."

One of the basketball players hailed Tucker. "Hey, Tuck," he said. "Heard you played a hell of a game in the joint."

Tucker shrugged.

"How about it?" the thin man urged. "Two bucks a point?"

Tucker gave a lopsided grin. In the last twenty-four hours the big man had relaxed noticeably. He walked out onto the court, and was handed the ball.

He bounced it twice, and then went in, fast.

Waites was prepared to remain impassive, but was impressed. Tucker's reflexes were awesome for a man so large.

True, he knew that the man was a fighter, but somehow he didn't expect him to be a graceful athlete as well. Despite the bearlike girth, clearly that is exactly what Tucker was—an athlete.

He moved as lightly as a bird, pivoting so smoothly and easily that he was reminded of a top-notch high school basketball player. Or of . . .

He looked down at Troy, who studied Tucker, unblinking. Evaluating. Judging.

Oh, shit.

Derek's heartbeat accelerated.

Tucker made first one and then a second basket, without really trying. The men scrambled around trying to defend against him, for all practical purposes utterly impotent.

They loved it, and finally broke up laughing, realizing that they could do nothing with him. He was faster than they were. His fakes were better, his timing superb, his acceleration a sight to behold. A man of his size just shouldn't have been able to do it, but he did.

Troy was almost smiling. Admiration? Derek wasn't certain.

One thin man slapped Tucker's shoulder. "You are absolutely too much. You should go pro with us."

"Niggers have taken over the sport," one of the others said. Tucker's smile didn't change.

"You got that right," the thin man said. "We could call ourselves the Aryan All-Stars, you know? Pound those spooks right into the ground—"

"He's not so *bad*," Derek heard someone say. Oh, shit, it was Troy.

"What?" the thin man said, incredulous that the dark-skinned victims of their hilarity might conceivably have an opinion, or dare to express it.

"I said, he's not so fucking *bad*."

Derek turned to Troy. "Let's watch our language—"

Troy rushed on. "I say you only think he's good 'cause you don't know shit about basketball."

The explosion of anger was instantaneous, and, Waites knew, entirely anticipated by his suicidal offspring.

"Fucking little bastard," one of the men said.

Tucker's face darkened. "You think you could show me something?"

Troy nodded confidently. "Bet your ass."

Derek held his breath. It was impossible for him to sort the different emotions warring in his heart at that moment. Shame, for placing his family in this situation to begin with. Anger, for the jibes and taunts that they had endured. And pride. He couldn't strike back, or at the very least hadn't been able to find a direct and safe way to do it. But his son, although just a boy, had made a challenge. In watching the boy, Derek made contact with something within himself that had been lost. Or . . .

Maybe he only *thought* it had been lost.

The thin man said, "Well, just come on out here, boy."

The menace was obvious, and Derek's heart broke. As fine a player as Troy was, he couldn't compete with grown men who wanted to hurt him.

Then something unexpected happened. Tucker put his hand up. He bounced the ball twice, and then caught it.

"No," Tucker said. "Just him and me." He looked directly at Troy, but Derek noticed that he had taken a small step sideways, subtly interposing himself between Troy and the other men. They seethed, but then relaxed, and nodded.

Troy looked to his father. His eyes virtually begged. Derek realized that Troy was at one of those terrible points that make or break human beings, and the relationships that bind them.

A thousand different responses seethed through his mind, but what finally came out felt like the most honest response, the one that came from the deepest and most genuinely compassionate part of his being.

"Kick his ass," Derek said.

Troy nodded, and walked out onto the court carefully, as if testing the ground every step of the way.

Tucker handed him the ball. Troy bounced it a few times, perhaps reassuring himself that it hadn't been booby-trapped. Then he looked up, David confronting Goliath. "Three points," he said. Tucker nodded, and Troy walked to the outside line.

From the corner of his eye, Derek saw that Rachel and Dee had appeared at the edge of the court. Dee looked a little sleepy, as though walking in semidream, but then woke up and seemed intensely interested.

Rachel, though, was in something close to a panic. "What in the world is he doing?"

"Shh," Derek said. "Let him go. He needs this."

"You mean *you* need this."

Troy exploded past the guarding Tucker, out onto the court. Derek caught his breath. *Damn,* but that boy was quick, and the almost percussive quality of the acceleration took Tucker by surprise. Troy shot past him, slid in like an ice-skater, pivoted, and shot. Tucker turned, too late, and the ball swished the basket.

"One," Troy grinned.

Tucker bounced the ball, watching Troy with what was clearly new appreciation. At the sidelines, the Lightning Dawn men hooted. "You gonna let that pickaninnie do that shit to you?"

"Kill his little black ass." The one who said that looked over at Rachel and grinned mirthlessly. "Why, I'm sorry, ma'am, is that your little nigger we're talking about?"

She remained silent, but her lips pressed into a thinner line.

Tucker took the ball out, bounced it, held it at his waist, and crouched. Even through the baggy pants, his enormous thighs bulged. Damn, but he was a big man, and the sheer size of him continued to make its sneaky impact on Derek.

Tucker faked left, and then drove right, the fake so good that Derek would have sworn the man would have to take the step out onto the court. What caught Derek completely by surprise was that Tucker's movement was as fast as Troy's. Troy was such a hummingbird—he would have expected Tucker to be like a rhino. But no, Tucker moved so lightly it seemed some kind of movie special effect. With that belly, and the heavy arms, it didn't seem possible that he could have an almost effeminate grace—but there it was.

But as fast as Tucker was, Troy still snuck in and stole the ball, pivoting to the left. Tucker faked a stumbling step, then reversed himself and stole the ball back, went for the shot. Missed. Troy got there half a step ahead of him, and managed to get the ball. Jesus. *He got the ball.*

A few stragglers at a time, a crowd began to gather. The inhabitants of the camp straggled in from other amusements, distracted from other tasks.

Some of them were men, many were younger, and puzzled, wondering what all the excitement was.

Derek concentrated. Tucker was as fast, but not as agile, not at this game, and his shooting wasn't quite as good. Maybe.

He made the basket on his second attempt, after an exchange of moves so blinding fast that Derek could barely distinguish them. And then something hit him: Rachel's concerns were groundless. Although Tucker was playing hard, he was also playing fair. He wasn't using his size or mass difference against the boy.

To play fair, or to humiliate him by winning with pure skill?

Troy went out, faked, and then went in on the original line with a movement so fluid he might have been dancing. He caught Tucker literally flat-footed.

Rachel's mouth was open. "I didn't know that he was that good," she whispered.

Derek thought, *If CBC covered high school basketball, maybe you'd show up for a game.*

But what he said was, "I didn't know *anyone* was that good."

It was true—and downright weird. Troy and Tucker were moving so fast it almost defied belief. The combinations of move and countermove pinged back and forth, faster and faster—

Almost as if the two of them existed in a separate reality. But Troy, as good as he was, wasn't *this* good. As quick as he was, wasn't *this* quick . . .

Unless . . .

Tucker. Something was being communicated from the older man to the younger, something uncanny.

Troy made the basket. Tucker went out, Troy stole the ball, shot, was blocked by Tucker. Tucker stole the ball and spun, virtually levitating his enormous mass. He made his second basket.

Tucker, anticipating Troy's next fake, covered the wrong angle and Troy powered past him.

Troy stopped, dribbling the ball while watching Tucker, until Tucker went for the ball. Troy spun, dancing away. Shot. Tucker blocked the shot, and this time Troy collided with him. Troy went sprawling.

Rachel's breath caught in her throat. The LD men hooted, slapped their thighs as the small, thin boy sat there on the ground, looking up in shock.

"See, see—" Rachel said. The expression on Troy's face was pure pain.

Rachel started out onto the court, but Derek stopped her.

"Wait. You've got to give him the chance."

"To what?" she asked, but waited.

Tucker looked chagrined. He sighed, and wiped his hands on his pants. The LD men hooted and laughed. Troy looked up at Tucker, his eyes glistening. Derek had seen that look before, too many times, and flushed with shame. His son was about to cry, right in front of all of these sick bastards.

Tucker extended his hand, and said, "Sorry."

Troy looked at the hand without taking it, and pushed himself shakily to his feet. Tucker handed him the ball.

Derek prayed. *Continue the game. Continue the game. Please don't quit. Even if you lose, don't quit.*

Troy wiped his face—then, as his arm came up to cover his eyes, faked around Tucker so fast that a communal "Hey!" went up from the assembled crowd. Tucker was after him like lightning, virtually no time lag between cause and effect, but Troy got to the basket first, made a hummingbird-fast fake, and a layup and—

Swished the basket.

Troy's fists shot up in the air with a gigantic gotcha grin on his face, and he roared, "He shoots, he *scores!*"

Utter silence from the crowd. Troy caught the ball, bounced it twice, and then threw it to Tucker. Tucker caught it as if it had been drawn to his hands like a magnet.

"Not bad," Troy said, "for an old white guy."

The crowd began to disperse. They were stunned by the display of skill, and clearly torn. The older men shook their heads, and some muttered curses. Somebody said "jungle bunny."

But one of the younger ones, a kid of about fourteen, looked at Troy with open admiration, and said, "Goddamn, that was good. You maybe want to play some one-on-one later?"

Troy looked back at his father, who nodded. The other kid gave a huge, toothy grin.

I'll be damned, Derek thought. *Kid probably wouldn't want Troy marrying his sister, but he's happy to shoot some hoop.*

And in this place, that was good enough.

"Sister's probably ugly anyway," he said.

"What?" Rachel said, confused. She didn't wait for an answer, but gathered Troy into her arms as he came off the court. "Don't ever do anything like that again." She hugged him fiercely. "You could have been hurt!"

Dee looked up at her big brother, her eyes shining. And Derek felt something that he hadn't felt in at least a week.

Happiness.

*　　*　　*

Tucker bounced the ball, looking at the Waites clan, a hint of a smile creasing his mouth. His body had been full of light. And he felt it, *felt it* spark over to the kid. What was his name? Troy?

For an instant there, it was like playing ball with his own son, with Billy. And that was a good feeling.

The crowd thinned until only one person remained. Tonya. And there was a question in her eyes, one that refused to be satisfied by an easy answer.

She smiled at him.

Tucker tossed the ball back over his shoulder, still keeping his eye on her. The ball swished the basket, without touching the rim. Tonya nodded to herself, and made a clapping motion without her palms actually touching. Tucker grinned, picked up his towel, and walked away.

Neither of them noticed Krause, watching from the side of the latrine building. And there was no trace of amusement on his face.

29

It was three o'clock in the afternoon. With the honk of a horn, a Jeep appeared. Derek Waites appeared on the cabin's front steps, barely recognizing the man driving the jeep. It was Tucker, clean shaven and hair cropped militarily short.

Derek shook his head in amazed amusement. The disguise was almost perfect.

Dee drew him down and kissed him soundly. " 'Bye, Daddy," she whispered, and then added, "It's dangerous."

"I know," he said soberly. What use in lying? "What else can I do?"

Rachel's hands rested protectively on Troy's shoulders. "Two days," he said.

She wrapped her arms around Derek, touching her lips to his, then backing away as if she had touched a hot plate. She bit her lower lip hard.

Tonya stood only a few feet away, her expression cool,

but not hostile. For the first time, he spoke to her directly.

"They're all I have," he said.

Their eyes met for an intense instant. Her gaze flickered to Tucker, and then back again. "Only monsters make war on children," she replied.

Derek hugged Troy, and the boy clung to him for dear life. Derek had a terrible premonition. He would fail his family again. They would all die here in this hateful place. Or death would come for Rachel, and Troy, and Dee, and he wouldn't be there to protect them.

No. Not this time. This time I won't let them down.

He disengaged himself from Troy, and looked at the boy with deadly seriousness. "I'll be back," he said.

Troy smiled faintly. "Wrong accent, Dad." Troy lowered his voice, and went into his Arnold impression. *"I'll be back."*

"I'll be back," Derek repeated.

"Needs work."

Derek jumped into the jeep with Tucker.

"Nice family you have there." Tucker slammed the truck into gear.

"Yeah," Derek answered, not knowing what else to say.

"I hope you can keep them."

So did Derek.

The Piper Cub sat at the end of a narrow dirt airstrip. The pilot already had the engine running.

Derek carried a small duffel bag onto the plane with him, and buckled in as Tucker slammed the door.

He closed his eyes as the plane taxied down the runway, wheels juddering.

Oh, Lord, keep my family safe from harm. Take me. Take me if you have to, but let them live. Please.

And then they were airborne.

Neither Tucker nor Derek Waites knew that they were being watched.

The two men who watched them wore camouflage shirts and pants, and lay in a stand of bushes a few hundred yards away.

Their faces were darkened artificially. They observed the entire proceedings, the unloading and the preparations, the taxiing and the takeoff, through binoculars. They watched and then, when the small plane was safely into the air, one of them whispered quietly into a radio.

Then, without speaking to each other, as if at a prearranged signal, they faded away into the bushes.

30

The room was a place of shadows and flickering candles. Its curtained, shadowed walls were scribed with glyphs and concentric circles.

The chamber lay thirty feet below the surface. It was warm and very dry. Rows of steel pipes along the ceiling hummed as they carried water, electricity, communications cables.

There was a single post set slightly off-center in the chamber. It was six feet tall, of dark square wood perhaps six inches to a side. Heavy metal manacles were anchored in two sides, four feet from the ground.

From somewhere below the chamber came screams, muffled by the earth. The sounds of human voices, sounds of agony and despair.

In the middle of the room, three concentric circles had been drawn in blue and gold and red. In the center of the innermost red circle sat an enormous black man.

His chest and face were graven with scars. He sat cross-legged, eyes open, pupils rolled up and vibrating side to side rapidly. Forty-three television monitors lined the chamber's walls.

He looked almost bearlike, so thick and broad were his chest and shoulders. He breathed slowly, no more than four or five a minute. His face was more feline than ursine, with sharp, intelligent eyes and lips that were thin for a man of his complexion. His teeth, although flat, somehow seemed . . . *sharp.*

The black man's meditating image appeared on each of

the television screens. Suddenly, his image winked off, and the visage of a white man appeared instead. First one monitor, and then another, and another, until his image filled them all.

The Caucasian also gave the impression of power. A man used to absolute obedience. His red hair framed a high forehead, and his cheeks were prominent, suggesting a skull shape even though there was plenty of healthy flesh on his cheeks.

He stared out, as if he could see through the monitor screen. "Niles," he said. "They left the compound. Long-range sound pickups suggest they are headed to Chicago. I'm certain you know where. Your people can kill them there."

The black man began breathing more rapidly. His eyes rolled down a millimeter. His lips moved almost imperceptibly, but his voice was strong. "I will do what is necessary—but yours must do their part. They must not fail me again."

The white man's face tautened. "I'm not sure I like your tone of voice."

Niles allowed himself a slight, mocking smile. "Your former slave apologizes, my friend. I sometimes forget how much I owe you."

The white man laughed back. "You don't frighten me," he said. "Save it for those you intimidate." The African had already closed his eyes, sinking back into the dark dreams he loved.

DuPris's image winked off the monitors one at a time, leaving them dark as the African's skin. The darkness swallowed them both.

31

Their plane arrived in Reno in late afternoon and touched down at one of the smaller runways, taxiing to a hangar rented to small aircraft for standard maintenance. Tucker and Derek deplaned, and walked casually to the main terminal, where tickets awaited them for a flight to Chicago, under names that were not their own.

Derek felt every eye upon him, wondered when the pointing fingers would mark them out, when the accusing voices would raise in alarm. When the guns and batons would drive them to their knees, and handcuffs would click into place.

It didn't happen. Tucker walked on casually, talking about a nonexistent business meeting in Chicago. Anyone who came close would have heard a lot of low-information chatter about a line of athletic supplies, just enough to seem like a normal, distracted conversation, not enough to draw anyone's attention or invite a comment or participation.

A policeman strolled past, studying faces. Tucker nodded politely, then continued the conversation. His body language was so relaxed that Derek found himself struggling to remember their desperate circumstances.

It finally occurred to him why they were so unlikely to be stopped and questioned. Beyond a doubt, Tucker was described in the police reports as being a member of the Aryan Brotherhood or Lightning Dawn. And as such, traveling with a black man was the most perfect camouflage imaginable.

Right next to them, a newspaper headline blared about a search of the California-Nevada-Arizona tristate area for the escaped serial killer, the article emblazoned with a clear picture of the bearded desperado Tucker. The policeman looked at the newspaper, and then straight at Tucker without the flicker of an eyelash.

When the boarding call came, they stepped onto the American Airlines jet without a backward glance, and were seated without comment. Derek began to breathe again.

As they sat there, a stewardess passed out magazines from a well-stocked pushcart. *Business Week, Byte, People.* A lady three rows behind them selected *People* magazine and began to browse the pages. It was two weeks old, but still of interest. There was a where-are-they-now article discussing the black holes that had eaten Tatum O'Neal, Linda Lovelace, and John Travolta.

And then there was another article, this one toward the back of the magazine. It was entitled ''Mystery Celebrities.''

The article was the usual *People* magazine chatter, with a trace of the mysterious. It involved people of note who were reclusive, who remained out of the public eye for one reason or another. "Reclusive as Garbo . . ." one of them said. There was the usual sprinkling of aged matinee idols and sex symbols who remained out of the public eye. These hoped their video or celluloid images would be the lasting memory, not the drug-, food-, or time-wasted remnants of a once fabulous face or form.

But there were a few others, as well. One was a penniless European prince, once a notorious playboy, now a happy family man wedded to a shipping heiress. And in a box on the lower left corner of the page, there was another picture, another capsule description.

"DuPris," it said, "the reclusive pornographer, multimillionaire publisher of *Looker,* the biggest men's magazine in the country. Once the host of the most notorious orgies in Hollywood, whose guest list included governors and senators, the reported seducer of more women than any man in modern history. DuPris hasn't been seen in over ten years. . . ."

It continued, in panderingly lubricious detail and tone. That was all standard ops. The thing that might have seemed remarkable, had anyone noticed, was a telephoto shot taken of DuPris on his yacht. The photograph had reportedly been taken about twelve years before. The yacht was enormous, a seventy-footer. DuPris was yelling down to someone on the dock. His shirt was open to the waist. He was clearly in excellent physical condition.

The photo was grainy, overexposed, and indistinct. It was also, unmistakably, a photo of Austin Tucker, or of someone who looked so much like him that they might have been twins.

32

Their plane touched down at O'Hare International Airport at ten P.M. They collected their luggage quickly, took the red striped bus out to the Avis lot and rented a car on a fake credit card obtained from Krause.

They took I-190 to the Kennedy Highway, past an industrial center, in toward Chicago.

"Not sure I like the idea of ripping off Avis," Derek muttered.

"Bills are paid," Tucker assured him. "But in the name of 'Buster Silvers.'" The identity was often used by various Lightning Dawn men during different missions. If a crime was ever connected with the name, all papers associated with it were destroyed. This was a useful ploy, as it was impossible to put together a coherent description of "Buster Silvers." A 7-Eleven clerk remembered a tall, thin galoot. A piece of videotape at a service station showed a stocky short man, balding, who never quite showed his face to the camera. And a bank teller only remembered a tall, bearded man with the charisma of a movie star, who took a cash advance for a thousand dollars and flirted with her outrageously.

The Buster Silvers identity would probably remain in operation until its natural terminus—say, the execution of a Commisymp senator, or the bombing of an IRS office.

Tucker turned off the Kennedy at the southeast Clybourne exit, sliding through streets that looked more like industrial than residential districts.

Derek had thought himself inured to poverty and the extreme desperation it could produce. But the people on these streets seemed a different breed altogether from what he was used to in Los Angeles. These streets were darker, more cramped, and in some odd way he had the feeling they were visiting a Third World country.

Burned-out traffic lights snarled the sparse traffic. Liquor stores with gated windows advertised cheap beer, and even cheaper vodka concoctions. Stores were boarded up, factory doors chained. Streetlights were broken, creating endless pools of shadow in which indistinct human figures crouched hot eyed, watching.

Women prowled the streets hungrily, seeking to survive another night by whatever means necessary. From second-story windows blared music with driving beat and rhythm but little melody. The lyrics were muddled, but the tone screamed violence, rage, and raw sex.

Tucker drove, following a map clipped to the sun visor.

A wizened black man crossed the street ahead of them, pushing a cart that held all his worldly belongings. Tucker came to a stop. The old man looked at them with eyes that had once faced other men with dignity and hope. Little of either remained.

"I can't believe people live like this in America," Tucker said. "Where's their pride?" His voice said that he didn't expect an answer.

Derek's neck burned. "Maybe they're doing the best they can with the cards good old America dealt them."

Tucker laughed sourly. "I'd say God dealt those cards. Take it up with Him."

Derek had an almost overwhelming urge to smash his elbow into Tucker's throat, despite the terminal consequences. "Maybe I'll just send you up with a telegram," he said.

Tucker's laughter this time was genuine, and almost warm. "Big dreams, little man."

They turned onto Division Street, and Derek watched a gigantic row of buildings rise up on their right. As Tucker approached them, Derek saw that they were part of a complex of beige high-rises that looked more like factories than apartments.

However, apartment buildings they were, six, seven, eight of them. A mega-apartment complex. Gigantic, like nothing in California. They looked like prison barracks in some penitentiary of a dark, dystopic future. Four of the gigantic structures were spaced around the same city block. There was nothing green in sight, nothing but pavement and concrete. No trees. A few abandoned cars along the streets.

The buildings were about forty stories high. Fire escapes

winding up the sides were fenced off. The entrances were fenced.

"Metal detectors," Derek said, pointing. His intonation made it a curse. "Children have to go through metal detectors to get to their own homes."

Cabrini Green. During the entire flight, he had tried not to think about this, tried not to imagine how it would be to enter one of America's sickest social sores, a square block of hopelessness, and helplessness.

Tucker parked, and drew a nine-millimeter Glock automatic from beneath the seat, checked it carefully, slid it into a holster at the small of his back. He checked a holster beneath his left arm. It held a knife, and when he drew it out and checked the blade, Derek had the unmistakable feeling that the knife was a double-edged tool with a single purpose. Tucker hadn't been wearing the knife or holster when they went through the metal detector at the airport, of that Derek was certain. When, then, had he slipped it on? Derek had no idea, and it made him vaguely uncomfortable.

Across the street, lounging in front of the apartments, were several slender black youths. So far, they had paid no attention to the men in the car.

Despite that, Derek felt some fragile emotional barrier giving way, and he was more afraid here, among his own people, than in the middle of the survivalist camp. And for that, he felt utterly ashamed.

"Maybe," he began tentatively, "maybe I should have a gun, too."

Tucker studied the boys across the street. The youngsters bristled. Tucker chuckled, and slipped the knife back into its sheath. "These are your homeboys," he said mildly. "Hell, they'll probably bake you a bean pie."

Tucker was out of the car before Derek had decided what to do next. He hated the feeling that this bear of a man was just one step ahead of him at every moment, but there it was.

Derek locked his door, thrust his hands deeply into his coat pockets, and joined Tucker.

It was almost ten-thirty. A thin, shrill wind blew from the north, tumbling a few crumpled scraps of trash down the street. None of the tenement's windows were broken, which surprised him. But the impression remained that those windows were portals to an alien world, and that the street they crossed was a no-man's land between sanity and hell.

Distantly, a police siren wailed. It never came any closer, it never seemed to go farther away. It just started, and then stopped.

The four young men watched them as they approached, and Derek had little doubt that they would have accosted him if he had been by himself. But they sensed something about Tucker, had more sense than to mess with him. Maybe it was something about the way a man walks when he's carrying a Glock and a big knife. Or maybe it was just something about Tucker.

A curtain of steel mesh shrouded the front gate. It was dark back there, but Derek had the distinct impression of somebody hiding in the shadows.

As they reached the front door, a voice called out, "Whatchu want, dude?"

The voice came from lower than he expected. And it was a younger voice than he would have thought. His eyes finally adjusted to the gloom, and he made out a boy, no more than sixteen, sitting on a chair in the shadows.

"We're here to see Dahlia Washington. Fifteenth floor."

The boy dug out a scrap of paper. "Yeah," he said. "You on the list."

Five seconds later the entry buzzed, and they were in. Much to his surprise, Tucker's armament didn't set off the alarm.

The halls were narrow and claustrophobic. A couple of chain-latched doors opened, and faces peered out from behind them questioningly. The faces were curious and irritated, with little fear, but little expectation of joy either, as if the more extreme emotions had been flensed from their systems.

Beyond the front door, down the street perhaps, a gunshot rang out hollowly. Somewhat to Derek's surprise, Tucker jumped a bit, and plucked nervously at his collar. So: the Ultimate Warrior had nerves just like anyone else.

A door cracked open, and a little black girl opened it, looked out at them. She reminded him of Dee, not quite as pretty, but the eyes were huge and lovely. He couldn't shake the feeling that this girl had known genuine hunger. And yet she seemed plump. He couldn't quite reconcile the two warring impressions. An adult woman appeared behind the child, pulled her back into the apartment with sharp words, closed the door.

Derek and Tucker entered an elevator.

The interior was covered with gang symbols. They reminded Derek of glyphs he had seen drawn by outback abos in *National Geographic* magazine. One reminded him vaguely of something . . . a little man in a bottle, maybe. He was too exhausted to make the association. If he wasn't mistaken, he had had perhaps eight hours of sleep in the last three days, and it just wasn't enough. He was running on ephedra tablets and adrenaline.

A hollow-eyed black woman entered the elevator. Chronologically she might have been in her forties, but spiritually she seemed dead, hundreds of years old. Drained of all hope. She looked at Derek, and then at Tucker. Her face was dull and incurious. She let her gaze fix on the floor, and there it remained until the elevator paused on the twelfth floor. She exited.

"Why didn't the metal detectors pick up your cannon?" Derek asked.

"Glocks don't have much metal in them to begin with. This one's been modified with some pretty advanced plastics. About a third the normal amount of metal."

"And the knife?"

"Oh—that's *all* plastic. Won't hold an edge long, but it's a throwaway anyway."

Derek and Tucker continued up to the fifteenth floor, which was actually the fourteenth. What was he supposed to think of a society that castigated people for being superstitious, but then reinforced it by refusing to label the thirteenth floor the thirteenth floor?

Somewhere down the hall, a man was crying. Televisions and radios blared, the meaningless sounds blending one into another, melding into a symphony of confusion. Waites knocked at the door marked 15-Q.

There was a long pause, and then the door opened as wide

as a security chain would allow. A face appeared behind the door. The breath froze in his throat, and he felt the floor drop out from underneath him.

It was Rachel. No, it couldn't be, but this woman looked almost exactly like Rachel. A little younger, but at the same time more cruelly used. There was a wealth of dearly won knowledge in that face, but little of Rachel's intelligence, and none of Rachel's fierce clarity.

She wore a yellow housecoat that was tied in the front with a sash, and seemed in danger of falling open. The body beneath it was lush, almost overripe. She might have been as young as twenty-three, but had seen enough despair to last a dozen lifetimes. Deep circles ringed her eyes. Her hair was matted and nappy.

She spent another few moments sizing them up, and then said, "Yeah? What do you want?"

Derek spoke quickly. "I talked to you on the phone."

"How I know you who you say?"

"I'm married to your cousin Rachel. Out in California. Did you find the chest?"

"Maybe," she said, but made no move to unlatch the chain.

Derek dug in his wallet, and found a picture of Rachel and the kids in front of their old house in Santa Monica. He remembered that house too well. He also remembered being dragged out of it in front of his son.

He pushed it through the vertical crack she had opened. She plucked it from his fingers, peering with undisguised interest. "This some kind of trick picture?" she asked finally. He could almost see the gears turning in front of her eyes. That house had cost almost three hundred thousand dollars.

"It's not a trick," he assured her.

A crafty smile wound its way across her lips. "This your house?"

"Yeah, it's my house."

The door closed. He heard the chain rattle, and then she opened it wide. "Come on in, baby," she said.

33

Dahlia Washington motioned for them to sit on a couch that looked as if it had been bought at a secondhand sale, then refurbished by Kmart. A gaudy pastiche of yellow flowers glared at them from its slipcover.

A plastic slipcovered chair that almost, but not quite, matched the couch sat kitty-corner to the couch, and Dahlia plopped down onto it in an open-legged posture, arms and legs arranged apparently without concern for the impression they made on a visitor. But the subtext was unmistakable: an open, challenging sexuality that had never been completely harnessed to the emotional drives that supported it.

Derek scanned the apartment. It wasn't clean, but wasn't dirty, either. He had the impression that it was kept in a state of half-readiness, as if it could be made presentable with an hour's frantic cleaning. He suspected that she preferred, or at least accepted, the general clutter as a part of her daily life.

The appliances were incongruously expensive: a four-hundred-dollar Orek vacuum cleaner, a fifty-inch Mitsubishi projection television set, a fancy food processor that still looked as new as the day it left its box. He sensed a mixed message about the whole arrangement, but couldn't quite put his fingers on the meaning.

Dahlia flipped her head casually, indicating the entire contents and context of the apartment. "It ain't much," she said, "but my man, he pays for it."

"Where is he?" Tucker asked.

Dahlia laughed with genuine mirth, tinged with something just a little dark.

"Oh, you don't want to meet up with Scar Man," she promised them.

Derek was genuinely puzzled. "Scar Man?"

She ignored the implied question. "Why you want to see the wedding chest?" she asked.

"I'm doing a book on my wife's family. You know, the stories about Grandmama Dahlia?"

Dahlia Washington's eyes narrowed, caution and pleasure in them at the same time. "It's her chest all right. I got it, 'cause Mama named me for her. Should have gotten that old nightgown, too, but Aunt Dee got mad at my mama and held on to it."

"You should have gotten both?"

"That's the family story. But Aunt Dee gave it to her sister's girl, Charlotte."

Derek sat up with a jolt. "That's Rachel's great-aunt Charlotte. Was Dahlia really your great-aunt?"

"What?"

"Was she your mother's aunt?"

Dahlia Washington bobbed her head. "Yeah, I guess so."

"Shit," Derek said. "Great-aunt gave it to Rachel's mother, who left it in her will for Dee. So chest, and nightgown, and maybe other things were all supposed to go together, and got split up because of a family argument."

"So you just want to see it? A hundred dollars?"

Derek produced five twenties and passed them to Dahlia Washington.

The bills vanished into her pocket. As she opened a closet, she talked. "It's been in storage for years. Still a lot of furniture stored up. Fifteen a month, every month, just to keep it. . . ."

She bent, and then straightened, carrying with her a cedar chest the size of a large hatbox. She set it in front of Derek. His hands shook as he opened it.

The wood was smooth, and surprisingly warm to the touch. It seemed to have been stained a darker brown, with streaks of black, and thick metal hasps that looked newer than the wood. Someone had replaced the originals, maybe fifty years before.

The workmanship was excellent. "This belonged to Grandmama?"

Dahlia nodded.

Tucker examined it as well. "Fine work," he said. "Better than you'd expect a slave to have."

Within were several internested shelves, the first of them

empty. It might have held a folded nightgown. There were items of jewelry, and he examined these carefully. "Did you ever wear any of these?" he asked. One looked like a silver coil, but most of them were carved of wood, or bits of glass or base metal. Nice, but simple, and in some cases, plastic. Recent. Most of the things in the box had been purchased in the last fifty years or so, certainly between the turn of the century and the time when Dahlia placed the box in storage.

He took out the next nested shelf, and looked under.

More gewgaws. Some little glass-bead earrings, something bought at a county fair. A set of rings, probably not gold. Some crystal tumblers, and some sets of handkerchiefs. Derek held them up to the light, to see if odd dark threads ran through them.

Nothing.

"This is bullshit," Tucker said. "We wasted our goddamn time."

Derek sat, thinking. "No," he said carefully. "I don't believe that." He held the box up, examined its dimensions. "Doesn't the bottom of this box look a little *thick* to you?"

Dahlia Washington grunted. "Whatchu mean?"

But Tucker understood instantly. The bottom of the box was at least an inch thicker than the sides or the lid. "Shit. False bottom."

Derek felt around in the bottom of the box, and found nothing, then turned it upside down. There were four little leglets, one at each corner. Each was grooved like a screw. Derek pulled out his key ring. On it was a little multipurpose tool, and one of its attachments was a short, wide screwdriver.

"Now, don't you hurt that—" Dahlia said. Her interest was fully engaged now.

Derek examined the bottom carefully, pressed his blade against the first leg, and applied pressure. After a moment, it moved counterclockwise a half turn. He repeated the action with each of the other legs.

He turned the box over again, and probed inside. The inner wall didn't quite touch the edges of the wooden floor. A gap just large enough for the blade of his screwdriver had opened. He pried it up.

Hidden inside were two flat black leather books, each three quarters of an inch thick. Derek gingerly lifted them out, and looked up at Tucker, who nodded.

"I never knew. . . ." Dahlia said.

"Somebody knew," Derek said. "I bet that once upon a time the nightgown, and the books, and the family legend, and everything else were all part of the same thing. A few generations down the road, it gets fragmented, and nobody remembers, nobody teaches their children anymore. A heritage is lost." He gingerly opened the first book and turned a page. "Damned good paper," he said. "Somebody chose carefully. Looks like a diary."

He looked at the pages, touched them, examined the careful scrawl. He drew his finger along the page. The ink was a rusty brown-black.

He was holding more than history. He was holding something sacred.

Dahlia took it out of his hand. "That's mine," she said.

"I'd like to borrow it. I'll pay—"

Before he could finish his sentence, a linking door to another apartment opened. Another woman, very dark, not as pretty as Dahlia. She carried a crying baby. The baby was very dark. It wailed somberly, knotting and unknotting its little fists as if disturbed more by existential issues than the irritation of soiled Pampers.

The woman said, "Dahlia? You watch Sugar for a few? I gotta get to the store."

Dahlia said, "Sure, Glory."

Glory finally seemed to focus on Derek and Tucker, as if just realizing that they existed. "Who are you?" she asked.

Dahlia laughed again, and this time unease mingled with the laughter. "They wanted to see my wedding chest. And asking questions about Scar," she said, in the same way another woman might have said, "He wants to stick his hand in a blender."

Derek wondered what Glory's reaction would be. Alarm, disinterest, anger. He was surprised when Glory gave them a lazy, sensual smile. "He ain't like no man you ever seen," she assured them.

"What do you mean?" Tucker asked.

Glory handed the baby off to Dahlia. She extracted a pack of Kools from her purse, lit one and puffed twice before answering. "He knock boots with my auntie 'fore he took up with me. She old now. He still young."

Derek narrowed his eyes, alert for falsehoods. He looked at Dahlia. "I thought he was *your* man, Dahlia."

Dahlia laughed again, this time more genuinely amused. "Hell. He got seven, eight women, just right here. Kids, too. Takes care of 'em."

"Pays support?" Tucker asked.

She nodded. "And finds rich families to take 'em."

That one rocked Derek. "You . . . let him take your children?"

The air suddenly changed, and the two women looked at each other, then back. There was a flash of defiance, and maybe guilt, and just a touch of something unutterably weary in their expressions.

"They get better homes," Glory explained. "He a good man. But he too much man for you." She looked significantly at Tucker, appreciating his mass without being overtly impressed by it. "For both of y'all," she added.

That seemed to end her willingness to talk to them. Without another word, Glory left the room.

They waited for a moment, wondering what was coming next. They didn't have long to wait. Dahlia Washington levered herself up from the chair as if she were a much older woman, and said, "Heard that much, might as well see."

"See what?"

She placed the books back into the chest, and led them through the open door, into a linked warren of rooms. The first of them was much like Dahlia's apartment. A large-screen television displayed an old movie that Derek couldn't quite name, something with Peter Lorre playing a Japanese spy. Lorre did some kind of judo move on a German officer. The officer flipped through the air with the greatest of ease, and landed hard on the floor.

"Mr. Moto," Tucker said.

"Nope," Derek corrected. *"Invisible Agent."*

Tucker grunted.

The woman watching the television screen was very pregnant. Maybe eight months, swollen almost to bursting. She drank what he hoped was fruit juice out of a paper bag through a straw. The orange fluid rose and fell with each slow sip. She glanced up at them without actually seeming to see them.

There were three children on the floor around her feet, ages two to maybe six. They cavorted in a cleared play area, with toys that appeared new, and maybe even pricey, but impersonally chosen. As if someone who cared little had given a wad of money to someone who cared even less, and told them to buy tranquilizers for rug rats.

When Dahlia led them into another apartment, and then another, Derek saw that the scene more or less repeated: multiple children, single mothers. No sign of men around, no children older than seven or so.

The adjacent apartment walls had been knocked out to create this odd warren.

"Breeding pit," Derek whispered. He thought that the whisper was to himself. Beside him, Tucker nodded without speaking.

The children were huge eyed, and stared unblinkingly at the television screens. Some of them displayed shows, others were merely vehicles for violent video games.

There was no way that Derek could escape the thought that they were . . . waiting for something. Something. Not acting. Not planning. Barely thinking. Mostly just waiting.

"We all cousins," Washington explained, as if suddenly touched by the need to explain. "Glory, she my aunt Tessie's girl. Eva, she by my great-aunt Pearl—"

Tucker broke in. "Aren't there any other men?"

Washington shook her head. She also shook a cigarette out of a slender package, and lit it. She blew a smoke ring toward the ceiling. "They don't last too long," she said, as if her comment explained everything.

A question tickled at the back of Derek's mind, something that she had said and then glossed over. "You said that Scar finds homes for the children," he asked.

She nodded. "He take 'em to rich folks he know in New York, Florida, Texas. . . ."

She led them back into her apartment, and poured herself

a drink. Cigarettes. Alcohol. Televisions everywhere. This place was an addict's paradise. He wondered if cocaine, heroine or barbiturates were secreted about. Now that he thought about it, he was fairly certain that he smelled marijuana.

Her hands shook.

"What do you know about Grandmama Dahlia?" he asked. "Dahlia Childe?"

Something stirred in the back of her eyes. "Oh, yeah," she said. "Saved her family by leading troops back to the old plantation. I look mighty saved, don't I?"

He ignored the jibe. "Do you have kids?"

Her hands shook worse. She downed a slug of whatever the hell she had poured. "One," she said. "Ginger. Don't know where she is. Scar came, took her, two years ago."

She finished her drink, and started another one. Derek sidled around to where he could peer into the trash bin behind the wet bar. There were at least three bottles of what he could identify as a cheap vodka-and-orange-juice preparation.

"Why did you let him take Ginger?" he asked.

She laughed, and this time there was no trace of true mirth in it. "You don't say no to old Scar," she said.

She poured herself some more screwdriver, and held it with both hands, drinking greedily.

Tucker spoke, his voice utterly flat. "So he came, and took your baby to a wonderful new home."

She peered at him from over the top of the glass. "What you want from me? My rich cousin got some money for me?"

"I need information," Derek said. "I can pay for it. Is there anything about your ancestor Dahlia you can tell us? Anything about this man, Scar?"

She wagged her head with disingenuous sorrow. "He just come when he come. And we best be ready for him."

Derek persisted. "Is there any history of strangeness in your family? Or psychic phenomena?"

That, curiously enough, got her attention. "What?" She asked.

He pushed on doggedly. "Any little girls talking out of their years? Did you, when you were a girl, or do you ever now—"

* * *

Behind her, Tucker moved to the window, peering out and down. He wasn't happy with what he saw. Two cars pulled up in front of the building, and then a third. Eleven, maybe twelve men emerged, wearing heavy coats, hats, projecting everything that his senses told him meant danger. They exchanged greetings with the men sitting in the front of the building.

Trouble.

"What do you really want?" Dahlia asked. Her voice was shrill.

"The truth," Tucker said.

Washington had reached some kind of threshold. The entire building seemed suddenly too quiet. Derek's nerves sizzled.

"You best get out," she said. "Get the hell out." She threw her glass across the room, where it shattered, leaving a wet orange blossom on the wall. "Caught me drinking. I talk too damn much when I drink."

"What are you afraid of?" Derek asked.

"This all I got. You get out. My man's a good man. You just don't know what love is."

Tucker's ear was pressed against the door. Derek looked at him, at his face, and something in it froze the smaller man. One of Tucker's big hands motioned them out of the line of the doorway. He flattened against the wall.

Dahlia's eyes were huge, as if she understood but refused to believe that something was about to happen.

And then, the door burst open.

34

Two huge black men in gang colors exploded through the door. The smaller was armed with a Remington shotgun. He swept the room with a short, jerky motion, almost as if he were under the influence of some stimulant, not quite in synch with his physical responses.

But before he could fully register who or what was in the room, Tucker moved. The knife was in his hand. Tucker deflected the shotgun barrel with his left hand, stroked across the throat with the right, twisted, and suddenly the bleeding body catapulted into the second man, cartwheeling and spraying blood. The second man loosed an Uzi burst into the ceiling, but Tucker was there a moment later. The two gangsters hit the floor together, dying or dead.

Tucker slammed the door shut with his foot, then hit the floor rolling. A hail of bullets ripped through the doorway, blowing the top half of the door into splinters. Waites pushed Dahlia ahead of him into the next room. They were both screaming, Dahlia incoherent, Waites bellowing: "Out! Get the children out!"

Tucker crouched behind the wet bar, waiting.

Children ran past, one of them, a small girl in shorts, glanced at Tucker, her eyes wide with fear, frantic to ask a single question: *What is happening?*

He couldn't tell them what he didn't know. All he knew was that they had to move, and move quickly, or they were all going to die.

The third man through the door died before the fourth knew that there was still someone in the apartment. Tucker drew a careful bead on him, fired three times, twice in the body and once in the head, *tap-tap-tap*, blowing him backward against the wall, where he slid down with a surprised expression on his face, as if he had never truly contemplated the possibility of death coming for him. Anyone else. Everyone else. But not *him*.

"Guess again," Tucker snarled, and shot the next man in the head as he came into view.

A scream from the room behind him chilled his blood. He braced his back against the wall and kicked at the wet bar. It wasn't bolted into place, wasn't built in by the original construction crew. It was just hooked up to the plumbing with a wrench. Tucker toppled it onto its side. The joints groaned and ripped free. Water sprayed as it fell, blocking half the doorway.

Cheap, he thought, and back-rolled through the door, coming to a halt with the Glock cupped in his hands and ready to fire.

A gangster tossed a girl out of the way, trying to get through the second doorway. "Hey!" Tucker yelled, and the man half turned, spinning the girl around as a shield.

It didn't matter. From Tucker's low angle, even though the man crouched, eight inches of head were exposed. Inside Tucker lights knit into a blazing white cocoon. Time slowed to a crawl. He had all the time in the world to fire at an upward angle, taking the top of the man's skull off.

He barreled into the next room in time to see Glory shot in the stomach. She screamed, clutching herself. Red oozed through her fingers as she died.

Tucker was there in a long slow-motion stride, seized muscular wrists and pivoted. He hurled her killer into the window as if throwing the hammer. The gangster hit the window butt first.

Tucker saw the glass fragment, cracks spreading out like earthquake fault lines. The gangster bleated like a sheep, but was stuck there, stunned and cut by glass. He grabbed at the frame with bleeding fingers and tried to haul himself back into the room. Tucker took a short step and heel-kicked the man out of the window. He fell ten screaming stories to the street below.

Tucker tried to usher the children through the apartment into the next room, uncertain why he was doing it, or what safety might lie there. He heard glass breaking, smelled gasoline, felt the floor shake with the *whumf* of a Molotov. The lights died.

A giant of a man rose out of the darkness, and his gun flashed almost in Tucker's face. For an instant Tucker couldn't see. He crashed into the man, shoulder first.

At grappling range, sight was unimportant. The first touch told him where the rest of his opponent's body was. Fingers closed with crushing power. A head-butt broke the man's nose. The gangster forgot about the gun in his hand, forgot about everything except the sudden, terrible pain in his face. Tucker actually *felt* the bastard's will collapse. Spun him by his shoulders, broke his neck and let him fall without another thought.

Big, and strong and fast, but no *heart*. He sneered.

Fire licked into the room. Tucker heard screams from elsewhere in the building now, and it was clear that the organism called Cabrini Green was awake.

He finally managed to catch up with Derek and Dahlia, who crouched in the dark, waiting for . . . something. He could see the fear in her eyes clearly. "Who are they?" she asked, her teeth chattering.

Before he could answer, the door next to her was kicked open. A gangster charged in, grabbing Dahlia Washington, smashing Waites to the side. As Derek was flung back, he managed to get both hands around the gangster's gun hand, almost dragged him down. The gangster kicked Derek once, hard, but the programmer's fingers stayed glued to that gun. The gangster stopped trying to get it loose, and came at Tucker. Tucker's attention was split: he was firing at a man coming through the bedroom door. Click. The piece was empty. He whirled in time to see the gangster coming at him like a boxer, fists swinging.

Tucker brushed a right cross aside and hit the man precisely in the center of the chest with his palm, exhaling harshly, knees soft, hips dropping. It was a whiplash caress.

The gangster's entire body vibrated. He collapsed as if he had been boned. Dead without a mark.

Tucker turned to see Dahlia Washington gaping at him.

"Come on," he said. Smoke filled the air. The halls were filled with screaming chaos, women bundling children up and hustling them out. Dahlia and Waites each carried babies in their arms.

Tucker jostled past and tried to force a path for them through the crowd, which was panicking.

He looked down the hallway, which was thick with smoke now, and he saw . . . something like a stick-thin human being. It couldn't have been human, though—it moved too damned fast.

Reflexively, he drew a bead on it. It screamed and zipped from wall to wall, bouncing like a ball, trying to get close to them.

He fired a shot at it, and it disappeared into one of the rooms, and was gone.

"What the hell was *that?*" Derek whispered.

"I don't know, and I don't want to know. Come on."

Tucker slammed a stairwell door open. It was jammed with fleeing people. Almost at his feet, a small black child looked up at him with its arms outstretched, teetering backward as feet threatened to trample him.

Tucker bent to pick the kid up—and a cadaverously thin woman hit him in a blur, smashed into him from behind. She seemed to materialize out of thin air, attacking so quickly and fiercely that Tucker fell through the mass of people, tumbling down the stairs.

All the way down, the woman shrieked, raining blows on Tucker's face and chest. Tucker, stunned, could do little save cover up. Tucker's head slammed into the wall at the bottom of the stairs, driving his teeth into his underlip. Blood trickled from his wound.

He struggled to get his knife back out, but his coordination was gone. No magical flicker this time, just a slow-motion exercise in futility.

The witch snatched the knife from Tucker and reared back, shrieking in some kind of weird triumph, preparing to stab. She paused at the peak of her arc, eyes flaming.

Before she could complete her action, Derek ripped a fire extinguisher from the wall and bounded down the stairs, swinging wildly. He smashed the fire extinguisher against her head with a sound like a gong being struck with a leg of lamb.

She went down, hard.

Waites got his hands under Tucker's armpits, helped him up. There was a moment of hazy recognition, and then another moment when Tucker's lips moved, as if there were something he wanted to say, but couldn't quite phrase it. Then the three of them, and the children they held, were down the stairs and heading for the exit.

If Derek Waites had taken the time to examine the woman he had clubbed more thoroughly, he would have seen something that would have interested him. Around her scrawny neck was a rope, and dangling from that rope was a leather sack. Inside it, something the size of a woman's fist lay curled up, a thing of dessicated skin and bones.

It might have meant nothing to Derek. Conversely, it might have meant everything.

35

A crowd had gathered, clustering, pointing, as the fire engines arrived. Dahlia Washington had already handed off the children she carried to one of her cousins. She was shaking, her hair streaked with sweat and soot, but in some odd way, Derek found her more attractive now.

"What is this shit?" She was nearly babbling. "What happen in there? Why this happen?"

Derek gazed at the building. It poured smoke now. "You can thank Scar for that," he said. "He, or somebody like him, has been killing your family for two hundred years."

Dahlia Washington turned away, but Derek grabbed hold of her shoulders and turned her back.

"You listen to me," he said. "All of the children he took from you and your cousins are *dead.*"

She twisted as if he had hooked her through the middle. "No," she almost spat at him. "Ain't true."

He was merciless. The red revolving light of the emergency vehicles flashed on and off against his face, giving him a slightly satanic air. "You know it's true. And it will keep being true until it is stopped."

He dug into his pocket, pulled out the picture of his family. His hands were shaking.

He showed her the photograph. "This is Troy. My son," he said. "He's thirteen. He's going to die unless you help us."

Her voice sounded so small, so pitiful and helpless, that he felt almost sorry for her. Almost, but not quiet. "What can I do? Can't do nothing."

"Yes, you can. You . . . hold the secret. You, and my wife,

and my daughter, and Dahlia Childe . . . all share something. You can save my boy.''

Dahlia Washington stared at the photo in her hand, and then looked up at the building. Smoked gushed out of its windows now, even as tongues of water lapped at it, seeking its heat.

''We should have grabbed those diaries,'' Tucker said ruefully.

Derek looked at him, reached back beneath his jacket and extracted the books from between belt and shirt. ''You mean these?'' he said.

Dahlia Washington gaped. ''How you—?''

''Just as soon as you left the room,'' he said. ''One way or another, they're coming back with me.''

Tucker coughed and turned away, but Derek would have sworn the big man was grinning.

Dahlia's arms were wrapped tightly around her chest. She seemed small, and terrified almost beyond belief.

But she nodded her head, and said, ''All right.''

The Pan Am jet's turbo engines droned on in the early morning air, carrying Derek Waites and his strange allies to their destiny. Dahlia was asleep. Derek gazed at her, brushing a curl of hair out of her eyes.

Tucker watched them both.

''Jesus,'' Tucker said finally. ''Just like your wife. Fucking twins.''

Waites silently sank back into his seat.

There were a few more moments of silence, and then Tucker said, ''You saved my ass in there. That bitch had me.''

Waites was aware that he was being handed a compliment, and didn't know quite what to do with it. He was ready for many things between himself and Tucker, but not that.

He thought, and realized that there was something he wanted to say, something that he hadn't wanted to express to a man he hated. But now, at this moment, he felt none of the hate. ''I've never seen anything like what you did in Cabrini,'' he said truthfully. ''Never seen anything like you.'' *Except maybe that woman.*

"What was she?" Waites asked. "What is it that you have? And what was it that happened to Troy, on the basketball court with you?"

Tucker shook his head. "I don't know much. It's something in the blood. You have to be born with it, and then taught how to use it. Troy has some of it. So did that woman. I think she was a crackhead, too, by the look of her. Whatever it is that I've got . . . that Troy's got . . . she couldn't quite control it. Turned her crazy. Lucky, or she would have killed me."

They were both quiet. The adrenaline burn was long gone now. Little remained save complete exhaustion. And that, perhaps, made truth easier to come by.

Tucker actually smiled, the edges of his heavy lips tugging upward a little. The smile was a genuine one. There was nothing nasty or secretive or supercilious about it, and it virtually transformed his face. For an instant, Derek had a view of another man entirely. "You're pretty fucking smart," he said. "Good with that computer. I never saw you steal those books. And you don't piss yourself under fire."

Derek felt himself smile, and realized that he didn't want to. That some part of himself needed to dislike Tucker.

Tucker looked out the window at the lights and clouds far below them, as if measuring the distance between himself and the remainder of humanity. Then he looked back.

"What happened?" Tucker asked. "Between you and your wife?"

Again, Derek was surprised to find a genuine level of human inquiry there. The man wasn't the golem he had supposed . . . or had needed. Damn. What was he thinking? He tried to find an answer, and once again, perhaps he was just so extremely tired, he took refuge in the truth.

"Me and Rachel?" he asked. "We grew up together. Same elementary school—Alta Loma. Junior high school—Mount Vernon. High School, Los Angeles High. She was president of the class, I was the honors science student." He paused, flooded by memories. "God, she was beautiful, and by some freak chance, she loved me. Me."

Tucker nodded, as if this possibility didn't surprise him. "It happens," he said quietly.

"We dated after high school, and after I got my masters we got married. I had my own software firm, Prometheus Engineering."

Tucker laughed sharply.

"Rachel worked for CBC. Started as an intern, and worked her way up. I had a little fun on the side. Computer hacking. I called myself Captain Africa, King of the Cybernet. Shit. I could get into anything, and did. There was Captain Crunch, and Mr. Miracle, and Captain Africa. We were absolutely the biggest names in hacking and fone phreaking back in the eighties. Shit." He had to shake his head. In spite of the pain that those memories conjured, he had to admit that there was also a load of pleasure.

Tucker's voice brought him out of his reverie. "So what happened?"

Derek was shocked at how swiftly the positive mood soured. "One of my customers stiffed me, and I couldn't retaliate legally."

"Why was that?"

"I was under contract to his corporation, not to him personally. After I delivered nearly a year's worth of work, he folded his corporation, and started a new one—using my software. It was a type of legal theft."

Tucker considered. "Can someone *do* that?"

"You bet your ass. Happens all the time. I decided to get even. I broke into his accounting files, and transferred funds to my own account. Covered my tracks perfectly."

"So what went wrong?"

"Human error. I had six employees at the time. One of them was dating a girl in the accounting department of the other company, and never mentioned it to me. I made the mistake of hinting about what I had done."

He winced at the utter, complete stupidity of his actions. How could he have been so asinine? "Nothing direct. Just, one week we're almost totally broke, the next week everyone has his back pay. And I joke about how Mr. X had finally come through on his debts. Well, there was some pillow talk, and this girl knew that money had disappeared, and the next thing I know, the FBI is at my front door."

"That's a bitch," Tucker said with genuine sympathy.

Derek was hypnotized by the old pain now. "If I'd been white, I'd have gotten rich. Writing books, doing security consulting: 'How did you do it, Mr. Waites?' But they threw my ass in jail." He paused. He felt himself sliding down a bottomless emotional pit, and didn't want to do that now, didn't even know how he had gotten so close to the edge. "Something just . . . broke. Inside." He touched his chest, just over his heart. "Everything just . . . went downhill after that."

"How long?" Tucker asked quietly. "How much time?"

"Two years," Derek said. "I lost two years of my life."

"Because you're black." Tucker's voice was dangerously quiet, and only after Derek replied did he begin to see where Tucker was leading.

"What else?"

Tucker leaned back into his seat, and closed his eyes. "You did two years for a crime you actually committed, and it's because you're black. I did twelve years, for something I *didn't* do. Tell me, *Captain Africa*, who am I supposed to blame?"

Tucker turned away from him, toward the window. His short moment of vulnerability was over, as certainly as if it had never begun at all. Derek stared at him, realizing what he had done, what it had cost Tucker to open his shell for even the barest fraction of a moment, and that he was wholly to blame for rupturing the slender thread of trust that had been spun between them.

And stared out into the gloom of the plane, wishing that he could take the words back, as he had wished to undo so many actions, replay so many conversations, earn one more chance to make things right.

One last chance.

36

It was almost eight o'clock in the morning when they arrived at LAX and deplaned. They gathered their meager luggage and finally pulled away from the big green box of the National Rent-a-Car building, driving a Ford minivan rented with the Buster Silvers identity.

Tucker drove, his face impassive. He had said little since they landed, and nothing of any personal import. The radio was tuned to a country-western station, but as they crossed the security spikes leading out onto Airport Avenue, a news broadcast began.

"The final tally from the riot damage will reach close to a billion dollars." The words on the radio lacked full impact—the rest of the shock was rendered by looking at the twisted, burned buildings they passed on the way to the freeway.

Tucker turned it off. His face betrayed nothing.

"So what do you think about that?" he asked.

Derek considered. "When I heard the verdict, I think I wanted to kill someone."

"But you didn't."

"No. I have a career. A way of getting the things I want out of the system by playing by the rules. When things are working well, I make more money than most white people. I can be pissed all I want—but I'm not going to try to take the system down."

Tucker grunted. "Aren't we the buppie."

"What about you?" Derek asked. "What was your take on it?"

Tucker shrugged. "Looked to me like Rodney King pissed some cops off, and they beat the shit out of him."

Derek felt himself heat under the collar. "They're cops. They're not supposed to react like that."

"They're also human beings," Tucker said mildly. "You try chasing a speeding, erratic driver for miles. He might be crazy, on drugs, whatever—he's certainly a stupid, self-destructive man. You want to get home to your family tonight, and realize that this might be the asshole who blows your head off. Do you have any idea at all how high your adrenaline gets, at a time like that?''

Derek considered. ''Maybe I got a taste of it last night.''

''Yeah, right. Now, this asshole gets out of his car, and shakes his butt at you. Makes a fool of you. They're cops, but they're also men, you get it? And *men* respond to things like that.''

''If they can't keep their reactions under control, they shouldn't be cops.''

Tucker shrugged. ''You want the job?''

They drove on for a while, neither speaking. ''So you think they were right?''

''I think they were human, and that has to be factored in. Besides, he was fighting them. Resisting arrest. They didn't have any responsibility to get down on the ground and wrestle with him.''

Derek chose his next words carefully. ''So they were scared of him.''

''Damned straight.''

''Five white men, armed with guns, tasers, tear gas, batons, and backed up by twenty more cops, and they were scared of one black man?''

Tucker paused. ''You've never been there,'' Tucker said.

''I guess I haven't.''

Derek took a certain amount of dirty satisfaction in noting that Tucker's ears were reddening slightly. ''Tell me,'' he asked. ''Would *you* have been afraid?''

Tucker stared straight ahead at the road as he drove.

''Aha,'' Derek said. ''And you're used to dealing with men under stress. Men you can trust to back you up. Judging by their performance when confronted by one unarmed man, would you have wanted any of those cops to back you up in a combat situation?''

Again, Tucker stared at the road. After almost a full minute, he said, ''No.''

''Thank you,'' Derek said. ''So we can come to the conclusion that if they were good men, they were bad cops. In other words they wanted to be good, but hadn't the courage or training to do it. Or if they were good cops—in other words, they had the courage and training to do what was right—they chose not to, and were therefore bad men.''

''It's not that black-and-white—'' Tucker said, but then his face twisted into a grin and he started laughing. ''All right, asshole. You win that one.''

Dahlia hadn't really been listening to their conversation, she was mostly staring out the window. ''I never been to L.A. before,'' she said quietly.

A police car cruised past them, and was caught at a red light at the corner of Century and Aviation. Tucker seemed to shrink back into his seat. One of the cops looked at him very casually, and then continued talking to his partner. When the light turned green, the cruiser pulled on.

Dahlia was watching Tucker and his reaction. ''What kind of law trouble you got?'' she asked.

Tucker's semijovial mood had completely vanished. ''They killed my family,'' he said. ''I took the fall for it.''

Derek watched them both. She wasn't intelligent the way Rachel was, but did seem to have some kind of intuitive understanding. ''That why you *angry* all the time? Seems like you ain't got nothing inside you but hate.'' She smiled, and the smile had surprising warmth, took some of the sting out of her words. ''That ain't no way to live.''

''No,'' Tucker agreed. ''But it's a way to kill.''

She nodded. ''You good at killing. You hit that man in the heart, didn't you?'' She made a little pumping action with her palm, miming a martial-arts face. ''Some kung-fu shit.''

''Yeah,'' Tucker sounded tired. ''Some kung-fu shit.''

''Just stopped him cold, not a mark.''

Tucker's hands were locked on the wheel, and his eyes were fixed on the road ahead. ''Just stopped him. No marks. No pain.'' Beat. ''Better than the shitball deserved.''

37

Their rented car pulled through Lightning Dawn's security gate at a little past two o'clock.

Derek had grown increasingly anxious for the past hour.

Now, as the car came to a halt, and Derek saw none of his family, he knew that his predictions had been accurate. Visions of bloodshed and rape swam up to drown him. He searched the faces and forms that surged to meet them, looking for brown faces, brown arms, hoping and praying that his decision to bring them here hadn't been the worst mistake of his entire life.

It felt as if everything had stopped, the world gone silent. When Dee's blessed little form appeared, running toward him, he felt the impact of her smile as certainly as if she were a cardiac needle loaded with adrenaline. She swarmed into his arms, covering his face with kisses. Her eyes widened as she finally saw the woman getting out of the backseat of the car. Shock, surprise, and then understanding piled one upon another so quickly they were almost, but not quite, a single emotion.

Troy was right behind her, and he had yet really to focus on Dahlia Washington. "Hey, Dad!" he yelled. "Are you all right?"

Then he skidded to a stop as his gaze slid over to Dahlia Washington, and he fell silent. His mouth opened, and he looked back at his mother, who was coming through the group behind him, as if wondering if she had somehow managed to get ahead of him and switch clothes.

When Rachel appeared, she was brought up absolutely short, her huge chocolate eyes widening even further.

Dahlia Washington seemed to be enjoying herself. After all, she had had long hours to adjust herself to the new reality, and Rachel was still dealing with shock.

"Hey, cuz." She smirked.

Rachel glanced back and forth from Derek to Dahlia and

back again. The entire crowd was silent, as curious and cautious about the entire interaction as Rachel. *Must be sisters. Long-lost sisters. Cousins. Hell, they breed like rats—everybody humping everybody . . . who knows. . . .*

The two women circled each other carefully. The difference between them was instantly obvious. Despite living in the rude surroundings of the LD encampment for three days now, Rachel was still infinitely more elegant than Dahlia Washington. Somehow, she had managed to keep the same slacks and blouse clean and relatively neat, and even given them an illusion of being pressed. Dahlia Washington, wearing a simple dress purchased from an airport shop, seemed somehow dowdy in comparison.

Still, they were exact duplicates, as if a single soul manifested in two different bodies in slightly different times. Dahlia was ten years the younger, but her eyes were older by lifetimes.

She reached out and brushed a finger at Rachel's sweater. "Where you get the sweater?" she asked. "Ain't Kmart."

Rachel managed a small smile, and to pull back from Dahlia's grasp without seeming to reject her. "Fleming's," she said. "That's in Beverly Hills."

Dahlia Washington's smile was genuine, mixed with admiration, envy, and sheer urchin pleasure. "We *got* to go shopping, girlfriend."

Rachel's expression was a kaleidoscope of mixed emotions. The woman standing before her was like a dark mirror—what Rachel had fled her entire life: ignorance, poverty, moral disintegration.

Rachel's worst nightmare. "If you can help my son, I'll buy you anything you want."

Dahlia grinned again, and this time her face reminded Derek of Rachel's back in high school. "Word up," she said. It was strange. This woman seemed to be a very young Rachel, and a very old one at the exact same time. Somehow she had skipped right over her own generation. Odd.

Dee was the next to break the silence. She took Dahlia Washington's hand in her own small fingers. "I'm glad you're here," she said. "Everything will be all right now, I know it."

Derek heard those words and didn't really know what to think or feel. Everything seemed very fucking not-all-right, everything in the entire world but all right, but somehow when Dee said it, he found that he couldn't find the heart to say that she was wrong.

Krause ushered Tucker into his office. For once, his mood and tone were not deferential. He stormed in as if expecting Tucker to follow him closely, turned as if he expected Tucker to be hanging on his every word and action, spoke as if Tucker should be waiting for the Voice of Doom.

Instead, Tucker was at the first table near the door, leaning back against the wall, browsing a stack of survival, knife, gun, and girlie magazines. He thumbed a copy of *Looker*, glanced at the masthead, and then looked up. "You know, I used to have *Looker* number one? What is it? Forty years now? Shit, I could have sold that bad boy and retired." Two of Krause's men entered close behind him, standing ready.

Krause glared at him. "Other people breed chinchillas," he barked. "If you want to breed pickaninnies, do it somewhere else."

Tucker's voice remained calm. "This is important, Krause. More than you know."

Krause's chest heaved with emotion. "You know, I think I got it," he said finally. "You're related to 'em somehow, ain't you? Your grandpappy have a taste for dark meat? Or is there a nigger in the woodpile—"

Krause was in a half crouch, as if expecting some kind of physical intimidation. His two men, watching, were quiet, unsure what to make of the tableau.

Tucker slide-stepped up to the bearded Krause and suddenly Krause was against the wall with a boom that shook the entire building. The move wasn't particularly fast, or frantic, in fact it almost seemed as if Krause had cooperated with the motion. Somehow, Tucker's fingers were enmeshed in Krause's hair, and Krause's face was scraping against the wall.

"I think you might want your guys to leave," Tucker whispered. His hand shifted from Krause's hair to his shoulder. The two men looked at each other uneasily. When

Krause hesitated, Tucker added, "There's something I want to say, and I don't think you want them to hear it."

Something passed between them, then, and Krause managed to turn his head so that he was facing his men. "I'll be all right," he said. "You can wait outside the door." He said the last with a voice that parodied his former imperious tones.

The two soldiers let their hands drift away from the pistol grips, and left the room. Tucker eased up a little on the pressure. "Now you listen to me," he hissed. "You shut up, and help me here, or my memory's going to clear up. You know what I'll remember?"

Krause's expression was more rodent than wolf now. The man looked trapped, cornered. The hatred flaring from his eyes was enough to melt tungsten.

"No answer, Krause? You know what that makes me think? It makes me think that you've forgotten, too. Or maybe after all this time, you've actually managed to convince yourself that your little fantasy is the truth. Have you done that?" Tucker's voice was an ugly whisper. "Have you actually managed to do that?"

"Fuck you," Krause grunted, but in the back of his eyes there was something desperate, something that almost pleaded with Tucker to stop now, stop before something was said that couldn't be undone.

Tucker was merciless. "Know what I remember, 'Bro me? You. Stretched over a washing machine, with four men taking turns on your pale narrow ass. Four *white* men. And from what I saw of your ass, they must have been mighty desperate."

Krause was trembling now, a narrow thread of drool working its way loose from his lower lip, dangling. He sniffed it back.

Tucker went on, his grin as humorless as a shark's. "Not exactly the great Krause triumphant against a raging mob of buck niggers, was it?"

"Fuck you," Krause said again, but there is no heat in it at all this time.

"No, fuck *you*. I will do anything, anything at all, to avenge my family. And I need these people to do it. If you play ball with me, I'll tell these little no-nut G.I. Joe wannabes anything you want about how big and bad you were in the joint. I'll tell them about the time I got froggy with you, and you kicked my ass. I'll tell them you parted the Red Sea. But don't fuck with me on this one, Krause. Don't make that mistake. Don't. Fuck. With me.''

Like magic, the knife appeared in Tucker's hand. He brought it close to Krause's right eye, very close. Krause stared at it, and made a great intake of breath, as if preparing himself to scream. Then the blade veered, nicked his ear instead, no more than a quarter of an inch, just enough so that a single tear-sized drop of blood began to ooze from the wound.

Then Tucker slammed him against the wall again, and stormed out. Krause leaned against the wall and wiped at his ear with his grubby shirt, furious.

The bodyguards entered instantly as Tucker left, and stared at Krause. Krause's synthetic smile did little to improve his appearance.

"He's like my big brother," Krause said to them jovially. "Sometimes we piss each other off. A family thing. Don't sweat it." He paused. "When he cools off, get him to tell you about the time I stuck his head in the toilet." He paused. *"Before* I flushed."

The two guards looked at each other, then roared as if they had heard some great and rare joke. They nodded at Krause, as if he had reaffirmed their faith in the basic structure of the universe. They left the room.

After they left Krause's face changed again, utterly, a mixture of fear and rage and raw naked loathing—layering, never mingling, one layer after another surfacing in strange, rapid succession.

But the most dominant emotion was fear.

38

Evening shadows stole across the camp. This night, there were no twilight combat maneuvers, and no bonfires with the singing of odd pastiche songs about the rise of the South, or the reemergence of the old America, the real America, a land of blond girls and pink-cheeked boys that might return, that their own children might inherit, if only the scourges of Communism and immigration and Judaism could be eradicated from the land.

Rachel's face was tight, exhausted. "I don't know what to believe. What to think. I sure don't know what to do."

Dee toddled up to her mother, and took her hand. "Don't worry," she said in her own voice. "I know."

Rachel hugged her child, held her, and leaned her head atop Dee's.

Derek sat at Rachel's side, and held her hand. In the last week Rachel's life had gone from near paradise to utter hell. Her fiancé had been murdered, her children threatened. She was bruised, in hiding, and her ex-husband had broken a convicted murderer out of prison. Now she was in hiding in a redneck survivalist retreat.

How in the world she was coping, he couldn't figure.

Rachel yawned. "I got maybe fifty pages in. Then my eyes wouldn't focus anymore. Just wish I knew where this was going."

Very solemnly, Dee took the books from her mother's hand and placed them in the center of a cleared space in the cabin's living room. Tucker had gathered about fifty candles from Lightning Dawn's storeroom. Derek watched as Dee made a careful circle with them, each candle held erect by a makeshift cardboard candleholder fashioned by Troy and Rachel. With her permission, Troy helped her light them.

Then Dee took her mother by the arm and helped her step over the arc of flickering light, to the circle within. "Sit here, Mom," she said. "And Troy, you sit here."

She continued, placing each of them, forming a ring of five people connected to Dahlia Childe by ties of blood. Dahlia Washington, Dee Waites, Troy Waites, Rachel Childe—and a man named Austin Tucker. Rows of candles surrounded them. Dee sat between her mother and Tucker, holding hands with both. Tucker's gigantic paw completely swallowed her hand, but somehow, despite being dwarfed by the adults on either side, she still remained the focus of attention.

Dee, and the two leather-bound books in the center of the circle. Her tiny face was somber.

Waites stood outside the circle, two large buckets of ice at his feet, waiting. Ready. Praying.

Dee turned her head to look back at him. "Daddy," she said. "There's no danger now. The five of us can hold Grandmama Dahlia safely." She released Tucker's hand and beckoned to Derek. "Please," she said. "Join us."

He seemed almost startled, made uneasy by her request, by the earnest expression on her face. "Me?"

Dee nodded. "She wants you in the circle. She wants you to see."

Derek met his daughter's eyes squarely. A cold wind seemed to blow through the room, but the candle flames held steady. Distantly, he was aware of it, but was also aware of something else. The contact with Dee's eyes warmed him. She was connected to something, somewhere that he couldn't see and could hardly hope to understand. Something that he needed to trust, and to understand, if his family was to have a chance, any chance at all.

He joined the circle, sitting between Rachel and Troy.

He waited. Dee looked at them, and smiled serenely, as if they were the children and she the adult, the keeper of the ancient mysteries. "She's coming," Dee said. Then her chin dropped onto her chest.

The wind seemed to flow beneath the doors, swirled around the candles. The room grew very dark, the candle flames pinpoints of light in a limitless void.

The two books were set one atop the other. The topmost cover fell open, and the pages flipped until it was open precisely to the midpoint.

The brownish black letters blurred, and Derek rubbed his eyes, certain it was the light. They jittered, almost as if they were insects instead of ancient smears of ink and blood.

Then the black began to fade, leaving behind streaks of red that beaded and glistened, and flowed up out of the pages, first in a tiny trickle, and then in a torrent, to pool on the floor.

Derek realized that he hadn't breathed in almost a minute, that the sound roaring in his ears was blood, his own blood, that the rhythmic thunder was a heart starving for oxygen, and he forced himself to gulp air.

The crimson fluid oozed into a pool almost a yard across—and then began to rise at the edge like rising pancake batter. Threads coalesced in the center, thickening into dark stringy things, to pulse rapidly, growing into a network of veins that looked something like a horribly bloodshot eye.

They seemed to gain substance from the shadows, from the very darkness, twitched with the beat of a heart dead for more than a hundred years. They writhed like blood-gorged snakes or worms, stretched, stood in the darkness as a lacy crimson filigree, sucking light from the room, taking flesh before their eyes.

As they watched, the veins gathered flesh, grew stalks of white bone. Organs appeared briefly, then clothed themselves in meat until the glistening thing in front of them reared upright, teeth shining from its flensed skull for an instant before dark flesh clothed the webbing of muscle and fat.

For an instant a nude woman stood there, head thrown back, what they could see of her eyes rolled back in her skull as if suspended in some timeless place, suffused with either fathomless ecstasy or pain—

Then white threads appeared, covering her nakedness, and Dahlia Childe stood before them.

She glimmered slightly, as if not quite real. Her simple white cotton dress clung without being the least provocative.

Rachel spoke first, a touch of awe in her voice. "D-Dahlia?"

Dahlia inclined her head almost imperiously. *"My children,"* she said simply. *"There isn't much time."*

Derek found his voice. "Can you tell us who is trying to kill my son?"

She nodded. *"There are two men. The African. The European named DuPris."*

"Where are they?" Tucker growled.

"I can only see the things my children have seen," Dahlia said regretfully. *"As I can only enter this world through girl children of my blood, bearing my name, wearing the cloth I wove with my own hair."*

"What are we dealing with?" Derek asked. "I need information. Please."

Dahlia's image nodded agreement. *"I can show you,"* she said calmly. *"I must. Close your eyes."*

Derek was the last to close his eyes. There was blackness at first, and then Dahlia stepped through the blackness as if she had stepped through a dark curtain, and was suddenly there with him. She began to sway, moving in a dance that was old, utterly strange, yet somehow familiar.

Light and color began to dance at the edge of his vision, and then sparkled more fully, more magically, and suddenly the world was full of light, and collapsed into a hallucinogenic pastel swirl.

THE JOURNAL OF DAHLIA CHILDE

1.

The afternoon sun cooked that Charleston marketplace. The business of human flesh had been conducted since early morning, so much of the crowd had thinned, but some remained. The courtyard was in the middle of a marketplace which sprang up not two hundred yards from the docks. I could smell fish and sweat and the stink of fear. And more—I smelled my own blood, although none of it had been spilled.

I cannot remember ever feeling so miserable, so utterly adrift.

Why had this happened to me? Was I being punished for some slight real or imagined?

No, I think not. There are many ways in which my

story begins here, in this place. I could go back further into my past, into my childhood, where I played with Mistress Lisha and we seemed more friends, equals, than mistress and slave. But those bright days of games and frolic were too painful to look back upon.

Leave it be said that Lisha's family fell on hard times, and that I was one of the few remaining assets with which to enrich her dowry. And when it came time for her to marry, she took me to market.

I have to credit her with the dignity to do it herself. She didn't pass the task off on another. But we were both seventeen years old, slave and mistress. I had tightly curled black hair, and brown skin. She had blond hair and fair skin. I learned to read over her shoulder—it was illegal for slaves to learn such things, but her family allowed it. I eventually surpassed her in this, and many other things. For the most of our lives she took pleasure in my skills, for often games pit one set of girls against another. If I was on her side, and the games involved running, jumping, or dancing, Lisha knew that we had an excellent chance of winning. I could outrun any girl my age, and learn any dance after one lesson.

But despite my familiarity, our friendship, my intelligence or other gifts, when the day came that she was to marry, I was nothing but another asset to be considered, and we went to market for the last time.

Her father, a merchant fallen on hard times, had soft words with a pale-eyed graybeard of a man at the market. I had seen this man come to the house, weeks ago. They nodded and gestured excitedly, haggling.

I sat with my back very stiff, sewing a little blouse. It was a small thing, for a baby, and Lisha had watched me make it for the last few hours. I worked, without speaking, stitching linen fragments together carefully, humming to myself. Several times mistress had tried to speak to me, but I had said nothing.

Now she watched as I made the last few stitches. It wasn't finished, but I knew that she could complete the work. The final touch was my half of our signature. Over the years Lisha and I had made hundreds of skirts, and shirts, and tablecloths, and pairs of pants. And we had devised a little signature, an *L* and a *D* intertwined. Each of us would stitch our half, and the two letters were beautiful together.

I handed it to her.

"What is this?" she asked, knowing.

"It's for your first child," I said, looking at her squarely. "You finish this, and then you sign it," I said. I could barely control my voice, but I forced it calm. "And you tell him your friend made it for him."

Lisha stared at me, and I smiled. I would not let her see my feelings. I could not. I had to have that one small victory.

Lisha nodded, not knowing what to say.

A moan went up from the auction block, and I saw a cheer from the audience, and a fist in the air, waving money. A miserable colored man was led down from the block, and his bound hands given over to another man, no better than he, save for the color of his skin.

The colored man looked here and there as if hoping for support, encouragement, protection, but there was nothing for him, there or anywhere.

He was led away. Another man was led up the stairs to the auction block, and told to remove his shirt.

"You won't have to go through that," Lisha said, as much to herself as to me. "I can promise you that."

"I thank you, missy," I said.

"If there had been any other way. If we could have stayed together . . ."

If I had cursed at her, or blamed her, or tried to shame her, or begged for mercy, she might, in her quiet moments, have convinced herself that I deserved what I got, was no more than another ignorant and ungrateful Negro who didn't know my place in the world. But her expression left no doubt that she knew how she would have carried herself if the roles had been reversed. That my refusal to strike out at her was, in one way, the cruelest thing that I could possibly have done.

The bearded man broke with her father, and came to me, helping me kindly off the wagon. "We've already got a buyer for you, missy," he said. "His man will be here tomorrow for you, and meantime, we'll take just fine care of you. All right?"

I nodded, and let him help me down. I looked back over my shoulder at Lisha, who stared at me, remembering the games of dress-up, the dolls, playing tag. The times we had sworn to be friends for life. And she looked into her own heart, and perhaps told herself that she was merely grown now, and that one of the prices of adulthood was putting a lie to all you believed as a child.

They kept me in the pen with the other women that night. The other colored girls whispered to each other, and to themselves, about their eventual fates. They kept a little apart from me, even then. I don't know why. At seventeen people said that I was beautiful, but more than that, that I carried a bit of a quality that they could only call queenly. Yes. I liked that. Wherever I went, I decided, I would be a queen. There are ways. There would be a way, I was determined.

The first meal the next day was a bowl of hot cereal, actually not terribly bad. I have to admit they took decent care of their merchandise.

The door swung open, and a thin pale man in his midthirties walked in, carrying a roll of paper. He searched the room until his eyes met mine, and for some reason, we immediately recognized each other.

"Here, girl," he said, and I came to him. He lifted my chin, and for a terrible moment I thought that he was going to kiss me. He merely inspected my eyes, my face. And then nodded as if I had passed some minimal standard of quality. "We're going to get along just fine, ain't we?"

I nodded without speaking, and he led me out without chaining my hands.

Why should he? Where was there for me to go? If I ran away in Charleston, I wouldn't last a day, and might well end up dead, ravished, and abused by men who had no concern for the preservation of their investment.

There was a poster outside the door which read Slave Auction, May 17, 1785. I was aware that I was crossing an invisible line. Before yesterday, I had been able to pretend to myself that I was a friend, a companion, something near to a daughter to the people who had cared for me, nurtured me since birth. Now I was merely property, and I felt the earth open to receive me. I fell, screaming.

"Don't worry," the man said. He still hadn't introduced himself. "We're gonna get along just fine."

I was herded onto a wagon filled with other colored people. One of them was a girl my own age who seemed to have an odd element of dark mirth in her eyes. "What's your name, girl?" she asked.

"Dahlia," I said. "Dahlia Childe."

"Isn't that pretty," she said, and lay back against a bale of straw. Her legs were chained, like mine, to the side of the cart, but she didn't seem to notice.

We rode on like that for a time, and then the curiosity overwhelmed me. "What's your name?" I asked finally.

"Cherry," she said. "Was wondering if you'd ask, you being a house lady and all."

I paused, knowing that she was right, that she had drawn some kind of line between us.

"How did you know?" I asked, and she laughed, and the others in the cart laughed with her, as if they were all in on the same joke. I laughed, too, but had the uneasy feeling that I was on the wrong end of their humor.

"How did I know?" she asked. "Look at your hands, girl. And then look at mine."

I did look at my hands. I had always thought that my hands were pretty, but now for the first time I felt a bit ashamed of them, as if there was something wrong with having soft pretty brown hands. Cherry held her hands out for my inspection. They were well formed, a little larger than mine, and already callused. Stronger. Clearly, they had seen toil, and strife which mine had never known.

The Childes had run a big store in town. I had done only light housework, and been companion to their daughter. But now I had visions of laboring in the field. I remembered stories of miseries so bad they seemed like ugly dreams.

I had heard white people refer to Negroes as savages, but the things which it was whispered happened to blacks "sold south" to the rice fields seemed as barbarous as anything they had ever accused us of. I kept my mouth closed about such things, of course. It seemed to me that there was good in all people—the Childes had always treated me with kindness—and I didn't want to believe either set of stories. But now, rolling in the cart toward an unknown destination under a hot sun, I wasn't so sure.

I think that Cherry must have seen the worry on my face, because she suddenly let loose with the most extraordinary burst of laughter. "Don't you worry, girl. Ain't nobody bought you for your farm hands. I think they got something else on their minds for the likes of us!"

And the other girls in the cart laughed, and I looked around, finally paying real attention to the others. Yes, they were all girls, but—and I blush to say it, because of what it said about me—they were all real pretty. And—again, I blush, even all these years later—they looked uncommonly ready for the rigors of childbirthing.

Heavy, ripe bosoms and broad hips, and a lazy, smoldering something in their eyes, as if they had some intuition about the life to which they were headed. And were satisfied with the vision they saw.

For the first time I felt a wave of true terror overwhelm me. These girls were all, if not experienced in the ways of men, at least familiar with the secrets. This whole area was something strange to me. No one had ever spoken of it, but there were animals around the Childe household, dogs and cats, and a couple of dairy cows, and every year a bull was brought over to service them, that the Childe family might increase their herd. I had seen. Missy and I had hidden and watched, and I knew that that thick red wet thing he stuck in the cows had something to do with the mystery between men and women.

I knew that babies came into the world through the bodies of women—I had assisted in Mrs. Childe's third childbirth. She was a brave woman, and strong, but it had nearly killed her.

What was so strange, strange and wonderful, was that after the blood and the suffering, when Mrs. Childe held her newborn son in her arms, there shone from her eyes such an abundance of love and joy that the suffering paled in comparison. Its memory was dimming already.

I thought about this. I thought about the suffering with which animals brought their young into the world, and then the patient, loving way with which they nurture those hard-won children, and it seemed to me that out of suffering can come a blessing just as great.

I vowed to meet the sufferings in my own life with the same courage that I had seen in Mrs. Childe. I vowed that I would bring my own children into the world, that I might share with them both the joys and the sorrows, and in a strange way, I thanked God for letting me be who I was, and giving me a mind clear enough to see through the pain, into the glory.

But I knew nothing of sex, or lovemaking, and little of the rituals of courtship. Oh, I had seen the young men coming around Missy, seeking her attentions, and felt happy for her. But there were no male slaves at the Childe house except for Uncle Abner, and he was too old to be interested in a slip of a girl like me. Bessie would have put a shovel in his head, anyway.

Mr. Childe was a hardworking, God-fearing man, and loved his wife. His attentions never turned toward me—

not in that way, and that was the end of it. There were no other ways that I could have met men.

Oh, slaves from the outlying farms visited, driving wagons to sell milk or eggs or loaves of fresh bread, but Mr. Childe demanded respect for his womenfolk, slaves included. I suppose that I imagined that when I was of marrying age Mr. Childe would buy a man who might be a good husband for me, for he was a practical man, and I believe saw the value in couples working hard. I think that I might even have imagined that in that phase of my life he would allow my husband and myself to buy our way out of bondage, that our children might grow up free. Those dreams sustained me through the nights when, due to some mistake of mine in manners or habits, Mr. or Mrs. Childe found it necessary to remind me of my station.

This didn't happen often, but too often for me, nonetheless.

Now so much had changed, and so suddenly, that I was no longer certain of who or what I was. I had fallen into some other abyss, some side trip along that particular descent into a personal hell. I needed to come to an understanding of what had happened, and I needed to do it swiftly. As certainly as this old cart creaked up the road toward an unknown destination, my very survival depended upon my ability to learn what might be demanded of me, and learn it swiftly.

2.

After two days of travel, we passed a little town called Miller's Parish, and maybe five miles beyond it we arrived at a fence which, as we progressed, stretched around and around a piece of property, enclosing what seemed to be miles of land. It was green and knotted, untamed, and it was difficult to imagine what might be within. After another hour I began to see the signs of cultivated land, and men working thereon. Some of them were close enough to gape at us as we came closer.

The slaves seemed like other colored men I had

seen over the years, but there was something a little
harder about some of them. The overseers, who
lounged about with rifles over their shoulders—an unusual number of rifles, I thought—seemed to be harder still. Despite the warmth of the air, I shivered.

This, I thought to myself, might well be a more
difficult place to earn my way free of.

At last we turned down a pathway that led to an
enormous gate, perhaps eighteen feet high and made
of weathered logs, with a sign perhaps twelve feet by
four feet which read Bloodroot.

An old colored man opened the gate for us, watched
in silence as the cart passed by.

His eyes met mine, and for a moment I felt something like sadness from him, could have sworn that he
shook his head as if thinking thoughts that he dared
not express. But then the moment was past, and we
entered.

There was an odd sign above the gate. Like a little
imp in a bottle. It reminded me of stories that I had
heard as a girl, stories of magic, and once again that
familiar, uncomfortable feeling and sensation stole
over me.

The wagon trundled down the road for almost an
hour before it came to a row of cabins. In front of
some of them, women hung up clothing and cooked
in big pots. In the distance, there were fields where
both men and women worked. I saw few older folks.

It is odd about the old folks. The good slave masters
provide for the old ones, give them a little plot of land
to work. The plantations which have been in the family for generations have their own communities of
slaves with their own customs. The old ones take care
of the children, actually freeing the younger ones for
more work in the fields.

Then there are other masters who exchange slaves
too often to be concerned with the communities which
might or might not form. In such, howsoever, it is still
decency to allow the older ones to grow their own
food, and have homes, however ramshackle, where

they might live out their declining years. However harsh thin times or cold winters might be, the lot of such slaves was often no worse than the poorer whites who have no resources, indeed nothing in their lives to be thankful of save that they were not born black.

But then there are the ones who sell off the older slaves when they are no longer of use.

At least—it is said that they sell them off. But there are no laws protecting slaves, and rumors about what it truly means to be "sold south" come back, doubtless distorted. There are tales of aged, harmless Negroes murdered to save a few acres of land. At seventeen, I had never met a white man so cruel, but still, the rumors persisted.

And when I went into the place called Bloodroot, I found my eye searching for the older ones. Wondering what it would be like to grow aged here, praying that I would see such faces, if only for what it might imply about the people who now owned me.

I didn't see them, and I can't remember the exact thoughts that came to me about this, I remember only that it filled me with dread.

The third cabin in the row was empty, and I was taken down from the wagon and pushed into it by an overseer who was oddly gentle, as if unwilling to spoil the merchandise.

The overseer was a big man with a broad forehead, and very yellow hair. His gut sagged over his belt, but it was clear that at one time he had been a man of unusual strength. I could also tell that on some level he was attracted to me, but probably didn't want to express that, because I belonged to his employer. Never mind. My mind was already humming with ways that I might put that to my use.

I was naive, but not stupid, and there were few weapons for a woman in my position. I could do little save make the most of those few I possessed.

"Make yourself pretty," he said, holding my elbows tight, pulling me close. Close enough for me to smell his whiskey breath. "He's coming."

The cabin was mostly bare except for a mirror and a bed, and a wooden box with a few scraps of cloth in it. The man, who I later learned was named Mallick, left and came back a moment later with a dress. He threw it on the bed. Behind him in the door appeared an old, tired slave woman. She brought in a basin and a bowl of water.

She looked at me, up and down, as if I were a piece of meat, as if I were a calf being brought in for the slaughter. She cared, but couldn't afford to care, if that makes sense. She spoke at me instead of to me. "Best do what he say, child," she advised. "Do what he say."

I grabbed the dress and held it up in front of me, backing into a corner of the cabin, eyes wide and terrified.

Oh! When I think back on the girl I was then, when I try to remember what it felt like to be her, to have the questions running through my mind, to feel the heart beating so fast in my chest that I felt like it would explode. . . .

When I think about that girl, I wish I could reach back and comfort her, could tell her that although her life would be hellish that it would take her beyond pain and pleasure, beyond good and evil, that somehow she would survive.

Somehow.

But that girl just curled up into a ball in that corner, wondering what was going to come next, and thinking that if she was Cherry, that she would put that dress on and pretty herself up. That Cherry knew things about the world, about men that I would have given my soul to know. There were shadows reaching for me, and I could feel them coming, dropping the temperature in the room as certainly as winter fell, but no coat or blanket could possibly protect me.

Night fell, and with the night a thread of change to the sounds that filtered in. There was a hysterical celebration, a kind of giddy laughter, and somewhere far off I heard a voice that might have been a scream and it might have been a laugh, or something else, some combination of the two which again whispered of certain secrets for which I was unprepared.

The door opened, and a man entered. He was tall, almost six and a half feet tall, with blazing red hair, broad shoulders and a thick chest. As impressive as his upper body was, it was his eyes that caught my attention first. They were the kind of eyes which had seen things that I didn't want to speculate about. Eyes of terrible wisdom, and when they fell upon me, the mouth beneath them smiled, but the eyes remained unchanged.

"My name," the man said, "is Augustus DuPris." He closed the door behind him and spoke almost conversationally, as if we two were friends. "I own everything here."

He waited, as if for me to answer, to be impressed or to make an appeal to his vanity, for it was clear that he possessed an enormous store of it.

"I own everything here," he repeated, and took a single step closer. "And the most important thing to remember is that I now own you. You have nothing to worry about. You'll be treated well here." He paused. "You won't be beaten unless you try to escape."

There was something in his voice that gave me a moment's hope, made me dare to think that there was a chance that I might be treated well here in this strange place. Perhaps he had a daughter, and needed a house girl. For he didn't look at me with the lustful look that I had recognized in so many other men when they contemplated my hips and breasts. He looked at me as if . . . well, as if I were a tool. Not wholly a human being.

He looked about the cabin. "We can pretty this place up. Curtains, a table, a couple of chairs." As his mind began to paint in the furnishings I saw him begin to relax. I could almost see him begin to see me in a different light in the context of things, of furnishings, as if the presence of such things increased my own humanity.

Then, when he turned back to me, for the first time

I saw him peer at me with the kind of speculation that a man displays toward a woman, and the hope died in my chest.

"You'll be treated very, very well," he said. "There's just one little thing we have to get out of the way first."

He crossed to me in three slow strides, and with every step I seemed to become more real to him, as if human beings didn't quite exist except when they are close. Because by the time he reached me, those three steps seemed to have taken forever, but that forever occurred between one breath and the next.

Then he gathered the dress up in his hand, his giant hand—I swear that I had never seen a man so large— and hurled it to the side.

He grabbed my wrists and threw me onto the bed, and then his thick fingers shredded the cloth that was all that remained between us.

I do not know what it is like for other women. Their first time. Most of them, thank God, have that first experience in the arms of their husbands, or lovers. I would think that even under the very best of circumstances, there is a pain, a tearing, a sense of violation which only love and affection, and the respect and bonds of the marriage contract can ameliorate.

Even among slaves, that rude and simple contract which stands as marriage, which had no moment in white courts, was something which raised sex from a basic animal act to one of faith, of hope.

Yes, hope.

I have to believe that that is what it is, for that is the very thing which was torn away from me in that moment, the long moments to come. It hurt too much for me even to scream. I thought, I knew, I hoped that I would die then, before another moment of the abject humiliation and terror had a chance to pass.

But I didn't die, and the man who lay upon me, who roughly separated my legs, who spat upon his hands to slick his fingers and then guided them inside me, laugh-

ing as I stiffened in shame and smiled at my prayers
for release, this terrible man . . .

Who forced into me something larger than his fingers, something rigid and hot, something that tore at
me, burned me, thrust into me again and again, so that
my whimpers became wordless cries . . .

I knew in that moment that I had fallen into the pits
of hell and there was no one, nothing to protect me.

I entered a kind of trance, some part of me far away,
watching, watching this poor, slender black girl pinned
to a rude bed by a giant, the tears flowing down her
cheeks. He hadn't even disrobed, this man. Had merely
undone his breeches to draw out his thing, but his sweat
soaked through his shirt, and at last his eyes rolled up
as he began to lose control.

And that girl, that small, poor girl, at that moment in
the midst of her pain and humiliation, and her degradation, stored that moment up in the back of her mind.

I know that because when he left, soon after spend-
ing, left her with his fluid leaking from between her
thighs, her own blood staining the mattress, and she
curled into a ball, hurt in her entire body, wondering
how she would kill herself, something, some small
voice in the back of her mind replayed that moment.

He was out of control, that voice said. *And you were
watching. For all of his strength, for all of his power,
there was a moment when he was out of control, and
you were not. Hold on to that. Build on that. It is power.
A loathsome power. But in a place like this, with no
friends, and nothing but fear around you, seize on any
power that there is.*

Or you won't survive.

And even then, I was absolutely determined that I
would, indeed, survive.

39

Dahlia Washington wrenched her hand away from Tucker's, staring at him as if he were a thing unclean. The moment she did that the vision ended, and the five of them were back in their own time and place, their own world.

Troy cried soundlessly, hugging his mother, who stared at the wall, eyes unfocused.

Dahlia Washington's head was down. She whispered to herself. Tucker reached out to take her arm, his own face torn by conflicting emotions.

She jerked her arm away from him and spat out, "Don't touch me, motherfucker!"

Dee still held Tucker's other hand. She looked up into his face, concerned. Tucker looked ashen, stricken. For once, he didn't seem to know what to say.

"It wasn't *me.*" His voice shook.

Dee looked up at him, and when she spoke it was with Dahlia Childe's unmistakable voice. *"It wasn't him,"* she said. *"Tucker is not the man who did these things to me. Tucker is here to help."*

Rachel shook her head like a woman trying to shake off the last trace of a savage nightmare. "That's all," she said. "No more. I won't have my daughter go through more of this. I read some of the books, but I had no idea it would be like this." She shook Dee hard. "Dee," she said. "Wake up, honey." Her voice was low and soft yet on the razor edge of panic.

Dee didn't respond, was still in that trance state where Dahlia Childe pulled the strings.

She spoke, again in Dahlia's voice. *"We must finish what we began."*

Derek felt it now, a growing, gnawing fear of what was happening to their daughter, of the insanity taking hold in their lives. "No, dammit! She's just a little girl!"

"We must finish, or Troy will die. And more will die."

Derek cursed viciously, fighting to find the lie in Dahlia Childe's words, and unable to do so.

Dahlia Washington was the first to regain her composure. She wiped the tears from her face and glared around the room. Then her face softened. "All right," she said, and wiped her hand against the wet beneath her nose. "All right. Let's keep going. Let's see what . . . what she needs us to see."

Derek shook his head. "It was . . . it seemed as if I was *there*. Too real. I don't want that again." He shook his head again, trying to clear out the mists, mists that refused to disperse.

Rachel turned to Troy. "Troy? You don't need to see this. Please. Step out of the circle."

Troy looked at the ground. What had to be going through the boy's mind? Derek didn't know what Troy knew or didn't know about sex. He did know that if the boy's first experience of sex was witnessing the rape of his mother, or of a woman who looked exactly like her . . .

Such a trauma might take years to overcome. Years, or a lifetime.

Troy clung to Rachel. "Shhh, shh . . . it's all right, baby," she whispered to him. Her eyes were hollow, terrified.

Dee seemed not wholly present—thank God—as if it were true that two personalities had a difficult time occupying the same body at the same time.

But whatever miracle sheltered Dee hadn't helped Troy at all.

"It wasn't me, it wasn't me, baby," Rachel said. Troy turned, and spat in Tucker's face.

Tucker rose, and numbly wiped the spittle away.

Troy held his mother again.

"Don't watch," she said to him, over and over again.

He sobbed, but beneath the tears, Derek heard his son speak, and the words made him feel both unutterable sorrow, and a deep and affecting sense of pride. "Mom," he said, "there's nowhere to run. I have to know." He tried to smile. The effort made his small dark face seem even younger and more vulnerable. "Knowledge is power, right, Dad?"

His father nodded. "Knowledge is power," he said numbly.

Tucker stood apart from the circle, still staring at his glistening fingers.

His eyes seemed dead, as if he had retreated back into the shell where Derek had found him, a week before.

Dee/Dahlia caught Derek's eye, motioned to Tucker. Derek nodded.

Walking toward Tucker felt like walking across broken glass. The man was his enemy. The man was his ally. They had nothing, and everything, in common.

"Tucker," he said quietly. "It wasn't you."

Tucker's face twisted. "How do you know? You don't know who the fuck I am."

Derek fought with himself, fought with the urge to strike back. For an instant he saw something inside this man, and decided to take a chance. "Yes," Derek said. "I do. I saw you pick up a child. I saw *you*, Tucker. You don't make war on children. Or women. I know you, Tucker."

Tucker's eyes met his, and he searched Derek's face, looking for lies, pity, condescension, and finding none of them. The silence in the air between them grew until it was almost unbearable. Then Tucker nodded.

"All right," he said brusquely. "Let's do it."

His face was riven with guilt and shame, and pain. Then Dee was there. She took Tucker's unresponsive hand in hers, and pulled him back to the circle as if he were a big, tame bear. He seemed hollow, or almost mindless, as if his heart had been broken so deeply that his mind could hardly engage with his emotions.

He hadn't been able to reach out to the man. But Dee . . .

Maybe the children are our hope, Derek thought reverently. *Maybe our only hope.*

They rejoined the circle.

THE JOURNAL OF DAHLIA CHILDE

3.

I have little wish to speak of my life between that first day and the major events which followed. I write this now, after so many years, because I think that these facts may be important to one of my children. I have doubtless omitted many things, many small joys and brightnesses. It is not that they did not exist. It is only that I feel there is limited time to write these words, and I wish to say everything which may be of importance to those who follow.

I would have considered escape, but there was nowhere to go, I had no friends, no knowledge of how to get to the North.

And it was said that at night, creatures from hell roamed the roads. I didn't believe the stories, but some of the other slaves did. They believed so many things, so many terrible gods and demons. And why not? Their lives were hell itself. Why shouldn't Satan stalk its halls?

I will say of those times that my duties were light, consisting of little more than enough effort to keep me busy during the day, and no more than pleasantly tired by the end of that day. Washing, cooking, cleaning, but none of them the kind of heavy tasks which were the daily lot of the other servants.

I had the feeling that I, and some of the other women, were reserved for . . . special service. And the work was nothing compared to the burden of knowing how my nights would be spent.

There might have been thirty of us, the women who seemed to be a part of the household for the primary purpose of sexual chattel. He came to me at least twice a week. I do not know, but I have to assume that he went to the others as often, or nearly as often.

It alarmed me then, as it does now, what those numbers implied about his life energy.

Once I became pregnant he no longer dallied with me, but it wasn't for lack of interest in sex. I believe that he believed that continued union might risk the pregnancy, something that he could not afford to do, for reasons that I did not yet comprehend.

At any rate, as soon as my pregnancy became known to him, he beamed with approval, reduced my work, which, as I say, seemed mostly to keep my hands and mind busy, and assured me that if I brought a healthy child into the world my lot at Bloodroot would be easier still.

I began to feel that I had fallen into some kind of breeding kennel, a place where slaves were bred in order to be sold. I knew that the DuPris family had such investments in Mississippi and Georgia. I knew that Augustus was their last heir, and traveled, caring for his business concerns, which included gold mining, shipping, and growing a new crop called soybeans.

Perhaps I was nothing more than another business concern for him.

But if that was true, then it was strange that the slaves were strictly forbidden to have sexual congress with each other, except for a few pairs of mated slaves who were entrusted with duties around the house.

Well, then, perhaps we were his private sexual stock. There was certainly enough of that. I do not want to remember all of the things that he required of me, and those things I remember it would be improper to write down. Some were things that animals have the decency not to require of one another, things which have nothing to do with the reason God gave us the gift of sex. Things that had nothing to do with love, and little to do with procreation. But on the nights when I was summoned to his bedroom, or the nights when he visited my cabin—and he did fulfill his promise to furnish my miserable quarters—his physical drives were so powerful, and so numbingly urgent that I sometimes wondered if I lay with a man or some kind of demon.

But as I have said, his interest in sex changed the moment I became pregnant. He took a kind of pride and satisfaction that I have seen in other men at the announcement that their women are going to give birth. And yet there was an element lacking, and another element present which was difficult to explain.

There was pride, as any man might take in the proof of his masculinity. But there was no tenderness. And yet, if he intended to sell my child, then certainly there would be a kind of mercantile satisfaction, as of a farmer increasing his stock of pigs.

But this wasn't so. Instead of that kind of satisfaction, there was instead a kind of relief. I can't describe it in better terms than this. Relief. As a man might feel seeing his doctor enter the door of a sickroom carrying a bag of medicine and instruments.

Relief.

As the child grew within me, and I had more time to think, I noticed other things.

The company of the other women of Bloodroot was not denied me, but only the younger women. I noticed that none of the women of my circle had children over ten or eleven years of age. There were older women, but they kept their own council, and lived apart from us. There was one woman named Sadie who had a son of eleven, and on his twelfth birthday she was sent across the bridge, to the west side of the plantation. Most slaves never went there. The quarters were said to be better, the work lighter. But we rarely saw the Negroes who had been sent to West Bloodroot. When we did, they looked healthy in body . . . but somehow shrunken in spirit.

Sadie was one of those. After she went across the old wooden bridge to the west side, she never looked me in the eyes again, or spoke to me except on plantation business.

I saw her son, Steven, a few times, running errands here and there. But then one day I heard that he had been sold to another plantation. I never saw him again after that day.

As the child within me grew stronger and larger, the older women began to hover around more and more. And again, there too I couldn't completely understand their attitudes. There was an element of the joy that often accompanied the birth of a new child. But there were other feelings too, and those feelings were being hidden deep within them, not to be shared with a girl such as myself.

I wondered about these and other things, but ultimately there was nothing to do but to attend to the business of letting my body do what it knew to do.

DuPris would drop by from time to time with one of his overseers. And they would bring a little extra meat, or some sweets, and he would speak to me, chatting happily, lay his hand on my stomach and almost purr, happy as I have ever seen a man to be.

And I think that I can be forgiven for misinterpreting his interest. For not thinking more deeply about the implication of the things that I saw and heard. I was just a girl of seventeen, who had been sheltered much. But even if I had been a woman grown, there was nothing in the world outside Bloodroot that could have prepared me for the horror to come.

4.

By the light of candles I gave birth to my first child. I was of generous hips and healthy constitution. Although it hurt abominably, the primary memory that I carry to this day was one of joy so intense and transcendent that it transformed the pain into something almost holy.

I remember looking out through the rude windows of my shack, toward the house so far away, up on the hill, its lights blazing. In moments between the terrible contractions I wondered what the child's father was doing. Wishing, despite the part of me that loathed the man—and loathe him I did—that he would come down here, would be with me in these moments.

Would hold my hand. Would swab my forehead. Would care about me the way the father of children should. I knew, however, that this wasn't possible, that it wasn't even an idle dream. That it was the worst kind of self-deception. I was a breeding animal to him.

As for the women gathered around me, helping me, urging me, I cannot say what they thought of what was happening. I know that they were efficient, that they helped me through my pain.

And yet, there was something about their actions which reminded me of the way a farmer might assist a calf in coming into the world. The caring was distant. The compassion of an impersonal nature. I felt very much alone.

Back in Charleston, I had often felt part of a community despite the fact that there were few of us in the Childe household. Mr. Childe was quite protective of me. I suppose that the other Negroes in the area went out of their way to exchange little pleasantries, to weave into some kind of community the disparate and scattered remnants of African folk.

But here, although surrounded by others of my kind, for some reason I felt utterly isolated and alone.

And when the last push had been made, and my child was delivered into my arms, the midwife, an enormous woman named Aunt Coretta, looked at the child, and at me, and said in a voice as carefully neutral as anything I have ever heard, "It's a boy."

And I held my son close to me, and cried. Slaves have many reasons for crying when a child is born. It is precious to bring life into the world under any circumstances. Life is always a good thing.

But the slave knows that her son's life will not be his own. That he will not be able to be a man—a slave woman, though degraded, can function as a woman more fully than a male slave can function as a man. The mere attempt and commitment to protect his family could cause his death. I know that the lot of male slaves was one in which there is virtually nothing for them to take pride in, save their children—and the master had complete control over the sanctity of the marital union.

DuPris came at the very last part of the birth, as if to inspect his handiwork. At first, seeing him arrive at the door, in his high-collar shirt and long coat, I dared to think that he cared. But when he lighted a cigar in the doorway, and watched me the way another man might have watched the birth of a foal, all such hope left, and I felt an even deeper sense of loneliness than before he appeared.

Coretta, the midwife, was maybe thirty years then, a woman taller and broader than most men. With six children of her own, she kept busy on Bloodroot helping other women with their birthing.

"Push, baby!" she said to me. "Come on. Just a little bit more. Now come on . . ."

She was a plain woman with a flat nose and the smallest eyes I have ever seen. But she was fierce, and insistent, and I think that I might have died if she hadn't been there, urging me on and on.

I hear the white folks talking about the strong nigger women who birth their brats out in the fields and go right on chopping the cotton within that hour. They are animals, it is said.

But if that woman dies before she reaches thirty, of fatigue and sorrow, and a body racked by disease and hunger, nothing is said of it. Any woman can force herself to do things that it is unhealthy to do. But the ability to stagger on when there is no choice is used not as evidence of moral fiber, courage, or strength, but as evidence of the lack of humanity which justifies the treatment itself.

I was lost in pain, and fire, and hardly knew it when a baby's—*my* baby's—cries filled the air. Coretta held up my child for me—no, she held the child to Mr. DuPris, so that he could have the first look. The master nodded in satisfaction.

Only then was my own child handed to me. I suppose if I hadn't been so bone weary I would have felt some kind of insult in that treatment. I was beyond that.

Just to hold my child, just to feel him against my skin filled me with the most extreme satisfaction. Everything seemed right in the world.

"It's a boy," Mr. DuPris said. There was a strange satisfaction in his voice. I looked down at my child. He was lighter skinned than I, reflecting his parentage.

Mr. DuPris watched me, and looked at the baby, and then abruptly turned and left the room. I suppose that there was something in his eyes which should have made me feel more discomfort than I did. In some ways I blame myself for not seeing it, not sensing it.

But what mother, just through the throes of labor, and holding the product of that labor, feeling his heart beat against her breast, scenting his sweet breath on her face, wiping away the blood with the soft cloth, and planting her first kiss on skin more delicate than any flower petal . . .

What mother can believe that anyone could ever want to harm such a child?

5.

The years rolled past, and my life on Bloodroot took on a rhythm. My primary work after the first three years was the care of my own children. They were to be well fed, and healthy. There were light tasks, which the mothers shared amongst themselves, sharing the child-care duties. And we had time to ourselves, time to make our own world, and at times, living there on Bloodroot, it was difficult to believe that there had ever been another world, outside.

Oh, I heard word. A slave passing through told me that she had heard that Miss Lisha settled to the north, just outside Miller's Parish, not more than ten miles distant. She had married her beau, and had a child, much like mine.

And I wondered what our children might say to each other if they ever met. If they would realize that their mothers had been dear friends, but that one had sold the other to buy a marriage. And how those feelings might run. I wondered how that meeting might go, but never dreamed that I might have the chance to make it a reality.

I had four children by then, and had been on the Bloodroot plantation for almost thirteen years. Still, there were things about it that I did not know. I had never, to that day, been across the road, crossed the bridge to the encampment on the far side. I didn't know many things. But over the years, I had watched other women come and go, and many of them moved across the bridge. I had seen many men come to Bloodroot, and it seemed to me that they were all of a type—hard, cold, unfeeling. More so than the usual slaves.

But I excused that, thinking that I had little to compare it to. The other women and I were not encouraged to speculate about anything but the health of our families, and to occupy ourselves in their maintenance.

There were two dozen of us, and do not imagine that the master was our only sexual contact. Although the guards and the other male slaves were strictly forbidden to use us, there was a small group of other men who sometimes did.

These were strong, smiling brown-skinned men, sometimes seen around the plantation in positions of authority. No one knew for certain who they were, and they referred to DuPris as Mr. DuPris, but there was a feeling about them, some of them. Some of them were DuPris's age, and some older. Some in their early twenties. But there was a resemblance between them, a quality of carriage, of intelligence of eye, a similarity of visage which suggested that they were related. I think that at that point I speculated that they might have been bastard brothers, sired upon the slave women in a previous generation by DuPris's father.

No one I could find cared to answer such a question for me. And then there were those from across the west bridge, those haunted, sallow women. They carried some secret within them, its meaning I knew not what. And never would they speak.

From time to time DuPris would call upon me, or ask that I join him in his house. On such occasions I was encouraged to dress well, and indeed clothes would be sent for me. And I dressed in a fashion which might have pleased the best of the white ladies, and was encouraged to do so.

I thought on some occasion as that I might have been asked to move into the house itself, except that it would have caused more jealousy than such a gesture might have been worth to Mr. DuPris.

But I was one of the few to whom no other sexual access was allowed. Not his guards, nor the other slaves, nor even what I supposed to be his half brothers had such access to me.

And when I went to the house, that two-story white mansion which sat on the hill, with its pillars and many windows, walking up that gravel path, escorted by one of his guards, holding my petticoats as best I could, I could feel, almost, that I were a lady going to visit a gentleman.

How I managed to maintain such a fiction to myself, I do not know. I imagine that it is one of the things that we do in order to keep ourselves sane.

I would be welcomed into the long hall, and escorted to the dinner table. I remember the first time that this happened, after my second child was born. DuPris was much pleased with me. A second boy child, it was. For reasons which I did not then understand, this made him well pleased.

He called for me, and had me dressed, and I presented myself for the approval of the old woman he sent to prepare me. She had supervised all of my washings and dressings as if I was a little girl, or as if every detail had to be exactly right if the master was to be satisfied.

The moon was low and huge that night, in that curious way that the moon has of seeming so terribly close when full.

And the trees along the winding path leading to the low gate around the mansion seemed heavy with blossoms. It was in June, I believe now. A servant met me at the door, an old colored man bent as much by the weight of secrets as years.

He took me back to the dining room, which was furnished well. Such a profusion of white linen, and fine plate, and crystal chandeliers, such as I had never seen before. The Childe family had been genteel, but had certainly never furnished a room such as this.

Indeed, it was so blinding that had I not seen something of the world outside Bloodroot, I might have thought that white people were gods, that they all lived in such a fashion.

As it was, I merely asked if the crops grown on Bloodroot were sufficient to provide wealth like this, and to speculate that the master's businesses must have been far-flung indeed.

I was beckoned to sit at the table, and I sat in growing discomfort for almost half an hour before Mr. DuPris appeared.

He was dressed in his finest, exactly as if he was entertaining a lady from town.

And it was at that moment that something occurred to me. I had seen few visitors to Bloodroot, and no ladies at all. It had never occurred to me, but the master didn't seem to be on the best of terms with his neighbors in Miller's Parish, and I have to admit that I wondered about it.

In fact, by the way he welcomed me, never mentioning the fact that I was slave and he master, I was black and he white, it occurred to me that we were playing out a kind of charade. In it, I was a lady from the surrounding town, accepting his hospitality.

I knew this, and remembered what I could of the mannerisms I had learned at the Childe house. And what a little fool I must have seemed, fumbling over forks and spoons and such, struggling to speak intelligently.

"And have you enjoyed your day?" he asked me.

"Yes," I said, sipping my soup. My mind was racing. What was going on here? And then I formed the thought that of all the girls who had been brought here, I was one of the few who had belonged to a family, perhaps the only one who had been brought up as a companion to a young lady, and as such I had certain mannerisms which he might have found appealing, if for reasons that I did not understand he did not have access to the fraternity of the surrounding town.

"It was most kind of you to . . ." I paused, searching for the words that my mistress might have used.

For even then, at that early time, I perceived that there was something inside this man that I hadn't seen before. There was a lack. Perhaps only a woman might have felt it, but there was a part of him that longed for something that he had, clearly, forsaken title to. Perhaps the companionship of genteel women. Yes, that was it. His maintenance of a virtual seraglio of captive women would not endear him to the surrounding townsfolk. I had to suppose that they had that much decency. So perhaps that was it.

But I looked at him, those bright green eyes and flaming red hair, and thought that there might have been an opening here, a way to reach him, perhaps to gain extra favors for my children.

So I resolved to play the game, to be, in the best manner that I could, a lady for him.

We spoke of common things, of the business of the plantation, without ever mentioning slaves or slavery, or even the visits that he had paid to my cabin. He certainly never mentioned the children he had sired upon me.

And in time, after the dinner, he bade me take his arm, and we walked to the drawing room, where he offered me brandy.

I had never tasted spirits such as this before, and its taste was a burning thing on my lips, burning down my throat, hitting me like fire thrust into my heart, and my next sip was a smaller one. That is, the next sip after I ceased coughing.

He affected not to notice me, although I did notice

that he smiled over the rim of his glass as I came back to my senses.

A fire crackled in the fireplace, and the room was filled with the warmth and scent of cedar. We sat on opposite sides of the room, and he smoked a cigar, its vapors wafting and curling about him, as he watched me.

I felt the unaccustomed cloth upon my body, thinking thoughts that I had not dared to think for over five years now.

Mistress Lisha and I had played games. I had worn her clothes, and in fact there were times when it seemed to please the Childes to dress us as if we were actually sisters. I believe that it was out of the kindness of their hearts, and from some genuine affection for me. But there were darker days when I feared that it was to create a shadow for her, that they felt that the darkness of my skin placed me so far beneath her that to create contrast for their daughter, they dressed me up, as if the very comparison made her more desirable.

As I said, that is the dark side to my own thoughts.

But now, and here, wearing these clothes, I wondered if it might be possible to wear such finery more often, perhaps to move my children into the big house, to become Mr. DuPris's lady. And I have to admit that the thought did not repel me.

Perhaps it is a basic part of the nature of a woman to yield to the circumstances rather than to resist them, to find what is good in what is ordinarily intolerable.

Or perhaps, more specifically, it is our nature to accept the rule of a man, even a brutal man, if that man will protect our children. Because every man has his weakness, and they are always in direct proportion to his strength as a man.

I think that the more male a man is, the more desperately he needs a woman to feel human. He forgets what it is, and feels only a sense of longing so deep and pervasive that it can be crippling.

So if I, through my memories of the Childes, and

my basic wiles, could help DuPris remember what it was to be human, then I would gain power. Power to protect. Power to control.

This man had complete control over the lives of hundreds of people. He had fathered two children with me, and although those couplings had nothing of love or romance within them, neither had he been cruel. And out of the drudgery of my life, he had chosen to ask me to his house, to share a meal with him, and later, undoubtedly, a bed.

It would have been impossible for a slave girl not to be utterly dazzled by all of this, not to respond. To dream.

I found it difficult to keep my air of detachment, to keep the conversation light and smooth. I found that I wanted him to touch me, and felt shame and guilt for that very desire.

He looked over at me, and I could swear that he could read my thoughts.

"You probably have questions about me," he said finally. "I am pleased with you. You have given me two sons, who will . . ." He paused, as if deciding exactly how to phrase his next thought. "Who will serve me well. Yes." He nodded slightly, pleased with his own choice of words.

He took another sip of the brandy, rolling it around in the goblet which reflected the firelight so brightly. "Do you like the brandy?"

I nodded. "Is that what this is?" I said, and then caught myself. "I mean, why, yes. I find it delicious."

He laughed to himself, enjoying the game as much as I feared it. And yet, there was something else, once again that sense that in some small way this evening meant almost as much to him as it did to me.

I sipped, and learned to drink without coughing. In truth, I had had spirits before. Missy and I used to steal small amounts of it from the kitchen. Sherry it was, and nothing so fine as this. But I wasn't quite as used to the ways of the world as DuPris might have thought.

Still, when he looked at me, I had the uncanny feeling that he was looking at more than my skin, that my eyes were windows, and that through them he saw within me to places where no man should have been allowed to see.

"Do you have questions about me?" he asked again, almost as if he genuinely expected an answer. "I am in an expansive mood. I am willing to answer a question. A single question. Any question."

"Why?" I asked, and was a little surprised to hear how small and meek my voice sounded, even to me.

"Why?" He paused. "Because I think I see in you an intelligence lacking in the others. Even in the women in Miller's Parish. Is it true?"

I didn't answer. It didn't seem the kind of question it would be intelligent to answer.

"Do you wonder, for instance, how old I am? Where my wealth comes from? Where, in fact, I come from? I know that there are whispers of such things, and I wonder if you want the opportunity to ask the question directly?"

I wondered, and not for the last time, whether to ask the wrong question now was to risk going across the bridge, to that invisible island from which nothing seemed to return. "No," I said finally. "I don't want to ask."

He smiled again. "What do you want to know?" he asked.

"I want to know," I said, slowly, "what price might win my freedom."

He nodded. "I was right about you. You are intelligent," he said. "Well, let us see. Your value to me is considerable."

"But I might be more valuable still if I was able to believe that one day my life might be my own, that there might be some way for my family to be free."

The air around him seemed to crackle, and I knew that somehow I had said the wrong thing. Then with an effort of will he calmed himself again. "You, perhaps. And perhaps some of your family. There is still much you have to learn.''

He came and stood over me. I tried to rise, and his broad hands rested heavily on my shoulders, holding me down. They felt hot. ''How smart are you, girl? How smart, really?''

''I don't know how to answer those questions,'' I said.

''We will see. There are many ways to answer a question. The most direct is action.''

The mood had grown dark in the room, so much so that in some way that I couldn't understand, the fireplace seemed to radiate cold instead of heat, and I shrank back in my chair. For that moment, the veneer of a civilized meeting slipped away. For that moment, he was my master again, and more. I sensed that there was something that he wanted from me, something beyond my body. That within the green eyes lurked something that I could barely begin to understand at that young age, that even now, looking back over so many years, it is difficult to believe.

But I began to fumble out words, hoping that words would stem the tide of fear rising within me. ''I could be of service to you, in ways I haven't been.''

His hands, large and rough-smooth, cradled my chin. ''You have been of service to me,'' he said softly. ''And will be of greater still.''

''I know how to sew,'' I said. ''I can make things. Beautiful things. I . . . I should have been sold to a seamstress. . . .''

''I know,'' he whispered, and he was coming closer now. Close enough to kiss, or to bite. ''My purchasing agent looked for a woman like you.''

''Why?'' I asked, and realized that I had asked a second question.

His eyes glittered. ''Another question,'' he said, and there was bright triumph in his eyes. ''Tonight, you will do what I ask, and you will do it joyously. You will not hold back from me, in any way, or you will be punished, do you understand?''

I understood. "I agree," I said. "But my question?"

"My purchasing agent seeks out women of many kinds. Of fertility. Obedience. Health. Strength. But sometimes I grow lonely. So some of them are chosen for intelligence, and something else."

"What?" I said softly, thinking of the pale-eyed, gray-bearded old man who had come to my master's house, who said that he had heard a woman slave was being offered for sale. I remember the look in the old eyes, and something burned in the back of my mind.

"And something else. Something inside you. You have a strength. I enjoy that. It is worth possessing. Worth controlling. A spirit strong enough to be worth the breaking."

"This man of yours saw quite a bit," I said, trying to keep that element of formality in my voice. He was very close now, so close that his eyes, his green eyes, filled my world.

"Of course he does," DuPris said, and raised me up, one strong hand on each of my shoulders, held me so that even if I had fallen unconscious, I would not have collapsed to the ground. "He is not merely my man," he said. "I am his son."

And his lips came down on mine, blazingly, as he had never kissed me before. And it was in the middle of that savage kiss that I realized that I had not heard him correctly. That he must have misspoken himself, and that my mind, trying to find the sane within a situation which was growing more insane by the day, had rearranged what this man had said in order to make sense of it.

I had heard "I am his son."

What he had said was "He is *my* son."

The hair. The eyes. The age. The man who had negotiated my purchase was at least sixty years old. DuPris could be no more than forty.

Impossible.

Opening my mouth and my body to him, I surrendered.

6.

And so I became something more than a slave to DuPris—but less than a free woman. From time to time now he summoned me to the big house, and I would dine there, and afterwards we would talk. It assumed the nature of a ritual. And afterwards, we would retire to his bedroom, where he would take his pleasure with me. Apparently the pleasure I afforded him was great, because I gained greater and greater freedoms, and eventually he wanted to see what I would do if he furnished me with cloth to sew—he saw what I was able to do with the plain cottons given to the plantation women.

And I worked, knowing that every stitch brought me closer to the ability to bargain for the things I needed, for myself and my family. There are no words which can describe the feverish manner in which I worked. Far into the night, and early in the mornings. I made him things, and things for the house. And things for the overseers, until there was hardly a person on the plantation who didn't have a shirt, or a scarf, or a coat which I had made. There was no denying it, I was making myself needed as well as wanted on Bloodroot. The other slave women, who had no such unique skills, envied me, for most of them had nothing to barter with save their bodies, and there is one thing which is true: we may all take pride in the ripeness of our bodies, but the key to sexuality isn't the ripeness of the body, or the skills which one acquires along the way. It is purely and simply the degree to which a woman opens to the man she lives with. How sensitive she is to his needs.

I created, with my sewing skill, a nightgown of the richest cloths I could find. And every time he used my body, I took that nightgown off, folded it slowly and put it to the side. And I would look at it, as his body melded with mine, and I would remind myself that one day I would wear it in freedom, perhaps for a man who would love me for myself, and not for what he could wring from my body.

But then there was another part of me that knew full well that I would never have that in my life. That no man would come to me, want to be with me. I knew even then that there were things that I would do, as yet undone, which would take me far afield from the ranks of the women who can find men to accompany them through life. This was not to be my path.

The years passed, and my children grew. I had a daughter, and then another daughter, and a year after that, a son. Although he was disappointed that I didn't have even more male children, he seldom spoke of that disappointment. And at least once a month I would go to the house, and I would play my charade with the man with the flowing red hair. I came to sense a great loneliness, a great apartness in him, even as I puzzled on the riddle of the purchasers.

In truth, the man who had purchased me was one of several who did business for Mr. DuPris who had the master's flaming mane and high forehead. Some of the guards did, as well. Bloodroot seemed in some way a kind of family concern, and I wondered what manner of man his father, or grandfather was, for clearly it was such a man who had set up the concern in the first place.

But it was impossible to ask any questions of the guards and get answers of any kind. They simply didn't speak. And so I was left with many, many questions, questions which were for many years unanswered.

It was almost thirteen years after I first came to Bloodroot when the first of my deep questions was answered.

I still remember the day. The morning had been unusually cold, and the ground fog hugged the grass, looked as if it wasn't going to burn off until the sun had gone high. Then suddenly it was gone, and the trees to the north seemed somehow heavy with sorrow.

I haven't spoken much of my neighbors, the women who lived around me. Well, one of them, Mary, moved across the bridge when her eldest son turned twelve. I remember that day. Mary's son was sent for, and didn't come back, and the next day Mary and her family moved across the bridge. I saw her a few times after that. She said that her son had been sold north, to apprentice to a blacksmith. That there might even be a chance that he might buy his freedom one day. But there was something in her eyes that told me that she was lying, although I could never have guessed at the truth. And shortly after that she ceased speaking to me at all, avoided me, spoke only with the other women who lived across the bridge.

And I didn't ask. I didn't want to ask.

But I did want to know.

Life went on, for me and for the rest of those who lived on the plantation. And with the passage of days, you tend to forget that your world is a prison.

It wasn't as bad for me as it was for some of the other women. I suppose I fantasized that DuPris and I had a relationship of a kind. I thought of him, I have to admit, as more than merely my master. I thought of him as my lover. As my man. And I think that he encouraged me to feel this way.

Then came the day that everything changed.

It was on a spring day in 1801. I sat in a chair on my cabin porch, sewing. My life was fairly easy by this time. As I said, I had made myself, if not indispensable, quite valuable in ways that the other girls had not. As a result, there were many favors which came my way, and I was always eager to find a way to ingratiate myself to anyone on the plantation who had the power or authority to make my life, or my family's life, more comfortable.

My primary task was to breed, to produce children, and this was a labor of love. DuPris didn't come to my cabin, as he came to the cabins of the others. He called me to the big house, and there I donned dresses and sometimes wigs, and we played out our charade, one which invariably ended in his upstairs bedroom, when we would be swept, together, into a hurricane of passion.

There were times when he would spend, and then hold me tightly, and look at me with something like tenderness. And then turn away, as if afraid that he might speak the wrong words.

And one time when he did speak. When he said, "I gave this all away."

I asked him what he meant by that, and his breathing changed, and he said, "No decent woman would have me. Now get *out!*" He screamed the last words, and I gathered my clothes and dressed in the hall, and fled that house before he killed me, which I am certain he might have done.

I had two boys and two girl children by this point, and my eldest boy, Georgie, was about twelve years old. He was stirring a cook pot in the house, boiling down meat from pig bones. Later, we would begin to add more seasonings, and vegetables, and create one of the soups for which I was famous on the plantation.

Perhaps we would have a party. DuPris didn't mind the slaves having their own entertainments, and in fact would sometimes enjoy coming down and dancing with us, as though he took some kind of odd pleasure in proving that he could be more Negro than the blackest of us.

But this was, as I recall, a Thursday night, and the work of the week had yet to be concluded. So the soup would be for us. And perhaps for those of our neighbors who wished to share it with us.

I sat there on the porch, doing my sewing and enjoying my day, enjoying the scent of the fresh soup drifting across the porch, when I saw the master approach.

It was just dusk. There was a quality about twilight on Bloodroot which was almost magical. The mist which seeped from the ground morning and night swirled about your ankles. The trees grew heavy with shadows, and the night birds sang, low and plaintive, from their darkness. Even the stars seemed too clear and bright and cold, tiny marbles burning in the night.

In the thirteen years that I had been there, time had taken its inevitable toll upon me. I felt the changes in my bones and blood. I was a woman fully, at the height of my life, and as was the norm for slave women, knew that I would make a rapid descent soon. Work for most slave women was too hard, the diet too meager, the conditions too degrading. There was a quality of swift ripening, and swift rot that was a part of life then. I knew that I was at the summit of my life, and had, because of the twists and turns my life had taken, never found a mate. It was only natural under those circumstances to look at DuPris as my mate. I played games, childish games, I see now, telling myself why he was distant, why he didn't come to see me, why he didn't call me to his bed more often. And fancied that there were basic differences between the relationships that he had with other women, and the one that he had to me. I couldn't quite imagine his couplings with the others, but imagined them to be more animalistic, more degrading, than ours. Ours I fantasized into some kind of dark spiritual communion.

So when I saw him walking toward my cabin in the dusk, the first fireflies flickering in the gloom, I have to admit that my heart leaped. "Georgie!" I called, and the other children ceased their games to see what was about to take place, as if they could tell by the very tone of my voice that something special was about to take place.

Mr. DuPris was closer now. He took off his broad hat as he came up onto the stair, and made a shallow but almost courtly gesture, which made my heart pound. Georgie appeared on the porch next to me, a strong boy with rusty skin and reddish hair. "You bow to your father, now, Georgie," I said.

DuPris smiled at me, and it seemed to me that there was something in his smile that I had never seen before. I didn't know how to read it, and it sent a little thrill up my spine, although I have to admit that I wasn't certain whether that thrill was one of romantic excitement, or of danger. "Dahlia," he said, smiling broadly. "You're looking fine, as always."

"Thank you, sir," I answered.

"Yes, indeed," he said. Although the shadows had begun to fall, the day's heat was still in the air. He wiped his brow. "Yes, indeed. Hot today."

He looked at Georgie with what I imagined was affection. And this was where, for the thousandth time, I noticed something that I didn't want to notice at all.

In all the time that I had been on Bloodroot, DuPris seemed not to have changed a bit. Not a gray hair, not a line on his face. It didn't seem natural, and I suppose I thought to myself that his was a bloodline which aged slowly, and showed their years hardly at all.

"Well," he said to Georgie. "You're all growed up, boy!"

Georgie looked up at him. There was much of his father in Georgie's face. The eyes were brownish green. The shape of his face clearly suggested a father of European descent. Georgie's nose was not as broad as mine, and something in his carriage reminded me of his father.

And also something in his manner. "Yes, sir," he said, meeting his father's eyes unflinchingly.

It seems to me now, looking back on it, that there was some communication going on between Georgie and DuPris that I knew nothing about. Georgie knew something, and of this I am more certain the more I think back on it. Because it was clear that my boy was afraid, mortally afraid, but for some reason wasn't showing it at all.

And when I think back on that now, I think that he concealed his fear in order to protect us.

DuPris chuckled, and chucked Georgie affectionately under the chin. "I think that maybe it's time for you to come along with your daddy. I have things to teach you."

Now, finally, perhaps too late, I felt a feather of alarm trace my spine. I tried to keep my voice level, but it was impossible not to react to the sight of my boy trembling in the dusk. It wasn't just the cold. My boy knew, in that way that animals know, that death was reaching out for him. In his own small way, without saying, he was begging for someone, anyone, to stand between him and his fate.

I was his mother. It was mine to do it, but I had no power to intercede directly, and I wasn't smart enough to know what to do. "How long will he be gone?" I asked.

DuPris just smiled. "Don't worry your head about it. You have other children to tend." He paused, and then added, "For me."

I stopped my mending. The other children were very quiet now, as if they knew, everyone knew, what drama was being played out here. Georgie's eyes begged. He didn't want to go with his father. I believe that he would have gladly walked backwards through fire if it would have taken him away from his father.

"I've heard stories. About other boys going away. Not coming back. Is my boy coming back, Mr. Du-Pris?"

The air was very still, and I knew that I was very close to a line it might cost me my life to cross. That it was only the sessions in the house which allowed me to come this close without suffering.

He roared at me. "Don't question me, woman. Not now, not ever!" His eyes blazed. "You have other children. Do you want to keep them?"

Again, I froze. The threat was no longer subtle. No direct threat had been made against Georgie. He was merely to go with his father. And, I had very few doubts, we would soon be called to move to better dwellings.

Across the bridge. To the western side of Bloodroot.

My younger children looked up at me. I was, as mothers have been since the beginning of time, a captive of love. Georgie understood before I did. He looked at Mr. DuPris, and you wouldn't have known from his expression that he was the one who had lost, who was losing. That although I had no evidence, no proof, at that time knew nothing, my heart knew everything, including the fact that my boy was never coming back.

Still, he nodded, and quietly took off his apron, and looked up at DuPris, his master.

His father.

"I'm ready, sir," he said.

DuPris nodded. "That's good," he said. And the two of them walked off together. Once, and only once, Georgie looked back at me. And the expression on his face was one of purest terror.

7.

Night had fallen fully, and I busied myself with cooking. I kept looking out onto the porch, wondering aloud when Georgie would return, reminding myself to save enough food for Georgie, all of the little lies that I told myself to keep from going mad.

Aunt Coretta appeared on the step. Age was beginning to bow her, and the first gray had appeared in her hair, but she was still a strong, proud woman.

More than any other time I had seen her, however, there was a trace of that odd fear that I had seen in her. A sense that there was something wrong that she could never make right.

"Aunt Coretta?" I asked. I sensed that if I didn't begin the conversation, precious minutes would be lost.

She stared at the floor for longer than I think I've ever seen her do that, unable to speak, unable to leave, either. I thought for the longest time that she wouldn't be able to talk at all, but then she said, "Dahlia. I could get into bad trouble, but I brought your boy into this world. I can't just stand by. You got to know what gonna happen to your children." She paused. Now she met my eyes, and her eyes were wet, tortured, and there was something in them that told me that this distant but kindly woman, who had never had many words for the rest of us, was being completely torn apart by the knowledge that she carried.

"You hear me," she said. Her eyes watered. Her

round, wrinkled face seemed puffy, heavy. I think she must have been drinking. "It's best you cut their throats now."

Some part of me knew what she was talking about, had known for years what had to come next, but both of us had our roles to play out and regardless of the fact that it was a farce, we had to play them.

"What are you talking about?" I asked.

"You come with me tonight," Aunt Coretta said. "Come with me. And Lord have mercy on all our souls."

Coretta came for me after the rest of the plantation had gone to sleep. It must have been well after midnight. I can't count the number of times I had lain awake in bed, late, listening to my children's breathing. Leaving the cabins after curfew was severely punished, but I could still hear. And although the bridge was most of a mile distant, I swear that I could hear music, and the sound of human voices.

And although no one was supposed to answer questions, it was clear that something happened over there. And twice or so I had heard a name, or a description: the African.

It was just whispered. And there was, it was said, a path on the far side of the bridge, and up at the end of that path lived a man I had never seen. Whom no one on this side of the bridge had ever seen. And I only heard about it when someone was handed a poultice to place on the forehead of Mary's eleven-year-old boy when he was bad sick. He got well within two days, after two weeks sick. And the next month, after his birthday, he and his family went across the bridge, and we never saw them anymore.

It was said that the African had supplied the medicine.

So I suppose that over the years, he had turned into a kind of bogeyman. The children whispered about him, and the mothers sometimes used him to scare them into obedience.

He was ten feet tall, it was said, and looked like a gorilla. They said he had been alive for a thousand years, and was the power behind the master. People say all kinds of things, but I don't believe what I hear. Barely believe what I see.

But one thing I came to believe. Whatever the music was, whatever the lights, the rumblings . . . if they were connected with the boys who went across the bridge and didn't return, and the families who went there too, and afterwards seemed so changed, then the African was a part of it as well.

Coretta came for me, and she led me through the darkness to the very edge of the bridge. There was usually a guard there, watching that no one passed.

The bridge spread over a gorge. I could hear the water rushing below it, although at this time of the night I couldn't see the water.

I wondered where the guard was, and then heard giggling off to the side, and a rustle of bushes, and knew that Aunt Coretta had arranged for the guard to be otherwise occupied for a few minutes. Knew that if anything happened, and we were discovered to have passed during his watch, that it would go very, very hard for him.

I could hear drums to the south of us. As I have said, sometimes the sound of drums floated over the plantation at night, a low, terrible sound, which often made it impossible to sleep. There were many stories about what it meant, but I suspected that those who talked didn't know, those who knew didn't talk.

But now, pulled along by Aunt Coretta's hand, climbing through the bushes and creeping around the trees, I heard the drums not as a distant pulse, but as distinct sounds. I felt my heart speed up, and knew that my entire life was about to change.

I was going to see my Georgie, see him in a way that would kill me, and I was holding on to my heart, my life, to what remained of my sanity by a thread.

The undergrowth thickened, and then, some yards ahead widened into a flat area. Before we reached it,

Aunt Coretta gripped my arm hard, and pulled me to the ground.

Two male slaves were staked out in a clearing which measured perhaps a hundred feet across. Each of them was tied to an upright pole. It was difficult to tell exactly what was happening, because we were behind a stand of trees, and the boles of the trees stood between me and the clearing, standing and blocking me off, each of them cutting the light a little more until we were almost in darkness. But through the light, I can tell you what I did see.

I saw DuPris, stripped to the waist, wearing nothing but a loin cloth. His upper body was well oiled, glistened in the firelight, every muscle standing out like vines coiled around a tree trunk. His hips swayed slowly to the music. I searched, looking for Georgie, and finally found him.

Almost blocked by a series of trees, Georgie stood tied to a third stake, his thin arms above him. He was positioned between DuPris and the two slaves. And although his eyes were open, he didn't move. I knew my Georgie. That was fear, and something entirely beyond fear in his eyes. Terror.

I don't know where it began, but I know that I started to scream, and only Coretta's dusty hand over my mouth stopped it from splitting my throat.

"You can't help him," she said. "But maybe you can save your other children." Her eyes were very deep, and as hot as the torches.

The night was filled with fire. The fire blazed unnaturally hot, because I could feel the heat all the way back where we were. And it burned too damned bright, because the clouds over our heads reflected that fire.

No. That's wrong. Didn't reflect it. If I was to tell the honest truth, it was more as if the clouds overhead were boiling, edged with weird lightning, as if the fire had got inside those clouds. There hadn't been any storm when I left the house. The weather had all seemed fine, except for the deepness and darkness of the night. But here, it didn't seem crazy to think that the weather was completely different. For some reason it felt as if I had crossed not a mile, but an entire world. I didn't know where I was, or what land this was anymore, but I knew that anything could happen, and I was afraid for my Georgie, for myself, for my children, and it was all I could do to keep from losing all control.

I swear that the things I write here are true. I have no reason to lie—there is too much about me which is soiled by the words in these pages. It is only by telling the truth, including the truth that brands me as a monster, that I can, I hope, establish my own sincerity.

The lightning crawled from the sky. It danced around the edges of the clouds, and as the music continued, it shifted and danced until it was clear that that music moved to the beat of the drums, or else the drums somehow anticipated the movement and roll of the lightning. I don't know which I considered to be more reasonable, which seemed to be more likely.

Coretta grasped at me, but I fought free of her hands and wiggled closer, thinking, planning, trying to come up with some means of freeing my Georgie. I think that a dozen mad schemes found their way into my mind, means to distract, disrupt. I suppose I even thought of just running out into the clearing and grabbing my Georgie up and fleeing into the night.

But what of my other babies? I suppose that if it hadn't been for them, I might have thrown all caution to the winds and done what my heart said. But something told me that to be seen here, to disrupt this, would bring death to us all.

And so it is with shame that I admit that I watched, and did nothing.

There is another reason that I did not act.

I finally saw the man who beat the drums, and the sight of him transfixed me.

He was huge, and black, and taller even than DuPris. His body was enormous, almost like one of the apes that stories said lived in the forests of my homeland. His eyes blazed. His shaven skull gleamed in the dancing light.

I had never seen a man like him, and to glimpse him for half an instant, in near total darkness, would be enough to tell him from a million other men.

He was—he had to be—none other than that one who others on the plantation referred to as the African. As I watched him, my breath quickened in my throat, and my blood roared loud enough to drown the beat of the drums.

But I could hear his voice, and he shouted, *"Chango Pollo Mayombe Jana Shay! Chango Kosha!"*

I heard those words many times after this, but I will not give the words in their entirety, and there are mistakes in what I write here, deliberate mistakes.

For these were words of power. I could feel them in my bones, know that my ancestors had heard such words, that the men who had shouted such words had kept my people crouching in the darkness. The dark powers summoned with such words love nothing of this world except the fear of its people, the smell of blood spilled from the bodies of our children.

I knew, with the instinct of a mother, that this man, and his words, and the awful rhythms summoned from his drum, and the dark fire coiling in the sky meant death for my child, and that there was nothing I could do.

As he chanted, his body twisted and turned through an odd set of contortions, as if each word summoned a response from a different muscle. I had never seen a body move like that. It was like a bizarre, blasphemous dance. But—and I am ashamed to admit it—there in the damp and the shadows of the dark fire, I could feel my own body respond.

The bodies of the two slave men responded as well. They glowed in the firelight, and the shadows around their bodies seemed to be the envelopes which held in the life force, the very fire of their inner existence.

And the lightning above them, the clouds, in a trick of light, a trick of my sight, were no longer high and distant in the sky. They seemed just over the clearing, boiling just over the fire, as if they were composed of smoke. The first of the lightning bolts coiled, seemed almost to hiss, and split the night, striking the earth— and one of the two men.

He shrieked and arched, and his scream was a scream of almost sexual pleasure.

If the inside of a human being was filled with light, if the life within us was light, and the thing that kept the light from rushing out was our skin, then what I saw would have made sense. The man at the stake distended, as if the inside of him was some glowing mass pushing and stretching at his skin. He howled, and in the light of the lightning I swear I saw the bones within him, saw the skull and the empty eye sockets. For the eyes and the skin and the very meat of his body dissolved for a moment, became as transparent as glass, turned to light, to fire, to lightning, flowing from his body, and then the other man's body in a pulse which seemed to dance in ungodly time with the very music.

It coiled, snakelike, and rose as if it were lightning rising from the earth. And mated with the lightning in the sky.

Then dove back down again, and struck my son.

My heart died in that moment.

I heard his scream. His shriek of pain blended with the howl of the wind, and my own anguished cry, and I swear that despite the risk, despite the inevitable destruction of my family, I would have crawled to him then and there, but for Aunt Coretta's hands upon me. Despite her age she was a huge woman, twice my size, but it took all of her strength, I am certain, to control me. Finally I panted in her arms, and she held me like a child, and I sobbed.

Georgie's small hands glowed, as if filled up with whatever was being drawn from those two slaves.

As I watched, the two slaves grew smaller. Shriveled. Aged. From moment to moment, their bodies shifted from that clear glassy state to normal human, and each time it did, with every pulse of some ungodly heart within the sky, their hair grew grayer, their bodies more stooped, and I finally understood what I was seeing.

From Georgie, a stream of light flew back, and it was the purest, brightest light I had ever seen. And that light flew into DuPris, into his chest. He roared, screaming with pleasure so raw and total it was like pain.

And Georgie, my Georgie—his hands shriveled, grew darker. His skin cracked and burned, as if consumed with a fire from within, as whatever flew from those two men swept through him, burned him up, used him up. As he filtered it for DuPris, so that he might receive the essence of the life of those two men, prolonging his own cursed existence.

And it was at the moment that I realized this, that I saw and understood everything, that my poor senses were finally overcome, and I fell unconscious, and knew no more of that place, or of my own existence.

40

There was utter silence in the room as the vision ended for the second time. Then, with a great racked gulping sound, Rachel staggered to her feet, took two steps toward the bathroom and vomited explosively. Dahlia Washington was up in a moment, her arms around her cousin, helping her to the toilet. Troy's face was ashen. He silently fetched a towel, and began to clean up the wet yellow splash.

Dee sat on the floor, as impassive as a little yogi, legs crossed. Face calm.

Tucker went outside. He shook a cigarette out of his pack, and lit it. He took great satisfaction in the fact that his hand did not shake. He took deep drags, not really thinking about anything, just feeling.

Out across the compound, Lightning Dawn's flag waved. He fought a little wave of nausea, determined to keep his own private feelings his own, come what may. There were few sounds from the rest of the compound: some tinny music from one radio and the ranting of some ultraconservative talk-show host from another. Laughter from the listeners, something about the man, who was far to the right of Rush Limbaugh, being a pinko faggot.

Behind Tucker, the door opened. He knew from the footsteps that it was Waites. Heavy footsteps, untutored. Uncertain. The man had no body discipline.

Waites stood beside him for a while, saying nothing, gazing out into the night. Tucker offered his cigarette pack, and somewhat to his surprise, Waites took it. Offered a light, again taken.

He stared out at the trees. Waites drew deeply, then coughed.

"Don't smoke, do you?" Tucker said.

"No," Waites admitted. "But I need the nicotine."

"An honest man." Tucker chuckled mirthlessly. "What do you think about what we just saw?"

"Used that boy," Derek said. "Like a fucking strainer. Used him to purify something that he drew from the other slaves."

"What?"

"Energy. That's too broad a term, but it has to do. I don't have a better one right now. DuPris stole something from those men that he used to keep himself alive. He needed a child related to him by blood."

Tucker nodded. He was astounded at how difficult it was to say the next words. "I remember the autopsy on my boy." He choked. "They showed me the photos of what they thought I did to my boy." And then he was silent. He wanted to run, to just get away. He hated himself, hated what he saw in the vision. Hated the fact that DuPris looked so much like him. God.

"Yeah," Waites said. "The same thing." Waites took another drag, and then Tucker knew that he was staring. Waites was staring at him. Into his heart, the last place he wanted any man to look.

"He's not you, you know," Waites said quietly.

"What?"

"DuPris. He's not you. That was a long time ago. He passes something down through the generations. And he kills his own children. You were as much a victim as your son. He's not you, Tucker."

Tucker turned and looked at Waites, and for a moment didn't recognize him, felt as if the man were someone he had never seen before, and felt a flash of killing anger. *Take this man. Break him. Kill him now.*

Tucker buried it. "How can you be sure?" he asked quietly. "Maybe I did do it. Maybe I won't let myself remember."

Derek Waites looked at him, and finally shook his head slowly from side to side. "No," he said. "Dahlia said that you weren't the man."

"And if she's wrong?"

"I say she's right," Derek said quietly.

"How the hell can you know?" There was something in Tucker's voice that he didn't like to hear there. A plea. God, he wanted to believe.

"I know," Derek said. "Because my daughter believes in you."

Tucker looked at him, and realized, to his chagrin, that in some way that he couldn't quite understand, this black man and his family had become the most important people in his world. This man's daughter was a doorway. And on the other side of that doorway was the light he craved more than life itself.

He was torn in six directions at once, and knew that the next moment of his life would be crushingly important. He could run, he could fight, he could learn.

What the hell.

Tucker felt himself to be in some place beyond sanity or even rage. He was ice again, an ice-cold animal that walked and talked like a man. But somehow, subtly, his position in the universe had shifted. "All right," he said coldly. "Let's finish this fucker."

And together, they returned to the cabin.

41

"No," Rachel said. "It's over. I won't let her continue."

Dee pulled at her mother's arm. "Mommy—"

Rachel was near hysteria. Her mouth trembled as she spoke. *"No!"* she screamed. "Just . . . no."

Dahlia Washington took Rachel's arm strongly, as if lending her cousin strength. "It's all right," she said. "That last time, the last thing we seen. Felt like a tug. Here." She touched her chest, over her heart. "I think I can carry the weight. I think that Dahlia Childe can come through me."

"Are you sure?" Derek asked.

"No," Dahlia Washington said. "But I'll give a try. This ain't no thing for a child, nohow."

Suddenly the air in the room grew cold. Dee looked at them, and her face shifted again, and Dahlia Childe was in the room with them, beautiful, and serene and long dead. "If you are willing to take the risk, take the cloth, take the nightgown, and place it next to your skin. I will try."

Without ceremony Dee quietly peeled the nightgown away. She stood clad only in her panties. Rachel draped a blanket around her, then she tottered to a corner of the room, and leaned against the wall.

Dahlia Washington looked at the garment, holding it at arm's length, regarding the scrap of cloth as if it were a living thing that might turn to bite her. It was much too small for her to wear, but she folded it twice, and raised her sweater, tucking it up against her heart.

Her breath caught in her throat as she did so, and she stiffened. She seemed dizzy for an instant, and then caught herself against the wall, and said, "I'm all right." She sat, and they formed the circle again.

"This ain't no thing for a child," she gasped. She looked at Rachel, eyes hard. "We need you in the circle," she said.

Rachel still trembled. "I need to be here," she said. She hugged Dee, and then came to sit again. Dahlia regarded

Dee. "Can you handle the ice, cuz?" Dahlia asked, trying to smile.

Dee nodded soberly. "You bet, cuz," she said.

Dahlia smiled. "You the best."

Then Dahlia closed her eyes. She joined hands with Troy, Tucker, Rachel, and Derek. The candlelight flickered on her face, and the rest of them closed their eyes. As they did, the room slid sideways and—

THE JOURNAL OF DAHLIA CHILDE

8.

I ran for my life through the cane groves, pulling my children behind me. I don't think I stopped to think much of anything. I wasn't afraid of the night creatures that legend said roamed the roads. I just moved as quickly as I could, stumbling over the roots and ruts in the road. Where the grass played out, there was a stand of trees at the edge of a road, and that was where the wagon was waiting.

"Bless you, Aunt Coretta," I said, I prayed, thinking that this was the best thing anyone had ever done for me in my entire life. I hoisted my children into the back of the buckboard, and climbed up into the seat. I hadn't much experience in driving a thing like this, but there was no time to learn.

What I had seen destroyed me. All of my excuses, all of the games that I had played, all of the things that I had seen on Bloodroot that I hadn't let myself understand, all of them came flooding back to me in a moment.

I tugged at the reins, and urged the horses down the road. If Aunt Coretta was right, the gate would be clear, everything relaxed after the ceremony was over.

The moon was gigantic, huge, seemed to sit like a great swollen spider at the top of the trees as I lashed those horses, driving them on. Where I was going, I didn't fully know. I only knew that Bloodroot was death, and I had to get myself and my children the hell out of there, even if I had no idea what might lie ahead.

I hadn't gone for fifteen minutes, the wagon leaping and bucking beneath me like a horse, my children white eyed with fear in the back of the wagon, before disaster struck.

I looked back over my shoulders, and in the moonlight, I saw three things in the road. Black and clawing at the ground, all lit up with fire, and I couldn't see more than a little glimpse before I had to put my attention back on the road. I could hear them pawing and snorting. The shape was like nothing human. Maybe they were four-legged, but they were bigger than horses, and there was fire around them. As we rounded one bend after another I saw the glow in the road behind us, through the trees, and pushed the cart on faster and faster. They were gaining on us.

Then I knew that the stories I'd heard all those years ago were true. There were monsters on the road, and now they would kill me and my little family, and all was lost.

Then three men galloped out of the shadows in front of me, torches in hand.

I had never seen them before. The first was a thin man who blocked my passage, and hailed me to stop.

"Run!" I screamed. "They're coming! Oh, God, they'll kill us all!"

But they just laughed at me. Their rifles leaned back against their shoulders.

"Where you think you're going, girl?" the biggest of the three asked. His teeth gleamed in the moonlight.

The second one . . . I suddenly realized that I had seen him before, out to Mr. DuPris's place. "Ain't this Dahlia?" he asked. "Luscious little thing belong to Mr. DuPris, don't she?"

I looked back over my shoulder, and saw the fire coming, saw the demons coming around the bend. . . .

And then knew myself for a fool. There were two men on horses. They wore sheets that covered them all up, and carried torches. In the night, in the shadows, they looked like something other than men, but men was all they were.

I knew then that the stories of demons on the road were just that—stories, spread by the masters to keep their slaves afraid and quiet. There weren't any demons. Just night patrols.

I cursed, all the possible lies on my lips suddenly dying. There was just nothing to be said. I decided to try to tell the truth. "Please," I sobbed. "Help me. You don't know. He's the devil. The devil!"

They laughed, winking at each other. "He beat you?" the thin one asked. "Come to your bed too often?"

I hardly heard them, plowed on, still hoping against hope that they could hear me. "He killed my boy," I sobbed. "Killed my Georgie. He tied my boy up." The words were tumbling out now. I saw the look on their faces, and knew my words were falling on deaf ears, but had to speak anyway. "He tied my boy up. Only twelve year old. Just killed him, burned him up."

There was silence. What I was most afraid of was that they knew. That they were in on it.

The truth, in its way, was even more horrible. They looked at me blankly, and it was obvious that they had never been a part of such a ceremony. One of them looked at the others a little nervously, as if the words I spoke had been voiced before, and he felt uneasy about them.

But these were, truthfully, good God-fearing men. My misfortune was that they were God-fearing white men, and could not believe that one of their own race could do such a thing.

The fatter man looked at the thin one. "She's talking crazy," he said, and tilted his hat back on his head.

I knew that I was lost, but I couldn't stop myself, had to continue to talk even if it was, indeed, hopeless. "He made fire come down out of the sky," I babbled. "He burned Georgie up."

Now the two men looked at each other, and I could swear that there was some silent communication between them.

I wondered then how many slaves had escaped down the same road I had flown, been intercepted. How many times such tales had been told. And knew that every time it was told, the whispers about Mr. DuPris would grow a little stronger. I knew then why he mingled so little with the townsfolk. I knew then the price of his powers.

I knew, but none of that knowing helped me. I was still desperate to find a way to get these men onto my side. They were good men. They had no part in the devilish goings-on at Bloodroot. If they knew, and believed what happened there, perhaps they would take action, but there was no way that they would believe a fleeing slave over the word of one of the wealthiest men in the state.

"Fire?" The fat one scratched his chin. "You're talking crazy again."

In the wagon behind me, my children cried softly.

"Come on, now—we'll take you back. Pretty thing like you—I don't think he'll have the heart for no serious whipping."

They thought that my fear was fear of being punished, the fear of the runaway slave that her master would punish her for theft of his property—namely, her own body.

There was no way these men, good men, could understand. I screamed "No! No, dammit!" and lashed my horses.

The sudden ferocity of my efforts startled the night riders, and they pulled back from me. I lashed the horses into a frenzy, and sped the wagon down the road. I was like a madwoman, I am certain, and if I had been able to watch myself rather than being swallowed completely by my own fear, I would have seen a slender Negro woman with three screaming children in the wagon behind her, horses galloping and snorting, wagon bouncing down the road. The night riders sped after me. At first, so insane were my efforts, that I actually pulled ahead of them, speeding down that road in the darkness, only the gigantic, swollen moon to lend us light.

Then came the evening's second disaster. The left front wagon wheel came undone, spun off. The wagon heeled over onto its side, and crashed, and I flew screaming from the seat and pitched into the darkness.

I pitched into a bush, was torn and scratched, but no more than that. I crawled back to my children, guided in the darkness by their cries.

Mercifully, I had sustained the greatest injuries, and my children were only frightened, and a little bruised. They threw their little arms around my neck, and held on for dear life.

The two horsemen pulled up, and hopped down, angered. Angry enough to place shackles upon my arms. "Whoa, there, missy!" the thin one panted. "Trying to kill yourself?"

I was completely out of my head now, and able to do little more than babble. "He's the devil! The devil!"

While my children sobbed in the night. Sobbed because their mother had failed them.

9.

I remember little of the trip back to Bloodroot, I was dazed, in pain, sick in heart and mind and body. The distance passed in a blur. The next thing that I remember clearly was actually standing in DuPris's study. I remember him handing each man a few bills, and whispering thanks.

It should be said that the night riders seemed faintly uneasy in DuPris's presence. I think that they could hardly wait to leave. I have smelled the night when a storm is approaching. There is a heaviness in the air, a swollen quality. There is something dark and cold coming, and everything in the world knows it, even if it is yet to be seen and felt.

DuPris was dressed in a silken dressing gown. I had

made it with my own hands. I knew every stitch, every fold at the collar or ruffle on the cuff.

There was no trace of the man who had capered in the moonlight not six hours ago. This man, apparently awakened from his slumber, sipped brandy from a crystal snifter. His eyes were very calm, too calm, as if they were only windows behind which something dangerous beyond all conception waited to see which way I would run before leaping.

And yet in another way there was a quality of bemusement in his attitude. He watched me. I stood in the middle of the room. My children had been taken from me, and I could do nothing, nothing but feel more fear, and more sulfurous hatred, than I had ever felt before in my life.

"Dahlia," he said finally. "Dahlia. I thought that you were more intelligent than this. That you understood that there is no escape for you . . . or your children."

He stood, came to me, caressed my face. His fingers were as cold as ice. I didn't move, was afraid to move, to speak, to do anything. But behind him, on the desk behind him, I saw a letter opener. As sharp as a knife.

And I thought that I knew what I might do.

"You have afforded me such pleasure," he said, with mocking regret. "And now this. Exposing my affairs to the townspeople. Did you really think that they would believe you?"

I hung my head, and shook it, shamed, broken. My head went into my hands, and I made as if I fought to keep from sobbing. It didn't require a huge amount of skill to act thus. Once I had decided upon a course of action, I was frozen into that path.

My eyes drifted past that letter opener, without fixing on it. I betrayed nothing of my intent.

"I've given you special food," he said. "Special lodgings. And this is how you reward me?"

I leaned against him, sobbing as I had so many times before, utterly helpless, begging forgiveness, and I felt his body relax.

Behind his back, I reached for the letter opener. Without making a sound, I plunged it clumsily into his back.

And screamed in agony. At the moment the blade touched his flesh, I felt a blade slash my own flesh, a searing, burning agony that froze me.

We stumbled away from each other, and his hand groped back to the wound, as mine did. I dropped the bloodied knife.

I wheeled searching the room, looking for the person who must have struck me. His hands were empty. He had wielded no knife, and yet . . .

And yet . . .

His hands came from behind his back, and his fingers were stained with blood. He rubbed them together, and then licked the blood from his fingertips.

I collapsed to the floor, convulsing with pain.

"I can heal my wounds," DuPris said harshly. "I can control my pain. But what of you? Was it worth it, to inflict such a scratch?"

He knelt very closely. "Do you think you are the first to try to kill me? It is not so easy. There are ways. Means. Any blow dealt me reflects back to the assassin. Think on that more carefully, before you try again."

I don't know how long it took for me to find my mind again, but when I did, it felt as if the world was spinning out of control. "What are you?" I whispered. "You're not a man."

He smiled at me, and there was nothing of love, or laughter, or joy in that smile. "No," he said. "Not anymore. Once I was. But there are ways to . . . transcend humanity. I will live a thousand years."

"Who are you?" I asked dazedly.

"I am the man who owns the African," he said. "He gave me the Gift. The Gift requires certain . . . sacrifices from such as you. I need boys of my own blood. You are breeding stock. When you run dry, I will throw you away. If you try to run again, or to hurt me again, you and all of your children die. Do you understand?''

He towered over me. At that moment he seemed to be the tallest man in the entire world. I could only nod my head, miserable.

"Good," he said. "Good." He wiped his bloodied fingers on his shirt. "Now. I think I'd like to start tonight, making a new boy."

He swept his arm, wiping books and bric a brac from his desk. With a clatter, it fell to the ground. Crystal goblets splintered like shattered dreams. I was defeated completely. And the worst thing of all was that DuPris knew it. Right down to the depths of his being he understood that he had won. He stared at me, through me. "Take off those bloody rags, slut," he said.

The pain in my back was terrible. I wanted to faint. Trembling, I took my bloodied blouse off, wincing at each motion.

And there, on the desk in his study, our blood and sweat and sex mingled, and my degradation was completed.

10.

Years passed. My family and I were removed from the general compound and taken across the bridge to West Bloodroot. Things were a bit more comfortable there, but there wasn't really as much difference as people had imagined. The shacks were still shacks. The main purpose of the separation was partially to isolate the slaves who had given up children to the master.

There was a further exclusionary area, as I have indicated, the area where the ceremonies themselves took place, this was across the bridge, and to the south of either compound. And the second compound was patrolled by armed guards day and night. It was five times harder to imagine escaping from this place, and my hopes sank even more deeply.

Still, I did not give up. I took every errand I could,

hoping that by learning as much as I could about the plantation, I might find some way out of the hideous trap into which I had fallen. I saw the other women, saw the hopelessness in their eyes. They were broken. They told lies to each other about how their children had been sold to fine masters farther north, were in households, saving money to buy their own and their mother's freedom.

But they didn't believe it. They didn't know what to believe, but from time to time another of the boys would reach twelve, and be taken away. And a mother would weep, and hold on to the desperate lie that somewhere, there was a better life for her lost child.

I don't know who will read these words one day, who will judge the things that I say. I can only say that when there is no hope, you hold on to whatever hope you can find. We were trapped by our color, within an entire country who would use that color to mark us, and return us to the master. There was no escape.

I remember, one day Cherry, the girl who had come with me in the wagon all those years ago, tried for her second time to escape. There was no ceremony. There was no trial, not for a slave. She was just taken to the center of the square, and whipped to death. We were forced to watch as her shrieks turned to sobs of pain, and then to nothing, just nothing, nothing but the twitching of a body no longer controlled by a rational mind.

And then her children went to live in the long wooden cabin at a corner of the compound, DuPris's orphanage. Maybe a dozen children without mothers lived there—with not even the minimum of love and affection, nothing but the lonely nights, huddling together, listening to the wind and wondering which night the men would come for them, counting the birthdays until they would be sold north, or until the girls were no longer children, and would be taken to hutches of their own, to begin to breed.

I don't know why, but I never stopped looking,

never stopped believing that there was a way out, and one day in 1803, just a few months shy of Derek's twelfth birthday, I decided to take a chance.

I was delivering a basket of preserves to one of the little guard cottages on the outskirts of the southern enclave, and passed a gate. A sign above it read Keep Out. To one side lay the carcass of a gutted chicken, its body dried and rotted. One of the other slaves, an old man called Uncle Will, glared at me as I looked at it.

"Stay away from there, you know what's good for you," he said.

My heart thundered in my chest. "What's back up in there?" I asked. The road twisted up into the hill, all tangled up with brambles. It was hard to believe that anyone went up there much.

Uncle Will spat in the dust. "The African," he whispered, as if that explained everything. And then he hurried on.

I watched him go, and then thought, Two months for my boy and then DuPris comes for him. I was going to have to do something. For me, there were no pretty lies about "life up north." I could not stand by and do nothing. Escape, I was certain, was impossible. Yet I would have tried it anyway, to save my child.

What I proposed to do now was no less dangerous. Without another moment's hesitation, I slipped past the sign, climbed up the winding dirt path through ancient, twisted trees.

As I walked, I began to hear the sound of a drumbeat, a rhythm I had heard before, many times before, a sound dark and darkly sensuous. It grew louder with every step.

There were symbols, twisted things that resembled trees or lightning or rivers, or maybe unborn children. Animals, and hunters of animals. I knew without ever having been told or shown that these were symbols from Africa, the land of my people.

But whatever joys and hopes and dreams my people had known, this was their darker side. These symbols were of intestines spilled from dying beasts, of lightning striking the earth and creating fire, of waters rising to sweep away fishing villages. And of beasts turning upon the hunters, and rending them, or carrying them whole into the forests, to eat at leisure the living flesh of screaming men.

It is odd. The longer I looked at those drawings, the more it seemed that I could see the men, the beasts, the villages—not merely as represented in the drawings, but could see the things themselves, as they wavered in my sight. It was easy to dream in midstep, to mistake the shadows around me for the fingers of living things. The trees reached out for me, the sun seemed to sink prematurely behind the hills, and as I walked deeper into that cleft, I felt that I was leaving everything that I knew further and further behind.

Something caught my eye. It was a bottle, a tinted bottle swaying in the wind, and in it, impossibly, was a little man. The man's skull was too wide to have slipped through the top of the bottle, how he got in there I do not know to this day.

But when I looked more closely I saw that it wasn't a man at all. It was a baby, an unborn baby in a bottle, its flesh withered until it looked like a little old, shrunken man, its eyes staring out at me, pale and seeing nothing, seeing everything.

My hand reached out to touch it as it swayed there in the wind, and then in the moment before I could touch it, a hand reached out and grabbed mine and whipped me around with such force as I had never known, even from the hand of DuPris. Where DuPris sometimes seemed a machine, this was like a force of nature, like the touch of an animal in human form.

I looked into this man's face, and saw pure evil. Pure power.

He was heavily scarred, ritual slashes covering his body. He was heavily painted, as I had heard that red Indian men paint themselves.

He was naked to the waist and his chest and back and arms were covered with scars which ran together and apart and curled into a great mass of symbols. I had the feeling that they told a story, that I could look at him, and tell things about him which led my mind into dark and twisted pathways.

I felt such threat from him, but his threat was pure, it wasn't hidden behind a civilized mask, as it was with DuPris. These two men where like brothers, not slave and master, and if one of them owned the other, it was only in the sense that the bank defines the river, or the day ends the night.

"Why have you come?" he asked.

I was frozen with fear, unable to do more than quake.

He looked at me again, in curiosity, the way I might have looked at an insect I was preparing to stamp underfoot. "Did no one tell you that it would cost you your life to come here?"

I dumbly nodded yes.

"Is that what you wish? Did you come here to die?"

Finally, I found my voice. "You're the African?"

"That is one of my names," he said.

"You are the one who gave DuPris his power?"

The African smiled thinly. "Ah, yes.. His power. He told you. You are one of his women. What if I did?" he asked. "What is it to you?"

He came forward, stalking me. I've seen cats coming after mice like that. And that was the way he moved. Loose, like a cat—not the pretty, dancing way people talk about when they say that someone moves like a cat, but the way a cat really moves. Loose. Relaxed. You can see the muscles bunching under the skin, know what it's getting ready to do, but can never tell the moment it will do it.

Slowly, one step at a time, I was being driven back. I struggled to find words to fill up the silence. In the silence was death. "Why? Why did you give him the power?"

The African stopped, and I had the feeling that the summoned memories were painful ones. I wasn't certain whether asking him to remember was a terrible mistake, or in some way that I didn't understand, exactly the right thing to do.

"He was my master," the African said. "Now— not master. We . . . own each other."

We own each other. I knew in the moment I heard that that this man was the key to my struggle. My mind raced. "You could protect my family," I said. It wasn't a question, or even a prayer. It was almost a whisper to myself, spoken aloud.

"Why would I want that?" he asked, puzzled but in some way delighted with my courage. "You are meat to me."

He had backed me up another step. I was against the bush, and had no place left to retreat. I ran through all of the things that I might offer to this strange man, and realized that none of them would be enough. My body? He would have any woman on the plantation if he wished it—that is, any woman not claimed as DuPris personal breeding stock. My skills? I sewed, but again, that skill could be his on demand. There had to be something.

Screwing up my courage, I twisted my body into a pose similar to the one I saw him use in the ceremony. As I said, I could learn any dance, just show it to me once. I screamed, *"Chango Pollo M-Mayombe Jana Shay! Chango Kosha!"* I stuttered, but I managed to get the words out, just barely.

And he stopped, taken aback. I swear that the wind ceased to blow, that there was no sound in the entire world for that moment. "Where did you learn that?"

"I watched you in the grove," I said.

His brow wrinkled. "How many times?"

My voice sounded small and frightened, even to me. "Just once."

"Once?" he asked incredulously. "Once?" My breath froze. He walked around me slowly, and again that feeling that he was some kind of vastly powerful jungle beast, that I was the deer he meant to claim for meat. "Say *Chango Kosha!*"

As he said that word, he did a whirling step, twisting through a savage and darkly exhilarating dancelike step.

I have always loved to dance, but never did I think that my life, or the life of my family might depend upon my abilities. Summoning all of my courage and skill, I imitated the moves as best I could and screamed the words he had barked at me.

When I was finished, I was panting, even though there had been no more than a half dozen motions. Every muscle in my body seemed locked in unyielding tension.

The African grinned. "You learn . . . quickly," he said. "You have a mind." He sniffed at me, at the sweat on my brow, sniffed the place between my legs. "Your people. Do you know where your people came from?"

"Charleston?"

His laugh was ugly. "Of course you wouldn't know. But girl—you have the gift. You wish to . . ." He paused, as if considering his choice of words. "Learn?"

"Yes," I whispered.

He walked almost all of the way around me, inspecting. Slowly, examining every inch. I stood straight, barely daring to breathe.

"You wish to . . . serve?" he asked.

"Yes," I whispered again. Oh, God, I prayed. Let this be an answer. Please.

The African might have been reading my thoughts. "Yes," he said. "I have use for you. DuPris will hate it." His grin broadened. "Good."

11.

It stormed again that night, but the driving rain and the lightning which split the clouds far above, and the rolling thunder, were all nothing compared to the human fury in DuPris's study.

Truly, I was a mouse between two cats. I did not know what it was I had done, but my courage, my intelligence, the fact that I had been DuPris's special plaything, and an ancient animosity between these two men had created a balance of some kind. Along with the skills I had shown in imitating the ritual steps and voices had created a tiny opening for me to wiggle through. My body and mind were of no true importance, but this man, the African, had chosen it as a battleground to strike back at the man he both needed and hated, DuPris.

I cringed in the corner as they raged, that night in 1804.

"No!" DuPris screamed. "It is impossible!"

The African's voice was falsely soothing. "Nothing is impossible," he said. "I have shown you this. You, of all men, should understand this. I told you I needed apprentices!"

"I gave you apprentices!"

"No! You gave me stupid, lazy toads!"

DuPris sputtered.

The African paid him no mind. "This woman is of the proper blood! Her people knew magic. She can learn!"

DuPris was almost speechless with rage. "You cannot have her! She is using you to shield her children!"

The African came close to DuPris, closer I think than any other man would have dared come. "Do you not want power?" he asked. "Life? We need her. You have other women. Take their children. This one is mine."

DuPris almost spat in his face. "You black bastard—"

The African raised a single thick finger. "Be very careful," he said softly. "We need each other—for now."

"Your own people sold you," DuPris hissed. "When I found you, you were just another naked savage."

The African didn't back down, and this in itself I found amazing. "A savage you need."

"As you need me."

The African drew back, as if stung by those words. "I will not always need a white face," he said. "The world will change."

DuPris laughed unpleasantly. "Yes," he said. "In a thousand years."

The African didn't back down this time. Their faces were so close together that they could have kissed. "I count the days. Hear my words. You may take pleasure from this woman's body, but her life—and her family—are mine."

I expected DuPris to strike the African dead at that instant, but something that I didn't understand held him back. He said not another word, but instead whirled and stormed from the room, pausing only to cast one terrible, burning glance back at me. Then he was gone.

The room was silent, but for the crash of thunder outside the window. I blinked, not certain what might happen next. The African came to me, and took my face between his hands.

"Make no mistake," he said. "If you fail me in any way, you will long for the simple agonies of hell." Then his grip fastened upon my wrist and he led me out of the house and back across the plantation to begin my education.

12.

And so began the end.

I served each of my masters in a different way. The African had little interest in my body, seeming to take pleasure only in the fulfillment of rites of power.

I danced with him, and learned to sing his strange songs, and slowly, slowly, began to understand the ways of his magic.

And I continued to serve DuPris in bed. His interest in me redoubled, as if he strove to achieve dominance over me in that way, seeking to touch my soul more deeply than did the African. And such was my existence at that time. Caring for my children, sexual subjugation, and the dark arts of the continent my people left far behind them.

There was a difference between my sexual relationship with DuPris, before and after the African came into my life.

I had power now. I had stopped him, and he knew it, and I knew it, and it made for a contest between us. I had found an area of weakness, and perhaps he might have killed me and my family, and dared the African to do something in retaliation. But instead he chose to accept the battle, and strove to master me in bed.

The African taught me many things. He taught me the rules of magic. One must have both natural talent, and training, and a source of power. If a wizard had ten sons, perhaps one of them would be truly fit to teach. And that one must study hard, and must acquire a source of power. There are certain stones, and plants, and places in the earth with power. But the greatest power is that which comes from stealing life itself.

There is also the magic of similarity. A wizard's children and grandchildren bearing his name will be more powerful than those who do not. Things shaped as other things may inherit and influence their power. Things which are a part of other things may also influence or share their power.

It was this knowledge that led me to preparing the way for my children. I would name my next daughter after me. And I began to weave strands of my own hair into my garments, especially the nightgown I often wore to bed with DuPris. These garments I would pass down to my daughters, to be given to their daughters who would carry my name.

What happened to me must not be forgotten. I don't understand everything that I can accomplish in this manner, but I trust that I am doing the right thing.

There is another fact. I once asked the African if he knew everything. He laughed. Then he said that he knew "most everything a man could know."

"I'll know more after I die," he said. "Those who live know less than the dead, but the dead are sealed into the afterlife. If one could come back, that one would be more powerful than any sorcerer who ever lived, so it is good that door is closed."

My sexual relationship with DuPris was no longer rape, or seduction. In some way that is difficult to explain, it became a game between equals, my knowledge of what motions and pressures would most likely force him to lose control, pitted against his urge to wring sexual response from me before that moment arrived. This game that favors a woman, who can climax again and again while a man's single orgasm forces him to rest a time, even a man so powerful as DuPris.

I had power.

I also learned of the strange connection between my two masters, a story which, as far as I know, no other human being knew in its entirety.

The African told me that story one night after long hours of working with the bones brought from a local cemetery, bones and flesh of a child and mother who had died together in childbirth.

"The bond between mother and child is strong," he explained. "It is the core of the magic I make. It is the most powerful magic in the world, and goes far beyond the wall of death. It is this magic which cost me my kingdom—"

And then he said no more, and I dared not ask. Not that time. But over time he became well pleased with me, and one night, after he had almost drained himself with dancing and chanting, he drank from a pouch of something fermented that he kept behind the stove in his little hut.

His eyes burned, and for one of the very few times that I was with him, I saw the human being behind the mask of power.

One thing that I have learned is that the most powerful man still holds the memory of being held in his mother's arms, long ago. And a woman who can, through softness, evoke that memory can control him as direct force never can.

And despite what he had become, when he believed himself to be in control of the learning process between us, when he saw no challenge in me, nothing but the urge to serve, he began to relax. And it is another truth that a man of power can truly trust no other man. Those relationships, all of them, need to be relationships of power, of fear, of shared ambition—but not of trust. But the yearning always remains to trust a woman. Most of the time this trust can only be found with a woman that such a man possesses, but the yearning remains.

And so it happened that one day, after a day spent disemboweling sheep and chickens, and teaching me of the dark things, he told me about himself.

And he told me the ultimate secret behind all magics. The secret is this: The darkness outside of us, the dark thing, the dark gods that lurk in the shadows, that devour the light, are one with the darkness within ourselves. The doorway is the human heart.

And you have only to kill the parts of yourself which are attached to the light in order to see the darkness more fully.

The things we did together opened my mind to the dark precisely because they were abominations, precisely because that which was good within me recoiled from the deeds, from the sights.

And I think that when I had dampened that goodness, when the screams of protest no longer echoed in my heart, there were two choices: First, I could progress to some greater, darker evil, something which made the previous deeds seem like flowers in comparison. Second, I could feed off the innocence of others, which of course these men had done. I resisted this, trying to find some way to keep going, despite the nights I spent shuddering, holding myself and praying.

Praying that somewhere, in some manner, I would find a way out.

But on one night, when the sheep intestines were cooling, the African told me his story, and here it is, as nearly as I can remember it. Incredible as it seems, I have no reason to doubt its truth.

13.

The African was born almost four hundred years ago, near the area that Europeans call the Congo. There, he was royalty, the son of a king, the eldest son, and in line for the throne. There was no dishonor in the things that he did to ensure the safety and well-being of his people, and they lived in peace and prosperity.

It is true, though, that the other nations feared and hated him, because he practiced what they called black magic.

But he was willing to do anything to ensure his people's safety and security, and so cared little what the others thought. And as he looked more deeply into these secrets, he found answers which most men would have turned away from, answers which extended his life far beyond the normal span.

The African says that there was no one else to take the reins of power, that if he had allowed himself to grow old and die like other men, everything he had built up would have fallen apart.

I don't know if he believes this, if he believes he was doing these things for his people. I only know that he did what other men might have done, had they access to the same secrets.

And the worst of them involved the death of his own children. Even worse, the death of his children unborn. I know that on at least one occasion he got a woman with child and then, before she could have her baby, cut her open and put the baby in a bag, and wore that bag around his neck. He said that the woman was of no consequence, a captive of war.

I think that he was playing with me, that he knew what those words did to me, would have done to any mother, but he said them as if it explained everything.

And even as I know that these words horrify you, my children, and horrified me, this man began to frighten his own family, the very heirs of his power.

But they could not kill him.

For what DuPris referred to as the mirror spell was a part of the African's power. And any man or woman who tried to poison, stab or club him would have died in the same instant, and all his family knew it. To kill him would cause the death of anyone who held the knife, or threw the spear. That person had to be willing to die, in order to kill him, and that kept him safe over the years.

Until one day they came up with an answer.

There were slavers coming upriver, buying captives of war. And the African's own family grouped together, and they bound him, and sold him to the white men, who took him to their ships, and took him to the new land.

Oh, how he raged! But he was separated from his source of blood relatives, and unable to perform his ceremonies, he began to age like a normal man, in fact, faster than a normal man. His was the body of a young, strong man in his twenties, although he was over two hundred. By the time he reached the Americas, he was a man in his late twenties. All of the protections he had created for himself were gone. A world away from anything he had known, he was no more than another black slave, one withering, aging a year every month.

He was purchased by a sugar cane plantation in Haiti, and sent to hard work. Such work burns the life from ordinary men, and that may be what his master thought was happening to the African. But a year in that heat, and he had aged ten years. He felt it, even if those around him didn't realize what was happening to him. And he knew that in five years he would be dead.

What was there to do? He had tried to talk to his new masters, but they would not hear him, and were Christian folk. They would have no interest in helping him in his terrible ceremonies. But other men came and went, and he hatched a plan.

The African says that the basic truths of magic go

beyond a country or a time. That they are based on
life and death, birth and aging, the turning of seasons,
sun and moon, tide and land, air, and fire and water.
Basic realities that are the same all over the world.

And because of this, a magician of one people can
talk to a magician of another people. All up and down
the Nile, magicians from the southern tip of Africa
could trade with Egyptian priests if they forgot their
languages and wrote instead in the mystic runes that
form the very basis of their dark arts. And the Egyptian priests had told him that they could do the same
with the men and women who came from even farther
north, from Rome and Greece and England.

It was on this idea that he placed his hopes.

I had wondered at the scars that covered his body,
the grooves and puckers and ridges in his flesh. How
long it took to create them, and at what cost in agony
I cannot say. But create them he did, and I can only
imagine the nights, sleepless and dark, when this half-
crazy black man from the heart of Africa, horrified by
flesh shriveling ten times faster than a man's ever had,
cutting himself, burning himself, to create symbols.
Symbols of the darkest, deepest evil.

They became infected. He tossed and turned, burning with fever, but continued to cut.

He worked, blood seeping through his shirt, chopping cane in the day, and then tearing at his own flesh
at night, swollen and bloated.

His owners whipped him, beat him, tried to make
him stop. But how can you stop a man who is willing
to inflict more pain on himself than you are?

And so at last they considered him crazy, and left
him alone.

I can only imagine what he must have been like,
fevered, flesh rancid, this hot-eyed man aging a year
every month, laboring in the fields under the sun. The
other slaves shunned him. His masters whispered
about him to the other townsfolk.

And he labored there, his shirt undone, and at last
his entire body looked like a mass of scars, but their

ridges took shapes that must have drawn the gaze as surely as the obvious agony of their infliction forced the eye away.

How he could have kept going day by day? A gaunt, dark figure chopping cane in the fields all day, throwing up what little food he could force himself to eat, and tossing with fever all night. I do not know. It might be that only the fear of what might wait for him on the dark side of the grave kept him going. I don't think I ever met a man who feared death more, or with better reason.

It was his third year on the plantation that it happened. By then, he looked to be an old Negro man of sixty, only a shadow of his old self, and I think that he had lost all hope.

But rumors have a life of their own, and one man tells two other men, who tell two others, and so news of something dark and unusual spreads far, finally reaching the ears of a man named Augustus DuPris.

DuPris was a wealthy Carolinian. His father had been wealthy. And one of the ways that they had grown rich was with the use of certain small magics. They knew things. There was a book which had been passed down in their family which taught certain secrets. I think the DuPris was a family of witches, who kept their secrets carefully hidden from the outside world.

DuPris was traveling on business, and his travels took him to the islands. He was buying trading goods—sugar, cocoa, and other things, and while he was there he heard the story of the strange black man. And he was intrigued, and he made a business trip to the small plantation where the African served out his ghastly time, and I can only imagine that first meeting.

The African says that he was working out in the field. It was the hottest day he could ever remember enduring, and he wanted to die.

The glare of the sun was such that he didn't really see DuPris approach. DuPris rode up on a great horse, and stared down at the old withered Negro that the

African had become, and said, "Take your shirt off."

By this time, the African had almost forgotten who or what he was. He had lost so very much. But with fingers which were numb and fragile, bleeding and swollen from the work, he unbuttoned his shirt and peeled it back.

DuPris climbed off his horse, and examined the scars. The African says that he didn't even know what the man was looking at. His mind was nearly broken, as the pain of a dozen lifetimes crowded in on him, robbing his nights of sleep, filling his days with fatigue so deep that it transcended agony.

"Who made these scars?" DuPris asked him.

The African stared at him. He says that he weighed not more than a hundred pounds, and his flesh must truly have hung on him like a coat of leather. But he wet his lips and mumbled, "I did, sir."

And DuPris looked at him.

I am sure that DuPris could not have been certain what he was seeing, but he must have had suspicions. There must have been references in the books he pored over in search of information, always information, what he called "arcane lore."

And he looked into the depths of the African's eyes, and saw something. And the African looked into DuPris's eyes, and saw that this man—this man and no one else in this world—could set him free of his prison.

DuPris made up his mind first. "You're lying," he said simply, and turned away.

And the African reached out with one withered hand, and took DuPris's sleeve. "No," he said, his English very poor. His mind had aged so rapidly in the three years since he had left his homeland that his grasp of the new language was terrible, but he fought to pull some pieces of it together. "I make signs. I teach you . . . if you help me."

DuPris looked at him, with just a little more interest in his eyes. "And why should I help you?"

"Because I can make you live forever."

The two men looked at each other, and despite the fact that one was white, of wealth and fortune, and the other was, in all appearances a hunched-up old nigger man, barely able to speak English, DuPris believed, at least enough to risk the money necessary to buy the African away from his owner.

DuPris brought the African back to America, and to his plantation—not Bloodroot, but another owned by his family, this one in Mississippi. And there, the African languished in chains until it suited DuPris to come to him.

And DuPris did, after almost a week. The African, chained hand and foot, waited in shadow for DuPris, and when DuPris came, the European said, "You said things to me when we were in Haiti. If you have more to say, you had best to say it now. If you were lying, or if you choose not to speak, I am afraid it is going to cost you a great deal of pain."

The African told DuPris everything, and in the end, DuPris believed. All the African asked for was the chance to prove that what he said was true. To do this, he needed a woman, a woman who was fertile. The African doubted the ability of his body to perform, so the woman had to be unusually appealing, alluring.

And one was found, a nineteen-year-old slave named Marie who had already had a child. She was mulatto, and purchased for her appeal. Again, it cost DuPris, but there was little risk, really. If the African couldn't do what he claimed, DuPris would still own the woman.

She was told that she could earn her freedom by bearing a child by the African, and that the child would belong to DuPris, but that she might be able to earn the child's freedom. She agreed, and presented herself to the African, and his body wasn't as decrepit as he had feared. There was still one last act of lust left in it, and then another, and then another over the weeks, as he aged even more rapidly now. He managed to perform as a man only by the most extreme acts of will.

And Marie became pregnant. The African tried to wait for the full term of the child, but his unnatural acceleration of aging became even more severe. He was losing his faculties, until even his mind, at last, nearly failed.

Marie was only five months pregnant when the African felt his heart almost go. By this time he was like a man of eighty, all bone and loose flesh, and terrible eyes burning behind a shaven skull.

He knew he could not wait four more months. He could not wait four weeks. Marie must have known that something terrible was in the air, because when he came to her hut, she tried to flee. But he still had the strength to catch her by the hair, and to stab her down.

And there in the hut, he used that knife, and removed from Marie's body the living child he had given her. And without cutting the cords that bound the babe to his dying mother, the African then performed a ceremony. I will not detail it in these pages.

All I will say is that when the overseers followed the trail of blood back to the shack that the African had been given, they were afraid to enter—DuPris had agreed that no one could enter that building without his permission. And when DuPris came, he challenged the African, and was horrified by what he saw, and leveled his pistol.

Then the African said, "See and believe!" and before DuPris's eyes, the child, who was somehow alive even though ripped from its mother's womb, began to shrink, and shrivel, with streams of living light flowing from it as it did. And the light covered the African. And right there, before DuPris's eyes, the African began to grow younger. His body straightened, his hair grew, and grew darker. And his skin filled out. In that one act, the African became again a man of thirty.

And DuPris looked at him, and lowered his pistol, and said, "What must I do?"

And that was the beginning of their relationship.

* * *

The obligations are simple to understand. DuPris protected the African, and provided him with women to impregnate, and later, men to drain. I do not understand everything about the ceremonies, or what is happening. I do know that the life force can be taken from adults, but it must be filtered through a child of the same blood, or it may prove fatal.

According to the beliefs of the African, the human soul is like living fire, or lightning, woven tightly by the mind and will of the human being it animates. But that soul can be stolen, and taken apart, and its heat and light taken by the man with the knowledge to rip it apart. It can kill, it can heal, it can give back youth. It is power, and can be used for almost any purpose.

There is a saying in the land of the African: "Soul and skin are linked: Soul can lead skin. Skin can call soul. Both soul and skin can be stolen or torn apart. Shun the man who would tear skin—for he is evil. But fear the man who steals the soul, for that man can steal the stars from the sky."

I have seen it do many things, this power. But always, there is a price. The magician drains himself, or must drain others. It seems that there are three things necessary for a magician. I said before, I will say again: First, you have to have the talent. It seems that this is passed in families, like height or shade of skin. Without the natural talent, the effort is futile. Second, you have to have a source of power. The souls of other men are the best. Third, you must be trained. Knowledge is important. Without all three of these things, there can be no magic.

The African kept DuPris alive. They needed each other, for different reasons. And the partnership has lasted nearly two hundred years. They have had to move at least four times, when members of their community began to wonder why DuPris never aged. But this was not difficult. For there were family businesses in several parts of the country, and new farms could be bought. I never traveled beyond the confines of Bloodroot, but I know that on at least one occasion, Augustus DuPris returned to a place he had visited sixty years earlier, presenting himself as his own grandson.

When he was gone, I had permission to use the library in the big house, and I did, improving on the lessons I had learned at Lisha's side, reading the way a starving man feasts.

And also, of course, I trained with the African.

These two hated but needed each other. In the one part of the Americas where the African could find human beings to slaughter and defile, he himself was considered less than human. And that means that he needed the help of Augustus DuPris. Both are slave. Both are masters.

I served each in a different way. The African had little interest in my body. DuPris took little in my mind. Yet each in his own way strove to possess me.

And I learned, studying every night, until I began to dance at the ceremonies, I called down the lightning from the sky. I watched as the children of the other women died, screaming. They hated me, those women. Hated me because my children lived, while theirs died. Hated me because I had managed to do what they would have done, had they had the ability so to do.

I do not say that what I did was right. I would not say such a thing.

I only say that I would do it again, if I had to.

I still remember, though. Remember the lightning, streaking from the sky. The lightning, and its victims. Shrouded in flame, cursing my name as they died.

I would do it again.

14.

Somehow, time passed. My children grew. We lived in quarters separate from the others, and took our meals at a somewhat more luxurious standard.

But I worked hard, both body and soul, for that protection, and struggled with myself.

What was the struggle? Can you not guess? Is it possible to wield, or be near such power, and not feel its pull? I could not. And I fought to keep my mind. I fear that I had already lost my soul.

I served my two masters for sixteen years, and knew them as no one else did. No one in Miller's Parish knew when he was at Bloodroot or abroad. DuPris had lawyers and other men who separated him from the community. And because he rarely met with the same ones twice, they would whisper about him, but were never sure: was he son, or brother? Or grandson? Or the same man?

Many times he changed mode of dress, and the way he wore his hair. Beard, mustache. He painted his hair gray on the very few occasions that he did take the carriage into town on this business or that.

I know that the people in the town talked about him, that they carried tales, but they were also afraid of him, and could prove nothing.

But over the years, I changed. I began to change in my body, and my hair grayed. I bore children for each of these men—The African would sometimes use my body for a ritual, always of power. Two children, one a son, the other a daughter, sprang from these unions. I bore three more children for DuPris.

But most of my time I spent in study, or taking care of my children. I could see the changes brought by the years. I was older, and some of the life gone from my step. My hair was streaked with gray. My face was lined.

I had never seriously considered using the ceremony myself. It terrified me, even though I was a central force in its practice.

But one day, as I made a shirt for the African, spinning his hair into thread, and stitching that thread into the fabric, he came and squatted behind me.

He moved silently, and I didn't turn, but I knew he was there. He had an animal smell. Not a smell of dirt or corruption, but the strong smell of a male animal, one which, even though he didn't take his pleasure with me, kept me in readiness at all times. And I knew that he was behind me.

He stroked my hair.

I wondered what it was that he wanted, wondered even if he intended to initiate sex, but the sound of his voice told me that quite a different thought was in his mind. "For you to serve me," he said, "you must extend your life. One lifetime will not be enough."

As he said it I realized that I had always known that this day would come. Known it, and feared it. "Why not?" I said.

"Do not ask questions," he said. "Accept the Gift."

A thousand objections filled my mind, but the first to pass my lips was most obvious and the strongest of all. "I can't kill one of my children in order to live," I said simply.

"How like a woman." The African laughed. Then all humor dropped from his voice. *"Chango Jaya Mala Chango—"*

He said more, but I will not repeat the words. There is power in words. Some of you might be tempted to attempt some of the things I have described. Know, then, that I have changed things enough to render the words and rituals useless. Please, my children. Do not follow in my steps.

But even as he spoke, I felt the strength of his words in my body. My back grew straighter. Around me, the air glowed as with a flaming mist. And I felt something which was not warmth, not cold, but which had characteristics of both. The light grew harsher, tighter, and finally took on a shape and form within me. The shape of an unborn child, very young, floating within my womb.

The African whispered the next words. "There is no need to kill one of your children. There is life within you. We can use that."

The understanding, the true comprehension of his

words came a moment after I took their general meaning.

I fought panic. "No," I said. *"Wait—I can't do that!"*

"Make your choice," he said coldly. "The life unborn, or the children you have swaddled and taught to walk. Either you are of use to me, or you are not! Choose!"

I looked into his eyes, seeking escape. There had to be a way out of this. How could I do this? The only way I had been able to justify my actions was with the thought that everything I did, I did to protect my children. If I took this step, for any reason whatsoever, it would change all of that. I would be lost.

And yet . . .

What kind of liar would I be if I did not admit that, at the same moment I realized that I was completely trapped, that for the good of the children living I would have to sacrifice the child unborn, that there was a kind of dirty joy inside me? And that that joy was the part which had sat, watching as I explained away one sin after another, saying that all of them, all of them were for my family.

And knew all along that it would come to this moment, knowing that I had the chance to receive a gift that men and women have dreamed of as long as there have been people.

I did not argue, or struggle. My head went down.

The African gestured, his fingers writhing as if they had independent life. I saw the child within me. It hung there, suckling at my body, wanting nothing but to be born, the very seed of life itself.

Suddenly, it began to twist, to writhe as if it were in awful torment. I cannot relate the pain it caused me to see and feel what was happening within me. I screamed, and my scream was drowned out by the scream which came from within me, a scream that accused me, damned me. I will never forget the sound of that scream, no matter how long I live. I felt the pain of its death. I clutched at my belly, and fell over onto my side. The pain rolled through me in waves, and I sobbed. But as I lay there, I saw my reflection in a mirror. Gray had streaked my hair, and lines of age were plain upon my face. Although the travails of my life weighed upon me less sorely than many of my slave brethren, still it was a heavy burden, and had left its mark.

As I watched, that mark faded. I felt the power of the life within my womb flow out, as if a small fire flowed through my veins, and my entire world flowed with light.

I lost all of my senses.

When I awoke, I looked at myself in the mirror. Tears streaked my cheeks. I was a girl again, a girl of no more than nineteen, and the mixture of terror and guilt and a dirty joy poured through me. I was immortal. I was a goddess.

I was damned.

"This is the Gift," he whispered. "Kings and queens would give all their kingdoms for what I have just bestowed upon you."

And although I knew that it was true, I watched a single tear slide from my eye, and down my dusty cheek.

15.

The years passed, and my family grew. I bore more children for each of my masters, and my children played more with each other than with the other children. Although the other men and women on Bloodroot were afraid to offend me, they subtly discouraged their children from playing with mine.

I was the mistress of the ritual. I tried to have influence where I could, and have the slaves who were killed during the ritual be of the most spoiled and violent nature, but there was nothing that I could do to keep the truth from being the truth. It was murder, murder by any name. And there was nothing at all I could do to keep from knowing that every year, at least one of the children would die. All I could do was concentrate upon the children who remained to me. I arranged for each family to lose no more than a single child, and then for the rest of the family to be sold to another plantation. They never knew what happened to their children. But no longer was there the singular dread, wondering when the next boy would leave. Only boys were sacrificed—probably because the girls were more valuable as breeding stock.

None of the little things I did to make life easier for the other slaves, to find them better food and work, stand as anything but what they were: the baldest possible attempt to save my own soul, an attempt to buy myself back from purgatory.

But the nights that I stayed awake, wondering what would happen to me when I died, were too numerous to count. It seemed that sleep eluded me entirely.

The nights belonged to fear.

I was the matriarch of the plantation. A woman older than most of the other slaves, who never aged herself. Oh, I would gain perhaps ten years, and then grow younger again. I felt the life within my womb reabsorbed into my body again, and again. This I could bear, as I could never have borne the death of a child I had heard talk, or taught to walk. Were they any less alive? I do not know. I hope so. I truly do, but I sometimes fear that I lie to myself.

I heard them scream.

One day, more than thirty years after I first came to live there, a woman came past my house.

She was old and gray, and bent. By custom more than by law, old slaves were often cared for by the masters who had had the use of their minds and bodies for their productive years. So it was not unusual to see such, even after their useful years had fled, doddering about the plantations, often working small patches of land given them by a master who had reason to feel grateful for their decades of service.

At first I didn't know the woman, but she stared at me, and I finally realized that I did know her. She was Coretta, the midwife who had shown me the truth. Coretta, who had tried to help me flee, who had implored me to kill my children and myself if I could not escape. I had not seen her for almost twenty years. Our eyes met.

I wanted to speak some words of reassurance, of thanks. I wanted to thank her for her warning.

But her face twisted into a mask of such loathing as I have never seen. She hawked and spat into the dust at my feet, and shuffled away.

I held my child, my fifteenth child. For a brief moment, I wanted to call after Coretta, to explain to her. I had done the things I did only to protect my family. That is all. But I couldn't speak. I never spoke, I just watched her walk away, every step that she took closing another small door in my heart.

I had made my deal with the devil. My family was safe, so long as I abided by it. My obligation was to them, and not to anything else in this, or the next world.

And so, I thought, it would remain.

16.

The world changed, for me and for the whole of my people, in 1861. The rumors and stories had of course been flying. Carolina, and other slave-holding states, would secede from the Union. Shots had been fired at a place called Fort Sumter. The Confederacy had the strength of King Cotton, and didn't need the men of the North.

But I believe that no one really thought that war would break out, and that all were surprised when it actually did. The one thing that everyone was certain of was that the fighting wouldn't last. The Yankees, it was said, just didn't have the stomach for war. They would rather sit and prattle on about the customs of the South, but when "the claret began to flow," and their precious sons began to return from the South on stretchers and in boxes, they would soon lose all taste for war, and sue for peace.

In many ways, it didn't really affect us much on Bloodroot. Oh, we saw supplies rolling up the roads, and sometimes men in military gear came to the plantation on this business or that, but the harshness of the war didn't really affect us.

But the slaves, the other slaves—I knew that they were abuzz, even though they didn't really speak of such things when I was around.

A victory for the North would mean freedom. The plantation was filled with speculation on what freedom would mean, where we would live, and how the Yankees would treat us. I wish that I could have been a part of that, but the whispers and laughter died away as I approached. I was not a part of their world, any more than I was truly a part of the white world. I lived in a land of shadows between white and black, a thing of evil who clung to her memory of the one good thing that she had—her family.

But I knew that news of every Yankee victory flowed down the pipeline, the slave rumor line, like water down a river. During this time, slaves from some of the neighboring farms would come to Bloodroot on one bit of business or another, and I would hear eagerly recounted stories of Yankees slaughtering Southern troops, laughter as they spoke of "Master so-and-so" brought back in a box or legless on a stretcher, even as sad faces were given to the white folks.

I knew of at least a dozen cases where a slave would cry in front of the parents as a Southern son came back, crippled or blinded or dead, and then that same Negro would fall on his knees in his own hut, thanking a God he didn't quite believe in for humbling a hated master. Every dead Southern boy meant a Northern victory was closer.

It amazed me that whites often believed that their slaves were actually rooting for the South. It was one of the things that convinced me white folks were no smarter than anyone else. People will believe whatever they need to believe, no matter how little sense it makes.

I remember a day standing by the fence, watching beaten Confederate troops trudging past Bloodroot. They were bloodied and bandaged, and I think I began to realized for the first time that the war might actually end badly for the South. The look on these men's faces was of the lost and the hopeless. Men in hell might have such faces.

They were beaten, and knew it.

Refugees streamed south, away from the advancing Union army, carrying with them the substance of their lives. Then refugees streamed north, as General Sherman's troops were said to be advancing from the south. It was a pretty dance those fine, proud people did.

Then came a special day. For the first time, we could hear cannon fire, musket fire from afar. It sounded like sharp thunder crackling in the sky. The Confederacy attempted to stop the advance, but rumors said that the Union troops were no more than a few days away.

I turned and ran back to the house, uncertain of what I should feel. I didn't know what such a change would mean to me and my family. I was afraid for my soul, and happy for my people.

Up at the main house, the servants were packing frantically. The house was stripped of paintings and silverware, all were placed in wooden boxes. Wagons had been streaming south for a week now, emptying the house, but so filled with wealth was DuPris's house that it took days before any real impact was made.

Augustus DuPris stood in the middle of his living room, directing servants. I slipped behind a curtain, next to one of the floor-to-ceiling windows, and listened. He never saw me there. For only the second time in the sixty years I had known him, he seemed close to be losing control. "No!" he screamed. "Take the paintings, damn it! Forget the china. It will break."

One of the colored servants asked, "What about the gold plate, sir?"

"Yes, of course the gold plate. And hurry."

An enormous overseer named Mr. Bright strode into the room. Bright was a cruel, stupid man, quick with the whip, quick with coercion and a careless smile for those women not under DuPris's protection. A muscular thug—with DuPris's bright red hair. "The soldiers are no more than three miles away, but the line is holding at Tampico Bridge."

DuPris seemed to radiate contempt. "It won't hold," he said. "The men will be back day after tomorrow. Give the order. I want the livestock killed. All of them. Anyone who knows the truth."

I froze. I had heard him use the word livestock before, and always to refer to the women who bore him children.

"Yes, sir," Mr. Bright said. "What about the woman Dahlia?"

I think I must have held my breath as he considered the answer to that question. All of the hopes and dreams in my heart were pinned upon it. There was no doubt in my mind that DuPris stood to lose much if the stories of free Negroes were ever tallied carefully.

After a considered pause, he said, "Dahlia and her spawn are protected. But all of the others die, do you understand?"

The window latch was undone. I opened it, and slipped out.

I do not think that I can convey the mixed feelings which I experienced. We were safe! He would keep his word!

And yet, and yet . . .

At what price? I tried to tell myself that it did not matter, that nothing mattered except the lives of my family.

But it was a lie. All a lie. In a few hours, days at the most, I would be free. And in that state of freedom, I would have the opportunity to reflect on what I had done in order to survive.

And I had an advance taste of it, then and there. I saw the faces, all of the black faces who had suffered and died that monsters might live. That my family might live.

And whatever price I had paid over the years, whatever justifications I had made, one thing was clear: Before, nothing I could have said or done would have saved those boys, those slaves. Yes, I participated in those ceremonies, and ultimately profited by them. But I comforted myself that there was nothing I could have done to save them, and made the excuse that people have made since the beginning of time, that if it hadn't been me, it would have been someone else, and the evil would have continued. No more people died—but no fewer, either. I merely affected the list of names to spare my own blood.

And if there was sin, it was the sin of a mother doing what had to be done, when there were no alternatives at all.

But now I knew what was going to happen. I knew that the coming dawn would see the death of over three hundred innocent souls. And if my mind and heart trembled with the burden I already carried, there was no chance at all that I could justify this.

There was a chance, however small, that I could save them. I would have to risk my own family to do it, but it was a chance, and I could never live with myself were I not to take it. It was a chance to save three hundred lives.

And just perhaps, my own soul.

17.

The cannons fired all through the day, and although the night brought a cease-fire, I knew where to go. I fled through the woods, fleeing not for my life, or even my freedom, but for the one slim chance at salvation that I would ever be given in this lifetime.

I came to a road, a road crowded with Confederate supply wagons. It was packed also with refugees, and one more fleeing Negro woman attracted no attention at all.

I saw a man on that road. He was an old, old man, and haggard, and looked as if he had been through the bowels of hell.

Thanks to the African's gifts, my mind, my eyes could sometimes see things that others would miss, and I knew at once that this aged graybeard was one of the night riders who had stopped me on the road, fifty years before.

He rode on a wagon, barely able to keep his head up, exhausted utterly. The substance of his life had run out, but he still went on, like some kind of clock whose battered face no longer tells time, but the wind-up works just keep ticking and ticking away without purpose.

His eyes met mine, and there was something, some momentary stirring in them, perhaps recognition.

I cannot say. There were many emotions that ran through his eyes in the moment that we faced each other. But if he recognized me, he couldn't have allowed himself to admit it—it would have meant too many things, too many for his mind to bear.

So he might have thought to himself that this slave woman was familiar, and left it at that.

I knew that I was drawing near the lines. I cut east across a field, walking and running when I had the strength, and it seemed that strength just flowed to me that night, as if there was no end to the resources that I could call upon.

I had always supposed that the strength and endurance which I enjoyed as a result of the terrible ceremonies were gifts of the devil. But now I wondered, wondered if they weren't merely the release of some strengths already within me, unleashed through those terrible deeds.

Whichever it might have been, I ran, ran all the night, ran until my feet and my legs were sore and raw.

At last I came to the place I sought. The Conway

farm. A green two-story house spread in the midst of carefully gardened acreage—not farmland, this was the home of a man who had made or inherited his money, and sought out a place of comfort.

The land was dotted with drab tents and slow-moving, bandaged men. Many merely lay on the ground, moaning. Some slumped on boxes or rude chairs. A few leaned against trees, staring numbly off to the horizon. They were tired, exhausted, barely aware of my approach as I limped up.

These were the faces of the beaten. To my left, a scream seared the early morning, and the smell of blood and smoke and seared flesh.

I walked through the outer reaches of the encampment. This was a kind of makeshift medical facility, a temporary hospital. They had taken over the Conway farm. The exhausted horses looked more alive than the soldiers. Wagons creaked out along the curved pebbled road, carrying away the wounded and the dead, and in makeshift tents, by torch and lantern light, I saw the bodies of men as they screamed for God to take them as the doctors worked on their bodies, hacking away limbs.

I hope that I never come closer to hell than the things that I saw there.

There was a scream from one tent, and a frightful figure lurched up, escaping the men who fought to hold him down, a big burly man, an Irishman, I think. His arm was sawed off at the shoulder, and the stump spurted blood. He could no longer stand the pain and tore himself free and out of the tent, running, screaming in pain, flailing his limbs in such a way as I have never seen before, until struck by three men who finally held him down. And he lay there in the mud and looked up at me, his eyes blinking, as they put the torch to his wounds, and the smell of seared flesh rose up. He looked at me not as a white man might look at a Negro woman, but as a child might look to his mother.

"Please..." he said... and I felt myself start to

kneel, to cradle his head in my lap, his rough and callused hand in mine.

Never had I experienced so much pain from another human being, and as his hand closed on mine I felt him shudder, and his great eyes closed, a single tear squeezed from beneath the lids.

Then they gently pried him away from me, but as they carried him away, his eyes remained locked on mine, and I swear that they were saying "Thank you." He thanked me, for doing nothing but holding his hand when he was in pain.

He was a Southern man, and in another time might have ordered me to do anything, including lie in his bed. Might have killed me without fear of meaningful retaliation. But his pain and grief made him just a man. And I had been just a woman for that moment, and held him, and there had been a bond.

Trembling, I rose, and went on.

I came to the house. An aged black servant greeted me at the door, and inquired as to my business. I asked him if Missus Conway was there, and to tell her that I had a message from an old friend of hers, from a long time ago. The message was important, and for her alone.

He stared at me, only a little curious. It didn't profit Negroes much to pry in the affairs of white folk. He disappeared in the house, and I stood there in the early morning air, listening to the whimpers of the men who had sworn to throw the North off their land in six weeks.

I felt more tired than I ever had in my life.

The old Negro man returned, and bade me to enter the house, and to enter the parlor. I walked into that house.

I had wondered often what had become of Lisha. I wondered if her marriage had worked out well, if she lived a life of comfort. And hated her for the things she had. She had, after all, purchased her happiness with my misery. I hoped that she had thought about that every day.

But now, as I drew close to her, my feelings changed.

There sat before me an elderly woman. She must have been seventy, and not a healthy seventy at that. Only her eyes seemed truly alive.

"You may stand there, girl," she said, and she was doing something with her hands. Sewing, it looked like. Her hands were knobby things, but clearly she had been sewing all of her life, and skills practiced so consistently often remain after other faculties have fled. The old woman smiled slightly, tiredly. "I hear that you have a message for me," she said. "You know, it seems that these days everyone wants to talk to me. A colonel's widow is still very much part of things, you know."

"You are widowed, ma'am?"

She nodded. And I saw in that sad, sweet gesture the girl I had hated, for all of those years. "Yes. He was called back to the regiment during the Mexican War, twenty years ago. And died. But I've been well taken care of. When they needed me, they knew they could count on me. All of these boys. All of these good boys."

I saw her hand falter just a little. She sat in that alcove, with the sun coming up behind her through the leaded glass, and suddenly I could see her, doing her sewing, looking out upon the world she had known and knowing that it was going to change forever.

She cleared her throat. "I suppose that it had to happen, the sins, you know."

"What sins, ma'am?"

"In this life, you must earn everything that you get. And we took things that we didn't earn," she said. "The South is paying for what it took." She looked at me shrewdly. "Your people will pay, as well."

"Excuse me, ma'am?"

"Everything is going to change. And you will be no wiser than we were. And you will take what isn't yours, and in time, you will pay for it, I am quite certain."

I felt confused, and had no idea how to answer that.

"Now, girl. What is the message that you bring to me. And who is it from?"

"It is from Dahlia Childe," I said softly, and watched her.

She continued to sew for a few moments, and then she stopped. She looked at me, very carefully, and she put the sewing aside.

"Dahlia Childe," she whispered. "That is a name that I haven't heard in fifty years. I have thought of her, though."

"You should, ma'am," I said.

"Yes." She looked at me carefully. Very carefully. "You . . . remind me of her, girl."

I knew that I had to be very careful here. "I'm glad," I said.

She studied my face for longer than I thought it would have taken for her to make up her mind about something, and then returned to her sewing.

"She was my . . . grandmother," I said.

"Yes," she said. But her hands were shaking a little. "I suppose you know that she and I were friends once."

"A long time ago," I said. And sat, quiet.

She reached up and pulled a bell cord. A slim, attractive mulatto appeared, wearing a maid's dress. "Adelpha, would you please bring me some milk?" she asked.

She smiled to me in an apologetic way. "My stomach won't tolerate much more than milk these days."

I nodded. Her hands were shaking more, and she finally put the sewing down and looked at me. "Would you . . . care for a glass of milk? I recall that your grandmother loved milk."

I nodded. Adelpha left with the two orders.

"What is your name, girl?" she asked.

"Dahlia," I said. She nodded. I saw something float behind her eyes, something that neither of us were about to admit.

"And you live over on Bloodroot?"

I nodded. She nodded. Outside, somewhere, I heard a man scream. She flinched.

"We never had much to do with the DuPrises. They were said to be wealthy, but they didn't mix in society.

Sometimes one of them would be seen in town. I suppose I've seen a DuPris twice in my life. There's . . . a strong family resemblance, I hear.''

She was watching me. I nodded.

"I have to admit, hearing things over the years, I often regretted selling your grandmother to the DuPrises. I wasn't certain that it was a good thing to do.''

I decided to ask a question which, for a slave, might be considered impertinent. "Then why did you do it?"

Lisha couldn't meet my eyes. "He offered the best price,'' she said.

"She was your friend?'' I asked.

"You may believe it or not—'' Her voice started with a touch of defiance, but there was too much deep sorrow behind it to sustain that mask. "But I have regretted my decision. In fact, about three years after we sold her, I attempted to buy her back.''

I felt something happen in my heart that I wouldn't have expected. "And what was the problem, ma'am? Was the price too high?''

She shook her head. "No. The DuPris who owned Bloodroot refused to sell her. I talked my husband into offering quite a handsome sum, almost twice what we sold her for, and DuPris refused. I could talk my husband into going no higher. I tried twice more in the next few years, but Mr. DuPris's representatives refused finally even to discuss it, and so I forgot the matter.''

I sat, stunned. I had not known. I wanted to rush across the room, and embrace my friend, to tell her that her words meant the world to me, but there was no way that I could without revealing more than I dared. "I am certain that my grandmother would have wanted to hear that.''

Her next words were chosen very carefully. Her voice was almost breaking, and I suppose, her heart might have been, as well. "Is she not alive, then?''

I thought. "No,'' I said finally. "She died when her oldest boy was thirteen.''

We were both quiet, and Adelpha returned with the

milk. It was warm, and delicious. "So tell me, Dahlia—how might I help you?"

"I fear for the safety of the slaves on Bloodroot," I said.

Her hands stopped moving.

"And why is that?"

"I think that you have heard rumors over the years. Some of them are true. I believe that DuPris is afraid of what would happen if his slaves were freed."

I saw her face, saw the impact of my words sinking in. "What is it that you wish me to do?"

"Do you believe that this war can be won by the South?" I asked.

She shook her head slowly. "No," she said. "Once, I thought so. We were so proud, so certain that we knew what was right, and that God was on our side. That our cause was right. But as we've lost the war, it seems that something within us is collapsing. That the moral rock on which we stood was merely sand. I see the faces, girl. All of those young boys. They've died . . . for *nothing*."

"Help me save three hundred lives," I said. "Help me. I need to help the Union troops break through the lines. I know where the supply lines cross the river. I could lead a group of men there, force the Southern troops to fall back, get Union men to Bloodroot a week ahead of schedule. They could save my people."

She looked at me in naked horror. "What are you asking me to do? I can't do that! You're asking me to betray my own!"

"For my grandmother—"

"No! Never! How dare you!" She stood. "I welcomed you into my home, treated you politely, as you were the granddaughter of my old friend, and you insult me like this? Leave! Leave at once; no, wait here, I will have you confined to this house—"

She raised her hand to summon the servant again, and I said sharply, "Lisha. Do it for me." My voice was strong. The pretense had dropped away. "Lisha. You owe it to me."

And my voice was dead, and deadly serious, and she turned and looked at me with dread in her face.

"No."

"Look at me," I said.

She refused to, but her hand didn't pull the bell.

"Lisha," I said, and my voice was commanding. "Look at me."

Slowly, as if she were the slave and I the master, Lisha's hand dropped away from the bellpull, and she looked at me. Her old eyes focused, and she studied me. She was not trying to decide what the truth was. She was, rather, trying to lie to herself, to dissuade herself from believing what she knew to be true.

"You know who I am," I said. And again, she couldn't look at me. She did not resist as I pulled a bit of cloth from her hand, and plucked the needle from her fingers. She watched as I wove that needle a dozen times in as many seconds in and out, stitching, turning, my hands moving almost as fast as the eye could see— sixty years of practice with young, strong fingers gives that to a woman.

And I handed it back to her. The old initials were there. The D and the C. They awaited her intermingling signature. She took it from me, eyes still too widely open, mouth open, and she studied it, and took the needle from my hand, began to stitch, and then stopped— and stared at me again.

I took a step closer. Her eyes were wet dark holes. I think I have never seen an animal so trapped. Her mouth shook.

"But . . . but it's not possible. You haven't aged."

"But I died," I said. "There have been whispers. You know there have. And when you heard them, you tried to buy me back. You know you did. And I thank you. But you sold me. You sold your friend so that you could have a comfortable life. A good marriage."

"I had the right—"

"*You had no right!*" I screamed. "You had the *privilege.*"

The gaunt old manservant appeared in the doorway,

eyes questioning, but she waved him away. "No," she said. "I am all right. Leave us alone."

He looked at her, and then at me, questioningly, and then obeyed.

"How did this happen?" she whispered.

"He is the devil," I said. "I did what I had to do, to protect my family."

She looked at her hands. I still remembered when they were small, and held mine so softly. I remember, as though it were yesterday. And then she stared at mine, and I could imagine the thoughts in her mind.

"You are a good Christian woman," I said. "I knew you when you were a girl. I knew your mama. The price is too high," I said.

She looked into my face then, and in some way I felt that she was really seeing me for the first time, and what she saw there broke her heart.

I thought myself, of all of the nights, all of the rape and the death, the price that I had paid, and I think that as I thought those things, she read my mind, or something very like it. Somehow the space between us vanished, that wall was gone, and we were in each other's arms, crying for all of the years lost, for the things done and the things left unsaid.

For a few moments we were just Dahlia and Lisha again, two friends, who loved dancing and sewing and cool milk on hot days, poetry and song, one of whom had the misfortune to be born with black skin instead of white, and that had made all the difference in the world.

18.

Oh, and I could have remained there forever, holding the old woman who had been my dearest friend. I had never had a friend in my life but Lisha, and I hadn't realized how much I missed it until those moments, when she revealed her heart to me. When she told me she had sought to purchase me from my bondage.

We had both done what we had to do, and her sins were less grave than mine. There is no way she could have dreamed what fate she had consigned me to.

"What can I do?" she asked finally.

"I have to save them. I have to. It is my only chance."

"But I can't. . . ." she said, but her voice wavered.

"It's my only chance to undo what I have done," I said. "My soul." I couldn't say any more, and she searched my face.

She was a Southern woman, a slave owner, who had been married to a man who, had he lived, would certainly have fought for the Confederacy. She had sons, and grandsons who fought for it. And I was asking her to betray it to save a few hundred colored folk.

I had no right to ask it, but I did.

"I need to think," she said. "Would you leave me for a few minutes?"

I nodded, and kissed her cheek, that old cheek which had once been young, and which I had kissed so many times, and went out into the yard. The sun was higher now, and still the moans of the dying drifted like night shadows across her dairy farm. To the north, cannon boomed.

I suppose that there was a part of me which might have felt some joy that these boys were dying in the defense of such a monstrous cause, but I couldn't find it within myself to hate them. We are all born into the world, and God tells us where we land. Some have power, and some are victims of it. And it is our job to find grace, whatever our position. Some of the Northerners no doubt were good men, others not. Some men of the South were good, and others not. I know that I had failed my own test, that somehow I lost my own way.

It was not my place to judge.

The gaunt old colored man at last summoned me back to the parlor, and I stiffened my back and went there without the slightest idea what to expect.

Lisha stood near the window, head bowed and

hands behind her back. "Dahlia," she said. "We have lost the war. If I was not certain of it, no matter what I might owe you, no matter what has happened, I could not help you. But enough damage has been done. What I want is to prevent any more bloodshed than there needs to be. And just maybe, this will help to bring the whole damned thing to a close a day earlier, and save a few lives."

She looked at me, and her expression was pitiful. She was seeking some way to make excuses, to justify what she knew had to be done, and there was no way out for her which was honorable.

"Yes," I said. "It will save a few lives."

She nodded. She looked at me again, and through me, I think. I suspect that she had heard more rumors about Bloodroot than she could admit. I suspect that she had thoughts about what price I might have paid for the gift of youth. I suspected that she would look at her face in the mirror tonight, and every night for the rest of her life, and wonder if she would pay the same price, if she were given the opportunity.

And that she was glad she had never had the chance to find out.

"You will be given a wagon. Take the north road. I have heard that there are snipers there, but a lone black woman should have no trouble. You will carry a letter on my husband's stationery, saying you are on urgent compassionate business for me. This will get you through the Confederate lines. What happens after that is up to you."

She couldn't meet my eyes. The morning light seemed almost to shine through her. "And now, if you will excuse me, I have young men to see after." She handed me the letter, with a small round red wax seal upon it.

She took my hand one last time. Our eyes locked, and I knew that there was something else that she wanted to say, and I knew also that she couldn't find the worlds to say it.

Her eyes dropped, and she left the room. I looked at the letter in my hands.

I never saw her again.

19.

The rest of it, the travel along the road, being challenged by Confederate troops twice, showing the letter, and crossing into Union territory supposedly to fetch medicine for dying soldiers, need not be told in detail. I will just say that I at last found my way to the camp of Colonel Fields, an intense, bearded man serving under General Sherman who listened to what I said about the supply lines, and found that it matched his own information.

The prospect of a guide who could take his men through that passage gladdened his heart, and I don't think I have ever seen a man who was in more need of gladdening. I swore to help them, on the condition that those men, once having cut that line and taken the bridge that supported it, would help the folk at Bloodroot. He promised, and I was happy to find him a man of his word.

The idea was to help a few dozen men through a route known to the slaves who passed between plantations during these war days, a path which got around the Tampico Bridge.

That journey was cold and wet and harsh, but no man there moved with more purpose than I did.

We came up from behind the soldiers at Tampico, and they never had a chance. I wish I could take some kind of pride in what happened there, but it was just a slaughter, with men caught in the meat grinder, and chopped up and spit out, dead before they really knew they were in danger. A few surrendered. Most never had the chance.

Medical treatment was given to the few survivors, and the Union sergeant, a good man name of Grunwald, held that bridge but put a group of men together to take back to Bloodroot. The wagons traveled for almost an hour to get there, and a small group of soldiers tried to stop us, but the line was broken, and men were fleeing south to try to regroup again.

The soldiers poured behind me. There were supplies—food and ammunition and weapons on a plantation to the south of Bloodroot—and the idea was to get to them before they could be moved, which suited me fine.

The soldiers streamed onto the plantation, headed toward the main house, and I led the way.

Mr. Bright, the overseer who had grinned at me so often as I came and went from the house, who had passed into old age as I remained a girl of twenty, was shot down by the troops as he rushed at me, screaming, cutting at me with a sword.

I ran into the main study, hoping to find DuPris, hoping that Union troops would try to kill him, that they would see that their efforts were fruitless, that he would be exposed as the monster he was.

But he was gone, only his hateful portrait staring down at me. The house was deserted. I stood in the study, where he had bent me back across the desk and ravished me those long decades ago, and prayed that he was gone forever.

Outside, Union soldiers swept out, streaming across the grass. They were celebrating, and streaming farther south. I saw Negro folks, slaves today, but free very soon. I cried, knowing that it was not too late, and that in some small way, a victory had been won.

I began writing this journal after Bloodroot was freed. I wasn't certain where I, or my folk, would go. I knew only that everything in my life would change forever, and that when things change, memories of the past sometimes dissolve into mist, and are gone forever. I did not want that to happen. So I found bound books in Mr. DuPris's house, and I began to write at night, hiding the journals in the bottom of a wedding box. It will hold the mementos—maybe a little money, the nightgown with my own hair woven into it, a wedding dress I plan to make—and will be passed down from one daughter to another.

I do not plan to teach the terrible things I learned under the African—who has also disappeared. But it seems to me that the facts as they occurred might be valuable to those who come after me.

I trust that if that is ever the case, that these journals will be found, and some knowledge in them put to good use.

It's been two weeks since I wrote here. Bloodroot is a Union encampment now, and troops move through here easily. DuPris's former slaves work happily for the Northerners, cooking, cleaning, fetching. Some of the women offer more than that, and some of the soldiers accept.

Male slaves from the neighboring plantations come here now, and the situation has changed so much, so quickly, that it is hard to believe what has happened.

The slaves know that I was the one who brought the soldiers. They hate me still, but are grateful, and none of them speak of what went before.

My family is safe. I remember the moment at which a stone rolled from my heart. I sat in my house, surrounded by my family, including daughters who look older than me. They call me sister. They have sworn never to speak of what has happened.

Union soldiers walk past, smiling and greeting. Because of me, perhaps some hundreds of their comrades are alive who might otherwise have caught a ball or a bayonet.

I do not know what will happen tomorrow, but I write about what happened today.

Today Aunt Coretta, who brought my children into the world, walked by the cabin. She looks to be almost eighty years old, and life has been hard on her. She carries the knowledge that she was bringing human cattle into the world, and that they were ill used.

She walked only with the help of a stick, and every step was like an ordeal. "Dahlia," she said. "I need a word with you."

"Yes," I said.

"DuPris got away," she said. "Nobody know about the African. He gone, too."

"I heard."

She looked at me, cocking her head to one side like she was some kind of bird. "I heard what you done. You risked everything. For us."

For myself. I thought. For my soul. But then, I know what she meant. "I owed you that much," I said.

She nodded, slow. "That you did. What you done . . ." She looked away, and I looked where her eyes pointed. Two old women, only one looked like the other's granddaughter. "All them years. That's on your soul. We hated you. But you ain't all bad. Maybe you only done what you had to do. What I would have done, if I'd had the smarts. What I want to say is . . ."

"I know," I said. "And I'm so sorry. For everything."

The wind blew kind of cool then over Bloodroot. Somewhere to the south of us, I heard cannon. Sometimes freedom is a painful thing.

She sighed, the way only an old woman can sigh. "I guess the good Lord will sort it all, in His time."

"In His time," I said.

I only hope that God is kinder than those He made in His image.

Been a while since I wrote here. The war is over now, and we are free. The Union men let us take some things from Bloodroot, and wagons, and we are moving north, up Illinois way. Hear tell there's good farmland up there.

Most of my family is coming with me, we're sticking together now, for a while, anyway. Strange, since all this happened, I can feel tired all the time. All the time. Maybe . . .

I don't know. Maybe I'll write more, later.

May 1866, Sweet Valley, Illinois

I have got to write this down. We are in a good place here, and we have a place to live, and a piece of land to call our own. My family takes care of me, and they watch over me. They're worried.

I'm worried, too. I know what happened to the African, all those years ago, and it's happening to me. I think every month is like a year. In the two years since the end of the war, I must have aged twenty. I got my gray hair back, and I think that scares everyone, but not me.

We got our land. Things are hard now, but the worst is behind us. I get feelings sometimes, feelings that it isn't over, but after everything that's happened, it would be natural to feel the fear.

I dream sometimes. Dream about the long years. About the master. About the things I did.

In those dreams DuPris says he's coming after me. He'll find me. He better hurry. The feeling in my bones says I'm aging fast, he better hurry, or I'm going to cheat him again.

Because I beat him. I did what I set out to do. I was just a poor nigger woman, but I used what I had, the way I could. I don't expect God to give me an award for what I did—I'm ready to pay any price He asks. But I'll say now, looking out over the valley, on the porch of the home we built together with our own hands, looking out on the cornfields tilled by my children and grandchildren—

I'd do it all again.

Thursday, May 14

42

Derek was the first to struggle his way up from the depths of trance. Slowly he oriented himself to the cabin, focused on the five other human forms in the room, and on the shimmering image of Dahlia Childe.

Dee was staring at the ground. "About a week ago I had a dream," she whispered. "DuPris and the African came. They called you terrible names. And killed you."

Dahlia nodded. "Yes, dear. I died. I betrayed them. And they cursed me to witness and share the pain of my family, down through the generations. And so I have."

"DuPris." It was Tucker who spoke now. "DuPris is my great-grandfather."

Dahlia nodded. "Yes. Several times removed. His blood is strong. He had his own magic even before the African gave him the gift of life. Some of my children married whites, and in time their skin grew lighter."

"The African," Dahlia Washington said. Her voice was weak, and she looked faint. "He's still alive. We call him Scar Man. Oh, my dear Jesus. He gave me my baby. He took my baby. . . ." She began to sob. Deep racking convulsions that seemed to be ripping her apart. Rachel put her arms around her cousin, and held her tightly.

Rachel looked at Dahlia Childe, and swallowed hard. "You helped them kill other children."

Dahlia's voice was a whisper. "Yes."

"To save your own."

Again, the whisper. "Yes."

Rachel looked as if she wanted to curl up and die. "You were my hero," she said. "I named my daughter after you."

"Mom," Troy said urgently. "She rescued everyone at Bloodroot during the Civil War. Right? Didn't you?"

Dahlia hung her head. It was impossible not to feel her pain. "They caught me," she said. "They killed me, and cursed all of you. I didn't save you. I damned you. For a hundred and thirty years I've felt every pain inflicted on my family, died every death over and over again." She made eye contact with each of them in turn. "You have to stop them. You are the only ones who can."

The image flickered, as if she were a dying television image. "I've shown you everything I can. It has to be enough. If I can help again, I will. For now," she said, "good-bye. Try to forgive me."

The floor beneath her seemed to turn liquid, swirled like a whirlpool of melting wood. Slowly, Dahlia sank down through the floor, and was gone. The floor solidified again.

The room was silent except for the soft, insistent sound of Dahlia Washington's grief.

For almost five minutes, the cabin was silent. Derek finally sighed, and then said, "So. We know the truth now. Rachel's family is descended from Dahlia's children by this African. You, Tucker, are descended from Dahlia's children by DuPris." He smiled thinly. " 'Bean pie,' my brother?"

Tucker groaned. "Would you *please* just shut the fuck up?"

Troy held Dee's hand. "What can we do?" he asked. "Where's the African?"

Tucker's voice and face were grim. "No idea—but we have the other bastard's name. DuPris. That *has* to help."

Rachel finally seemed to pull herself together. "Is he still alive?"

"Bet on it," Derek said.

Dahlia Washington seemed incredulous. "Won't he have changed his name?"

Tucker seemed lost in thought. "I don't think so," he said. "I've heard the name. Somewhere." He suddenly snapped his fingers. "I've got it!" A lightbulb suddenly went off behind his eyes, and he stormed up and ran out of the room, excited. The others looked at each other, and after him, wondering what in the world had excited him.

He was back in three minutes with a stack of magazines. He dumped them on the table. Their covers were well-composed color shots of fleshy women in negligees and outfits that, while technically considered bathing suits, bore the same relation to swimming or tanning that cigarettes bore to healthy outdoor living.

Tucker stabbed his finger at the masthead of the top magazine, which said *Looker* in three-inch-high letters.

Directly under those words, in somewhat smaller letters, it read, "A DuPris Entertainment publication."

Rachel immediately leaned back, and her face creased thoughtfully. "DuPris Entertainment?" she asked. "Isn't he the mystery man?"

Derek began to thumb through the magazine. It was high-gloss sleaze, a cross between *Hustler* and *High Times,* barely legal to distribute through the mail or across state lines, a celebration of every erotic pleasure known to man.

"What's the mystery about him?" Derek asked.

"He's a recluse," Rachel said. "Hasn't been seen in a decade. He's very wealthy—or the family is. Nobody's certain who runs the business. It might be DuPris's grandson."

Tucker's smile was flat and grim. "Now, why do people wonder that?"

Rachel closed her eyes, as if trying to find something in a mental filing cabinet. "*People* magazine got a picture," she said. "It looks about the same . . . as a picture taken . . ." Her face suddenly changed, as if a sudden realization were dawning upon her. "Thirty years ago."

43

It was four o'clock in the morning, and Tucker was very, very drunk. Crumpled beer cans lay all around his feet. He drained a Coors, gazing off into the eastern mountains. The sun was only a few minutes below the mountains. When evening fell, dawn would rush at the Lightning Dawn camp like a blazing tide.

Derek approached him nervously. "So," he said finally. "Where are we going?"

Tucker looked at him blearily. "Not 'we,' " he said. "This is personal."

"For both of us," Derek said. "I have a stake in this, too."

Tucker laughed, a flat, harsh, ugly sound, and for a second Derek clearly heard DuPris's voice in Tucker. He had the feeling that Tucker heard it, too, and was disgusted with himself.

"You want the truth?" Tucker said.

"Sure. Give me the truth.

"You're not up to it. I don't have time to wet-nurse you."

He turned his back, and popped the top on another beer. Derek seethed for a long moment, and then grabbed Tucker's shoulder.

"You fucking will listen to me. I got you this far—"

There was something that felt like the whirling of a savage wind, something invisibly fast and primally strong. Derek felt the air *whuff* out of him as his back slammed against the wall. His eyes wouldn't focus. Tucker pushed his face up close.

"You got us here," he said, "because you have disk drives where most men have balls."

Derek could see every pore, smell the beer on Tucker's breath. "Be happy," Tucker said. "A live wimp is not necessarily a bad thing to be."

Tucker gave Derek's throat a little squeeze. It was almost affectionate, as if just letting Derek know that he was an old and dear friend. Derek turned his head to get away from the beer smell.

When he turned his head, he saw Troy. Slender, small for his age, eyes wide and unimaginably hurt. He ran back inside.

Derek's head slumped in shame and defeat and corrosive self-loathing.

Tucker was oblivious. He released Derek, then trudged off, weaving drunkenly.

"Now," Tucker said, "I'm going to take the most heroic shit of my entire life. And tomorrow, there is a man I have to kill." He paused thoughtfully. "Slowly."

Derek looked back toward the cabin doorway. Rachel held Dee, whose face was buried against her mother's chest. Dahlia Washington approached him. "It's all right," she said. "He's drunk."

"He's drunk," Derek snarled, "and he knows exactly what he's saying. And he's sure he's right." He looked at her. "And he's not."

He shook her hand off, and stormed after Tucker, angrier than he had ever been in his entire life. Troy watched, holding his breath. And praying.

* * *

Tucker was almost too drunk to find his way into the latrine. He was enjoying the feeling of being drunk, because he knew that when he came down from that feeling, there would be a world of pain to deal with, a state he would postpone for as long as he possibly could.

He began to sing to himself, to the tune of the old Coasters' song "Poison Ivy":

"Vietnam, Vietnam
Late at night, while you're sleeping
Charley Cong comes a-creeping arouuund—"

He staggered into the nearest toilet stall, dropped his pants, and sat. The door of the stall swung shut behind him. He sighed massively.

A sound outside the cubicle. It registered on Tucker's blurred senses that someone was outside the door, and he squeezed his bladder sphincter closed and leaned forward, preparatory to getting up. The door flew open, and in doing so, struck him squarely in the face.

He felt pain and shock and surprise. Mostly surprise at the identity of the man responsible.

Derek Waites charged in. Tucker was caught with his mouth open, eyes wide, and started to raise his hand too late as the trash-can lid in Derek's hand smashed down into his face.

He saw stars, and struggled to get up off the toilet to defend himself. But his drunkenness, the surprise, and the state of dishevelment combined to create a vulnerability so total that he could barely think.

Tucker managed to get one massive arm up, and with it blocked blow after blow from the trash-can lid, enough to get to his feet. With the other hand he gathered his pants up in a bunch. The trash-can lid hit him a solid one in the right temple, and he heard something suspiciously like a whimper escape his lips. He screamed, as much at himself as at Derek, and tried to balance himself for a kick. The stink-slippery latrine floor betrayed him and he went head over heels, smashing through the thin wooden wall with a crash to end worlds. He smashed over a bench and somersaulted over a

trash can, trying to reclaim his balance, to buy himself room
to think or act.

But Derek didn't allow him any room or time at all, just
came after him like some kind of goddamned machine. What
made it worse was that the man was screaming something at
him, something he could barely hear over the cacophonous
crash of the trash-can lid against his head.

"Is *this* the only thing you understand?" Derek ranted.
"I am so *sick* of your macho"—*clung*—"warrior-ethic"—
clung—"dick-measuring"—*clung*—"*bullshit!*" He screamed
the last word, and punctuated it with an especially fierce swing
of his can lid against Tucker's ear.

A few Lightning Dawn men straggled out of their barracks, alerted by the groans and clungs. They stopped, frozen
in amazement by the sight of the slight, scholarly Derek
Waites flailing away at their hero with a garbage-pail lid,
Tucker struggling mightily to pull his pants up so that he
could concentrate on defending a less important target.

Tucker's face was cut and bruised, but his pride was hurt
far worse. He hooked his fingers around his belt, and yanked.
The trash-can lid came in, and he grabbed for it, but stumbled, losing his balance, and as he fell, Derek clobbered him
again.

It wasn't fair!

The LD men hooted and laughed. Tucker forgot about the
pants and lunged forward. Waites twisted like a bullfighter,
and bashed him with the trash-can lid again.

It seemed to go on forever. Little actual damage was inflicted, but the pain and humiliation were almost unbearable.

Then Waites paused. "Had enough?" he panted.

Hunched over, Tucker stared at multiple, wavering
Waiteses. There were three of the skinny wraiths in front of
him, weaving about like ghosts. Tucker hit the one in the
middle. Finally, this time, he connected.

It only took the one. Derek Waites staggered back, his
mouth opening into an O of surprise as the blow landed in
the middle of his chest. Tucker hit him twice more—once to
the belly, and once to the face. Derek went down hard, onto
his hands and knees, drooling blood.

Even sucking wind, Waites radiated defiance.

Grimly Tucker stalked over to him, bent, gathered Derek's coat collar up in one massive hand and drew him up. His right hand balled into an enormous fist. Waites glared at him, unafraid. Even with the bloody nose and sliced lip . . .

Glared at him.

Tucker looked around. Troy and Rachel and Dahlia Washington were watching. And Dee. The little girl. Damn her, she was terrified that Tucker would hurt her daddy.

He looked back at Waites, who awaited the final blow. And never flinched.

Tucker let Waites go. The black man staggered and almost fell, but stayed on his feet. He still stared at Tucker. And finally he said, "I'm . . . going with you."

Tucker shook his head. And then he laughed. "I guess you are," he said. "I just guess you are. One thing—next time you're winning a fight—don't stop to admire your work."

Derek gasped for breath. His stomach muscles must have been killing him. "I'll . . . remember that."

The men of Lightning Dawn guffawed until they were stomping around in circles, slapping each other on the back to keep from choking. They had no idea what they had just seen, but they did know one thing—they'd just had a week's worth of belly laughs watching a skinny-ass egghead with a trash-can lid give the Great Tucker a helluva bad time for about forty seconds there. And that, as the saying goes, was worth the price of admission.

44

Rachel screwed down with her thumbs, eliciting a groan from her husband that would have done credit to the darkest pits of the Tower of London.

She tsked. "Such a baby." She bore down again on his shoulders, working her way carefully around the most damaged areas. He lay on their futon, face up, naked to the waist. An ice bag lay on the side of his face, where Tucker's single blow landed. His lips were puffy and discolored. He yelped again when she tried to change rhythm on him.

"You look like one big sore spot," she said.

He groaned again. "It's been a busy week."

She stroked his back with her fingertips, grazing the spine, and bearing down on the muscle. "Bruised ribs, a broken tooth—it could have been a lot worse."

"You should feel it from this side," he groaned. "It *is* a lot worse."

Despite herself, and the seriousness of their situation, she couldn't help but laugh. "You know, watching what you've been willing to do for Troy . . . for us . . ." She sighed. "It makes me wish that things were different. Had worked out differently."

Her eyes were with him, and then away again. She lowered her head. "Medford," she said.

"He loved you a lot," Derek said. "And the kids. I never liked him, but even I knew he only wanted good things for you."

She nodded, so filled with hurt that she seemed about to explode. "Everything was so right, and it's all gone so wrong. I can't even feel the pain. Everything is just . . . compressed reality. I'm just trying to hold it together. Does that make any sense?"

He nodded.

"And now you're going to go away and get yourself killed."

"I'll be back," Derek said, mimicking Troy's Terminator voice.

She wasn't amused at all. "I don't know how much more I can lose right now. If this ever . . . when this is all over, I want to put my life back together. I don't know what part you might play in that."

He touched her face, and she turned it slightly, not a rejection, so that the warmth of her cheek rested against the palm of his hand.

"I love you," he said.

"I know," Rachel said softly. She took his face between her hands, and looked deeply into his eyes. "No matter what I've said, or have trouble saying, I could never stop loving the man who gave me my children. And is willing to fight for us.''

And then, somewhat to his surprise, she leaned forward, and kissed him softly. ''Come back to us,'' she said.

45

Derek had his computer case and overnight bag in hand as he appeared in the front doorway of the cabin, but was taken aback by an odd sight: Tucker deep in an argument with Dee and Dahlia.

He couldn't hear what they were saying, but as he came closer he saw Tucker's expression turn to one of exasperated despair. The big man threw his hands in the air. ''This is just fucking *classic!*'' He snorted.

He stormed past Derek into the cabin, pausing only to say, ''If it's going to be a goddamn parade, where are the fucking elephants?''

More confused than ever, Derek turned to Dee and asked, ''What was *that* all about?''

It was Dahlia Washington who answered. ''We had a dream,'' she said. ''Dahlia wants me to go with you to-night.''

He was stunned into silence, and fought to find something intelligible to say. Before he could find the words, Dee cautioned him. ''Uh-uh, Daddy. You can't argue with dead people.'' Her face was so round and calm, so infinitely wise beyond her eight years, that he was struck absolutely dumb. Finally he nodded numbly, and went to the side of the cabin where Tucker sat on a stump, smoking.

Tucker grunted his greeting, and shook out a cigarette, lighting it for Derek. Derek took a single drag, and coughed harshly.

''Things'll kill ya,'' Tucker said sympathetically.

Derek took another pull, hacked again. When the fit had passed, he said, ''We could both die tonight.''

''Figured that out, have you?''

Derek sucked on the cigarette again, and this time managed to keep a little more of it down. He let a long, thin stream of smoke into the air, feeling as if he had poured kerosene down his throat and ignited it. There was something that he wanted to say, and for some reason, it hurt more than the smoke. He coughed, this tremor mild enough to shield with his hand. "I just wanted to thank you," he said.

Tucker grunted. "This isn't for you and your brats," he said roughly. "It's for my son. My family. That's all that matters now. All that keeps me going. I want to kill DuPris. And die." He said it so calmly, so matter-of-factly, that Derek almost missed the last word.

"Die?"

Tucker exhaled a long, long plume of smoke, as if he were emptying out all of the anger and sadness within him. "All my life," he said. "All I ever wanted to be was a soldier. Served my country. Got all the medals. Great warrior." He took another drag. "The one time. The one goddamned time it mattered . . ." He stopped, and Derek suddenly had a very real and deep sense of what might be going through this man's mind. The scene in Tucker's house. The death of his daughter, and the climax, standing in a courtroom, accused of the very deaths he had been unable to prevent.

God. How had he remained sane?

"My boy," Tucker whispered, and turned to look at Derek. Derek thought that never in his entire life had he seen a man with eyes more haunted than Tucker's. It hurt just to look at him. Pain radiated from him like waves of heat.

"My little girl. My wife." He dropped his head into his hands, and held himself as if afraid that he might come apart if he didn't hold on tightly. "Great fucking warrior," he whispered.

He looked up and into Derek's face. His eyes were bone dry, but Derek knew that on another level, on and in another part of this man's existence, Tucker was shattered. "I just want to stop hurting," he said.

Derek took a slow, steady pull on the cigarette, and exhaled it. He said nothing. There was nothing to say.

*   *   *

Dee hugged her father tightly. Tucker's car was loaded with gear. Guns, climbing equipment, her father's computer, and bags of things that explode, and pierce, and kill.

Behind her, in the door of the main office, Tonya watched. Krause's arm was tightly possessive around her.

Even thirty feet away, Tucker could see her black eye. His stomach tautened, and he wasn't sure why.

Some of the men of the LD were crowded around him, helping him load, shaking his hand.

"Kick ass, Tucker."

"Take care of business."

Leaning close, a whisper: "And if a bullet catches the nigger while you're at it, that's a shame."

A tiny figure pushed through the ring of burly men. Tucker hardly noticed it at first, wasn't really aware until he felt the tug at his arm.

"Take care of my daddy, Mr. Warrior, sir."

He looked down into her face, and for just a moment, he saw his own daughter's face in Dee. He didn't like seeing that, or feeling the things that he felt because of it. But he nodded. She loved her father. This he could understand. He couldn't speak in answer, but he did understand.

He climbed into the car. Dahlia Washington sat in the backseat. Waites climbed into the seat beside him. He turned the key, and the engine coughed to life. They drove away.

Behind them, Rachel and the children waved, surrounded by people who disdained them, but were more afraid of the man who was leaving, a broken warrior named Tucker.

The gates closed behind them.

If Tucker had been paying more attention, he might have seen that some of the shrubbery across the road from the LD encampment had been disturbed, was pushed slightly out of alignment with the bushes around it. Deeper into the brush an entire bush had been clipped neatly away, the severed branches used to disguise a little multiterrain vehicle. Two men sat inside. A computer screen the size of a lunch box was positioned between them. Its green grid lines glowed palely. A pencil-point-sized light dot flickered to life on the screen, and the computer screen beeped. As Tucker pulled past them, it beeped more rapidly, then slowed again as they pulled away.

One of the two men picked up a cellular phone and speed dialed a number. With a click, it was answered on the other end by a dry, passionless voice.

"Yes?"

"They're moving, Mr. Timms," the observer said.

Then pushed a little red button to the left, hanging up the phone.

46

The Looker mansion was a square block of outrageous luxury in the middle of Brentwood, California. Its arched roof was barely visible behind high walls crested with barbed wire. At the corners of the walls, lurid feminine torsos with painted breasts postured for neighbors and passing drivers. A fierce and ultimately futile zoning battle had been waged over the images. Derek vaguely remembered reading about it, and cursed himself for not remembering the name Augustus DuPris.

Cautiously Tucker and Derek slipped out of the car in a miniature park across the street from Casa DuPris. Tucker leaned back in to speak with Dahlia. "Make a loop," he said, "and be back here in fifteen minutes."

She nodded, then slowly pulled away. From the park, Tucker scanned the walls and dense shrubbery carefully with his binoculars, talking aloud, more to himself than to Derek, as he did.

"Barbed wire," he said. "Electrified. Motion sensors." As an aside to Derek: "Swiss. They'll be tough." He clucked, but for some reason didn't seem discouraged.

"So," Derek said. "What do we try?"

"Bravado."

He zipped his jacket and slicked back his hair. Moving quietly, he jogged across the street, but motioned for Derek to stay back out of sight as he approached the camera at the guard gate.

"Excuse me," he said, a bit apologetically. "Listen—who's on duty tonight?"

A beat, and then a guard's voice crackled back from the speaker. "Mr. DuPris? I thought you were out of town, sir."

Tucker laughed self-consciously. "Got back early. The car broke down three blocks out. Buzz the gate, will you?"

There was a very brief pause. On some subliminal level, although the man in front of him looked and sounded like his boss, especially over a video relay, the guard had to sense something amiss. But the guard said, "Yes, sir," and buzzed him through.

The gate slowly swung open. Derek squelched his astonishment and grabbed the gear bag, skirting the security camera and walking straight up to the mansion.

They walked up a circular drive to the main door. A Lexus, a Rolls, and a silver Jaguar were parked on the circular drive. Over to the left was a sealed garage. Derek sourly assumed that the more valuable vehicles were parked therein.

As they reached the front door, a huge man opened it. His swollen arms and shoulders were almost a parody of fitness, the kind of physique that only comes from monomaniacal focus on iron plates and anabolic steroids.

"Sir? I—" He peered more closely at Tucker, and suddenly realized that something was wrong. There was no time to react. Tucker hit him so fast that it looked as if the body builder had been shot. A pistonlike motion of the right arm, fingertips burying themselves in the notch where the ribs join at the top of the abdominals, traumatizing the diaphragm and the inferior vena cava.

Unable to breathe, the guard crumpled to his knees. His face purpled and his mouth opened and closed like a beached fish. He slumped forward, and Tucker caught him. Derek tied the body builder's thumbs together with a twist of copper wire. Tucker crept inside, and Derek followed.

The interior of Casa DuPris was cavernous, ceilings three stories high, so distant they were swallowed by the shadows. It felt like walking into a museum, or an aircraft hangar.

Their flashlights stabbed into the gloom, illuminating first this statue, and then that classic painting. They were salacious, but rendered in a classic style. Every painting, every statue had a disturbing sexual undertone. He felt almost dirty scanning the never-ending vistas of hips and gleaming thighs, gaping mouths and blood-gorged organs.

"This looks like a Rembrandt," he whispered. "But I don't think he ever did a nude self-portrait like *this.*"

The next painting solved the riddle for him. It was in the style of Giovanni Battista Tiepolo, and on first glance looked much like the painting "The Erection of a Statue of the Emperor."

But closer inspection revealed that the group of women were indeed erecting something immense, and indeed it belonged to someone or something of imperial dimensions. There, however, the similarity to the original ceased.

So the mansion of Augustus DuPris was filled with very clever forgeries, all with a common debauched theme.

Tucker grunted in disgust, and motioned them on.

The hallways were silent, then they heard a very distant scream. A single piercing shriek. A woman's voice.

Tucker raised a finger to his lips, and moved onward.

"Please. Oh, God, no more—"

They moved quietly down a luxurious, deserted hall, Derek growing more and more alarmed, as much by the silences between the whimpers as the pitiable sounds themselves.

"Oh, God—"

Then came another scream, but this time, curiously, music blended with it. Derek and Tucker reached a corner, and peered around it.

Derek felt disgusted. They were in a guard cubicle, and the guard in question was watching a sadomasochistic porn video. Whips and cuffs were deployed, thin rivulets of fake-looking blood trickled. Tucker stepped in swiftly.

The guard hadn't realized that someone was behind him when Tucker said quietly, "I hope that's one of mine."

The guard spun around, gasping, "Mr. DuPris?"

Tucker spun him and clamped an arm around his throat. The man struggled convulsively for a few seconds.

Derek watched the man go limp. "Is he dead?"

"Only morally."

Derek crossed the guard's thumbs behind his back and twisted wire around them.

Tucker opened the black bag, and handed a shotgun to Derek. Derek took it, trying to remember the half hour of instruction Tucker had given him at the Lightning Dawn encampment. His mind felt very clear, the fear pushed way back up inside himself somewhere. It was there, it was just as real as it had ever been. The only difference was that now he didn't care if he was afraid.

Tucker motioned Derek to the other side of the hall, and they began to creep through the darkness, flitting from shadow to shadow, occasionally risking a flashlight burst.

Tucker kicked a door open, and shone his flashlight into the darkness of a bedroom-suite-sized bathroom. It was deserted.

Derek examined the walls as they walked along the corridor. He tapped, prodded, examined, paused and tried to sense for odd air currents. A bare whisper of a breeze ruffled the skin on the back of his hand as he approached a floor-to-ceiling replica painting featuring some unknown artist's crude and predictable visual pun of Salvador Dali's melting clock motif. He felt around the edges until he found a latch.

"*Pssst.*" He crooked his finger at Tucker, and the big man slid over. "I think I have something."

Tucker nodded approval, and Derek triggered the latch. The painting slid back, exposing a hidden door.

It exposed a narrow descending stairway, a mouth into unknown depths. Tucker's flashlight beam stabbed into the darkness. Derek swore that he heard a distant, evil giggling sound.

Tucker raised an eyebrow. Together they walked down the stairway, Tucker slightly in the lead, with Waites taking up the rear.

The stairway was of carved or simulated stone, and twisted down and down through two stories of darkness. Derek felt as if a metal band were tightening across his chest, squeezing out his last breath.

He forced himself to take one more step, and then just one more. Each step was a victory over DuPris, over himself, over the African. The fear was hammering at the gates of his control now, and if he hadn't been with Tucker, he was certain he would have run, gotten the hell out of there. But he wouldn't let this man see him turn coward. The hell with that. They were in this together, to the end.

A heavy wooden door barred the end of the stairway. "Hold this," Tucker said, and handed his flashlight to Derek. Tucker bent and rummaged in his bag, and came up with what Derek recognized as a pick gun, a sophisticated locksmith tool.

Tucker fiddled for a minute, adjusting something, and then started working on the lock. Derek heard an irregular *click . . . click . . . click* sound as Tucker worked on. Five minutes. Eight minutes. Sweat rolled down Derek's back, soaking his shirt at the belt line. He held the flashlight steady on the lock as Tucker worked. The air at the bottom of the stairwell seemed to vanish, and the room began to spin. He had to get out. He had—

"Tucker . . ." he started to gasp, then there was a click, and the door opened.

The giggling sound was louder now.

The door opened into an artificial underground grotto. Faux stalactites grew from the ceiling, stalactites thrust upward from the padded floor.

Hookah pipes extruded from the walls. Derek sniffed at one, thinking that the residue smelled richer, more *electric*, than the best grade of hash he had ever smoked in his college days. Who said crime didn't pay? Little trash bins were littered with amyl nitrate vials and foil condom wrappers. There were a few low tables, their surfaces mirrored. Tucker ran his finger along its surface, picking up a residue of white powder. He sucked his finger, grinning. "The man lives well," he said.

Derek panned his flashlight around the room until he found the source of the ghostly giggling sound—a trickling waterfall running down a fall of artificial rocks.

"Nothing and no one here," Tucker said. "Let's take it back upstairs."

* * *

An examination of the far side of the den disclosed another flight of stairs. It took five minutes for Tucker to find the trigger. They climbed the steps and emerged in an elaborate game room crammed with video games, pool tables, and hundreds of thousands of dollars' worth of gleaming toys. Derek and Tucker beamed their flashlights around the room rapidly.

Derek's light whipped past a corner, then zoned back in, revealing a gleaming stainless steel Dungeon Quest platform. "Expensive toy," he said. "I worked on the code."

Tucker grunted. "Want to autograph it?"

"Not hardly."

It was Derek who found the next door. It opened into DuPris's private office. A wall map as large as a man was erected behind the desk, with red Xs and pushpins marking up the Los Angeles basin.

They began to search the office, the fact of the ticking clock paramount in both their minds. In the top drawer of DuPris's desk Derek found a gold Dungeon Quest key card. "Everybody's a fan," he mused, and dropped it into his pocket.

"What the hell is that?" Tucker said at his shoulder.

"Shit. Give me a heart attack, why don't you? Could you maybe make a sound now and then?"

"Old habit. How about I swallow a watch?"

"Sounds good. This card is a key to a computer game. May mean nothing at all, but my mind is struggling to make some kind of connection. I smell trouble."

"So do I," Tucker said. "We've got big trouble. And I don't know what direction it's coming from. There's nobody here—DuPris's employees think he's out of town, and I swear something's wrong. Let's get the hell out."

Outside, Dahlia Washington drove slowly, cruising endlessly like a shark, passing the front gate for the second time, then circling around to make another pass. She was more frightened than she had ever been in her life. Most of that life she had lived placidly, without asking questions, just taking what had been given to her.

Questions were for people with options, and she didn't have any of those. She'd always told herself she was doing the best she could, and on those few occasions when she couldn't quite believe that, grass, or pills could be relied upon to numb the pain. It was like sleepwalking through life. Then Derek Waites came into her world, and demanded that she wake up.

Damn him. Damn him anyway, with his big words, and his rich wife, and his life that was beyond anything she had ever let herself covet.

She wanted to hate him, but couldn't. In fact, she found it difficult to do anything but think of what her life might have been like if she had been able to find, and hold, a man like Waites. She looked at herself in the mirror. Hell, she looked like the woman he loved, and that woman didn't want him anymore.

Maybe. Just maybe . . .

"Come on," she hissed. "I don't like this. Not even a little bit." Dahlia Washington scratched at the back of her neck. "Damn you. And goddamn that woman Childe. She got me seeing things."

47

In the California Sierra Nevadas, Chip Maddox and his partners patrolled the Lightning Dawn encampment. Silent Doberman pinschers strained at their chain leashes. They seemed hyperalert, as if aware that the apparent peacefulness of the night was a mask, and that behind that mask something feral snarled its anticipation.

In the cabin, Rachel played a game of Go Fish with Dee and a reluctant Troy. A flashlight beam slid past her window, and she shivered. The past week had weighed on her as if all the hidden stresses of her life had emerged with a vengeance, attacking her simultaneously. The waiting was the worst— waiting for Derek, or Tucker, or someone else, to help her. She wasn't used to having other people take action for her, and it rankled terribly. But she just couldn't see a way to break out of the passive pattern that had taken hold.

Wait and see. Wait and see.

It was killing her.

Dee came to point, almost sniffing the air, beautiful little face screwed up as if she had caught a whiff of teargas. She had done this three or four times a day, every day, since this whole nightmare began, and usually, it meant nothing.

"Dee?" she asked, trying to lure her daughter back into the game. "Do you have any fives? Dee?"

"They're coming," Dee said.

And Rachel stared at her, then stood and peered out of the window into the night. The camp looked the same. Out at the periphery, guards patrolled the fence. Everything looked normal, but in her heart, she knew that something was wrong. Something *smelled* wrong.

The wait was over.

Maddox looked down and saw the laser dot focused on his chest. For a moment he didn't know what it was that he was looking at. Then he knew, but didn't have time to react. The stun dart hit him precisely on the breastbone, and he spun to the ground. "Gordo . . ." he sighed, as the waves of darkness flooded in on him.

The second guard spun and, too late, realized that something was wrong. He didn't have time to speak before a dart hit him, and he was stunned into unconsciousness, sliding onto the ground.

Just a moment before he was completely gone, his trigger finger tightened on his Uzi, firing a single burst, irrevocably shattering the evening calm. Cries of alarm went up from every cabin, all over the camp.

From every shadowed corner, crouched, camouflaged figures moved in, and the Lightning Dawn camp was sudden chaos. LD men raced from the cabins and tried to take defensive positions, and were cut down by stun darts before they had a chance. The shadowed figures never exposed themselves, never gave the LD a chance to fight back.

It wasn't a fight. It was a slaughter.

*   *   *

In her cabin, Rachel cowered with her children as screams and crystalline peals of broken glass rang out. A moan, and the sound of someone sobbing, followed by a heavy, dull impact. Then an eerie silence.

Krause lay face down in his office, hands covering his face. Tonya cowered next to him. Her face was sliced by a sliver of flying glass. Blood oozed onto her lips, dripped on the floor.

She started to hitch herself up, trying to get a better look at what was going on outside. Krause grabbed her arm and jerked her back down so hard that she slammed her forehead against the ground. "Get your head down! You want to get your ears shot off?"

The night was split by a megaphone-amplified human voice. *"Bring out the Waites children."*

Krause goggled disbelieving. "Shit. Is that all you want? Hell—"

Tonya blanched. "You can't. You promised Tucker."

"He isn't here."

"You can't—they're just kids."

"They're not even human. Hell. They're just mud people."

The voice called out again. "I will give you one hundred seconds to bring the children to the center of the camp. Ninety-nine, ninety-eight . . ."

Krause stood and crunched through the broken glass, held his hands above his head as he exited. *"Don't shoot!"* he screamed. "I'm getting the fucking kids!"

"Ninety-five, ninety-four . . ."

Krause ran out into the night, devoured by his own fear.

"No!" Tonya screamed. "You gave your word!"

One door. Front door already under observation. Find another route.

Without a word, Rachel grabbed Dee, and hauled her into Tucker's bedroom. She had caught a glimpse of a window there, facing out into the woods behind the cabin. If it opened . . .

"Check that window, Troy," she whispered. Bless his heart, he didn't ask questions, he didn't freeze, he just pried the window latch open, and pushed the window up.

"Go on," she said urgently. Again, Troy didn't hesitate, just obeyed, and scrambled out the narrow window. As soon as he hit the ground, Rachel lifted Dee up, and slid her feet through the window. Dee felt as if she weighed nothing at all.

Her daughter twisted as Troy's arms went around her, reaching back for Rachel. "Come on, Mommy," she said.

There was already a sound at the front door. "There's no time, darling."

Dee understood instantly, and the expression on her face was unutterable fear and alarm. "Mommy," Dee sobbed. "Come with us!"

"Run!" Rachel hissed. There was just no time.

"Mom?" Troy said, eyes wide with panic. She reached out and touched his face, his precious face, one last time, and then shut the window as a tall man with a beak of a nose exploded through the front door.

Tall man. In his forties. He looked like an Indian.

Rachel ran through the bedroom and tackled him, snarling and screaming like an animal, and the Indian spun and threw her against the wall.

She smashed into it, sobbing with the pain as her back crashed against the table, breaking it so that she went down in a heap with the broken pieces. She felt something go inside her. Maybe a rib. Maybe worse. It didn't matter.

The Indian turned and took a step toward the door.

Without a thought for her own safety, Rachel leaped, landing on his back, screaming *"No!"*

She allowed herself no doubt, no hint of question about the next moment. She screamed, and went at him with fingernails clawing for his eyes, taking his ear between her teeth, grinding hard until blood spurted. The Indian whirled and crashed her back against the wall, and the damaged rib did something inside her, something that felt as if a broken bottle were twisting in her lung. She slid to the ground and fought against the rising black cloud of pain and fear, and a tide of blood that chocked her throat.

Rachel rolled over and grabbed at his foot. The Indian stood, holding one hand to the side of his bleeding face, staring down at her, his eyes blazing. He screamed *"Bitch!"* and his foot came up, and then came down, and Rachel's world went black.

"Seventy-eight, seventy-seven, seventy-six . . ."

Troy sobbed for breath as he pulled his sister through the woods behind him, running frantically, just trying to keep on his feet. She stumbled, crying, and he gathered her in his arms and hid with her in a shadowy clump of brush. Listening.

Flashlights shone through the brush. Boots clumped around them. Troy fought to keep Dee quiet, without success.

"I'm scared," she whispered.

"Shh. So am I."

The searchers ran past, disappearing into the dark. Troy decided to seize the moment, and led his sister out. She took one step, and then her eyes went wide as Krause stepped out from behind a tree and grabbed her.

"Got you!"

Troy took a step, and punted Krause in the groin as hard as he could. Krause staggered backward a step, face reddening, but even as he bent, managing to swing one hand out at Troy.

Troy saw it coming . . .

And coming, and coming . . .

The world had slowed to a crawl. It was weird. There was something. Colors crawling inside him, trying to solidify like balls of Jell-O. And as they did, the world shifted, slowed down, so that he had all the time in the world to duck his head, spinning away from the blow, turning to grab Dee—

And stepping right into the hands of a second Lightning Dawn soldier, whose grip closed on his arm almost hard enough to break it.

Searchlights blazed out of the darkness, marking out a delivery zone. Krause and two of his men brought the struggling children into the light.

Krause cupped his groin with his right hand. Beneath his beard, his face still looked ashen. "All right!" he yelled. "Take them! Take them and go in peace!"

There was a pause, silence, and for an instant Krause might have hoped that his offer was accepted. Then a withering hail of stun darts cut him down.

Troy and Dee were the last left standing, and they stared at each other in astonishment. Before they could run, or react at all, men closed in from the darkness, cutting off escape. Struggling, they were carried to a waiting van.

Silence in the camp. Timms emerged from the shadows, a vastly satisfied expression on his face. A couple of other men emerged, in paramilitary gear. A truck backed into the compound. Against the sounds of the night, the sobs of women and children could be heard.

Timms waved his hands at the fallen men. "Get them, quick."

"There are more people," one of the camouflaged men said. "Women, and some kids."

"Five minutes," Timms said.

Even as he spoke, the bodies were loaded into the truck, and its tailgate slammed shut. More victims, some limp and unresisting, others struggling fiercely, were hauled out of the cabins. The sobs and wails in the camp were louder, more despairing. Then there was silence. Five minutes later the truck wheeled away, roaring.

The last few men disappeared into the bushes, and were gone.

For ten minutes there was no sound, and then a few survivors emerged from the bushes, utterly shaken, ashen, uncertain what to think or do. One of them was Tonya. She stared out into the night for almost three minutes, then walked on unsteady legs to the main cabin, and began to pack her bags.

48

Tucker and Derek cruised Sunset Boulevard, searching for a telephone booth. Tucker had said almost nothing since leaving the Looker mansion twenty minutes earlier. He remained silent as he pulled into a gas station and parked.

When the engine died, he said, "This will only take a second. My neck is burning."

Tucker walked to the phone, and dialed. Derek watched him. His stomach clutched like a big fist as Tucker's face darkened. First the big man yelled, and then spoke with deadly quiet into the phone. He paused and looked at Derek. After a long moment's hesitation, he gestured that Derek should come to the phone.

Feeling as though his body were on fire, Derek came to the phone and spoke, trying to steady the quaver in his voice. "Hello?"

It was Tonya on the other end of the phone. "Is this Waites?" she asked grimly.

"Yes."

"I only did this because I promised Tucker, you understand? It has nothing to do with you or your woman. I keep my word."

"What?" He felt dizzy, faint.

"She's gone," Tonya said. "And they took your kids. I'm sorry."

"Rachel? The kids?" He was stunned almost into immobility. He couldn't breathe. He couldn't think. "Where are they?"

"I don't know, dammit. They killed everybody, and then hauled the bodies away. I'm getting the hell out of here."

Then there was a harsh, metallic click as the line disconnected.

Tucker might have said something. There might have been sounds in the surrounding night. But Derek couldn't hear it, all sound and sensation drowned out in the fury of his own scream.

They found a Motel Six, up in Sylmar at the top of the San Fernando Valley. They pulled their car into the lot, three exhausted, discouraged people who weren't certain what move to make next, knowing only that something would have to be done. They booked two rooms, one for Tucker and Waites, and one for Dahlia Washington.

Dahlia watched the two men enter their room silently. She heard them talking and arguing as she undressed, and after she showered, they were still talking, far into the night. She turned on her television set to drown out the sound, and fell into a dreamless sleep.

Friday, May 15

49

Raymond Cross, former football hero, small-time thief and pimp, was jarred awake as a door somewhere outside his cell was suddenly slammed open.

He could barely think, barely move. The cumulative effect of two weeks' brutal confinement and daily sedation had reduced him to a jelly, an insensate mass that barely remembered its own name.

Nothing hurt. He might have been floating on a cloud. He remembered little of his life before this cell, this one dark, damp, stinking place.

Occasionally he heard someone crying, or screaming. Sometimes it was him.

But all of that was away someplace, removed from anything that mattered. All that mattered to him was sleeping, and drinking and eating and sleeping again. Most of the times he couldn't remember his dreams. When he did, they were ferocious, nightmares in which fanged plants dragged him into their tendriled maws, cannibals chased and cornered him and devoured him with dull teeth, cops wielding shrapnel-studded batons beat and beat and beat him.

But most of the time, there was nothing but dark, dreamless escape.

He dragged himself painfully across a wet, sticky concrete floor to the metal grate, and pressed his face against it. He could see shadows. Shadows of people carrying people. He heard someone groan. Heard a man's voice, heavy with pain and drugs: *"Can't do. Can't do this t'me. I'm . . . Krause! Got . . . friends . . ."*

The corridor between the cells was suddenly blocked, and Cross saw two men carrying a third. Another man opened the tiny cell across the corridor.

With a jolt, Cross recognized him. The Indian-faced motherfucker. The Indian said, "Throw him in—"

And the man who called himself Krause went into that cell hard, like a bag of bones.

The door was locked, with a terminal clang. Krause lay crumpled there, a long skinny dude with a Jesus haircut, wearing army surplus shit.

The Indian looked at Krause, and then at Cross. "You two should get along fine," he said, and walked away.

Cross managed to turn over onto his side, and focus a little better on the man across the way. "Hey, dude—you look like shit," he said.

Slowly, as if in great pain, Krause managed to reply. "Shut the fuck up, Sambo."

Cross laughed, the first and only laugh he had had since he woke up in this terrible place. "Sambo? *Sambo?* Is that the best you can do, you long-haired redneck faggot motherfucker?" He gasped for breath. Damn, it felt good to laugh. "You better take a nap. Try again later. . . ."

He wanted to say more, but was losing consciousness again. Losing everything. Except one thing. A memory of what it felt like to laugh. And a mounting fear that he had better try to remember that laugh.

That it might be the last one he ever got.

50

In the morning Dahlia showered again, using up two tiny bars of hotel soap, lathering as if there were no way to put enough soap and water between herself and the world. She donned the clothes they had purchased for her the night before. She felt clean, and crisp, and calm in a way that she hadn't in years.

It was strange. Every mile that she put between herself and Chicago blurred that entire world. It was as if she had viewed and lived her entire life through a cloud of smoke. The veil was lifting now, but she had the terrible feeling that it wasn't lifting quickly enough.

She went outside, and found Tucker sitting on the stoop outside the motel room, smoking. His gaze was far away.

"Where's Derek?" she asked.

"Still at it," he said. "All night. Tough bastard. Hasn't found a goddamned thing."

She stared at Tucker, and then knocked at Derek's door. There was no reply. She entered.

The room was strewn with paper printouts and pieces of plastic, maps, and cards strewn across beds and desks. And seated on the edge of a chair, leaning forward toward the desk, was Derek Waites.

He looked frail and hollow-eyed, as if his will animated his body like a puppet. He didn't even realize that she was standing there.

"You haven't slept in two days," she said.

He looked up at her, his eyes mad. Then he went back to the search.

"Where?" he muttered, having looked straight through her, then turned back to his work. "Where in the hell? The mansion. No. He never went back there. I checked the surveillance inputs at his beach house. Nothing. Looker corporate headquarters in Chicago ... no, dammit. Has to be here.''

She looked at him for a long time, and then quietly left the room.

Dahlia closed the door behind herself, but didn't let the latch slip into place. Tucker still sat on the stoop, but this time he looked around at her as if she existed. She stood over him for a minute, and then said, quietly, ''Would you leave us alone for a while?''

He stared at her. ''I hope this isn't pity,'' he said. ''If it is, you might as well shoot him. Be quicker.''

''Not pity,'' she said. ''He just needs some rest, that's all.''

''Rest,'' Tucker grunted. He flicked his cigarette off, watched it spin into the parking lot, showering sparks. ''It's what this whole damned world needs.''

She held her room key out to him. ''Here. You take this. I'll call you in a while.''

Tucker nodded. ''You do that.''

Dahlia Washington opened Derek's room door. Before she closed it, Tucker said, ''Dahlia?''

She turned in profile. ''Yes?'' She looked exactly like Rachel.

Tucker tried to smile. ''Be good to him, all right?''

Her nod was almost shy, and then she was gone.

51

''Derek,'' she said softly. He looked up at her, and his eyes didn't even seem to focus. She thought that she had never seen a human being look so worn, so lost.

He stared through her. ''I can't do it,'' he said, and his voice was a rasp. ''I can't. There's just too much information. There's no way to sort through it. . . .''

She took his weary face between her palms, and kissed him. At first he tried to pull back, murmuring ''No . . .''

But his eyes were a child's, a frightened child's, bright

and hot and fierce, frantic thought and effort the only thing holding back an eternity of pain.

"Shhh," she said. "You can't work no more now. You got to stop a while."

"I have to—"

She shushed him again with her lips. "Come on, now. I got all the flavor you need, right here. You just take it, for a while. You just be here with me, for a while. . . ."

She kissed him again, and he pushed back again, but more weakly this time. Then his mouth softened and he kissed her back, responding like a man literally starved for love.

They swept all of the evidence, the cards and maps, the computer printouts, onto the floor.

Exhaustion had almost crippled him. His fingers shook so badly he was unable to unbutton his own shirt. She had to help him, guide him. Comfort and nurture him. Hold him close. There was urgency there, and passion, but most of all, understanding.

And when the passion had cooled, she held his head carefully, softly, and said, "Derek."

He was very close to sleep, the stress and horrors of the past hours giving way to something that might heal him, might allow him to rest enough to access his mind, and find an answer. He nestled close to her, and said dreamily, "Rachel . . ."

Dahlia froze, but held him, staring into the wall in the darkness, a darkness she had been born into. Somehow, somewhere along the line, she must have had a chance to escape it. She must have.

Hadn't she?

52

In a shadowed, cavernous place, a small dark boy was chained to a post. His thin arms were stretched above him, and his wrists ached in their manacles.

Troy was awake, but his mother and sister were still unconscious, chained low against the wall to his left. The room was the size of a basketball court, and lined with television screens. At least a dozen wrist or ankle shackles protruded from the floor, and he didn't have to ask himself what they were for—he could hear the moans of captive men, somewhere in the shadows behind him.

He twisted and fought until his wrists bled, and fought to keep any trace of a whimper from his voice.

He had no doubts what this place was, and what it meant. Dahlia had given him visions far too explicit. The fear raging within him was enough to make him physically weak and almost paralyzed.

Still, he struggled, because there was nothing else to do, because to do nothing would be death itself.

He heard a door open behind him. He tried to turn around, but couldn't twist quite far enough to see it. The door clanged shut, and he heard footsteps.

The footsteps indicated that the visitor was huge. Troy began to quiver, to shake almost uncontrollably. From behind him, a gloved hand reached out to caress his face, almost lovingly. He tried to pull away.

He heard the voice then, the voice that he had heard in Dahlia Childe's nightmare. Impossibly deep and resonant.

The voice of the African.

"Soon . . ." it crooned. Another stroke of gloved fingers. "Soon."

53

At a little after two in the afternoon, Tucker's phone rang. "Yeah?"

"You can come on over now," Dahlia said.

She answered his cautious knock on the second rap. She and Derek were both awake and dressed. Derek stood as Tucker entered, smiling a little sheepishly. Without speaking, he went to the window and stared out over the parking lot.

"So," Tucker said finally. "What do we have to work with?"

Derek didn't answer, just stared out. He had managed only three hours of sleep, and yet his mind was clearer than it had been in days. Even that new, hard-won clarity couldn't make sense of the facts he had to work with.

He turned, and as he did his eyes passed his portable computer. Its squarish bulk sat on one of the room's two wooden chairs. There was something about it, and the more he thought about it, the more it niggled at him.

His mind, still fatigued and yet invigorated, flashed back to Rachel's apartment. Troy had a video machine made by Advanced Graphics, a machine with the same odd symbol on the side.

He went to it and knelt. He stared at it. What was it supposed to represent? So stylized was it that it might have been an eagle, or a strange cloud. It was like an inkblot test—he wasn't certain that it really meant anything at all.

Maybe it looked like a genie in a bottle.

His mind was flipping now, going back and forth. The next vision was the image from Dahlia Childe's vision, a vision that matched the descriptions in the diaries.

A human fetus in a leather bag. The source of the African's strength. A human fetus . . .

His mind was turning them over and over again. He stared at Tucker, and there was something there, something that made his mouth open in sudden realization.

Tucker started to speak to him, and Derek's hand shot out, warning him to be quiet.

"What's wrong with him?" Dahlia Washington's voice said. But she was far away. Farther away than the Advanced Graphics building, with the symbol emblazoned thereupon.

Derek suddenly clicked back into the room, and everything seemed very clear, shockingly clear. "Tell me," he said. "Tell me everything we know about the magic. What we've seen and heard and felt."

Tucker was the first to speak. "It extends life."

Derek nodded. "And it can accelerate the time sense. And cause that reflective damage effect. There might not be a practical limit."

"If you have the energy, the human beings, to suck dry," Tucker said.

"But there is one thing that I'm not certain of. How did they track us to Chicago? How did they know we'd left the Lightning-Dawn camp?"

"They could use the same magic, couldn't they?"

"Maybe—but I think that would be like using a whale net to catch a minnow. In Dahlia's story was there any indication that DuPris knew she'd run away? That she was hiding in his mansion, overhearing him? That she had gone to the African? That she had run off to get help from the soldiers? No. None at all. Which says to me that if you can trace people's *location* with the magic, it's not easy or simple. Apparently *years* passed between the end of the Civil War, and the time that DuPris and the African caught up with her. No." He slammed his palm down on the table. "I think that they used something a lot simpler. I don't think they needed magic at all."

"So how did they . . ." His eyes narrowed. "They've been tracking us?"

Derek opened the computer case, and pointed to the Advanced Graphics logo. "The embryo symbol," he said. "The African used it. We saw it."

Tucker stared at the symbol, turned his head this way and that, and his mouth suddenly dropped open. "Jesus. You're right! I see it!"

Derek whipped a modem cord out and plugged his computer into the telephone line, and began typing.

"Advanced Graphics came to *me* with the offer to help program Dungeon Quest. I thought they'd been referred by one of my old contacts."

"Makes sense."

"Yeah, but I'm not so certain that's what happened. Now, I think that what they really wanted was a way to keep tabs on Troy."

He dug out three pairs of goggles, and three right-handed virtual gloves, and plugged them into the computer. He handed one to Tucker, and another to Dahlia, and donned the third pair himself.

"I want another look at that game," he said grimly.

54

It was a world of jarring angles and naked contrasts, neon intensities, colors brighter and stranger than anything found in nature.

M. C. Escher might have designed the game, or Giger, or Hieronymus Bosch, but certainly there was no precedent for it anywhere in reality.

They walked through corridors tiled in light, up impossible, dizzying angles, and through a dark and twisted maze filled with indistinct shapes and grunting shadows. This was the adult version of the game Derek had allowed the children to play—more extreme, more disturbing, the images more threatening.

He turned his head. Motion sensors in the goggles immediately adjusted, and he saw, to his right, two knights in silver armor. They both looked like white males with square jaws and blue eyes.

"Wait a minute, Dahlia," Derek said absently. "I'm making some changes."

The sound of computer keys tapping invaded the virtual world. And the farthest knight took on darker, more feminine features, an armored amazon. He walked past a mirrored wall and examined himself—he now looked rather like Mike Tyson.

"Thanks," Dahlia said.

Forward motion was controlled by pressing and rolling a finger of one of the virtual gloves against a hard surface. When later point accrual added powers like flying, various hand gestures, the addition of a left-handed glove, or even a foot pad would be necessary to keep up with the new abilities.

There was an enormous animated bronze door in front of them. Its surface shimmered. Derek's simulacrum extended its hand, and the door opened into an infinite honeycomb of corridors and connected rooms, a maze of interlocking stairways set at impossible angles.

There were other players already in the dungeon, in fact, everywhere they looked animated figures stalked monsters and each other, hopped from one stairway to another in defiance of gravity, and died screaming, reborn with adjusted hit points.

Spaceships zoomed incongruously through halls designed as optical illusions. As they walked past a green pastel alley, an alligator head popped up, and snapped sleepily at their feet.

When a player zapped a monster, his color brightened, and numbers flashed above his head.

"Nothing's attacking us very seriously," Tucker noticed.

"They can't see us," Waites said. "I'm on a programmer's pass. We aren't really in the game. Watch this—"

In the real world, Derek Waites fumbled and found a silver-colored key card, and inserted it into a slot on the side of the machine.

All of the animated figures became skeletal lines of light. Some were appended with Post-it note-type squares saying, "Please fix this image," "This barbarian looks too much like Conan. We're risking lawsuit," and "Isn't this spaceship a little too Trekkie?"

"What's all this?" Tucker asked.

"This is the level that I play on. I actually create this world. It's like fixing robots on the *Pirates of the Caribbean.*"

In the motel room, Derek removed his glasses and went to the closet. He fished into his coat, and found the gold-colored key he had taken from DuPris's mansion. He donned the glasses, and extracted the silver key, inserting the gold one in its place.

"These cards are magnetically encoded with gamer information. They store points, time credits, they decide whether to give you a G- or R-rated game, and they let you into different levels. Let's just see . . ."

The world abruptly cleared. A hovering embryo symbol appeared.

"Please enter code word," it said in a flat, metallic tone.

The sound of Derek's typing fingers drifted across the illusion. The word "DuPris" appeared on screen. It was followed a moment later by the flashing red word "Incorrect."

"Try 'Advanced Graphics,' " Tucker suggested.

Derek typed. The word appeared on screen, again followed by a flashing "Incorrect."

"*What* was the name of the plantation?" Dahlia Washington asked.

"Bloodroot?" Derek said, and began typing. There was a pause, and then the screen went black. Then the images appeared again.

It was strange. They were back in the previous world, only the perspectives had shifted somehow. It was the same . . . and yet different.

"There's something about this . . ." Derek said, cautiously.

"We're seeing it from the monster's point of view," Tucker said.

"Shit," Derek said in shock. "You're right."

They watched a monster devour a player. The scorecard beneath the monster skyrocketed.

The embryo symbol appeared again, but this time there was a skull visible behind its skin. Its voice was a deep, resonantly synthesized voice. One disturbingly familiar.

"Welcome," the embryo said. "What program would you like to run?"

"Good Lord," Tucker said. "The African."

"Then he's still alive."

"Both of them. Somewhere."

A list appeared. The header said "Categories: Successful Operations, Training Exercises, Theoretical Applications, Etc."

They were silent for a few moment, and then Tucker said, "Try 'Successful Operations.' "

A pointer appeared, and clicked onto the first category. A list of names and places appeared. Derek scrolled through them.

"What the hell?" Derek muttered.

A terrible suspicion was forming in his mind, but Tucker was the one who spoke the unspeakable. "All right," he said. "Type in 'November twenty-seven, 1980.' "

The date was typed in, and the view cleared. The words "Tucker, Billy. Lancaster, California" appeared.

"Oh, shit," Derek breathed.

The animation resumed.

The animation was the image of a quiet, suburban neighborhood, one with quasi-Spanish architecture.

Derek heard the breath catch in Tucker's throat. The point of view moved fluidly. As if the camera were attached to the leader of a wolf pack. The image rotated to an aerial view, illustrating a pincer movement attacking the front and rear doors of a house simultaneously.

The images of the Tucker family were flat, two-dimensional, and cartoonish. An animated dart gun rose into frame, and a flash followed. A little girl cartoon went down like a puppet with its strings cut. A boy cartoon was netted. *Flash.* A woman-shaped cartoon went down. *Flash.*

Tucker's left hand gripped Derek's arm painfully hard. A cartoon soldier appeared, wearing a foppish green beret. He *kiai*ed and made a few buffoonish kung-fu moves, and then was down, flopping like a fish, *X*s across the eyes.

The embryo appeared. The skull beneath the cartoon was clearly visible. It smiled. "Ninety percent effective," the African's voice said. "One fatality."

Derek tore his glove and goggles off.

"What is this?" Dahlia Washington said.

Derek held his finger over his lips, and made a crooking motion with his finger.

"Outside," he mouthed silently.

They went out onto the stoop, and Derek led them farther away, near the motel's swimming pool.

Tucker's face was turned slightly away from them, and he wiped at his face before turning to look at them again.

"If I'm right, then there's a tracer in that damned computer. Maybe even a microphone."

"Then why didn't they get your son when your family was in the motel?"

"They'd just made one big effort, at the condo. Probably needed to regroup. I was only at the motel for maybe fifteen minutes, then I was on the go again—and the computer was with me. The next time I was with my family, and the computer was stationary for any period of time, was the Lightning Dawn camp. I think that's how they found us.''

Dahlia nodded. ''All right, then. What the fuck is that game we just played?''

''It's a training school for killers,'' Tucker said coldly. ''A computer simulation bank. The military was experimenting with stuff like this even before I went away.''

''Can you really train people like that?'' she asked.

''In strategy? You bet your ass. In combination with live maneuvers, a system like this could walk your people through any battle you could program, allowing them to actually see the applications of textbook strategy. Then they turn them loose to hunt the players in that damned maze. It's fucking brilliant.''

''Most of the time the customers hunt the monsters,'' Derek said. ''But if you have a gold key, and know the code word—''

Dahlia Washington finally was up to speed, at last understood what they were saying, the horror beneath the surface. ''You get to be a monster. Hunt the customers.''

''You could train a street gang like that. Train rogue cops. DuPris would need an army to do the things he's done over the years. A secret army. And this is one of the ways he trains them.'' Tucker paused. ''But does it tell us anything about where your kids are? Where we can find DuPris? Or the African?''

Derek nodded grimly. ''Everything leads back to Advanced Graphics. It all makes sense. It's the place to look.''

55

The sun had set almost an hour before, flooding the Pacific with a wall of red clouds that clotted to black and then died, spawning an armada of cold, prickly stars.

Tucker, Derek and Dahlia lay atop a hill, overlooking the

Advanced Graphics installation. Through binoculars, Tucker could pick out armed guards, but not as many as he had feared. He guessed that an electronics firm couldn't project the image of an armed camp.

Most of the buildings were dark, but a few lights were still on in the central office, marked Building C. A police van was parked near the back, and he saw a few dark figures flitting back and forth.

Through the binoculars, Tucker watched as bodies were unloaded into one of the buildings from the back of a police van.

Waites rolled over onto his back. "Well, what do you think?"

"Piece of cake," Tucker said. "Motion sensors on the fence have to be calibrated so that gusts of wind and fucking birds don't trigger the alarm. You do your part, we shouldn't have a problem."

Derek turned to Dahlia. "Are you sure you want to do this?"

She nodded her head rapidly. "This don't end, Scar Man will kill me. I need to see him dead. If he can die."

He met her eyes. So much like Rachel's. He reached out and touched her face, and her eyes closed. She looked as if she hurt, and he started to pull his hand away, but she grabbed it, and held it tightly against her face.

"Come on," Tucker said, and started down the slope.

Stealthily, they approached the fence. Derek felt the wind pick up behind them, howling up over the bluff, blowing in from the ocean. The ocean smelled foul. It smelled like death.

Tucker paused, watching tree branches bending in rhythm with the wind. He watched for a full five minutes. When the tree branches bent, Tucker clipped a wire. He waited for the next gust of wind, and the tree branches to bend again. Somewhere inside those buildings, guards were watching the indicators. The pressure had to come in a familiar rhythm lulling them into a false sense of security. He clipped at the height of the wind. He repeated the process a third time, by which time there was a space wide enough for them to enter through, and they crept onto the grounds of Advanced Graphics.

"Your turn," Tucker growled.

Waites nodded, and opened the duffel bag he had brought with him. In it were two things: the Advanced Graphics computer case, and a box reading "Radio Hut Model 554-987 Treasure Detector." The picture on the box was a man in Bermuda shorts using a disk-shaped metal detector to find a coin chest.

"Pressure sensors around the fence," Derek whispered. "I saw them putting in the lawn almost a year ago. The gardeners exposed part of the pressure grid."

He switched the detector on. It beeped, letting him know that the batteries were good, and settled down to business.

It hummed strongly, indicating metal in the ground. When he shifted a few feet to the left, there was no signal. He led the way, using the treasure-hunting device as if it were a mine detector, threading their way through the maze of pressure plates, taking them all the way to the nearest building.

They raced across the parking lot into a concealing shadow, panting. There was a door only a few feet to their right, and he checked it. "Electronic key card," he muttered. "We can't break this."

Tucker examined it, and cursed. "What do we do?" Dahlia said.

"Let's try this," Derek said, and took DuPris's gold key card from his pocket and inserted it into the slit. The door clicked open.

Beyond the door was an abandoned lobby.

"Been here before," Derek said. "Mostly executive offices here. The other buildings are programming and testing. I saw a big black man go through here—couldn't see his face. Could have been the African. I don't know."

Tucker pointed to a security camera, and motioned to the extreme left, away from its beams. They would have to hug the wall.

"We should split up," he said. "Try to work your way around to where we saw the guard activity. If you can find your kids—pull a fire alarm. I'll try to find you."

Derek shucked the computer case out of the duffel bag.

Tucker shook his head. "I don't know about that," he said.

"I hope I don't need it. But I need an edge." He felt something near panic at the idea of being separated from Tucker, but choked it back. "What are you going to do?" he asked.

"Kill DuPris," Tucker said simply.

"Tucker," Derek said. "If I don't make it. Find my children."

Tucker nodded, and then slipped away into darkness.

Tucker melted away, leaving Derek Waites and Dahlia Washington in the shadows. Derek motioned away from the surveillance cameras, moving very carefully indeed.

Twice he stopped her, pointing toward a camera that swept through its arc with mechanical precision. He timed it, and they slid along a wall, out of its range of vision.

They passed a piece of abstract artwork. With some deep, unconscious part of his mind Derek registered that the artwork hummed, that it seemed to be more than an inanimate statue, but although his senses were completely open, he failed to realize what that sound might mean.

He made it down the next hall, very carefully, proud that he remembered the location of the cameras, that his memory of previous trips to Advanced Graphics was serving him so well.

He suddenly stopped. There was no sound, but his hair had an odd frying sensation. An entire row of glass doors seemed to vibrate with a tone that was below the threshold of hearing. "Did you hear that?"

"What?" Dahlia asked.

With heartbreaking suddenness, a hidden panel opened on either side of them, and two men stepped out, each with a gun in his hand. Dahlia and Derek froze. Derek raised his right hand. The computer case dangled in his left.

The bigger of their captors had a hawk face with bandages along the left cheek, and over his right ear. A blandly lethal intensity shone like a searchlight from his eyes. He leveled a police .38 at Derek's nose.

"They said you'd be along." He sneered. "Frankly, I

didn't think you'd be that stupid. But God, I am glad I was wrong."

He radiated joy, seemed charged with some kind of electricity, and Derek knew he was only a moment away from death.

"Timms," the second man said. "DuPris wants us to bring them in."

Derek said nothing. Timms's finger eased back on the trigger pressure.

"You even brought that damned computer," Timms said. He touched the side of his face. Bandages shrouded his ear and cheek, and Derek remembered the night at his mother's house, remembered kicking that face, and felt a cold and savage satisfaction.

"Well, I think that your bitch wife will be happy to see you."

"She's here?" Derek said, his voice husky.

Timms smiled. "Oh, yes. She's here. I should have killed the bitch. Kicked her fucking ribs in. But she's still alive, and she's here."

Derek felt something boiling inside him, anger such as he'd never felt before, and he fought to keep himself focused. *Focus. Focus.*

He inserted the ring finger of his left hand into a nylon loop threaded to the inside of the computer case's handle. He tugged, pulling it an inch, an inch and a half, felt it tauten and then grow slack as a slip of insulating plastic slid from its position inside the case.

He tried to keep his voice steady. "This damned computer had all the clues I needed to find this place. How many machines are out there? You can't kill every programmer on the project."

"I don't need to." Timms grinned. "I only need to kill you. Take the computer," he said to the other man.

Derek set it on the ground, releasing the silvered metallic tape newly wound around the handle. Releasing a tiny trigger button soldered into place only hours before.

Armed.

He raised his hands to shoulder level, his breath roaring

in his ears, as the second man bent, and grabbed the computer.

Inside the case, a relay was thrown, and three lithium batteries sent a combined charge of a hundred and fifty thousand volts through the handle.

The guard's body jerked erect, eyes and mouth flying open. His legs straightened spastically, sending him crashing into, and through, a glass wall with a crash that was echoed an instant later by the shrieking of an alarm Klaxon.

But before the alarm sounded, while Timms was still staring at the incredible, impossible thing that had just happened, Derek drew the knife that Tucker had given him, and ran it into Timms's side.

The cop screamed, whipping around, the side of his gun smacking against Derek's face. Dahlia started toward them, and Timms tried to get a shot off at her, but Derek grabbed his arm and the shot went wild, spanging off a sculpture next to her. Steel splinters flew, cutting her cheek. Dahlia reeled back, terrified.

Derek grabbed the knife again. Timms was shrieking now. He fought desperately to throw Derek off, find a moment's pause from the pain, a moment to think, to act, to do anything but *hurt*. Pain blinded. Pain ate thought. He should have been able to deal with this little bastard easily, but Derek Waites just didn't give him a chance to do anything but react. Waites kept hitting, and twisting, and driving him backward, and Timms's mind was filled by the awful pain, and hatred, and frustration, and shock—

But more than anything, more than everything, the *pain*.

He hammered at Derek as if he had forgotten that the piece of metal in his hand was a firearm, forgotten anything except the little man who twisted the knife in his side.

Together they pitched backward through one of the glass walls, smashing down onto the floor on the other side. Derek struck his head on a desk, and for the first time released the knife.

Timms dragged himself haltingly to his feet, and looked down at the knife, and the spreading blood—and Derek. For an instant he paused, shocked that the human buzz saw was no longer deviling him, caught his breath, fought to think what he could do about the wound in his side—

Then, from his position on the ground, Derek kicked Timms squarely in the groin. Timms doubled over, his scream pitched so high it was almost a whistle.

Derek staggered to his feet as Timms swung his gun hand back up. Before the cop could find his aim, Derek had found a desk telephone, had swung it up, and then brought it down with all of his strength, the corner of the phone making precise, and lethal, contact with Timms's skull.

Timms pitched forward and was still, a puddle of blood spreading slowly on the floor beneath him.

Derek sobbed for breath, and said, "Don't *ever* stop to admire your work."

Timms was beyond answering him, or anyone else, ever again. His open eyes stared at nothing. The crimson puddle continued to widen.

"Dahlia—" Derek said.

And turned in time to see two armed men zeroing in on them, weapons raised and ready, and knew that there was no chance at all.

They were taken to a hidden stairway, and, at gun point, forced to climb down into the depths of the building. The walls were dry, and vibrated slightly. Every step deepened Derek's sense of dread. He feared what he might find at the bottom of the stairs. His family dead.

Or, in some ways worse, his family, alive.

Dahlia Washington was so frightened she could hardly walk. She stumbled, and Derek caught her. "Come on," he whispered. "Stay strong. This isn't over yet."

She smiled bleakly, and kept walking.

At the very bottom of the flight of stairs was a heavy steel door. One of their guards rapped against it, and it opened.

56

The first thing that Derek saw was that the chamber was high ceilinged, rounded, lined with wall-mounted recessed television monitors. The second thing he noticed was that at least thirty men and women were staked out on the floor, fastened to metal cuffs at ankles and wrists. The number of white and black prisoners was approximately equal. They were arranged in a circle, creating an inner cleared space perhaps ten feet in diameter.

He thought he recognized some of the white faces from the Lightning Dawn encampment. In one wedge of dim light he recognized Krause, looking very much the worse for wear, jerking feebly against his chains. He didn't seem to know where he was. Krause seemed drugged.

The next thing Derek saw was Rachel. And then Dee, chained next to her. They were chained on the wall, not on the floor, as if separated from the others for some special purpose. A broad but crude bandage was wrapped around her waist. Derek cried out her name and tried to go to her, but something struck him behind the ear, forcing him to his knees.

All were unconscious, chained in an array similar to that displayed in Dahlia Childe's visions of Bloodroot plantation.

Then, almost as if his eyes were reluctant to admit such a sight, he saw the post erected at one point of the inner circle. There, Troy stood shackled and gagged. From this position, Troy's back was to him, the post between the two of them. But Derek could see the boy's thin arms raised to the shackle, could see the outline of his son's head, the leather gag strap across his mouth. Troy jangled at his shackle, tried to turn.

Alive. So far, everyone was alive. That was, he hoped, a blessing.

In the middle of the room stood Augustus DuPris himself. The rows of television monitors multiplied, amplified, reflected his image dozens of times.

"Welcome," endless rows of DuPris said. "You're just in time."

Derek heaved again, tearing himself free of his guards, and ran to Rachel. DuPris raised a restraining hand as the guards came after him.

Derek knelt beside his wife, and checked her pulse. It was strong. And then Dee's. Also strong.

"We'll ship her to our Arkansas breeding farm," DuPris said almost absently. "Dahlia's daughter, Ginger, is there, I believe."

"Why are you doing this?" Dahlia asked numbly.

"Because thirteen is the perfect age for a Purifier."

Derek smoothed Dee's hair. He was beyond any sense of fear for himself, but everything he loved was in this room. One word, one wrong act could kill them all. "Why?" he said softly.

"Oh, that. To live, of course. The meaning of life is to live. Unfortunately, it takes a little more life force every year. A hundred years ago, I only needed two lives every sixteen months or so. Now I need fifteen. In a thousand years I may need an entire city."

Derek moved back to Rachel, brushing his fingers lightly along her cheek. He didn't notice that Dee, although unconscious, had begun to sweat, just a little dampness at her brow.

Her eyes fluttered. She whispered a single word: "Tucker . . ."

Tucker crept down a hallway. Over and over again he stopped short of a camera's focus, hearing the very slight hum of a focusing mechanism, feeling, sensing, his senses open further than they had ever been before. He was very close to the man he had waited almost two decades to kill. Very close.

He would not make a mistake. Not this time.

Suddenly, and quite clearly, he heard his name spoken. A little girl's voice. Dee's voice. His head jerked up violently, and he turned, reversing direction.

Moving quickly down the hall now, running, still almost silently on crepe soles, so swiftly that he rounded a corner and collided with three guards coming the other way.

No one had time to think, but Tucker was not thinking, he was acting. More natural to him than his pistol, Tucker's knife was in his hand before he had any conscious awareness of what had happened.

He lived in a silent cocoon of light, colors dancing within him, flaring to white light, time slowing until he felt he was falling, falling. . . .

He was barely conscious of the fact that other human beings were there in this timeless space with him. There were arms to grasp. Legs to sweep. A screaming mouth, one of Tucker's thumbs distending the corner. A rolling motion, causing one of the men to tumble over Tucker's hips, colliding with the other.

And the knife. Here. There. Drawing a thin red line that widened, splashing light everywhere. Light. Light.

Flaring to blindness.

And then an awareness that he was alone in the corridor, that crumpled about his feet were three bleeding, broken corpses.

No. One man still crawled in a mindless, broken zigzag. Blood pumped from his throat in a rhythmic gout. He left a trail as he crawled, like some kind of bizarre crimson slug. He looked back at Tucker with blind eyes, those eyes blearily focusing, then widening with remembered shock, as if seeing something inhuman.

Then the man was still.

Tucker panted. He clapped his hands over his ears, concentrating on the voice within.

"Tucker," it said again.

Tucker wound his way through a maze of corridors, down a flight of stairs, led by the steady drone of the girl's voice in his ear.

He killed another guard.

He could hear Waites talking now, and then Dahlia Washington's voice.

"You got thirty people here," she said. "I thought you only needed fifteen—"

Before DuPris could answer, Tucker opened the door and stepped into the chamber.

57

For at least twenty seconds, the room was completely silent. Tucker and DuPris confronted each other, mirror images.

DuPris smiled, as if Tucker's appearance was completely expected. "Tucker," he said. "Unusually handsome fellow, isn't he?"

Derek finally managed to break out of his paralysis, and screamed, *"Shoot him!"*

Slowly, almost as if he were an automaton, Tucker turned his head to look at Derek, then turned back to DuPris. His eyes glittered. "This is personal," he said. He drew his knife, its blade already slick with blood.

This was the man who had slaughtered his family. Who had ruined his life, and brought him to the edge of insanity.

To kill this man, he would gladly die. Tucker drew his pistol with his left hand. DuPris's eyes narrowed, watching him closely. Then Tucker threw the pistol to Derek, and in the same instant, attacked.

DuPris blurred, moving impossibly fast as he slipped away. DuPris's fingers flashed at Tucker's throat, leaving red marks as Tucker reeled back out of the way.

Derek snatched the pistol out of the air. He cocked it, and held it in both hands, arms shaking.

He could fire. If he did, and hit DuPris, he would die. It would be worth it. But he wasn't certain that he could hit DuPris—the two of them were moving so fast now, their outlines merging and separating in an exquisitely accelerated ballet. He stood approximately the same chance of hitting DuPris that he would have had firing blindly into a catfight.

DuPris came at Tucker again, moving faster than any human being Tucker had ever seen.

The world within him was all light, and without sound. His pulse slowed, seemed to stop.

The universe was a blur. Nothing had a distinct edge

everything was a swirl of color, stop-motion crashing one instant at a time, DuPris's screaming mouth, clutching hands coming at him. Nothing human anymore, each moment the moment before death.

Even in this bizarre realm outside of time, there was no time for thought. Time only for the most economical parries with the knife blade, motion and strategy operating on a level beyond and above conscious thought. Without the knife, Tucker would have been dead in the first two seconds. If DuPris had possessed any skill at all, even the knife wouldn't have mattered.

For the first time in his adult life, Tucker found himself the slower and weaker of two combatants. And he used everything he had ever learned, every trick of angulation, distancing, timing, feint and draw, every understanding of a hairline-tight defense, every mental technique to clamp down on fear, so that the almost overwhelming, terrifying rush of DuPris's anger and will against him met not the vulnerable human being named Tucker, but the hard-won skill Tucker had accrued over a lifetime of combat.

And even that wasn't quite enough. DuPris blurred—and a burning sensation, a gash opened in Tucker's face. DuPris blurred again, and Tucker's ears rang with a savage cracking sound.

Tucker tumbled head over heels, smashed against the wall, barely managed to get out of the way before DuPris's hand smashed through a television monitor next to Tucker's head, showering Tucker's face with bits of broken glass.

DuPris laughed, withdrawing his arm from the spitting, sparking set. And for a bare moment, he paused.

And in that moment Tucker, in some dark hindmost part of himself realized that DuPris had insane speed, godlike speed—but was vulnerable to Newton's first law. Objects in motion tend to remain in motion. DuPris's acceleration, lightning fast as it was, favored a straight line. He displayed little ability to change directions once that explosion began.

DuPris blurred at him. Tucker dropped to the ground. He twisted sideways and extended the knife so that his arm and lat muscles and external obliques and the long line of his leg were like a Masai spear positioned against a lion's charge:

the butt end thrust into the ground for support.

And DuPris barely twisted out of the way in time to avoid being impaled, managed to lean to the side to minimize the damage to a deep, but nonlethal gouge along the left ribs.

Agony flared in Tucker's side at the same moment, and he clapped his hand over the new wound. In the same instant, in the same way that he had accepted the inevitability of his own death, he accepted the pain.

DuPris pulled back. Time seemed to hang in the air. DuPris stopped, turned, felt along his ribs. His fingers daubed at the wound, and he saw his own blood. His face was pale.

The silence in the room crackled. DuPris's breath rasped in his throat. "Even if you kill me," he gasped, "it will cost you your life."

Tucker's eyes closed to a slit. "I got no fucking life. You *killed* my fucking life—"

He lunged at DuPris, and for the first time, DuPris retreated before him and Tucker felt a savage exhilaration. He was alive, and this bastard was going to die. They were both going to die, together, Tucker and his evil twin, and that was just fine. . . .

Slash—he reached out and just touched DuPris along the jaw line, exalting in the pain in his own face. . . .

But at that moment he saw an image of his son, Billy. Smiling freckled face laughing. Laughing. Watching. Waving to him. Waiting for him on the far side of the grave.

Tucker shook it off, and in the next instant slashed DuPris's left palm, and the man screamed, *"N-No—!"* He felt the pain in his own hand—

And saw Dolly's face. Her loving face, the face he had kissed so many times—

He bore down and in the next instant DuPris stumbled over one of the unconscious prisoners, and Tucker swept his foot, and Tucker's hand spread out and grabbed DuPris by the throat, the knife already blurring home—

And there was a third, and final image. His wife, Crystal. "Can you handle me, buster boy?" Just a flash. So full of life, and love and hope. He was doing this for them, wasn't he?

No, he wasn't. He was doing it for himself, for his sense

of wounded pride, for his shattered ego. They wouldn't want him to die. They would want him to live.

And suddenly, quite unexpectedly, so did he.

But in that momentary hesitation, DuPris grabbed Tucker's right arm and wrenched it nearly out of the socket.

Time stopped.

"What do I do, Dad?" Billy asked.

He had no answer.

"Daddy, help, it hurrrts," Dolly screamed.

But it was too late.

"This will either be the best Thanksgiving we've ever had, or our last—"

Frozen time. Moments that cannot be changed. Only honored.

Tucker dropped the knife from his right hand, and caught it with his left. Grunting savagely, he stabbed it into DuPris's thigh, and ripped upward, severing his femoral artery.

DuPris staggered back, screaming. He released Tucker. Openmouthed, gasping for life.

Tucker staggered back, blood gushing from his slashed thigh. Femoral artery. A lethal wound—unless you can act swiftly, and decisively. Unless you have the kind of excellent training Major Austin Tucker had received, long years before.

He ripped off his belt, and tore at his shirt. "Help me!" he gasped. Derek and Dahlia were at his side instantly, removing and wadding his shirt, helping him position it, pressing it against his spurting thigh, cinching the belt tight. Then Derek's belt went around the compress. Tucker squeezed at it, the blood soaking the cotton shirt, sliming his hands. He felt his strength and life gushing from his body, and tightened the belt again, blood slip-sliming the entire procedure so that it was hard to find the notch, so that when Derek took over, placed one foot on the leg and drew with his other arm, pulling the belt tight, Tucker saw stars.

The bleeding slowed. Not stopped, but slowed.

The three of them, covered in Tucker's blood, finally turned to look at DuPris.

Augustus DuPris was in a blind panic. He flailed at his wound, and blood gushed between his fingers, spurted everywhere with an arterial pulse. It slimed his face, and clotted in his red hair.

He screamed.

Tucker struggled to a sitting position. "How does it feel, asshole? Time to die."

DuPris stared at him. He extended one crimsoned hand. "Help . . . help me. . . ."

"Your fucking spell cover this?" Tucker laughed nastily. "Sure, I'll help you. I'm just sure I have a Band-Aid around here somewhere. . . ."

He patted his shirt with one hand, as he kept pressure on the wound with the other. "Fresh out. You, Derek?"

"Must have left them in the car," Derek said faintly.

DuPris's life was pumping away. He fought to stand up again, and collapsed. He made a mewling sound, and then another. His hand relaxed on the wound, and the blood poured more freely, and then more weakly. DuPris shuddered, but there was no voluntary movement at all. He would be dead in minutes.

Derek held the gun unsteadily, sweeping it around the room. Nothing but unconscious prisoners, and the dying DuPris. And Troy. Forgotten in the savage combat, the boy was shaking almost uncontrollably.

"Dad?" He pulled against his bonds, and Derek checked them. Locked tight, but there had to be a key. "Tucker—"

Tucker collapsed against the wall, shaking. "Come on," he said. "I'm all right. Let's get your family out of here—"

Before Tucker could complete his sentence, something like a cyclone whipped through the room. An enormous black arm appeared out of the swirling shadows. It smashed the gun from Derek's hand. Dahlia Washington screamed, and a second blow cuffed her brutally to the ground.

The African emerged from the shadows stripped to the waist. His chest was graven with twisted masses of scar tissue, a dark masterpiece of vile art, a newly discovered continent of pain.

"Dahlia." Niles grinned. His smile was wide, and genuine, and terrifying. "My favorite niece. A long way from Chicago, aren't we?"

58

Dahlia backed away from the titanic figure, her hand at her throat. "Scar Man. I—"

"Shhh . . ."

The acid taste of utter defeat rose in the back of Derek's throat. This room wasn't set up for DuPris's ceremony. It was for someone older than DuPris. Someone who needed thirty lives.

"How very clever you are. Poor DuPris is not."

Augustus DuPris wasn't moving anymore. He lay in the midst of a vast red pool, curled onto his side in a fetal position. Dead, or dying.

"Intelligent in his way, but incapable of lateral thought."

Dahlia was breathing fast and hard. Tucker looked pale.

"A very clever solution, Tucker," the African said approvingly. "I'm not certain it has been tried before."

Tucker growled.

"DuPris and I each had our own clans, harvested our own blood—but sometimes cooperated in the hunt. My clan helped to harvest your family, Tucker." He paused. "Your son died well. Not easily, but well."

"You *fuck.*"

"Rarely," the African said. "I prefer power."

He turned to Derek. "Across the City of Angels, three hundred years of rage have come to fruition. Anger. Hate. Greed. Revenge. These are the Horsemen of the Modern Apocalypse. On these cornerstones will I re-create my empire."

He came closer to Derek. "You understand today's magic, the machines of this miraculous age. Advanced Graphics earned two *billion* dollars last year. I will re-create my kingdom. Old and new magic together at last. If you join me, I will give you your children, your woman, and your life."

Troy looked at Derek desperately.

"What do I have to do?"

"Kill Tucker," the African said. "Serve me as old Dahlia did."

"You betrayed her."

"Oh, no," the African said. His scarred face was almost obscenely jolly. "She betrayed *us.*"

He handed the gun back to Derek.

Rachel looked so pale, so still. The wound in her side was serious, but certainly not mortal. For just a moment, some dark and primal part of Derek flirted with the offer.

Was there any hope that they could all get out? All that mattered was his family. Tucker said he wanted to die. It wouldn't even really be a betrayal. . . .

Suddenly Dahlia Washington began to shimmer, a mild radiance flowing from her, filling the room with cool light. Through her lips, Dahlia Childe's voice said, *"Do not. Do not take the devil's bargain!"*

The African looked around swiftly, face suffused with an almost urchin glee. He took Dahlia Washington by the throat, and peered into her eyes.

"Dahlia Childe?" he asked in wonderment. "It *is* you, isn't it?" He searched her eyes, as if he wanted to crawl inside her head, and explore the shadows breeding there. His voice dropped to an almost reverent whisper. "You must have learned terrible things there, on the far side of death. But you can't reach me, can you? Two souls, one body. You'd burn this poor child right up. How sad. So close, and yet so very far away." He stroked her cheek, his mouth very close to hers, as if they were lovers. Then, regretfully, he turned back to Waites.

"Decide," he said. "Serve me. Kill this white man."

Derek looked at Troy, who was bound and terrified. And then at Dee. Tucker nodded: *do it.*

It wasn't a betrayal. All that mattered was his family.

He leveled his gun at Tucker.

From the corner of his eye, he could see Troy. The boy twisted his face away, his expression both relieved and ashamed. The African virtually glowed with triumph.

Tucker's lips drew into a thin line. His great barrel chest rose and fell. Rose and fell.

Then suddenly Derek pivoted. He pointed the gun directly

between the African's eyes, and pulled the trigger.

Click.

The African opened his hand. Two copper-nosed bullets rested in his palm. He chuckled nastily, then snatched the gun from Derek's hand. "Fool. You owed him *nothing!*"

"I owe myself," Derek said quietly. "I owe my family. Spilling innocent blood was Dahlia's mistake. You can take my life. I won't give you my soul."

Troy had turned back to him, and their eyes locked. "I'm sorry, Troy," he said softly.

Troy nodded. The boy trembled, but he met Derek's eyes without blinking.

"Touching," the African said. "Naive, but touching."

He strode to the inner circle, inside the array of chained bodies. He faced Troy's post, and raised his arms.

The room light dimmed, almost as if the African were sucking luminescence from the television screens and the overhead bulbs. Dozens of monitors around the periphery of the room reflected his image: arms outstretched and raised, legs spread wide, scarred chest expanded so that every scar stood out in relief.

Then the monitors began to flicker. Their screens crackled as if disrupted by a power surge. Derek watched a tiny electrical discharge leap first from one, and then another, and then every monitor in the room. The crackling sparks linked, flared brighter and wide, leaped into the air in arcs of blue-white lightning that formed a coruscating sphere around the African.

Electricity arced above the bodies of looters and militiamen, swirling, an impossible wind boiling in to accompany it.

Derek hugged the unconscious bodies of his wife and daughter, staring in horror at the spectacle in the center of the room.

Above the howl of the wind, he heard the African's voice.

"Chango Pollo Mayombe Jana Shay! Congo Kosha!"

A scream from one of the prisoners captured Derek's attention. He recognized the thin, bearded form of Krause as the man shrieked, and his body arched up with back-breaking intensity.

The scream went beyond pain, beyond fear, mouth distending until Derek was certain the man's jaw was dislocating. And then beyond that.

His eyes turned crimson and exploded. His face ran with blood, and then shriveled into a husk. Burned, twitching and leaping like an electrified frog leg.

The man next to him shrieked, and arched. And then another. And another.

Derek turned away from the sight, desperate to escape. The door. He ran to the metal slab, and pulled at it, using all of the strength in his arms and back.

Nothing. Nothing. He pulled until his hands ached, until his shoulder tendons felt as if they were ripping, but the door didn't budge.

Sobbing, he watched the African, shrouded now in rainbow arcs of blindingly bright electricity, lightning that arched from the ceiling, crawled up from the floor, flowed from the agonized bodies of the prisoners, and knew that he, and his beloved family, were dead.

59

Dahlia Washington watched the African's body glow with power, watched the awful spectacle as, one at a time, the prisoners were devoured by light.

This man, this terrible man had dominated her life since her childhood, had dominated the lives of her mother, her aunts and sisters. Had stolen everything of real value, giving only objects and trivial creature comforts in return. Watching him as he swelled with power, she felt she finally knew what he was, knew the depth of the evil she had enabled for so many years.

Curiously, she felt no fear. For the first time in her life, she knew what she had to do. Knew what she had been born to do.

Dahlia Washington closed her eyes. The darkness had always been a terrible place for her, a place where she had time and room to think of the utter nothingness that composed her life. A darkness and quiet to be avoided at all costs.

But this darkness was a comfort. In this darkness, she was not alone. In this darkness, a friend awaited.

"Come through me," she whispered. "Come into the world. . . ."

Behind her eyes, in the darkness, a swirl of glowing mist appeared. It moved slowly, and then quickly, almost as if in a reluctant dance. And it spoke with Dahlia Childe's voice: *"Two souls. One body. I cannot."*

A scream of mortal fear ripped her from her trance.

The walls of lightning coiled and hovered like ocean waves now, and they swirled around the stake where Troy hung, manacled. The boy screamed again, and this time, pain tinged the fear.

But Dahlia felt no panic, only a deep and pervasive calm, a sensation she had craved all her life. She bent to Tucker. His face was yellowish in the blinding storm. She yelled to be heard above the wind. "That heart stopper," she said. "The kung-fu palm thing. Don't leave no mark inside neither?"

"What the hell are you thinking?" Derek gasped, appearing behind her.

She ignored him.

"Does it . . ." She fought to find the words. "Just . . . make you stop?"

There was sudden, awful comprehension in Tucker's eyes. "Yes."

The sense of calm within her deepened. She knew everything now. Dee. And Tucker. And Derek. And her, Dahlia Washington. It would take all of them to stop this madness. Each of them with a part to play, and a time to play it.

And her time was now.

"Then do it," she said. "Give Dahlia a body. She can stop the African. I know it. Two souls, one body . . . she won't come through me while I'm alive."

Derek recoiled. "Oh, my God . . ."

Dahlia Washington screamed the next words, all of the intensity of a lifetime of repressed fear and hatred breaking through to the surface. *"Do it!* He killed my baby. He gonna kill Troy. Nobody stop him, he gonna live forever. Use it, damn you!''

Tucker searched her eyes, as if wanting to make absolutely certain that he understood the meaning of her words. Then he nodded. Dahlia Washington turned to Derek, took his face between her hands, and kissed him softly.

"Dahlia," he said. But she shushed him with her fingers.

"Shhh," she said. "Good-bye, Derek Waites. You take care of that woman you love. Raise that little girl right."

She nodded to Tucker. The big man struggled to come to a standing position. "Help me," he said to Derek. He put an arm around Derek's shoulder, braced his back against the wall, and got up. Tucker looked directly into the center of Dahlia Washington's chest, concentrating, blocking out everything else in the entire world. Nothing existed except this woman, this moment, this one act.

He exhaled, and his palm pistoned out, striking her at an upward angle, just to the left of her diaphragm.

Dahlia Washington staggered backward a half a step. Her eyes rolled up in her head, and she collapsed.

A savagely percussive wave of pressure coursed through her body, compressing air and blood passages, overloading her nervous system, jarring her brain. The shock bounced inside her, absorbed by soft tissues, reflected and conducted by bones, the shock waves crossing and crisscrossing each other, creating interference patterns that caused her heart to hiccough, and then stutter. . . .

And then stop.

In Dahlia Washington's body, there was silence.

She fell into an infinite void.

60

Within the sacrificial chamber, the electrical storm was growing more powerful, the whirlwind of sparks nearer Troy now, and the boy's screams were heartbreaking.

Tucker collapsed, utterly drained. Dahlia Washington's body was still.

"Nothing," Derek said miserably. "Nothing's happening. Why isn't anything happening?"

Tucker's face was tight with concentration. "Maybe . . ."

"What?"

"Maybe she can't start her heart again."

Comprehension blossomed in Derek's eyes. He rolled her over, and began to performed CPR compressions as the wall of lightning touched Troy for the first time. The boy's body leaped, and his scream was a single, prolonged note of horror.

"Shit! Come on! Come on, Dahlia. Please. Please." He pumped at her chest, then pinched her nose and breathed into her mouth.

"Chango Come! Jana Chango Kala Chango!!!"

The lightning grew fiercer still.

"Come on!" Derek screamed. He pumped at her chest again, frantic, the air above Troy sizzling.

Dahlia's fingers crooked and grasped at air, found his arm and bit into it with hysterical strength. She jerked upright, and her eyes flew open.

There was nothing human about those eyes. They were like blazing white marbles, shimmering with a distant, divine fire.

"Dahlia?" Derek whispered, aghast.

She smiled at Tucker, and then at Waites, and stood. She didn't move like anything human, moved rather like a marionette, as if suspended by strings from above.

She took a step, and then another step. Lightning coursed

around her, and she ignored it. She stepped into the inner circle.

"Jala Chango—"

The African turned and saw her, and his mouth fell open. "Dahlia," he said.

"I have come," Dahlia Washington said, in a voice that was not hers.

The African whispered, "No!" He retreated a step. "My hate matches your own. You cannot defeat me."

She shook her head, almost sadly.

"My tool is love, not hate. The love which tortured my soul for two hundred years. I do not hate you. I pity you. I know what hell awaits you, on this side of death."

Her body began to glow. Three spheres of light, so bright now that even Derek could see them. Blue, and red, and golden. The red light, pulsing at her heart, grew brighter, drew the lightning to her.

Into her.

"You told me once that one who has died knows everything," she said. *"It was not true. There is much I do not know. But there is one thing I have learned. It is this—you live because you stole from my family. And I now reclaim what is rightfully theirs.*

"I take back the lives you have stolen!"

Now the African was paralyzed with terror. His mouth opened, and he made a sound that couldn't have been a scream. No human voice could have held such horror, such pain, such animal hatred. His body began to dissolve into light, light congealing to lightning, lightning streaming out of him, unraveling him like a silkworm's cocoon unwinding, one nearly infinite glowing strand undone, a line of fire racing away from him, and off into a forestalled eternity.

It streamed out of the African and into Dahlia's body. And with the strands came shadowy, glowing forms. Women. Children. Men. Countless innocents gone for generations to feed his endless appetite for life.

The African aged with stomach-churning rapidity, his flesh rotting even as he still remained alive and in torment.

He shriveled, his flesh sagging and bubbling into liquid. He ran with every kind of carcinoma and disease of age. His shuddering husk collapsed. And ran to dust. And was gone.

61

Still shining with that inner light, Dahlia's legs buckled. Derek Waites moved just barely fast enough to catch her. She groaned and moved feebly in his arms, mewling like a sick kitten.

Hers wasn't the only weak voice. A few militiamen and looters were still alive. They were waking up now, sobbing and groaning, cursing and crying out to be released. He recognized the giant LD guard Chip Maddox. At first he didn't recognize any of the looters, and then he did.

Raymond Cross was burned, all the hair singed from one side of his head and his eyebrows crisped, but he was alive.

"I . . . know you," Derek said.

"Let me out of here, man," Cross snarled.

"You don't remember me, do you?"

Cross stared at him, then spat out a curse. "Naw, motherfucker. Just get me out."

"You took my girlfriend. You don't remember, do you? You ran in front of my car, two weeks ago."

Cross writhed, pulled against the manacles. "I don't know nothing about that shit." His face suddenly turned crafty. "Come on, brother man . . . cut me loose."

Derek looked at him quietly. "You don't have any idea what happened here today, do you? What almost happened. And you don't care, do you?"

"Cut . . . me . . . loose."

Something inside Derek, something dark and heavy, grew suddenly lighter, and for the life of him, he wasn't sure what it was.

"In your turn," Derek said. He went back to Dahlia.

She lay where he had left her. *"You saved my family,"*

she said. *"You are not of my blood, my flesh—but you are my son. I do not belong in this world."*

"What about Dahlia Washington?"

"She gave her life willingly. In so doing, she has redeemed herself. It is over for her. Do not pity her—she made the choices she made, and her final one was glorious. But there is one who loves you, and who you love. Your children need a mother. And you need a wife. Good-bye, Derek Waites."

She touched his face tenderly, then crumbled to the ground. The scintillant around her vanished.

Derek exhaled harshly, and laid her head upon the ground, as gently as he could.

He would find Troy's shackle keys. And Rachel's.

Tucker's Glock lay on the ground. Derek picked it up, and searched until he found the nine millimeter cartridges, and loaded it. Then he went to Tucker.

Tucker still sat with his back to the television screens, which now displayed, in their multitude, the place of sacrifice, the dozens of chained human beings, white and black, who had been brought here to die, that a monster might live.

Tucker's lips moved feebly. Derek couldn't hear him at first, and leaned closer.

"What a day, huh?" Tucker said.

"Yeah," Derek said, sliding down next to him. "What a day."

"So." Tucker said.

"So. Just what the hell do we do now?"

Saturday, May 16

It was almost three o'clock in the morning. The Advanced Graphics building still roared with flames, throwing a galaxy of sparks up to the clouds. They drifted back down onto the gilded roofs of Malibu, to the beaches, to the unchanged and uncaring ocean. Troy and Rachel and Dee were covered in blankets. Their backs rested against saplings two hundred yards away from the main conflagration.

Derek repeated his story to the police, to the firemen, and then to the police again, in endless rounds. The looters, the members of Lightning Dawn, the few surviving guards were being interviewed, and so far, no coherent picture had emerged.

It was clear that people had been kidnapped, and some killed. The extent of the horror was still to be determined, but Derek and his family were considered to be nothing more than victims in a conspiracy of uncertain but ghastly magnitude.

Detective Wally Hicks of the LAPD had been rousted from bed at about one A.M., and arrived an hour and a half later to participate in the questioning.

"How's the Beaver?" Derek asked.

"Thanks," Hicks said wearily. "I haven't heard that one all day."

He watched as one of Advanced Graphics's walls fell in. The Malibu Fire Department was doing its best, spraying water and foam on the wreckage, but to little avail.

"So what the hell happened up here?" Hicks asked.

"They took me, and my family, and these other people. There was some kind of fight, and some of us got free."

"That's it?" Hicks asked.

Derek said nothing. "Ask the others," he said.

"Don't worry. I will." Hicks looked at Derek, chewing on the end of a pencil. He scribbled something on a pad. He would scribble a lot more in the weeks and months to follow. Vast mountains of evidence would be extracted from the ruins of Advanced Graphics, and later from the Looker mansion. All of it would point to a vast and murderous conspiracy. None of it would answer Wally Hick's deepest and most disturbing questions.

He surveyed the grounds. There were body bags everywhere, and the survivors seemed to be divided into two distinct groups, one white, one black, each huddling with their own.

He saw a face he recognized. "Excuse me. Ms. Childe?"

Rachel sat with her arms around her children. Her ribs

were bandaged. Ambulances were still arriving, and soon she would be taken to have her wounds examined more carefully. "Yes?" she asked numbly.

"I'll need to talk to you later. You'll probably be asked to tell your story a number of times. . . ." He scratched his head ruefully. "I just wanted to say how sorry I am about all of this. Apparently, members of our own department were involved. Not many, but one is too much by a long shot. I just want to get this all straightened out."

She closed her eyes, as if trying to shut away the memories.

"That's all I want, too," she said. And held her children more tightly.

A section of roof fell in. Firemen yelled back and forth across the roar of the blaze, and radios crackled continuously.

Derek came to stand beside him. "A couple of the kidnap victims said that there was another man," Wally Hicks said. "It's weird, but the description corresponds to that of an escaped convict named Tucker. Was he in there?"

"Yeah," Derek said quietly. "He was."

"Where is he now?"

Waites pointed toward the fire as a spray of sparks spiraled toward the clouds. "There," Derek said. "I think he was there." He paused. "I don't think anyone here would be alive if it weren't for him. I think he was a hero."

"He was a killer," Hicks said.

Derek watched the fire. "You bet your ass he was."

Somewhere outside
Flagstaff, Arizona
September 10, 1992

Derek Waites held the wheel of his new Toyota truck hard, arms a little too tense to respond to the dusty, rutted road. In the jump seat behind him, Troy and Dee slept as they had for the last fifty miles, the early evening's warm air and the trucks jostling combining to create a powerful sedative effect.

"Are you sure you didn't miss it?" Rachel said, studying her map.

"No, but let's keep going for a few minutes before we turn around."

She had turned on the overhead light to study the creased chart, comparing it to the carefully typed directions they had received in the mail a week before.

Since those terrible days in May, they had endured much together. Answered questions together, lied together, cried and laughed, and ultimately healed together. She had taken a leave of absence from her job, time to sit quietly and think about her life, her family, her marriage. About the man who had died to protect her children.

There was a sadness in Rachel that might never vanish, but there was a quiet, too, as if her constant and all-important ambition was no longer the dominating force in her life.

Which was strange, because as soon as the notoriety had begun to die down, as soon as the reporters and policemen began to follow other leads, Derek had regained a sense of enthusiasm for his own work that he hadn't known in years.

Strange. Something had happened in there, in Advanced Graphics. To all of them. Miracle of miracles, no member of Lightning Dawn talked about Tucker—Derek's connection to him. There might well have been suspicions, inquiries, but the crimes of Augustus DuPris and the man known as Niles were a pit that loomed deeper and wider the longer the investigation continued. At least a hundred deaths were attributed to what the authorities were calling a satanic coven, and more were surfacing every week.

In the furor, the Waites family, which steadfastly maintained its ignorance, became just another statistic, and then, in time, of no moment at all.

Sometimes Rachel called Derek, just to talk. About their lives, their family. Of Troy's nightmares, or of Dee's. And how it might be a good idea for Derek to move back in with them, just for a while.

He did, and he found a balance with Rachel, a place where

they were both comfortable. More than friendship. Less than lovers.

Family.

Healing together. And he was content with this. Any more would happen in its own time.

Often, he wondered what had happened to Tucker. Wounded, bleeding, he had disappeared into the Malibu night, and Derek had been certain he would be found crashed into an abutment, bled out on some lonely road.

But no. No capture, no discovery, nothing. Tucker had disappeared. For months, Derek heard nothing.

Then came a postcard postmarked in Utah, with directions carefully typewritten for Derek to place an ad in the *National Enquirer* if he wanted to meet a friend who had lost a basketball game to his son. A follow-up letter contained directions.

"Drive to Phoenix. Eat at the Denny's at such-and-such a turnoff. Check into the Quality Inn. The next day, drive to Flagstaff. . . ."

Derek gathered his little family, and followed Tucker's instructions to the letter. And once he reached that Denny's he knew, without knowing *how* he knew, that he was under surveillance.

And now he felt the adrenaline burning in his guts as they drove down the dirt road twenty miles outside Flagstaff.

The desert scrub had been swallowed by shadows, and even with the truck's headlights going at full bore, the darkness outside was almost complete.

"There," Rachel said, and pointed at an abandoned Esso station. He pulled up next to a dusty pump, and blew his horn.

The theme from *Mission: Impossible* blared. Rachel sighed. Some things never changed.

For a long moment, there was no response, and then Tucker sauntered into the light. He was limping just a little bit, but the smile on his face was genuine, a bit sardonic, and he was shaking his head as he approached.

Derek got out of the truck, and scanned Tucker. "You look good, man."

"You, too."

The children were waking from their nap, and climbing over each other in efforts to be the first out of the truck.

Derek smiled. "There are enough supplies for a month in the truck. I've got about seventy-five hundred in cash. Figured it might help."

"You didn't have to," Tucker said. "Things are tight, but not that bad."

"What's it like up here?"

"Little ranch. You'll see it. You'll like it. Tonya's place." Tucker grinned. "Let's just say that things are working out all right—but it's nice to stay low for a while."

Rachel stood behind Derek, and she cleared her throat. "Are you sure it'll be all right with her for us to come up?"

"Did you bring the Mrs. Fields?"

"Three dozen."

"She'll be fine."

Rachel tried to laugh, but even after all this time, it caught in her throat. She extended her hands to him, and he took them. "Thank you," she said. "For everything."

"Thank you," he said. "All of you."

Tucker's hand suddenly jerked up, snatching a basketball out of the air. He tucked it under one arm.

Troy ran up, hand raised to high-five the big man. "Brought the ball, and a hoop, man. Gotta teach you some moves."

"Think I can learn something?"

"You're not bad," Troy said. "For an old white guy."

Tucker laughed. Then his face grew more serious. "There are some things I'd like to teach you, too," he said. "I would have taught my own boy . . ." He stopped, and something painful flitted across his face, and then was, for the moment, gone. "Anyway. With your parents' permission, I'd like to teach you some things. One day, you can teach your own son." He looked at Derek and Rachel. "Would you mind?"

"I'd be honored," Derek said.

"Like it or not," Rachel said quietly, "we're family, Tucker."

"I like," Tucker said. "More than I can say. I like."

"Let's get going, cuz," Troy said.

"Just a minute." Tucker bent down just in time to catch

Dee as she jumped up into his arms. He lifted her until they were face level.

"I had a dream, Mr. Warrior, sir," Dee said.

"What kind of dream?"

"Dahlia was there. She said to say thank you."

He sighed, and kissed her very carefully on the forehead. "If you see her again, you tell her the same for me."

"It was just a dream, but if I see her, I'll tell her."

Impulsively, she leaned forward, and kissed him on the lips, hard. And giggled.

Tucker hugged her to him so hard it almost crushed her breath. Derek saw something happen to Tucker's face, saw it soften, knew that in Tucker's heart and mind it was his own daughter who had kissed him, that it was Dolly's soft and warm body he held, her beating heart that pulsed against his own.

When he set her down again, Tucker's eyes were wet.

No one said anything, then Troy's voice: "Ooooh. Dee gets a check mark—"

"Do not." She stuck her tongue out at him.

"Do so." He bopped her with a Nerf football, and the chase was on.

She ran after her brother, shrieking, and the moment was over. When Derek turned back to Tucker, the big man's face was composed, his eyes dry.

"Well," Tucker said. "We have some serious driving to do. We're way up in the hills."

"Good way to stay away from strangers."

"Or to hole up with friends."

They piled into the truck, Rachel in back with the kids. Tucker slid in next to Derek. "About two miles east, there's a turnoff."

"You got it," Derek said, and started the engine.

They were almost a mile down the road when Tucker said, grinning, "Back at Malibu. The African's offer. You're an idiot, you know that? I would have killed you *twice.*"

Derek shook his head. "No, you wouldn't have."

"No?"

They went on for a little while longer, heading toward the

distant, invisible mountain, churning a plume of dust in their wake. Then Tucker said, "Are you sure?"

"Yeah."

In the darkness beside him, Tucker laughed. Then said, "Don't tell anyone, okay?"

"Sure," Derek said, consumed by a deep and almost overpowering sense of contentment. "Your secret's safe with me."

TOR
BOOKS The Best in Science Fiction

LIEGE-KILLER Christopher Hinz
"*Liege-Killer* is a genuine page-turner, beautifully written and exciting from start to finish....Don't miss it."—*Locus*

HARVEST OF STARS • Poul Anderson
"A true masterpiece. An important work—not just of science fiction but of contemporary literature. Visionary and beautifully written, elegaic and transcendent, *Harvest of Stars* is the brightest star in Poul Anderson's constellation."
—Keith Ferrell, editor, *Omni*

FIREDANCE • Steven Barnes
SF adventure in 21st century California—by the co-author of *Beowulf's Children*.

ASH OCK • Christopher Hinz
"A well-handled science fiction thriller."—*Kirkus Reviews*

CALDÉ OF THE LONG SUN • Gene Wolfe
The third volume in the critically-acclaimed Book of the Long Sun.
"Dazzling."—*The New York Times*

OF TANGIBLE GHOSTS • L.E. Modesitt, Jr.
Ingenious alternate universe SF from the author of the *Recluce* fantasy series.

THE SHATTERED SPHERE • Roger MacBride Allen
The second book of the Hunted Earth continues the thrilling story that began in *The Ring of Charon*, a daringly original hard science fiction novel.

THE PRICE OF THE STARS • Debra Doyle and James D. Macdonald
Book One of the Mageworlds—the breakneck SF epic of the most brawling family in the human galaxy!